The Weirn Books

Be Wary of the Silent Woods

1

SVETLANA CHMAKOVA

JY

The Weirn Books

BE WARY OF THE SILENT WOODS 1

SVETLANA CHMAKOVA

COLORING ASSISTANTS: Effie Lealand, Melissa McCommon
INKING ASSISTANTS: Young Kim, Effie Lealand
LETTERING: JuYoun Lee

JY
150 West 30th Street, 19th Floor
New York, NY 10001

Visit us at jyforkids.com
facebook.com/jyforkids • twitter.com/jyforkids
jyforkids.tumblr.com • instagram.com/jyforkids

First JY Edition: June 2020

JY is an imprint of Yen Press, LLC.
The JY name and logo are trademarks of Yen Press, LLC.

The publisher is not responsible for websites (or their content)
that are not owned by the publisher.

Library of Congress Control Number: 2020936433

ISBNs: 978-1-975-31121-6 (hardcover)
978-1-975-31122-3 (paperback)
978-1-975-31120-9 (ebook)

10 9 8 7 6 5 4 3 2 1

LSC-C

Printed in the United States of America

Table of Contents

Chapter 1

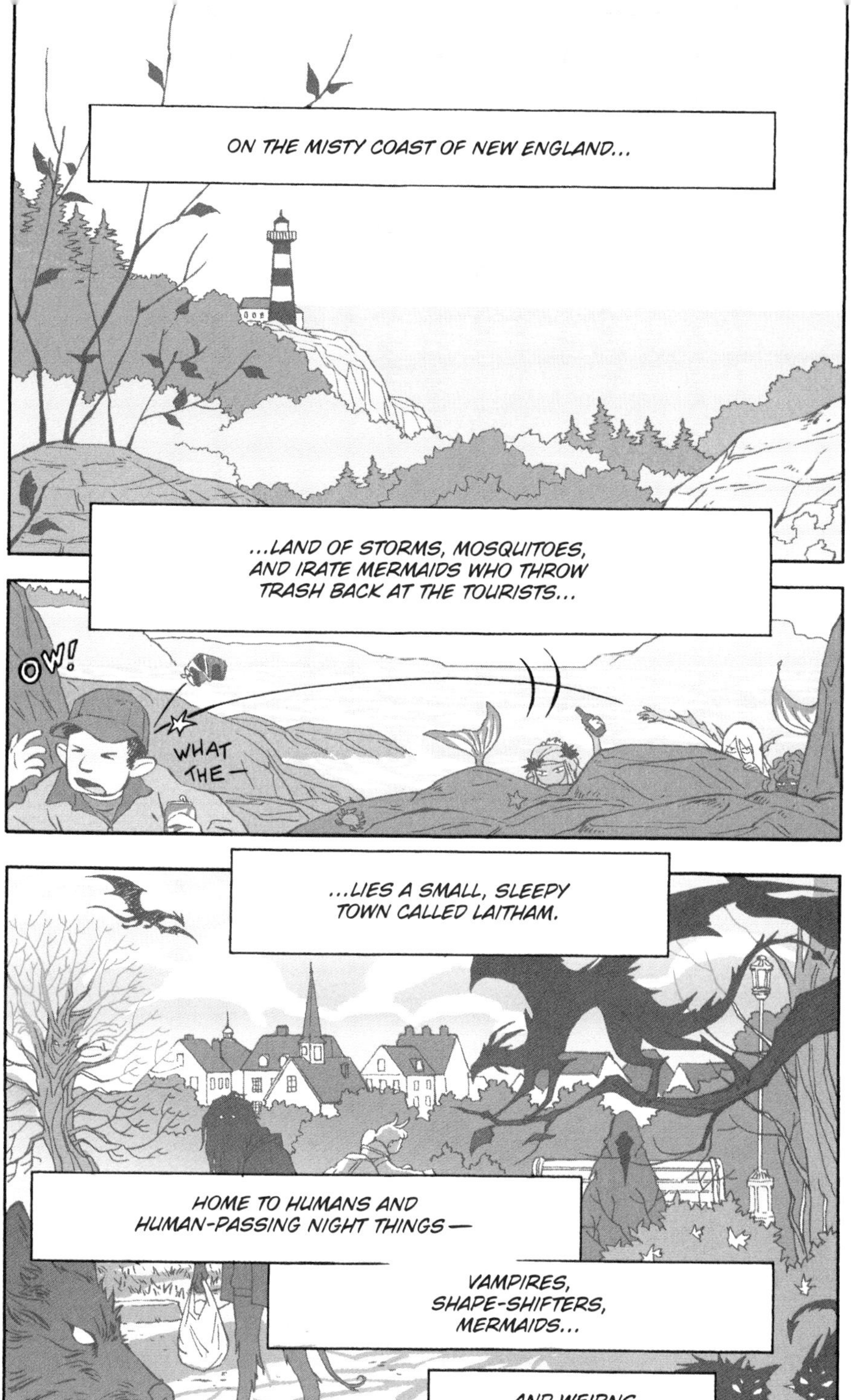
ON THE MISTY COAST OF NEW ENGLAND...
...LAND OF STORMS, MOSQUITOES, AND IRATE MERMAIDS WHO THROW TRASH BACK AT THE TOURISTS...
OW!
WHAT THE—
...LIES A SMALL, SLEEPY TOWN CALLED LAITHAM.
HOME TO HUMANS AND HUMAN-PASSING NIGHT THINGS—
VAMPIRES, SHAPE-SHIFTERS, MERMAIDS...
...AND WEIRNS.

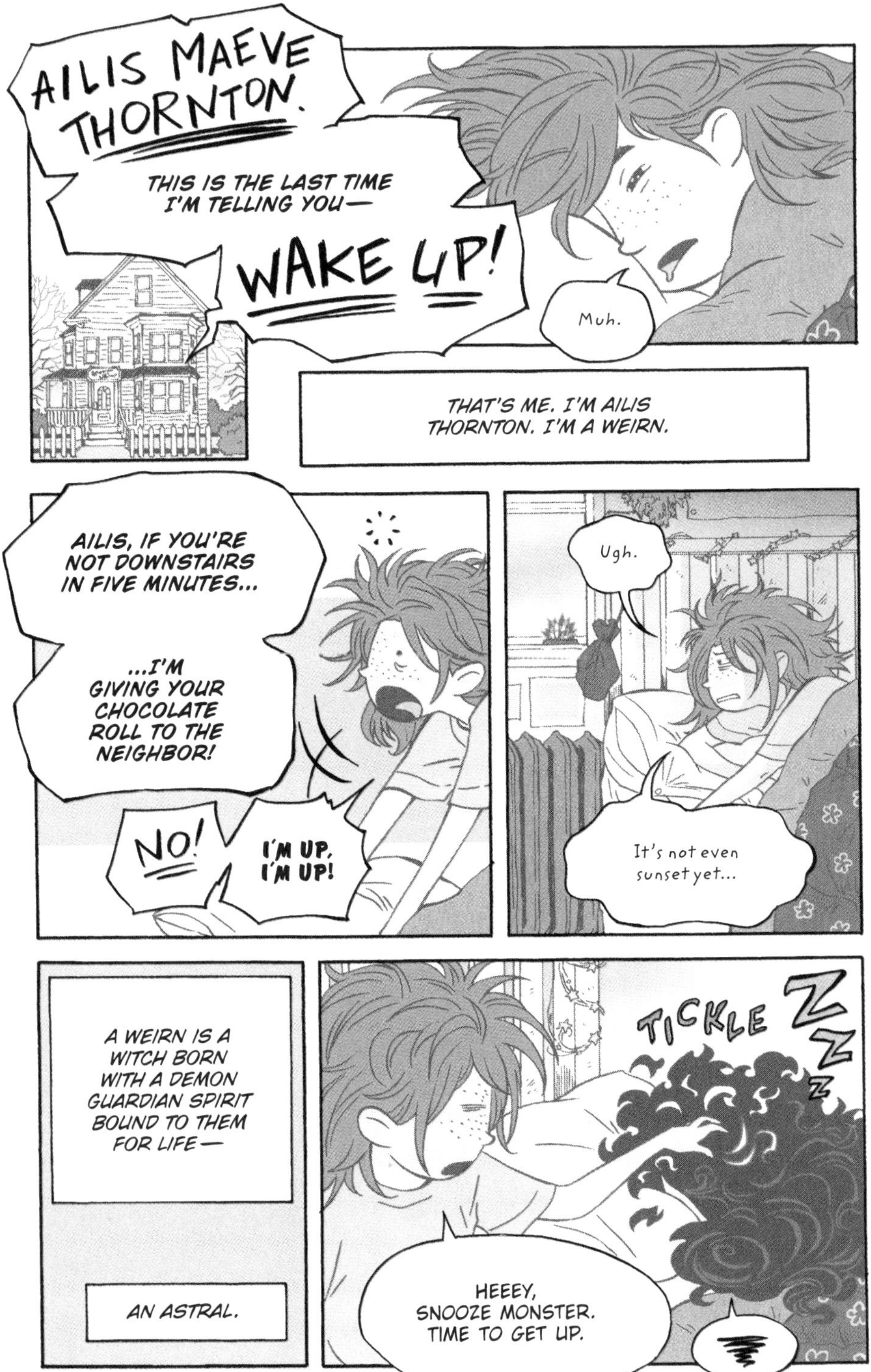
AILIS MAEVE THORNTON.
THIS IS THE LAST TIME I'M TELLING YOU—
WAKE UP!
Muh.
THAT'S ME. I'M AILIS THORNTON. I'M A WEIRN.
AILIS, IF YOU'RE NOT DOWNSTAIRS IN FIVE MINUTES...
...I'M GIVING YOUR CHOCOLATE ROLL TO THE NEIGHBOR!
NO!
I'M UP, I'M UP!
Ugh.
It's not even sunset yet...
A WEIRN IS A WITCH BORN WITH A DEMON GUARDIAN SPIRIT BOUND TO THEM FOR LIFE—
AN ASTRAL.
TICKLE
Z Z Z
HEEEY, SNOOZE MONSTER. TIME TO GET UP.

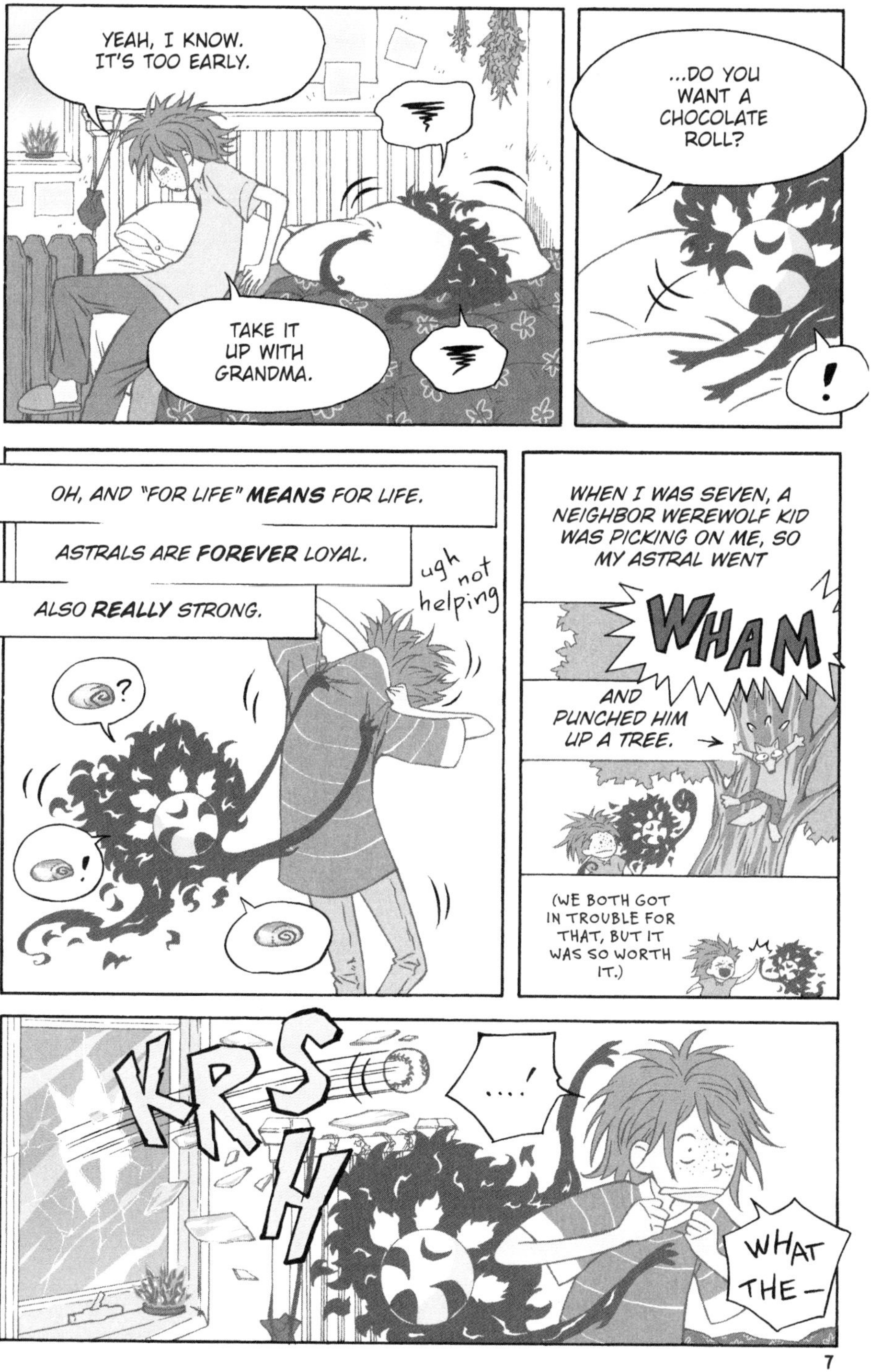
YEAH, I KNOW. IT'S TOO EARLY.
TAKE IT UP WITH GRANDMA.
...DO YOU WANT A CHOCOLATE ROLL?
!
OH, AND "FOR LIFE" MEANS FOR LIFE.
ASTRALS ARE FOREVER LOYAL.
ALSO REALLY STRONG.
ugh not helping
?
!
WHEN I WAS SEVEN, A NEIGHBOR WEREWOLF KID WAS PICKING ON ME, SO MY ASTRAL WENT
WHAM
AND PUNCHED HIM UP A TREE.
(WE BOTH GOT IN TROUBLE FOR THAT, BUT IT WAS SO WORTH IT.)
KRSH
....!
WHAT THE—

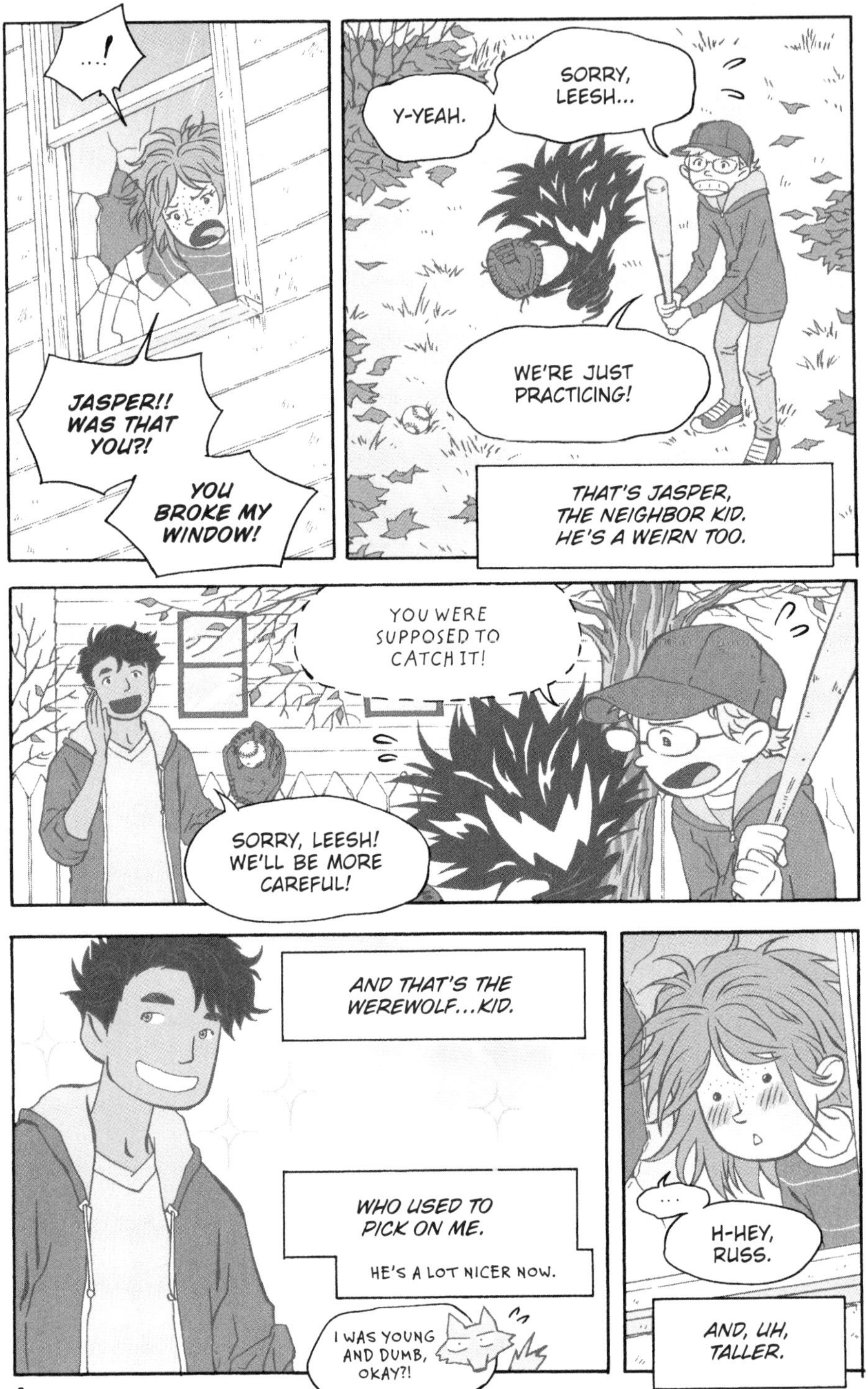
...!
JASPER!! WAS THAT YOU?!
YOU BROKE MY WINDOW!
SORRY, LEESH...
Y-YEAH.
WE'RE JUST PRACTICING!
THAT'S JASPER, THE NEIGHBOR KID. HE'S A WEIRN TOO.
YOU WERE SUPPOSED TO CATCH IT!
SORRY, LEESH! WE'LL BE MORE CAREFUL!
AND THAT'S THE WEREWOLF...KID.
WHO USED TO PICK ON ME.
HE'S A LOT NICER NOW.
I WAS YOUNG AND DUMB, OKAY?!
...
H-HEY, RUSS.
AND, UH, TALLER.

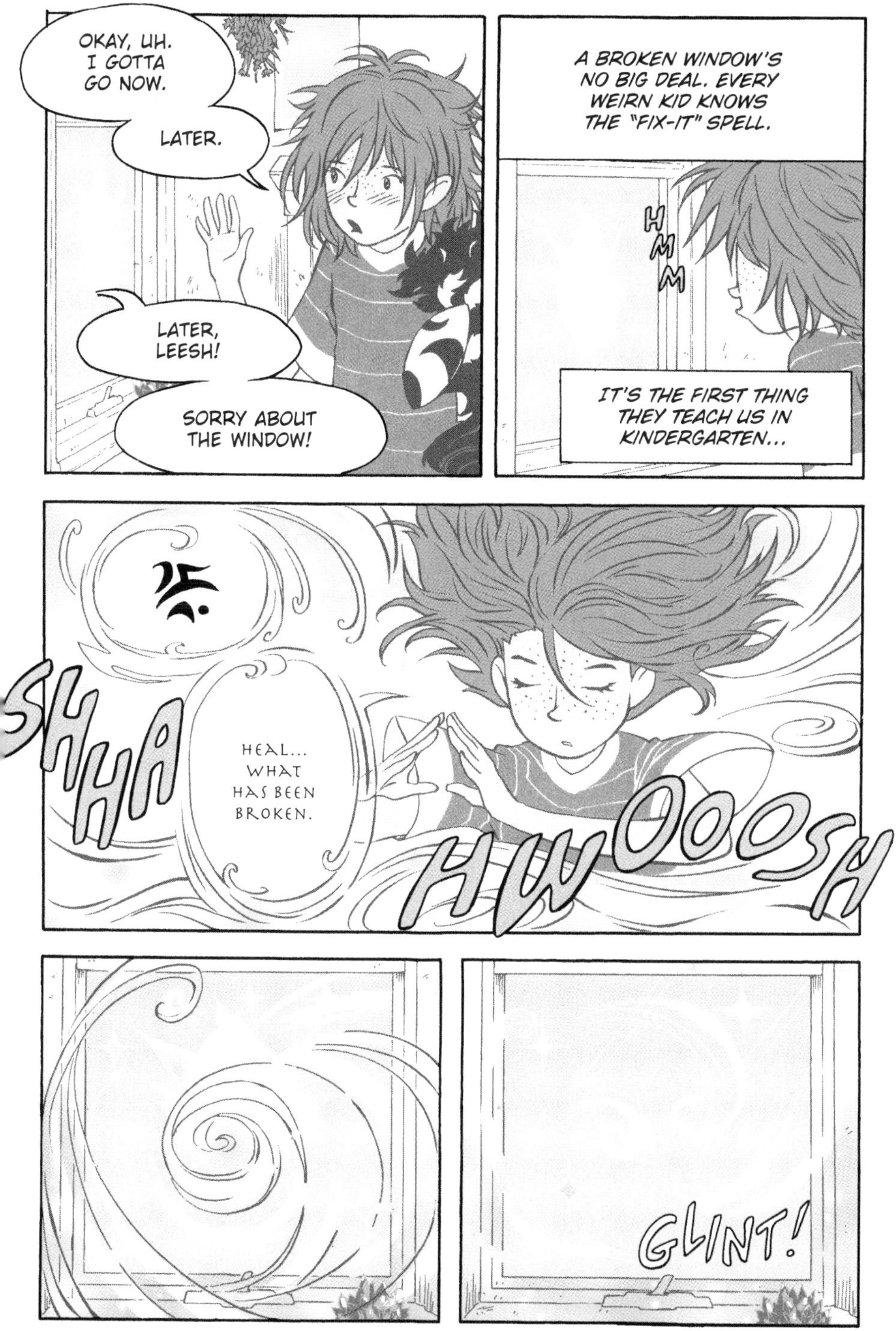
OKAY, UH. I GOTTA GO NOW.
LATER.
LATER, LEESH!
SORRY ABOUT THE WINDOW!
A BROKEN WINDOW'S NO BIG DEAL. EVERY WEIRN KID KNOWS THE "FIX-IT" SPELL.
HMM
IT'S THE FIRST THING THEY TEACH US IN KINDERGARTEN...
SHHA
HEAL... WHAT HAS BEEN BROKEN.
HWOOOSH
GLINT!

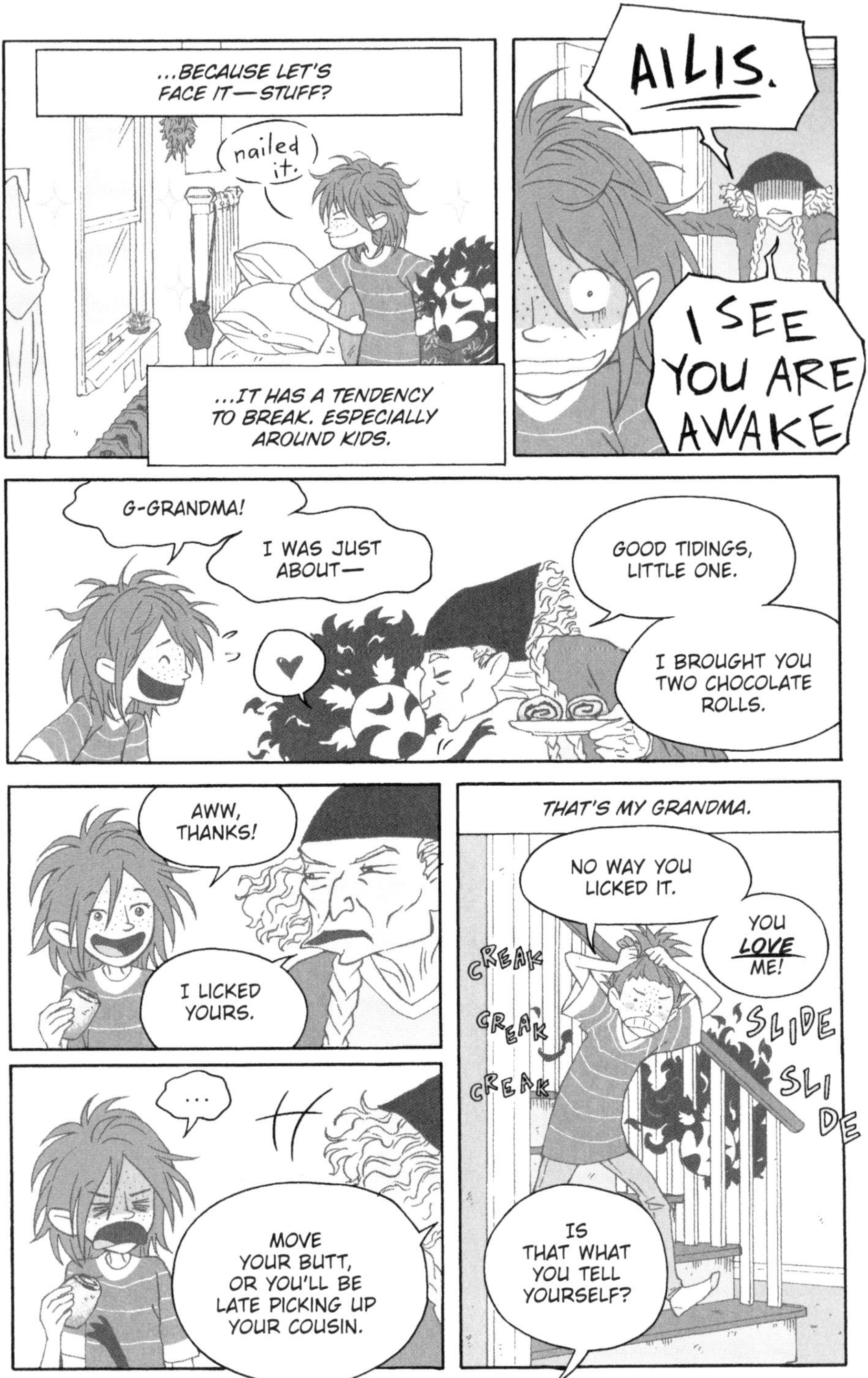
...BECAUSE LET'S FACE IT—STUFF?
nailed it.
...IT HAS A TENDENCY TO BREAK. ESPECIALLY AROUND KIDS.
AILIS.
I SEE YOU ARE AWAKE
G-GRANDMA!
I WAS JUST ABOUT—
GOOD TIDINGS, LITTLE ONE.
I BROUGHT YOU TWO CHOCOLATE ROLLS.
AWW, THANKS!
I LICKED YOURS.
...
MOVE YOUR BUTT, OR YOU'LL BE LATE PICKING UP YOUR COUSIN.
THAT'S MY GRANDMA.
NO WAY YOU LICKED IT.
YOU LOVE ME!
CREAK
CREAK
CREAK
SLIDE
SLIDE
IS THAT WHAT YOU TELL YOURSELF?

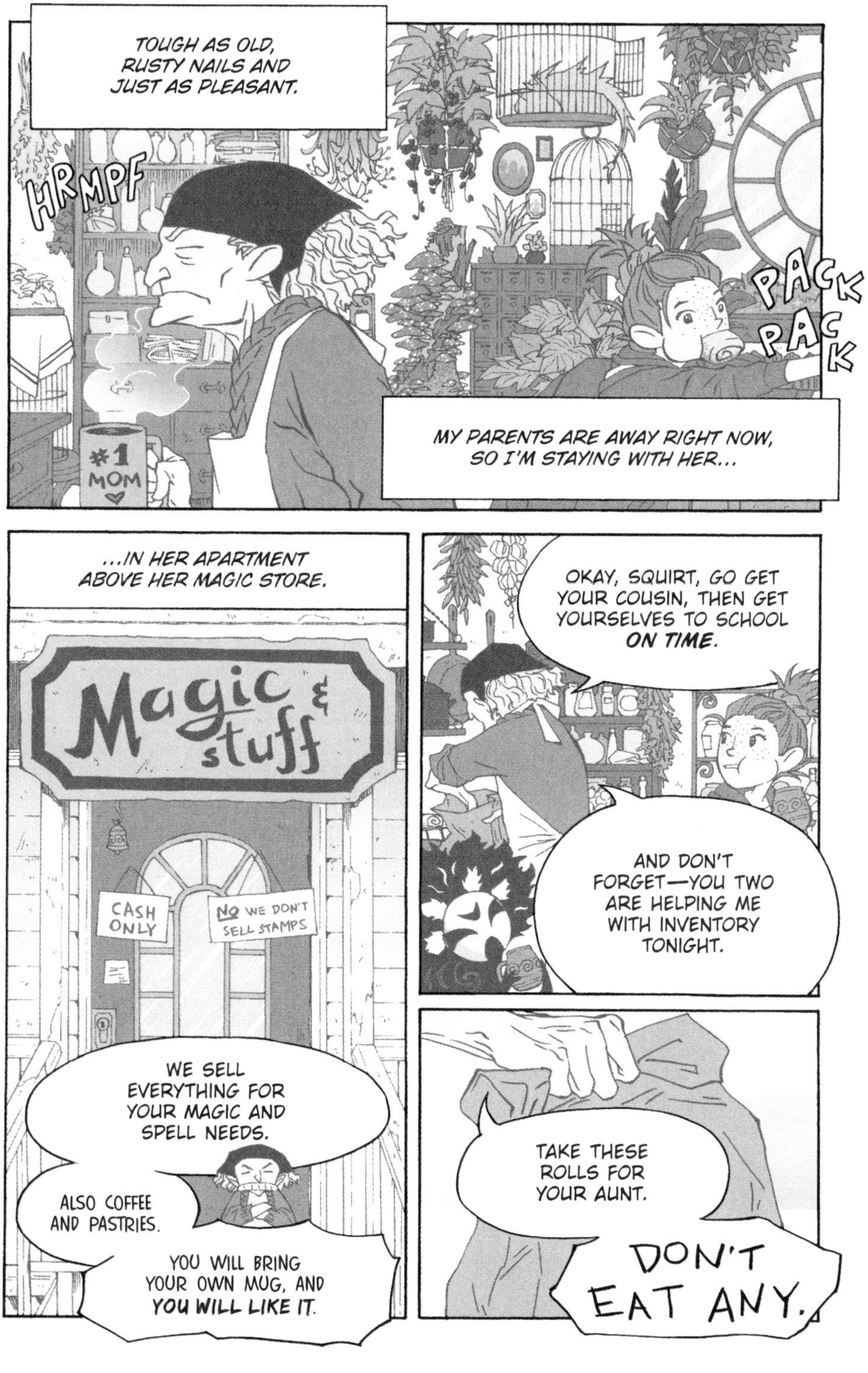
TOUGH AS OLD, RUSTY NAILS AND JUST AS PLEASANT.
HRMPF
#1 MOM
PACK PACK
MY PARENTS ARE AWAY RIGHT NOW, SO I'M STAYING WITH HER...
...IN HER APARTMENT ABOVE HER MAGIC STORE.
Magic & stuff
CASH ONLY
NO WE DON'T SELL STAMPS
WE SELL EVERYTHING FOR YOUR MAGIC AND SPELL NEEDS.
ALSO COFFEE AND PASTRIES.
YOU WILL BRING YOUR OWN MUG, AND YOU WILL LIKE IT.
OKAY, SQUIRT, GO GET YOUR COUSIN, THEN GET YOURSELVES TO SCHOOL ON TIME.
AND DON'T FORGET—YOU TWO ARE HELPING ME WITH INVENTORY TONIGHT.
TAKE THESE ROLLS FOR YOUR AUNT.
DON'T EAT ANY.

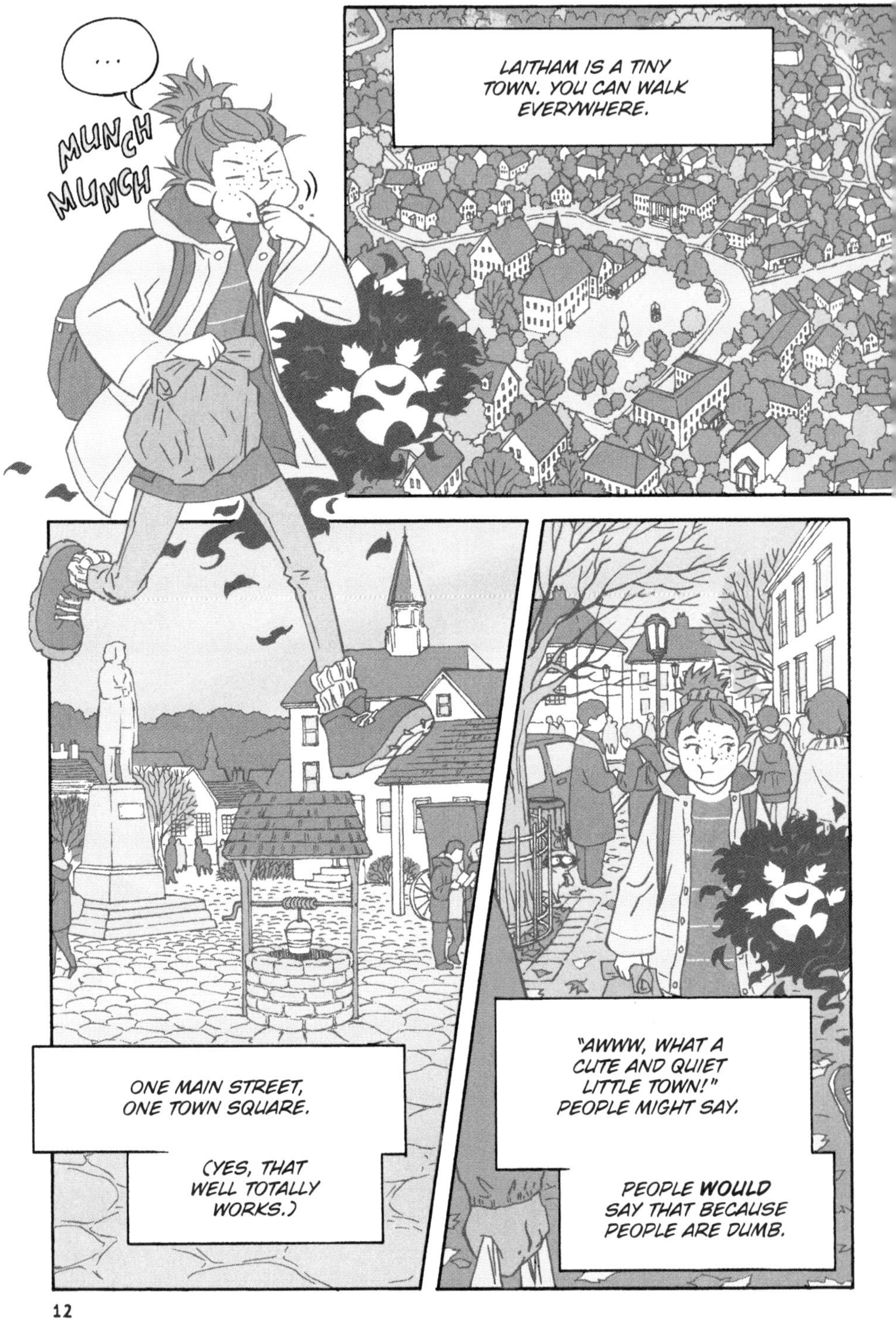
. . .
MUNCH MUNCH
LAITHAM IS A TINY TOWN. YOU CAN WALK EVERYWHERE.
ONE MAIN STREET, ONE TOWN SQUARE.
(YES, THAT WELL TOTALLY WORKS.)
"AWWW, WHAT A CUTE AND QUIET LITTLE TOWN!" PEOPLE MIGHT SAY.
PEOPLE **WOULD** SAY THAT BECAUSE PEOPLE ARE DUMB.

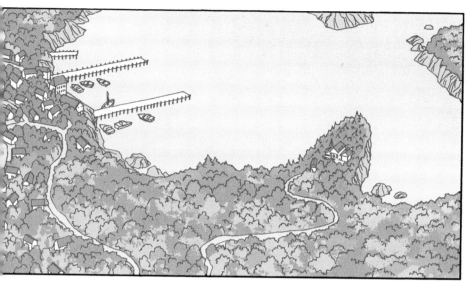

THE HUMAN PART IS SAFE AND BORING, I GUESS.

BUT THE NIGHT REALM PART? NOTHING CUTE OR QUIET ABOUT IT.

THE NIGHT REALM HAS THINGS THAT WOULD GLADLY EAT YOU FOR **DINNER**.

OR SNATCH OFF A PIECE OF YOUR **SOUL** TO PUT IN A JAR TO SELL AT THE NIGHT MARKET.

AND THE REALM ITSELF IS **LITTERED** WITH OLD FORGOTTEN MAGIC, ROTTEN CHARMS, AND TALISMANS THAT ARE PROBABLY ONLY GOOD FOR UNLEASHING END-OF-THE-WORLD EVIL BY NOW.

DON'T TRY **THAT** AT HOME.

13

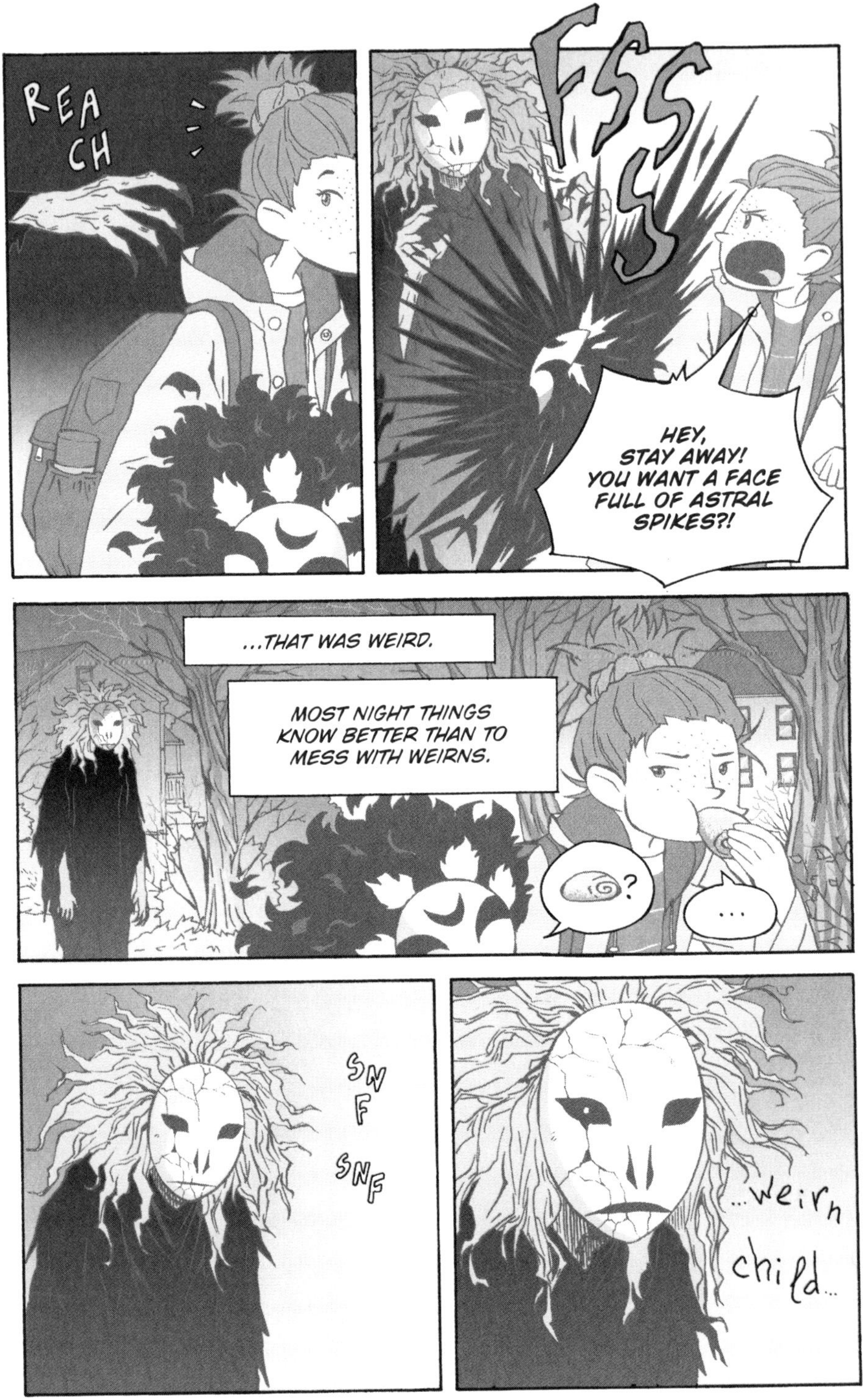
REACH
FSSS
HEY, STAY AWAY! YOU WANT A FACE FULL OF ASTRAL SPIKES?!
...THAT WAS WEIRD.
MOST NIGHT THINGS KNOW BETTER THAN TO MESS WITH WEIRNS.
?
...
SNF SNF
...weirn child...

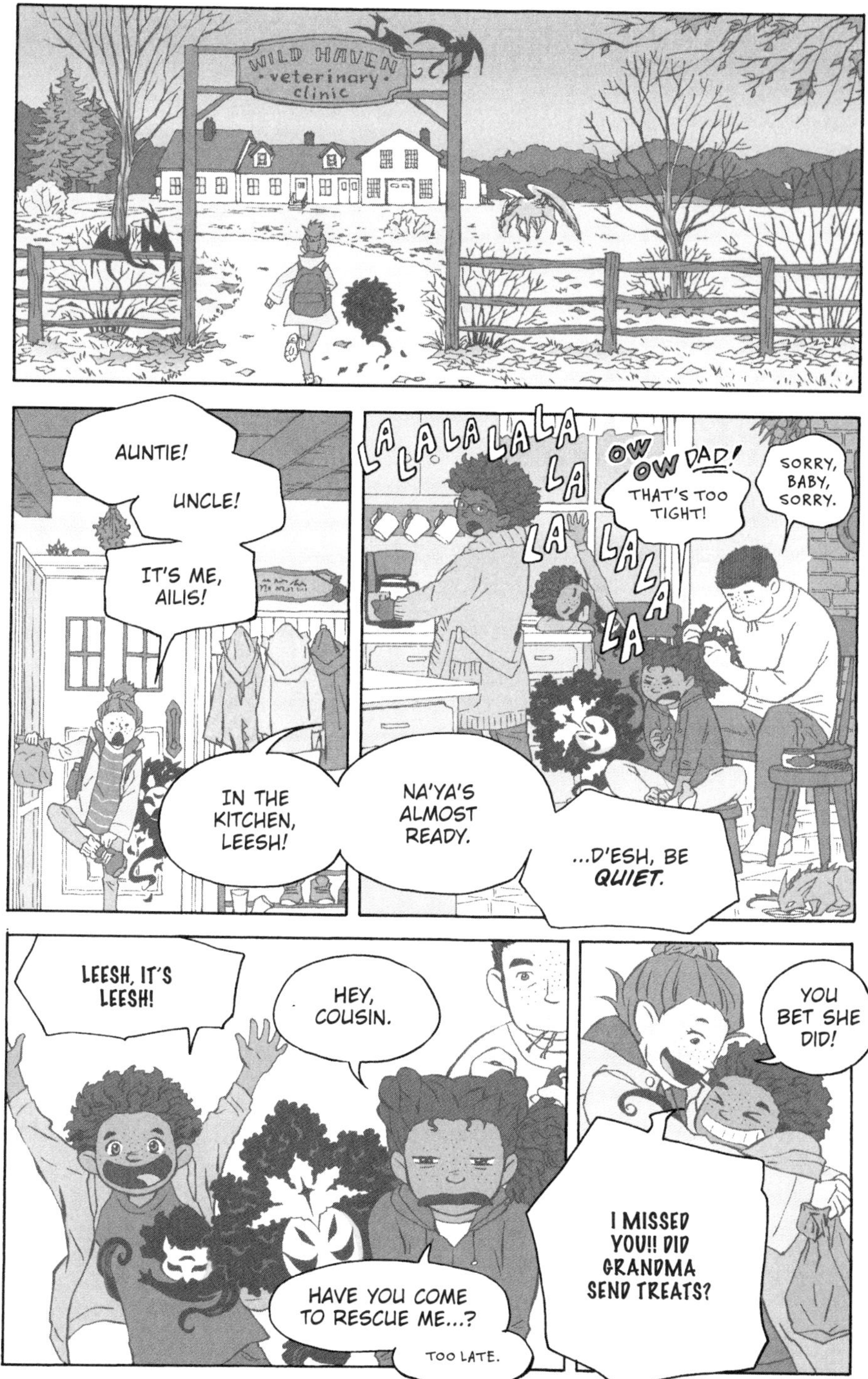
WILD HAVEN
veterinary
clinic
AUNTIE!
UNCLE!
IT'S ME, AILIS!
LA LA LA LA LA LA LA LA LA LA LA LA
OW OW DAD! THAT'S TOO TIGHT!
SORRY, BABY, SORRY.
IN THE KITCHEN, LEESH!
NA'YA'S ALMOST READY.
...D'ESH, BE *QUIET*.
LEESH, IT'S LEESH!
HEY, COUSIN.
HAVE YOU COME TO RESCUE ME...?
TOO LATE.
I MISSED YOU!! DID GRANDMA SEND TREATS?
YOU BET SHE DID!

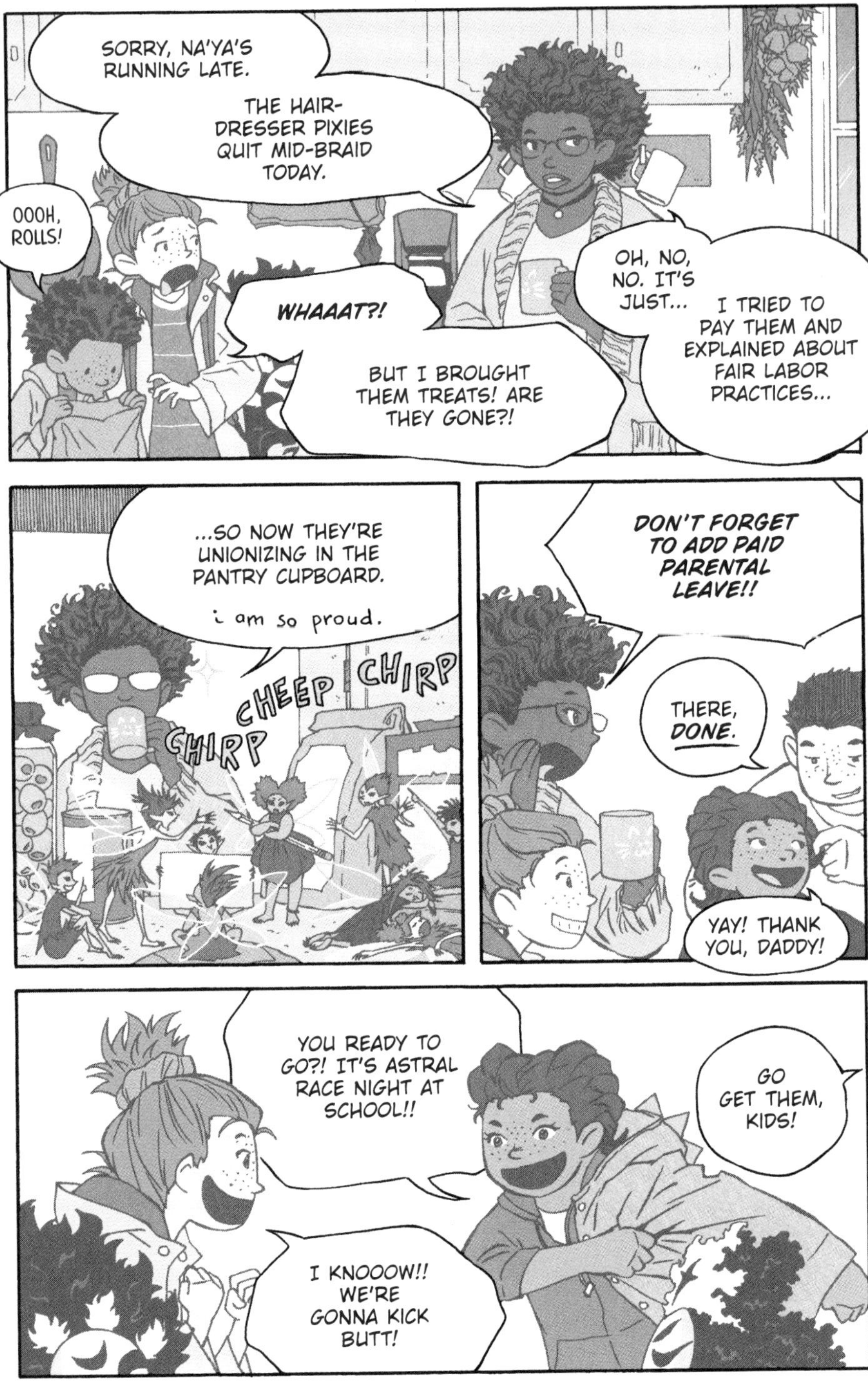
SORRY, NA'YA'S RUNNING LATE.
THE HAIR-DRESSER PIXIES QUIT MID-BRAID TODAY.
OOOH, ROLLS!
WHAAAT?!
BUT I BROUGHT THEM TREATS! ARE THEY GONE?!
OH, NO, NO. IT'S JUST...
I TRIED TO PAY THEM AND EXPLAINED ABOUT FAIR LABOR PRACTICES...
...SO NOW THEY'RE UNIONIZING IN THE PANTRY CUPBOARD.
i am so proud.
CHIRP
CHEEP
CHIRP
DON'T FORGET TO ADD PAID PARENTAL LEAVE!!
THERE, DONE.
YAY! THANK YOU, DADDY!
YOU READY TO GO?! IT'S ASTRAL RACE NIGHT AT SCHOOL!!
GO GET THEM, KIDS!
I KNOOOW!! WE'RE GONNA KICK BUTT!

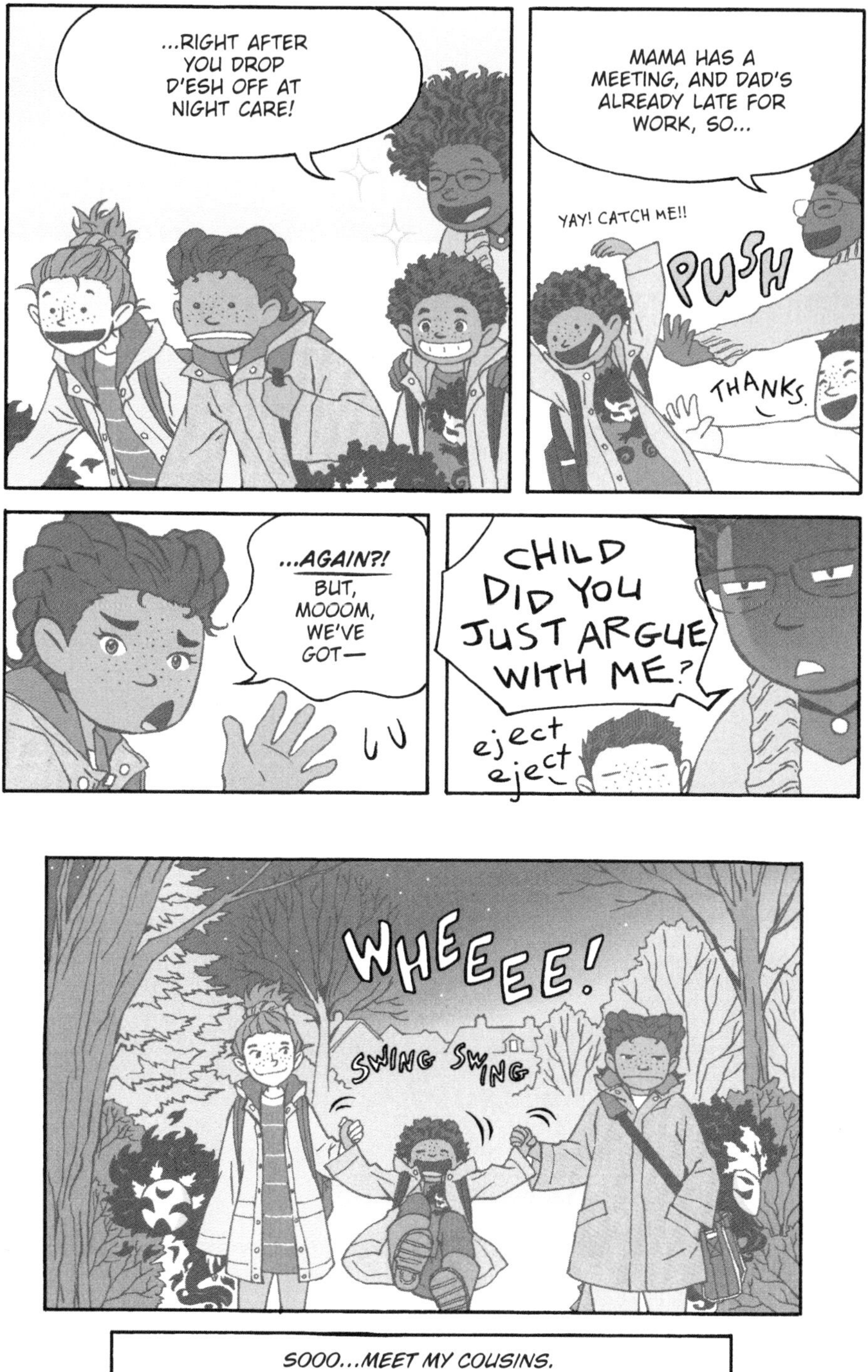
...RIGHT AFTER YOU DROP D'ESH OFF AT NIGHT CARE!
MAMA HAS A MEETING, AND DAD'S ALREADY LATE FOR WORK, SO...
YAY! CATCH ME!!
PUSH
THANKS
...AGAIN?! BUT, MOOOM, WE'VE GOT—
CHILD DID YOU JUST ARGUE WITH ME?
eject eject
WHEEEEE!
SWING SWING
SOOO...MEET MY COUSINS.

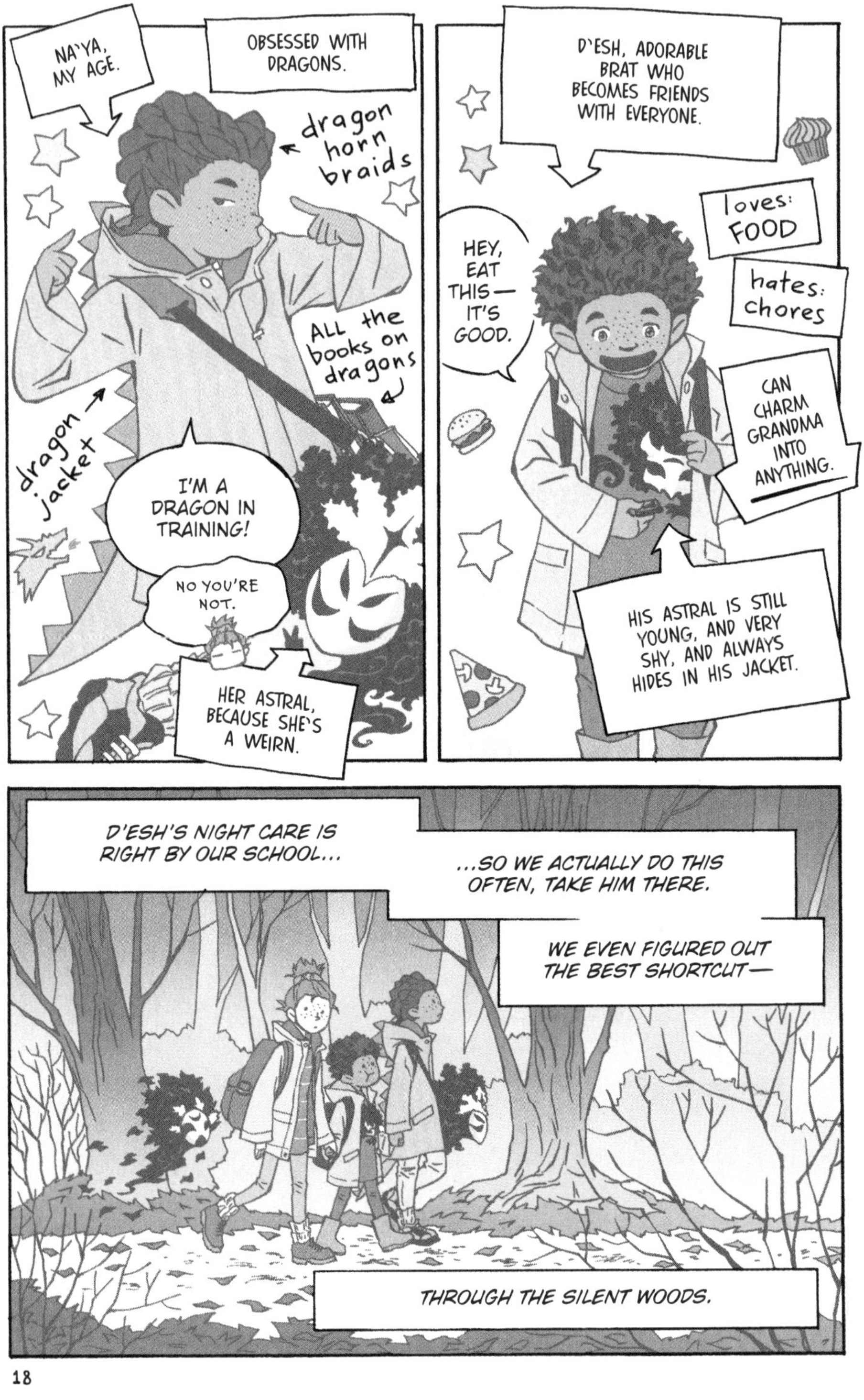
NA'YA, MY AGE.
OBSESSED WITH DRAGONS.
dragon horn braids
ALL the books on dragons
dragon jacket
I'M A DRAGON IN TRAINING!
NO YOU'RE NOT.
HER ASTRAL, BECAUSE SHE'S A WEIRN.
D'ESH, ADORABLE BRAT WHO BECOMES FRIENDS WITH EVERYONE.
HEY, EAT THIS— IT'S GOOD.
loves: FOOD
hates: chores
CAN CHARM GRANDMA INTO ANYTHING.
HIS ASTRAL IS STILL YOUNG, AND VERY SHY, AND ALWAYS HIDES IN HIS JACKET.
D'ESH'S NIGHT CARE IS RIGHT BY OUR SCHOOL...
...SO WE ACTUALLY DO THIS OFTEN, TAKE HIM THERE.
WE EVEN FIGURED OUT THE BEST SHORTCUT—
THROUGH THE SILENT WOODS.

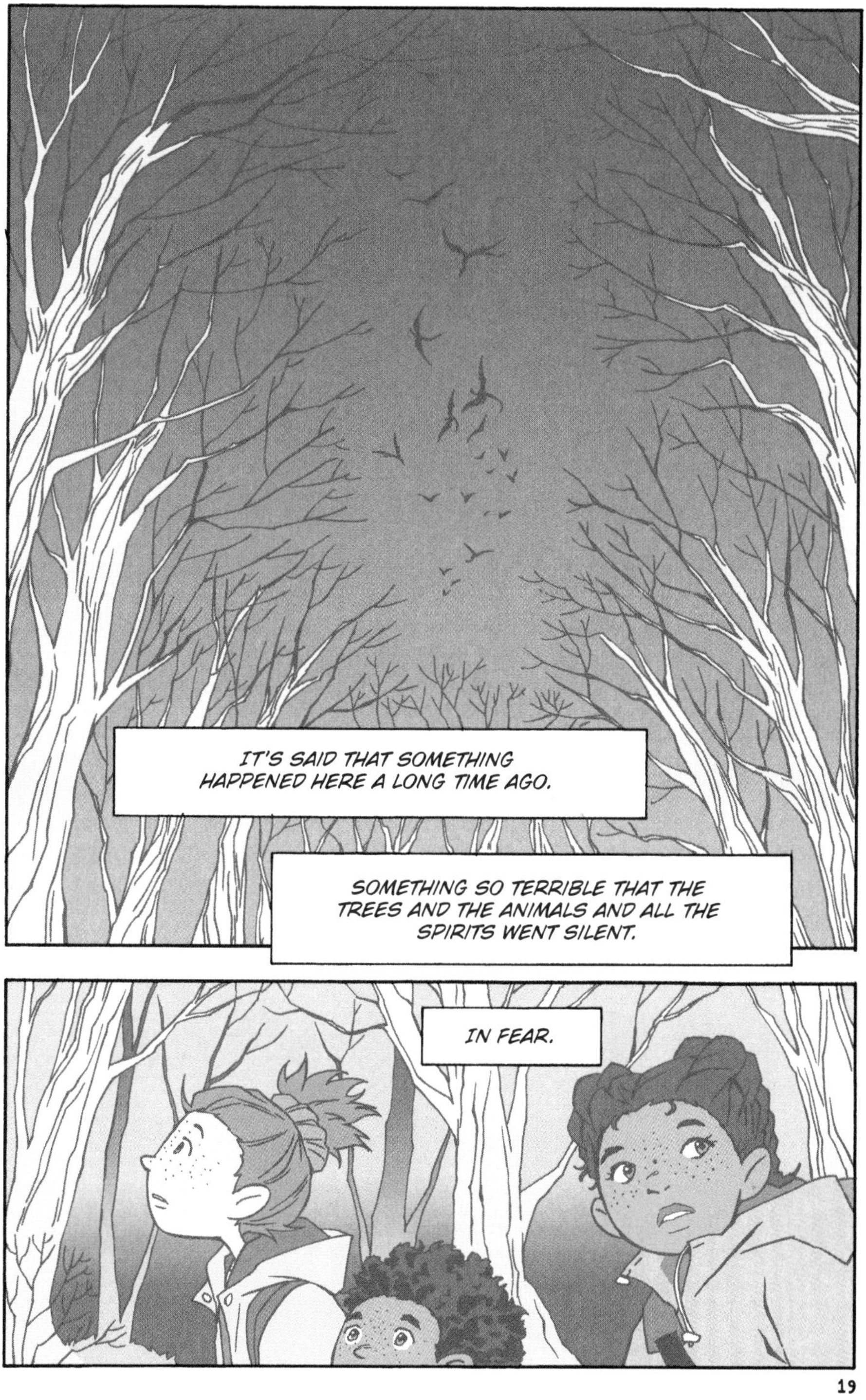
IT'S SAID THAT SOMETHING HAPPENED HERE A LONG TIME AGO.
SOMETHING SO TERRIBLE THAT THE TREES AND THE ANIMALS AND ALL THE SPIRITS WENT SILENT.
IN FEAR.

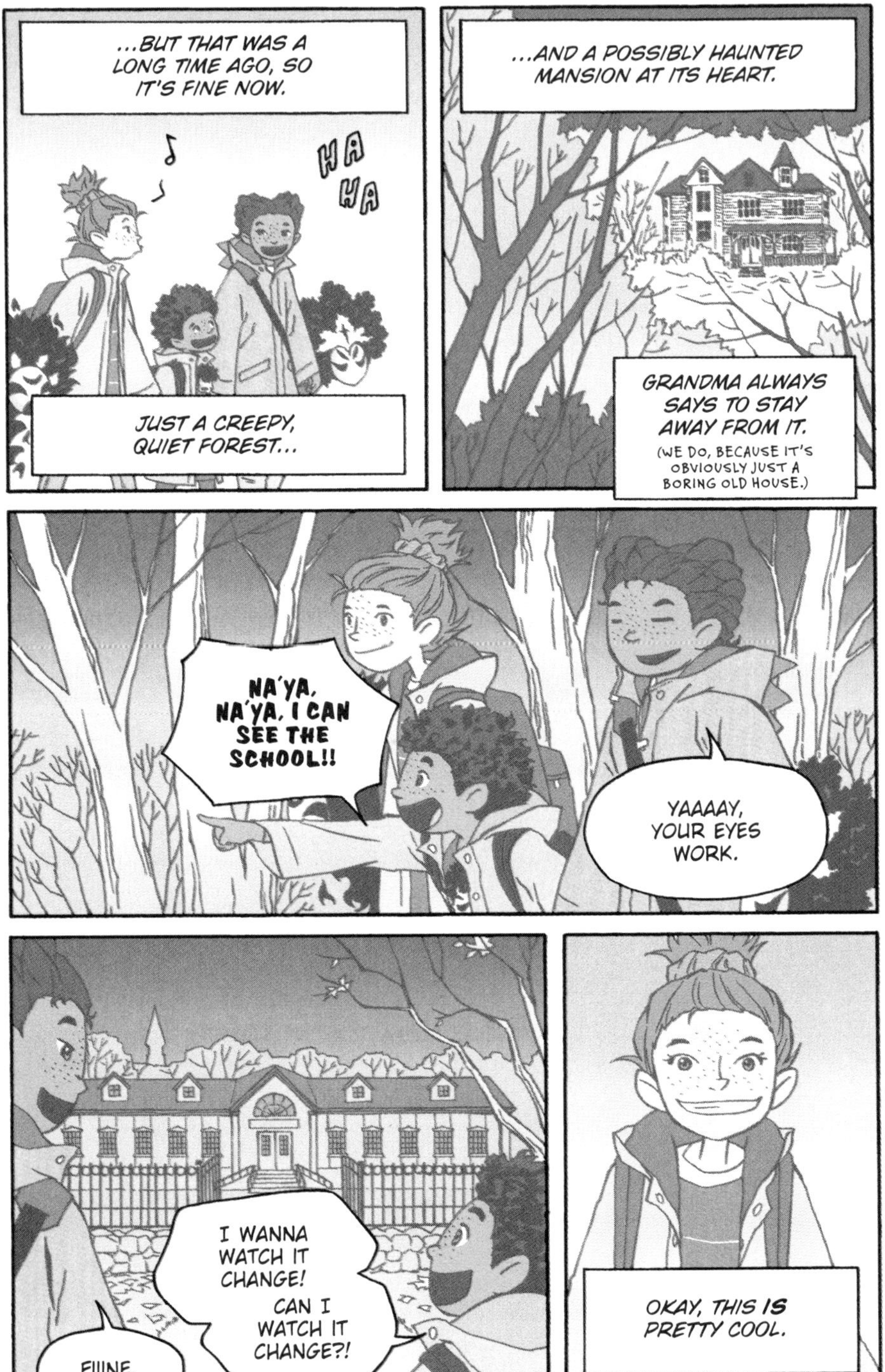
...BUT THAT WAS A LONG TIME AGO, SO IT'S FINE NOW.
HA HA
JUST A CREEPY, QUIET FOREST...
...AND A POSSIBLY HAUNTED MANSION AT ITS HEART.
GRANDMA ALWAYS SAYS TO STAY AWAY FROM IT.
(WE DO, BECAUSE IT'S OBVIOUSLY JUST A BORING OLD HOUSE.)
NA'YA, NA'YA, I CAN SEE THE SCHOOL!!
YAAAAY, YOUR EYES WORK.
I WANNA WATCH IT CHANGE!
CAN I WATCH IT CHANGE?!
FIIINE.
OKAY, THIS IS PRETTY COOL.

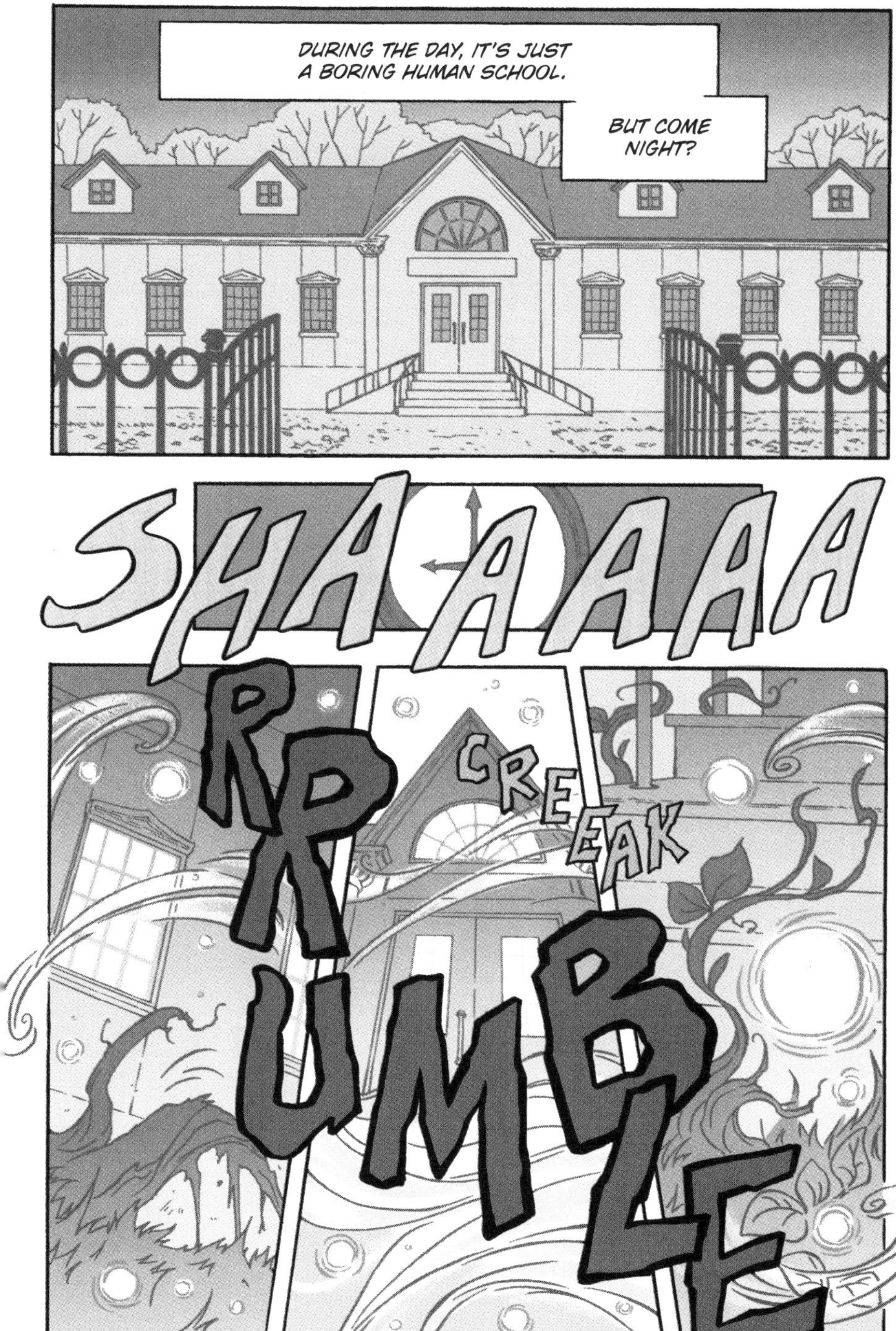
DURING THE DAY, IT'S JUST A BORING HUMAN SCHOOL.
BUT COME NIGHT?
SHAAAAA
RRRUMBLE
CREEAK

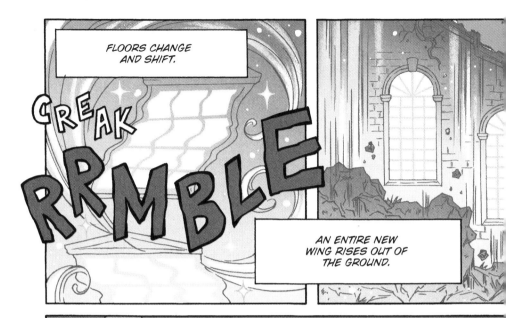

FLOORS CHANGE
AND SHIFT.

CREAK

RRRMBLE

AN ENTIRE NEW
WING RISES OUT OF
THE GROUND.

IT BECOMES
A SCHOOL FOR
US—

NIGHT
THINGS.

HWOO

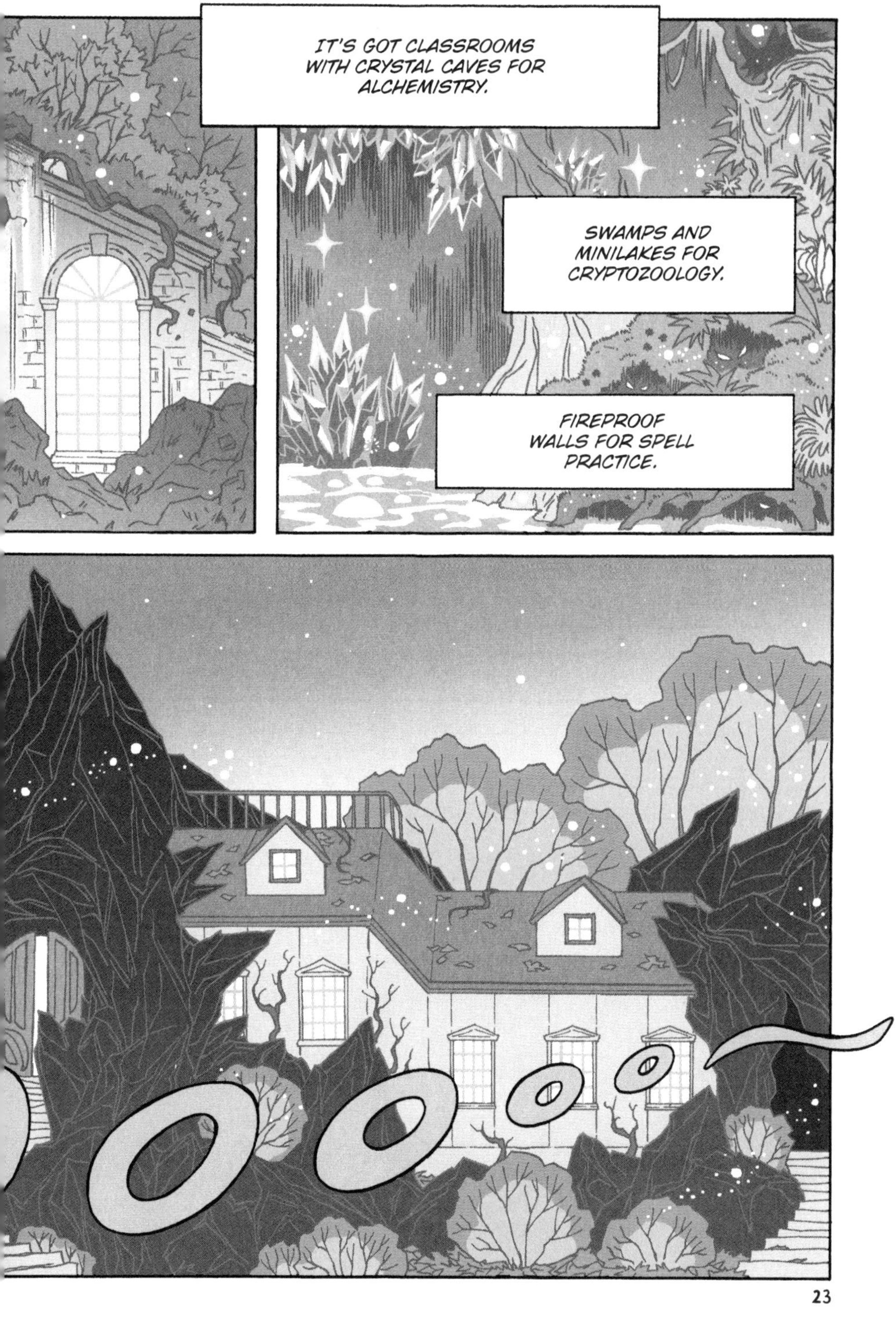
IT'S GOT CLASSROOMS WITH CRYSTAL CAVES FOR ALCHEMISTRY.
SWAMPS AND MINILAKES FOR CRYPTOZOOLOGY.
FIREPROOF WALLS FOR SPELL PRACTICE.
OOOOO~

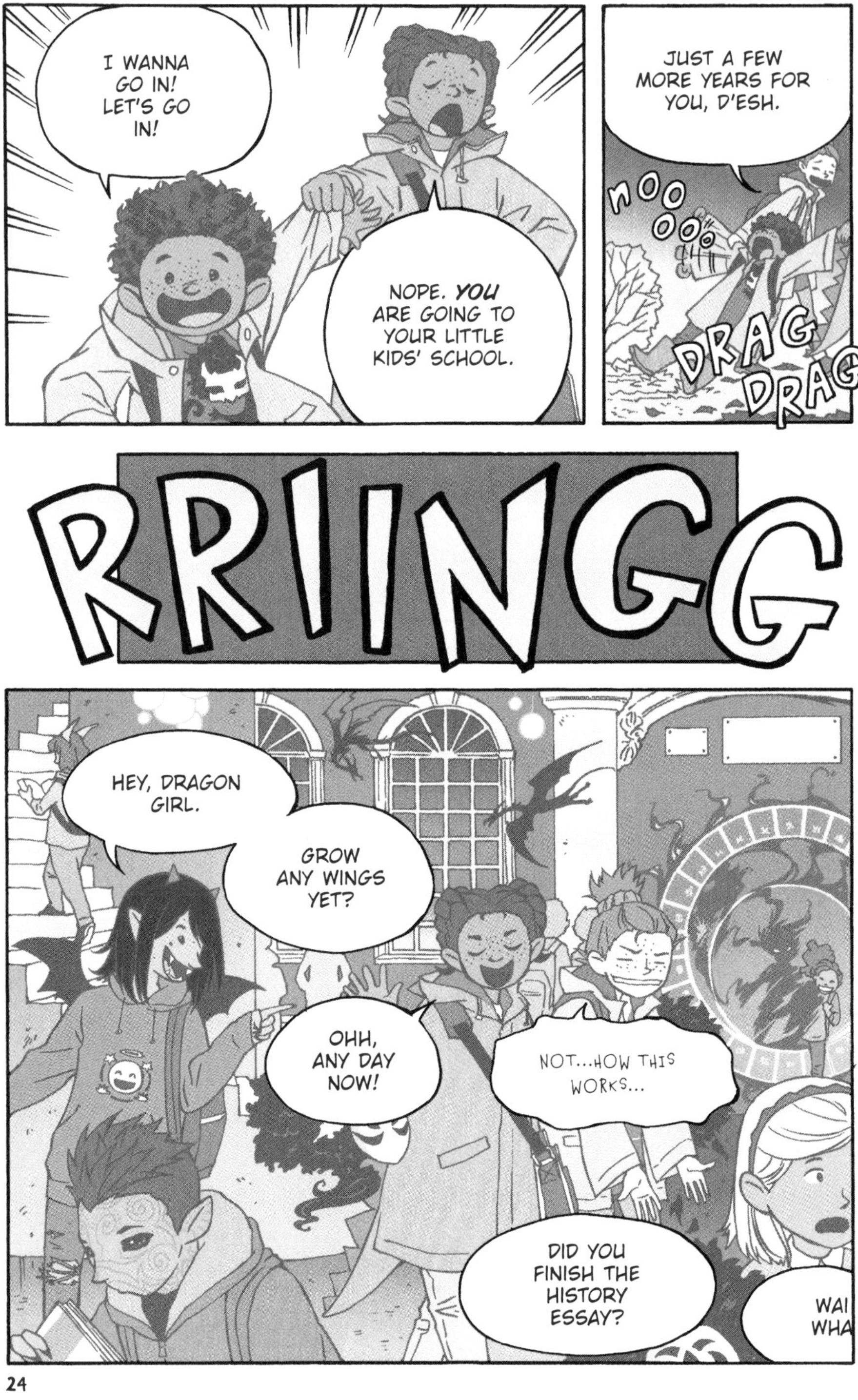
I WANNA GO IN! LET'S GO IN!
NOPE. *YOU* ARE GOING TO YOUR LITTLE KIDS' SCHOOL.
JUST A FEW MORE YEARS FOR YOU, D'ESH.
NOOOOOO
DRAG DRAG
RRIINGG
HEY, DRAGON GIRL.
GROW ANY WINGS YET?
OHH, ANY DAY NOW!
NOT...HOW THIS WORKS...
DID YOU FINISH THE HISTORY ESSAY?
WAI WHA

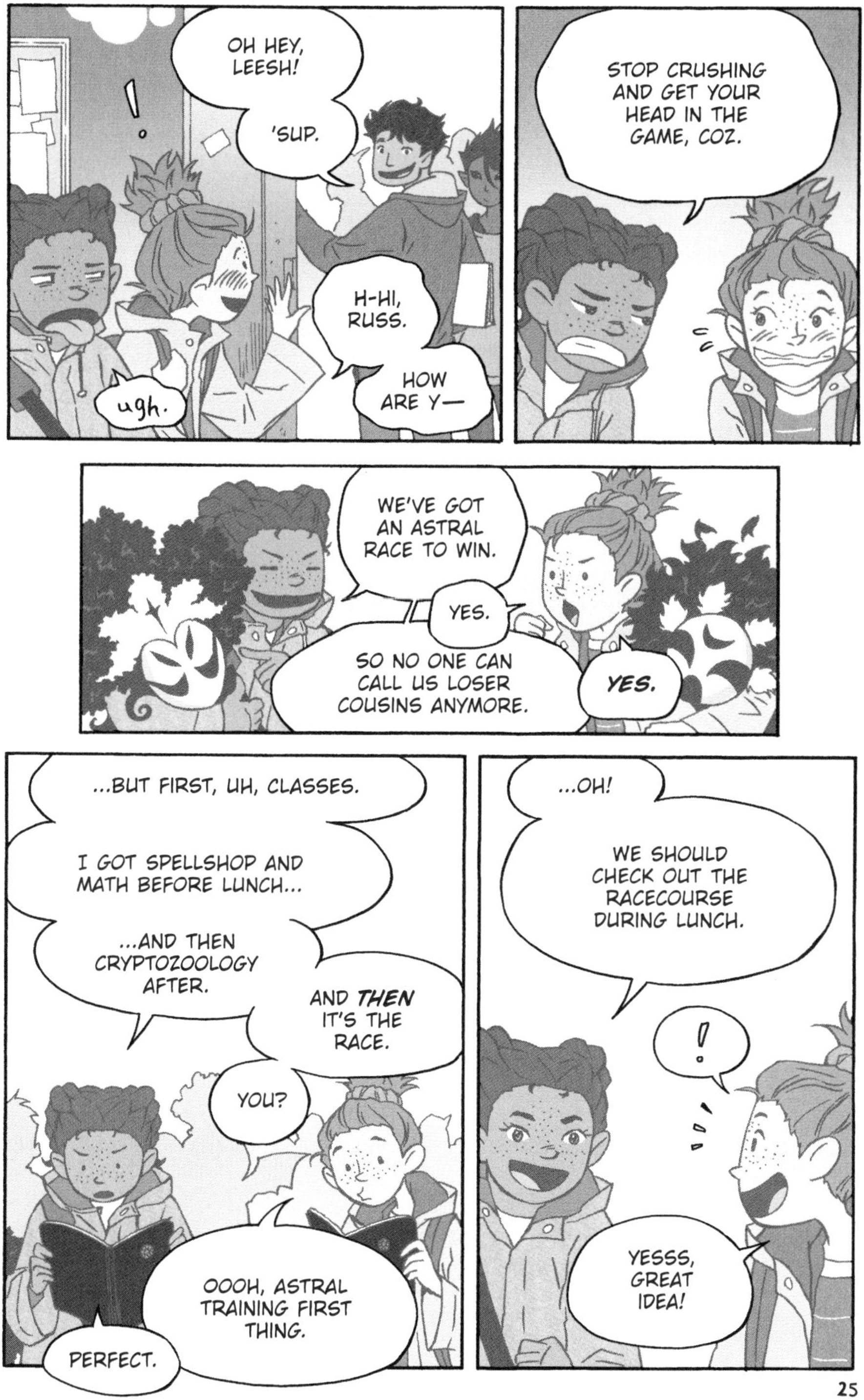
!
OH HEY, LEESH!
'SUP.
H-HI, RUSS.
HOW ARE Y—
ugh.
STOP CRUSHING AND GET YOUR HEAD IN THE GAME, COZ.
WE'VE GOT AN ASTRAL RACE TO WIN.
YES.
SO NO ONE CAN CALL US LOSER COUSINS ANYMORE.
YES.
...BUT FIRST, UH, CLASSES.
I GOT SPELLSHOP AND MATH BEFORE LUNCH...
...AND THEN CRYPTOZOOLOGY AFTER.
AND THEN IT'S THE RACE.
YOU?
OOOH, ASTRAL TRAINING FIRST THING.
PERFECT.
...OH!
WE SHOULD CHECK OUT THE RACECOURSE DURING LUNCH.
!
YESSS, GREAT IDEA!

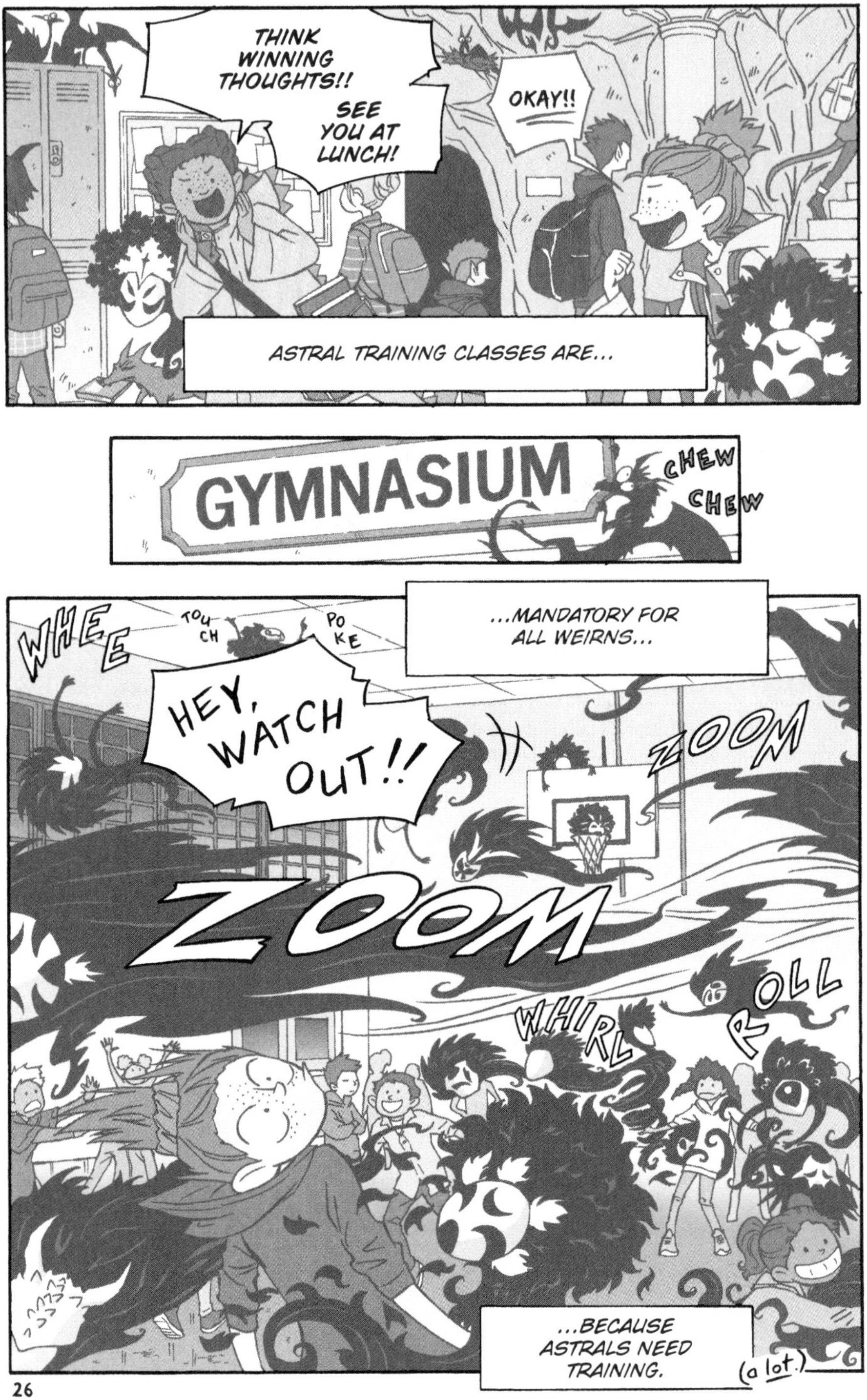
THINK WINNING THOUGHTS!!
SEE YOU AT LUNCH!
OKAY!!
ASTRAL TRAINING CLASSES ARE...
GYMNASIUM
CHEW
CHEW
...MANDATORY FOR ALL WEIRNS...
WHEE
TOUCH
POKE
HEY, WATCH OUT!!
ZOOM
ZOOM
WHIRL
ROLL
...BECAUSE ASTRALS NEED TRAINING.
(a lot.)

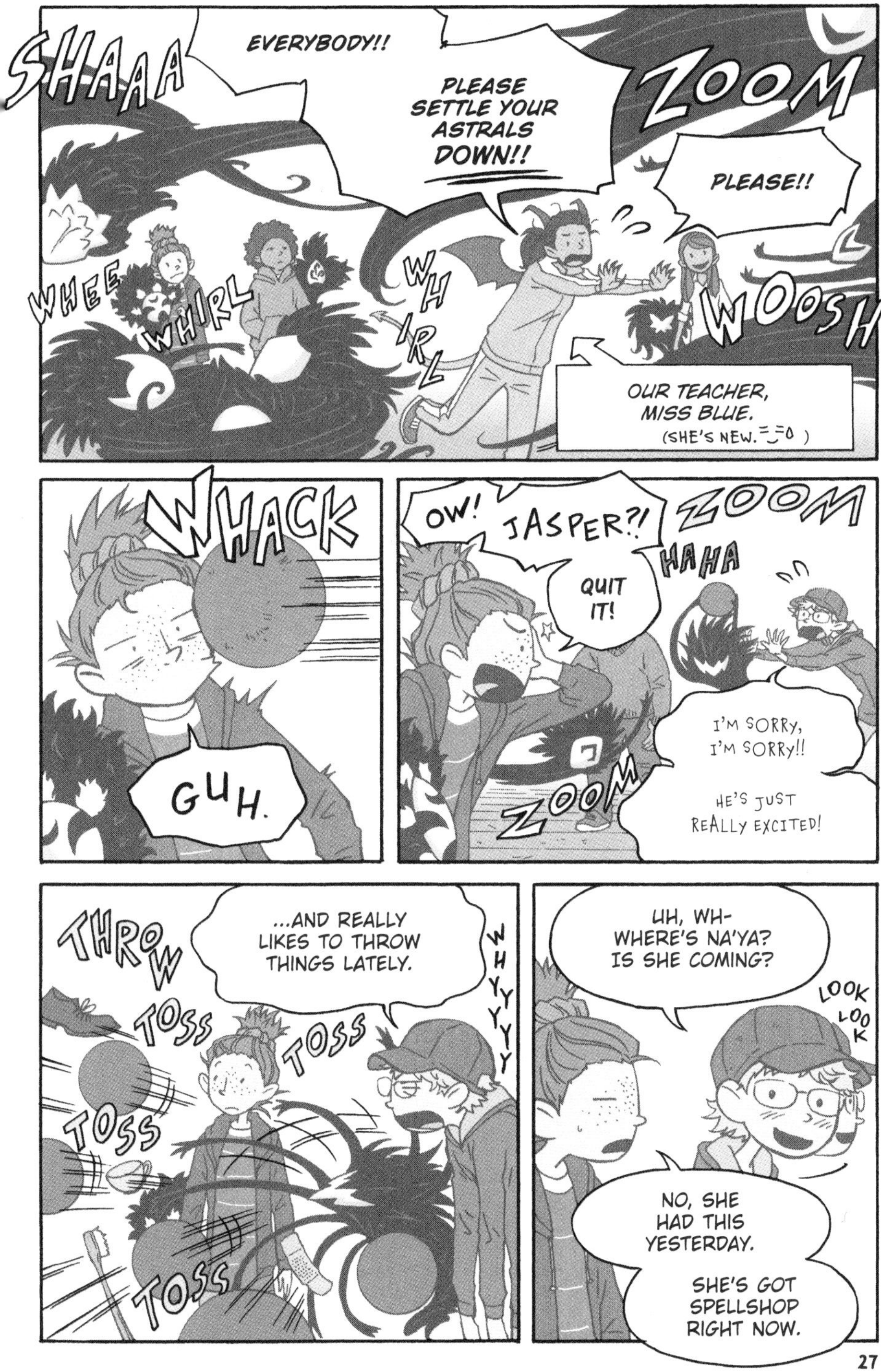
SHAAA
EVERYBODY!!
PLEASE SETTLE YOUR ASTRALS DOWN!!
ZOOM
PLEASE!!
WHEE
WHIRL
WHIRL
WOOSH
OUR TEACHER, MISS BLUE.
(SHE'S NEW.)
WHACK
GUH.
OW!
JASPER?!
ZOOM
QUIT IT!
HAHA
I'M SORRY, I'M SORRY!!
HE'S JUST REALLY EXCITED!
ZOOM
THROW
...AND REALLY LIKES TO THROW THINGS LATELY.
WHYYYY
TOSS
TOSS
TOSS
TOSS
UH, WH-WHERE'S NA'YA? IS SHE COMING?
LOOK LOOK
NO, SHE HAD THIS YESTERDAY.
SHE'S GOT SPELLSHOP RIGHT NOW.

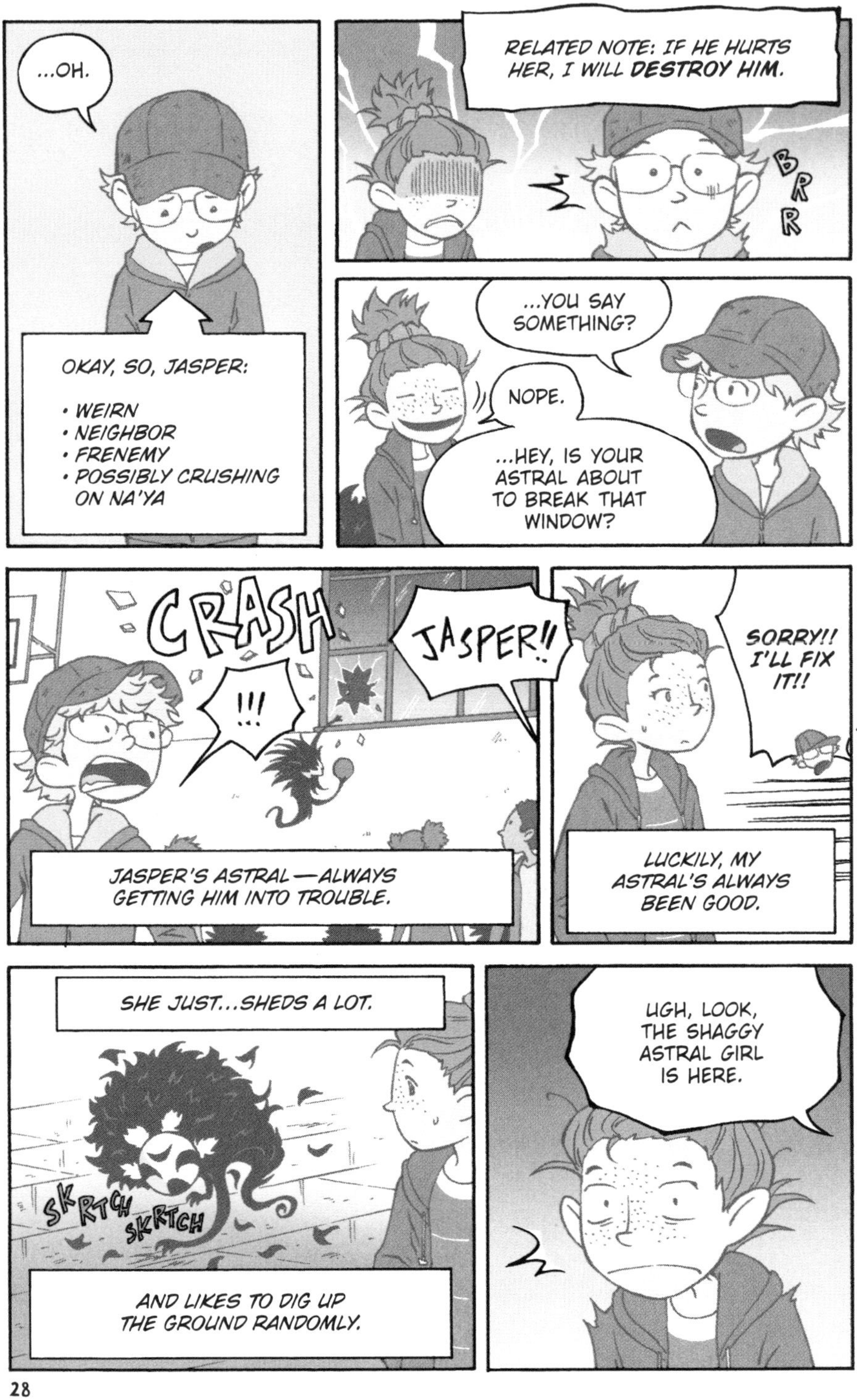
...OH.
OKAY, SO, JASPER:
• WEIRN
• NEIGHBOR
• FRENEMY
• POSSIBLY CRUSHING ON NA'YA
RELATED NOTE: IF HE HURTS HER, I WILL DESTROY HIM.
BRR
...YOU SAY SOMETHING?
NOPE.
...HEY, IS YOUR ASTRAL ABOUT TO BREAK THAT WINDOW?
CRASH
!!!
JASPER!!
JASPER'S ASTRAL—ALWAYS GETTING HIM INTO TROUBLE.
SORRY!! I'LL FIX IT!!
LUCKILY, MY ASTRAL'S ALWAYS BEEN GOOD.
SHE JUST...SHEDS A LOT.
SKRTCH SKRTCH
AND LIKES TO DIG UP THE GROUND RANDOMLY.
UGH, LOOK, THE SHAGGY ASTRAL GIRL IS HERE.

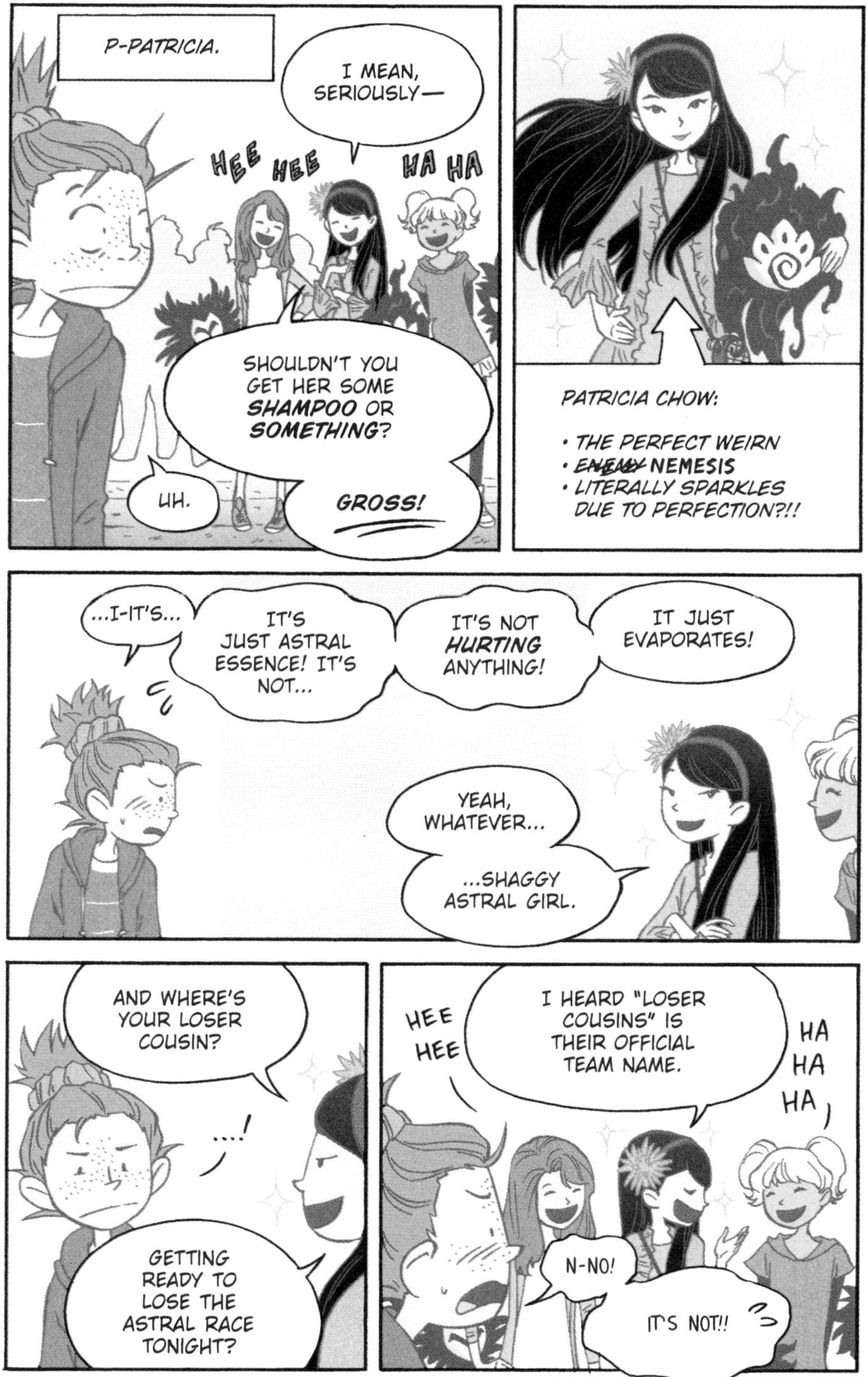
P-PATRICIA.
HEE HEE
I MEAN, SERIOUSLY—
HA HA
SHOULDN'T YOU GET HER SOME **SHAMPOO** OR **SOMETHING**?
UH.
GROSS!
PATRICIA CHOW:
• THE PERFECT WEIRN
• ~~ENEMY~~ NEMESIS
• LITERALLY SPARKLES DUE TO PERFECTION?!!
...I-IT'S...
IT'S JUST ASTRAL ESSENCE! IT'S NOT...
IT'S NOT **HURTING** ANYTHING!
IT JUST EVAPORATES!
YEAH, WHATEVER...
...SHAGGY ASTRAL GIRL.
AND WHERE'S YOUR LOSER COUSIN?
...!
GETTING READY TO LOSE THE ASTRAL RACE TONIGHT?
HEE HEE
I HEARD "LOSER COUSINS" IS THEIR OFFICIAL TEAM NAME.
HA HA HA
N-NO!
IT'S NOT!!

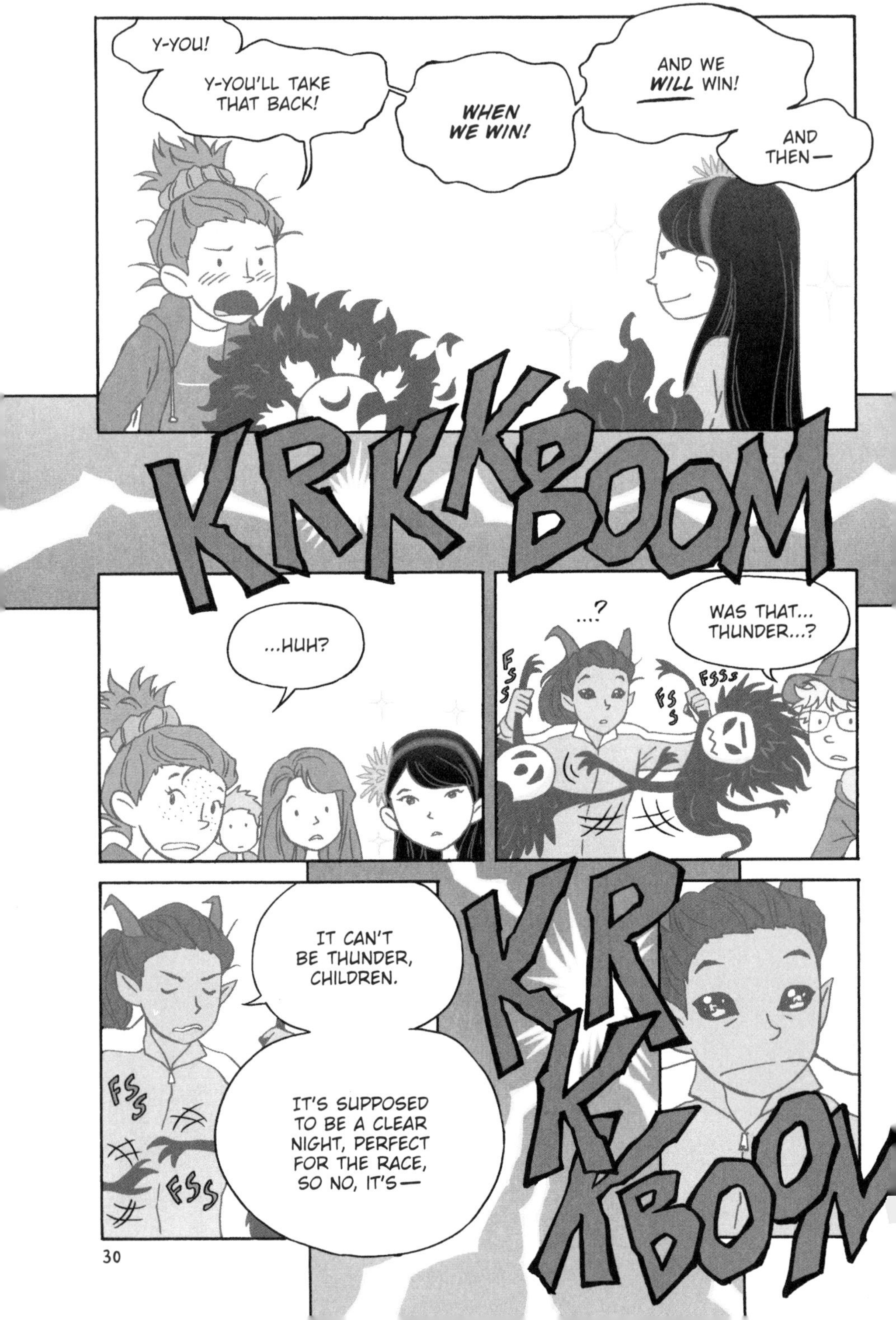
Y-YOU!
Y-YOU'LL TAKE THAT BACK!
WHEN WE WIN!
AND WE WILL WIN!
AND THEN—
KRKKBOOM
...HUH?
...?
WAS THAT... THUNDER...?
FSS
FSSS
FSS
IT CAN'T BE THUNDER, CHILDREN.
IT'S SUPPOSED TO BE A CLEAR NIGHT, PERFECT FOR THE RACE, SO NO, IT'S—
FSS
FSS
KRKKBOOM

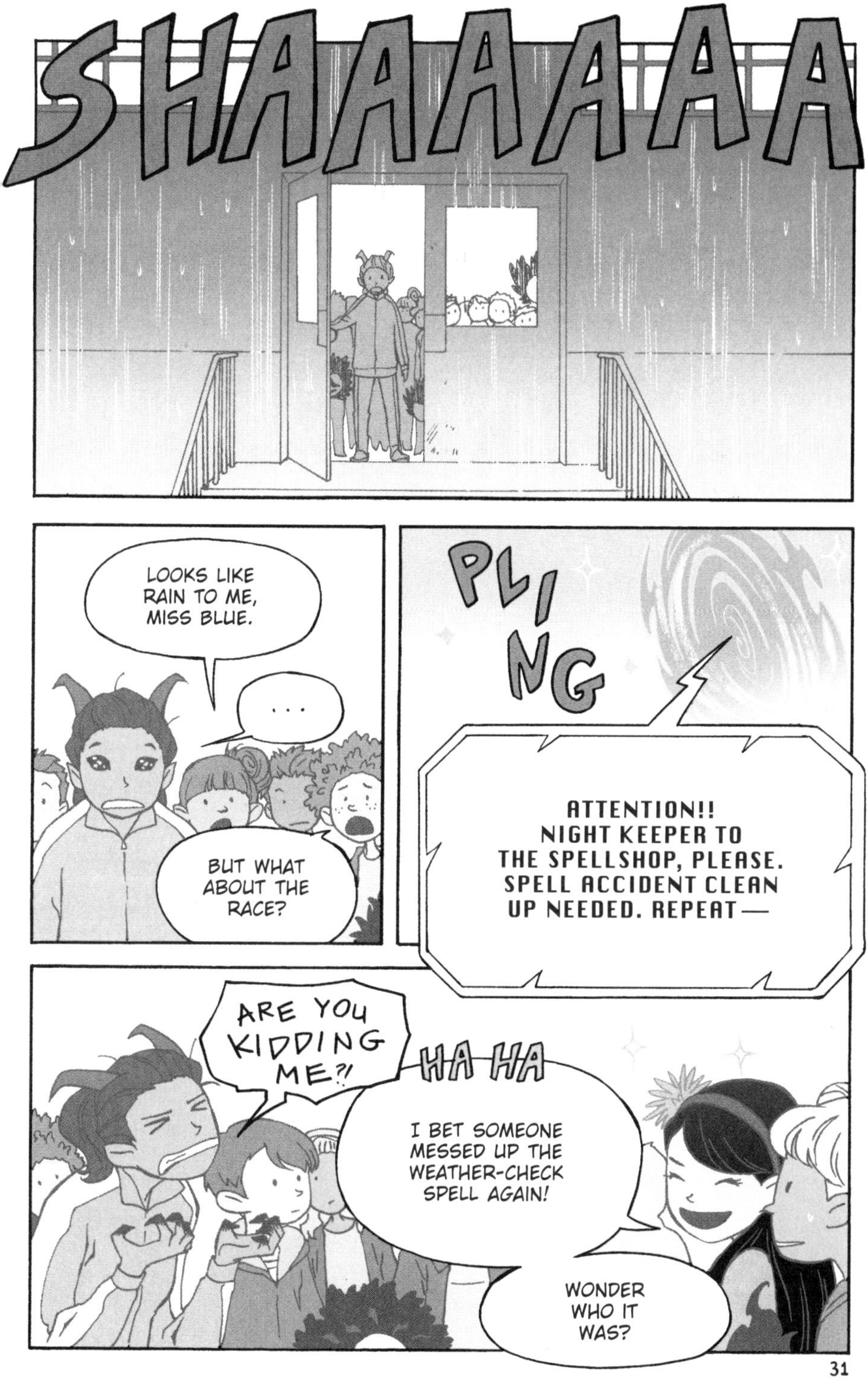
SHAAAAAAA
LOOKS LIKE RAIN TO ME, MISS BLUE.
...
BUT WHAT ABOUT THE RACE?
PLING
ATTENTION!! NIGHT KEEPER TO THE SPELLSHOP, PLEASE. SPELL ACCIDENT CLEAN UP NEEDED. REPEAT—
ARE YOU KIDDING ME?!
HA HA
I BET SOMEONE MESSED UP THE WEATHER-CHECK SPELL AGAIN!
WONDER WHO IT WAS?

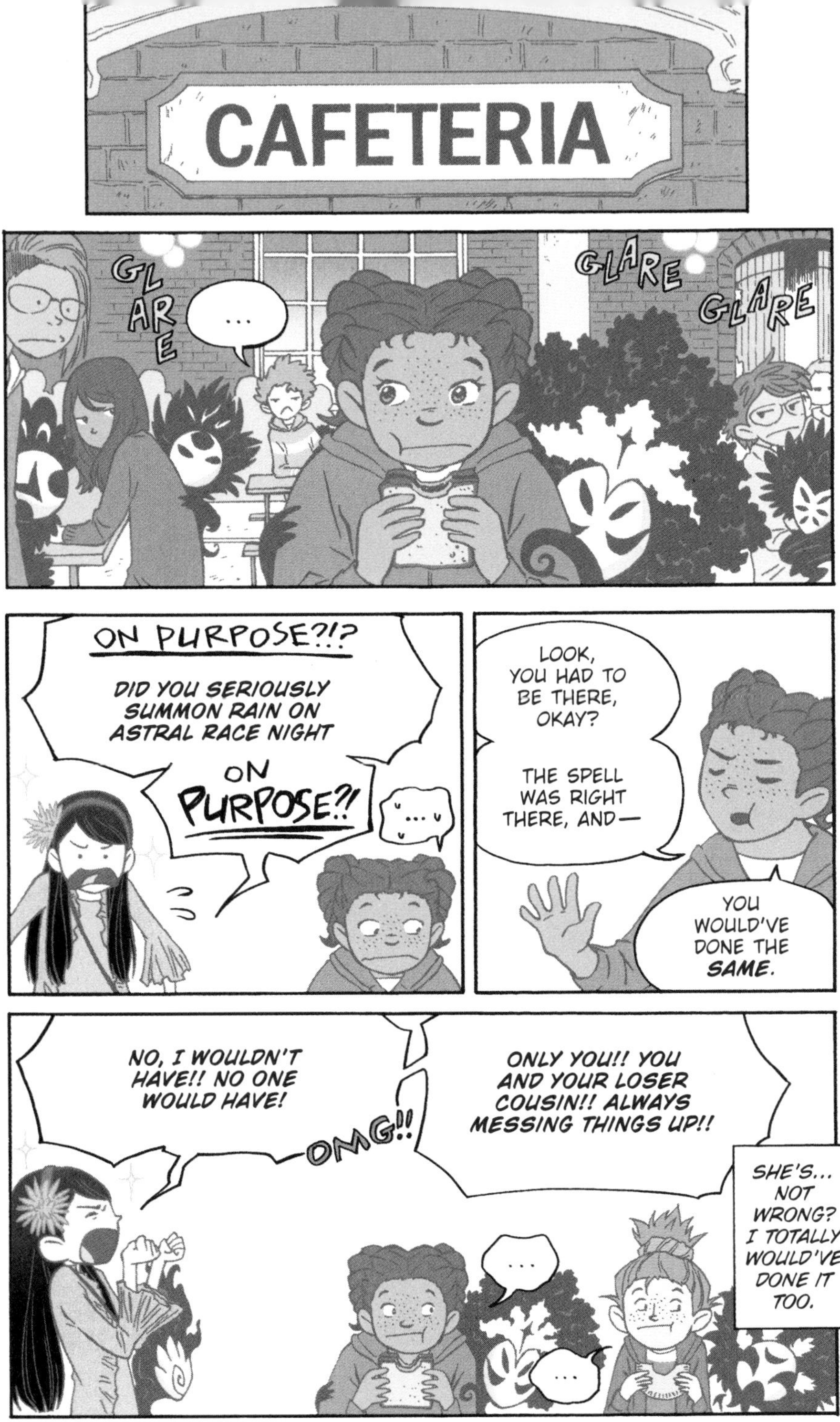
CAFETERIA
GLARE
...
GLARE GLARE
ON PURPOSE?!?
DID YOU SERIOUSLY SUMMON RAIN ON ASTRAL RACE NIGHT
ON PURPOSE?!
...
LOOK, YOU HAD TO BE THERE, OKAY?
THE SPELL WAS RIGHT THERE, AND—
YOU WOULD'VE DONE THE SAME.
NO, I WOULDN'T HAVE!! NO ONE WOULD HAVE!
OMG!!
ONLY YOU!! YOU AND YOUR LOSER COUSIN!! ALWAYS MESSING THINGS UP!!
SHE'S... NOT WRONG? I TOTALLY WOULD'VE DONE IT TOO.
...
...

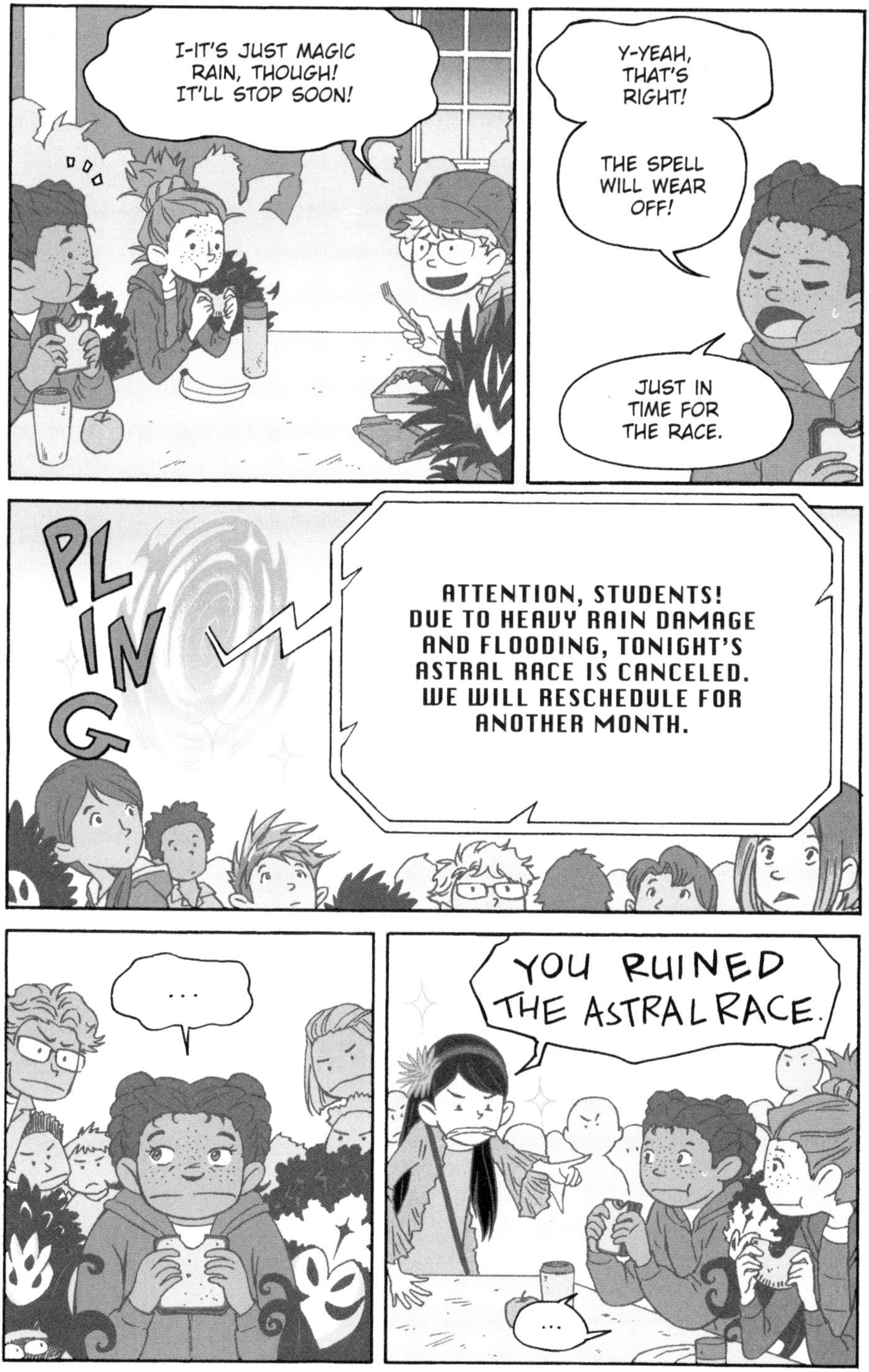
I-IT'S JUST MAGIC RAIN, THOUGH! IT'LL STOP SOON!
Y-YEAH, THAT'S RIGHT!
THE SPELL WILL WEAR OFF!
JUST IN TIME FOR THE RACE.
PLING
ATTENTION, STUDENTS! DUE TO HEAVY RAIN DAMAGE AND FLOODING, TONIGHT'S ASTRAL RACE IS CANCELED. WE WILL RESCHEDULE FOR ANOTHER MONTH.
...
YOU RUINED THE ASTRAL RACE.
...

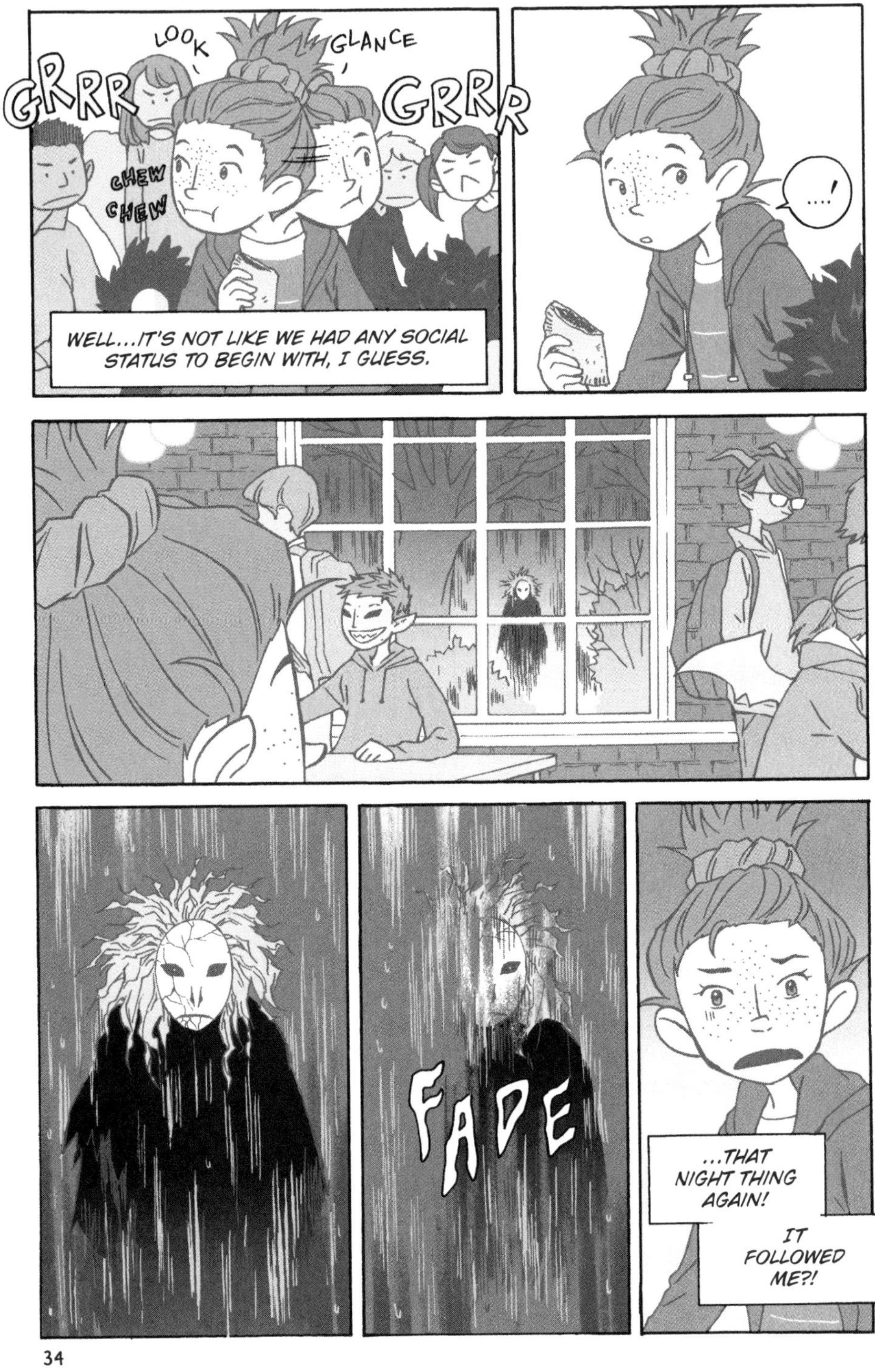
LOOK
GLANCE
GRRR
GRRR
CHEW
CHEW
WELL...IT'S NOT LIKE WE HAD ANY SOCIAL STATUS TO BEGIN WITH, I GUESS.
....!
FADE
...THAT NIGHT THING AGAIN!
IT FOLLOWED ME?!

Chapter 2

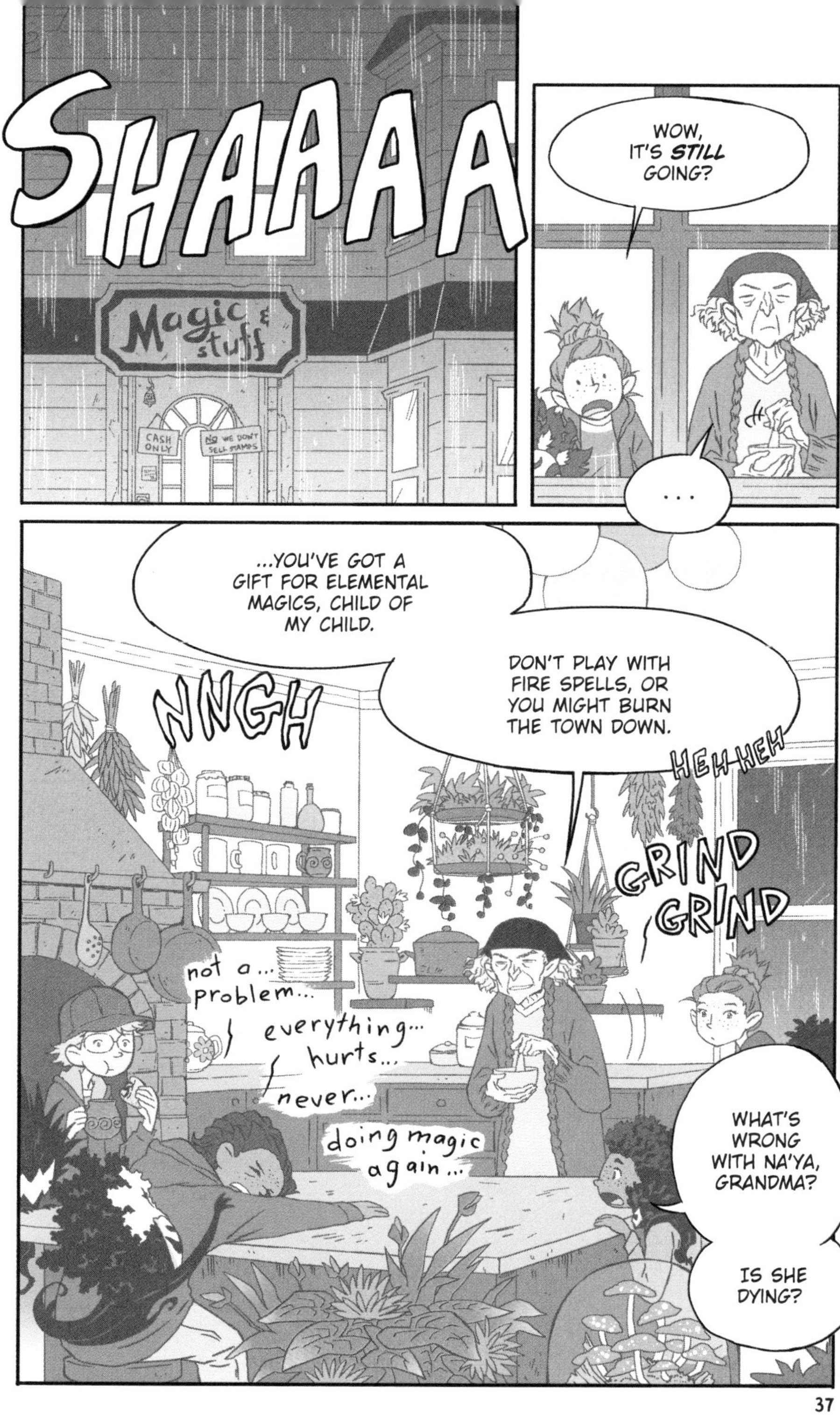
SHAAAA
Magic & stuff
CASH ONLY
NO WE DON'T SELL STAMPS
WOW, IT'S STILL GOING?
...
...YOU'VE GOT A GIFT FOR ELEMENTAL MAGICS, CHILD OF MY CHILD.
DON'T PLAY WITH FIRE SPELLS, OR YOU MIGHT BURN THE TOWN DOWN.
NNGH
HEH HEH
GRIND GRIND
not a... problem...
everything... hurts...
never...
doing magic again...
WHAT'S WRONG WITH NA'YA, GRANDMA?
IS SHE DYING?

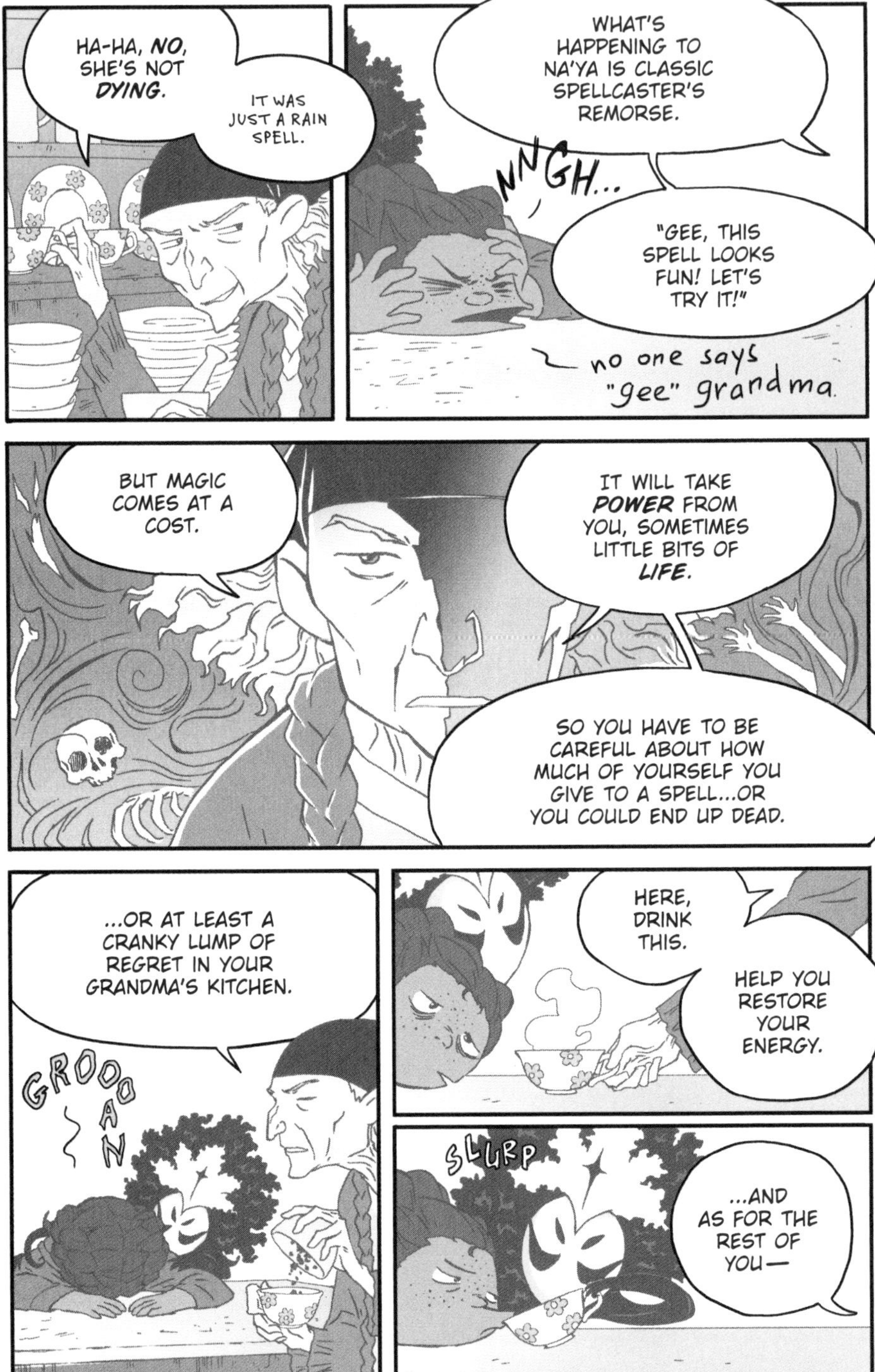
HA-HA, NO, SHE'S NOT DYING.
IT WAS JUST A RAIN SPELL.
WHAT'S HAPPENING TO NA'YA IS CLASSIC SPELLCASTER'S REMORSE.
NNGH...
"GEE, THIS SPELL LOOKS FUN! LET'S TRY IT!"
no one says "gee" grandma.
BUT MAGIC COMES AT A COST.
IT WILL TAKE POWER FROM YOU, SOMETIMES LITTLE BITS OF LIFE.
SO YOU HAVE TO BE CAREFUL ABOUT HOW MUCH OF YOURSELF YOU GIVE TO A SPELL...OR YOU COULD END UP DEAD.
...OR AT LEAST A CRANKY LUMP OF REGRET IN YOUR GRANDMA'S KITCHEN.
GROOOAN
HERE, DRINK THIS.
HELP YOU RESTORE YOUR ENERGY.
SLURP
...AND AS FOR THE REST OF YOU—

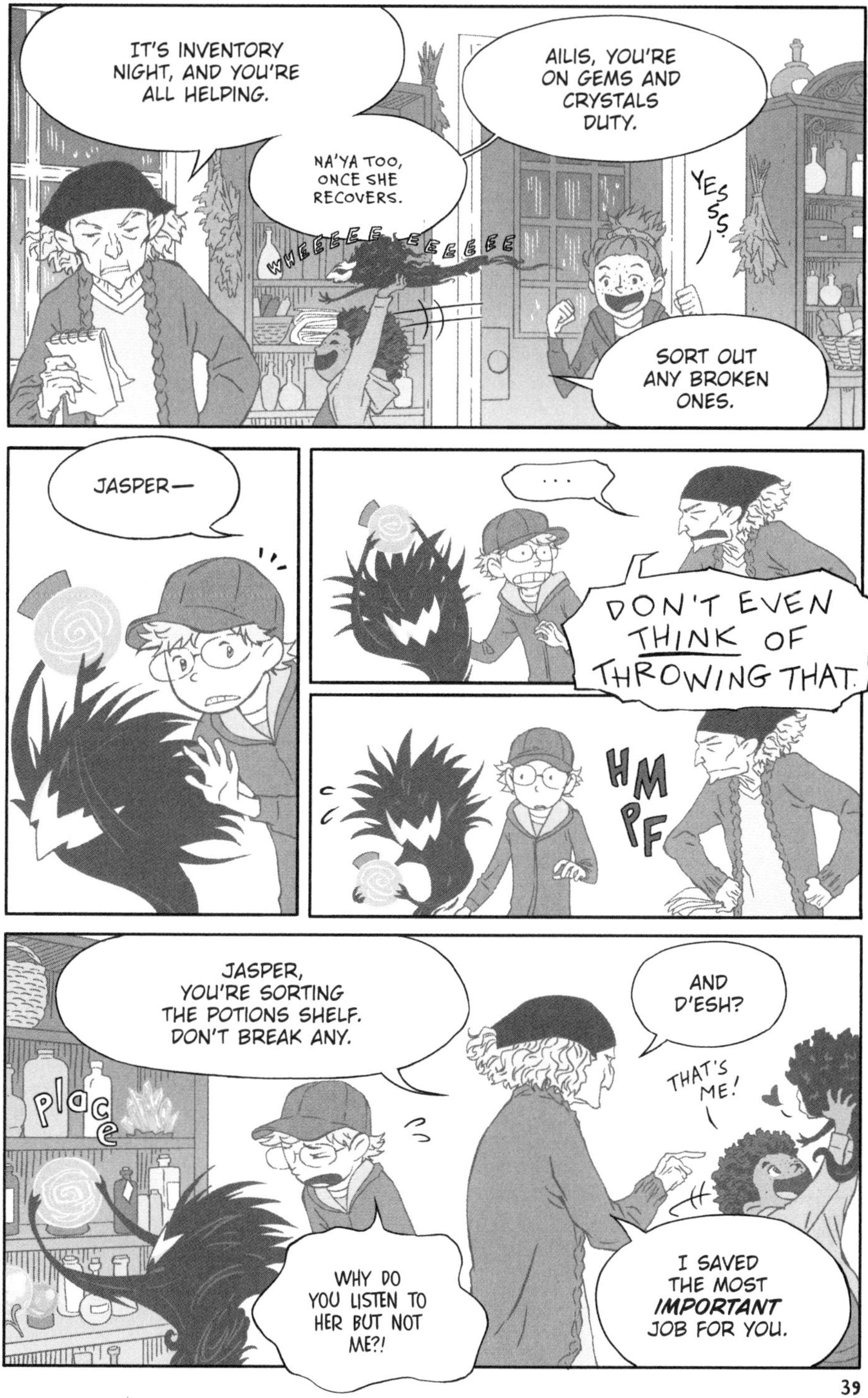
IT'S INVENTORY NIGHT, AND YOU'RE ALL HELPING.
NA'YA TOO, ONCE SHE RECOVERS.
AILIS, YOU'RE ON GEMS AND CRYSTALS DUTY.
WHEEEEEE EEEEEE
YESSS
SORT OUT ANY BROKEN ONES.
JASPER—
...
DON'T EVEN THINK OF THROWING THAT.
HMPF
JASPER, YOU'RE SORTING THE POTIONS SHELF. DON'T BREAK ANY.
AND D'ESH?
THAT'S ME!
place
WHY DO YOU LISTEN TO HER BUT NOT ME?!
I SAVED THE MOST ***IMPORTANT*** JOB FOR YOU.

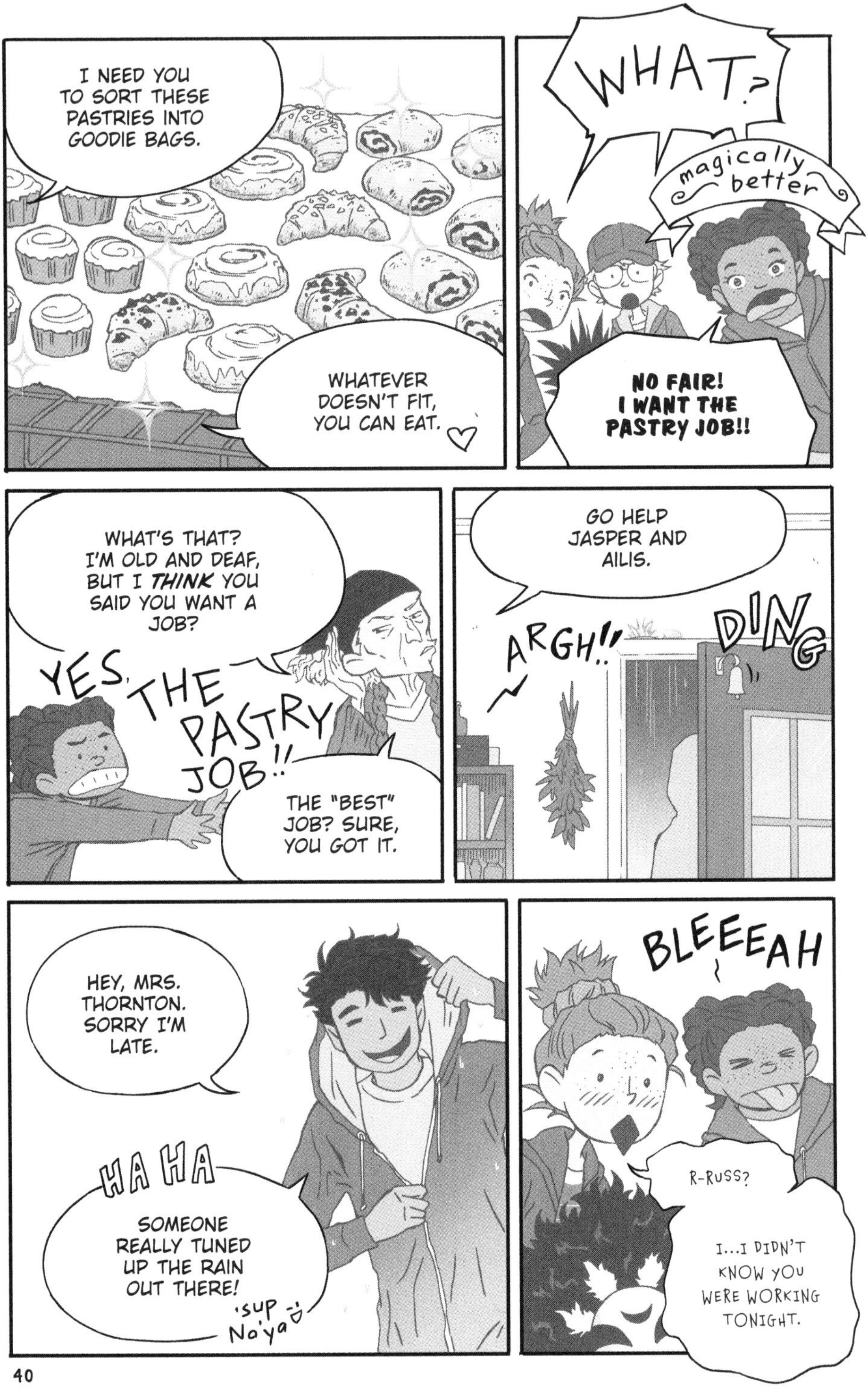

I NEED YOU TO SORT THESE PASTRIES INTO GOODIE BAGS.
WHATEVER DOESN'T FIT, YOU CAN EAT.
WHAT?
magically better
NO FAIR! I WANT THE PASTRY JOB!!
WHAT'S THAT? I'M OLD AND DEAF, BUT I *THINK* YOU SAID YOU WANT A JOB?
YES, THE PASTRY JOB!!
THE "BEST" JOB? SURE, YOU GOT IT.
GO HELP JASPER AND AILIS.
ARGH!!..
DING
HEY, MRS. THORNTON. SORRY I'M LATE.
HA HA
SOMEONE REALLY TUNED UP THE RAIN OUT THERE!
'sup Noya
BLEEEAH
R-RUSS?
I...I DIDN'T KNOW YOU WERE WORKING TONIGHT.

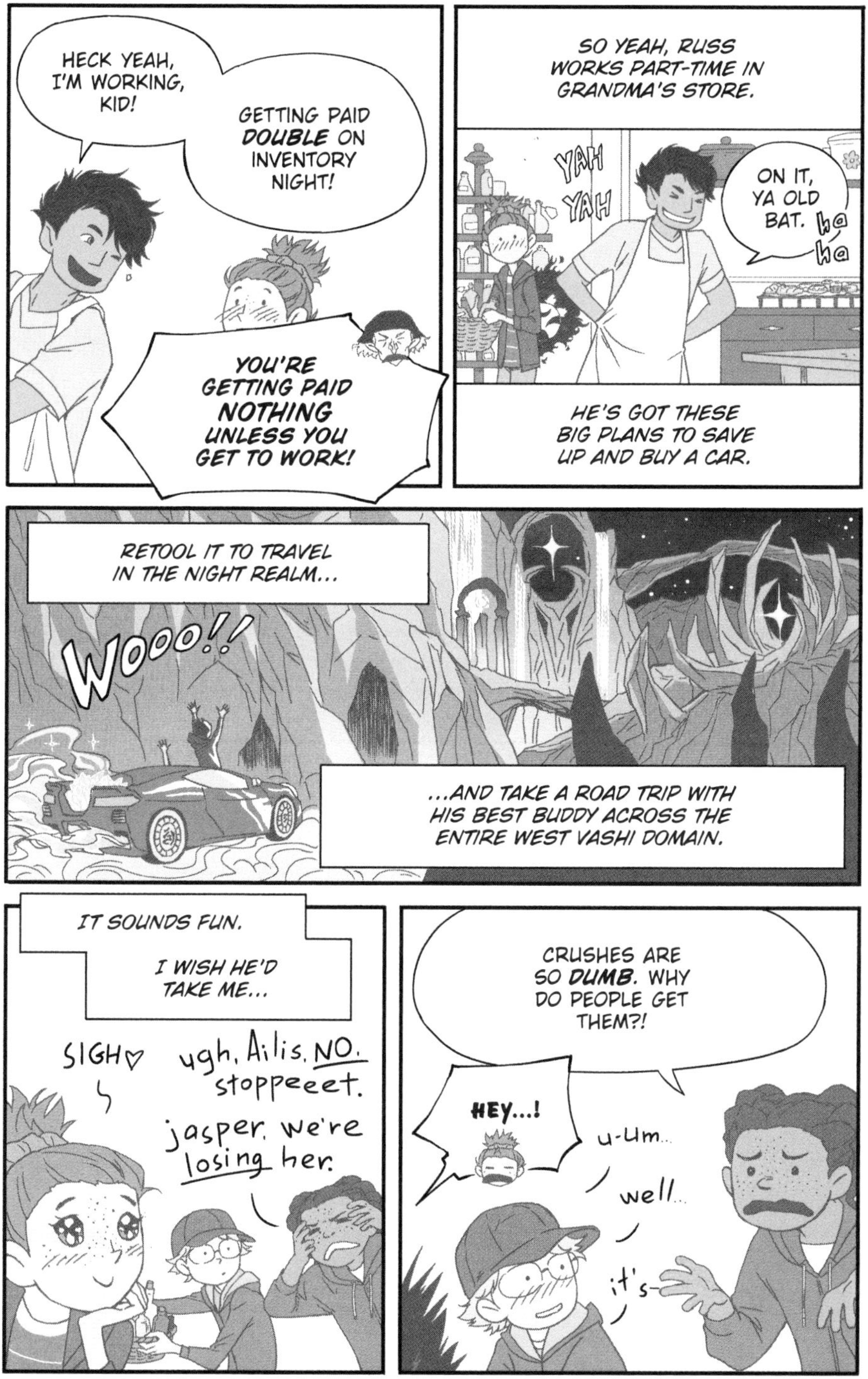
HECK YEAH, I'M WORKING, KID!
GETTING PAID DOUBLE ON INVENTORY NIGHT!
YOU'RE GETTING PAID NOTHING UNLESS YOU GET TO WORK!
SO YEAH, RUSS WORKS PART-TIME IN GRANDMA'S STORE.
YAH YAH
ON IT, YA OLD BAT.
ha ha
HE'S GOT THESE BIG PLANS TO SAVE UP AND BUY A CAR.
RETOOL IT TO TRAVEL IN THE NIGHT REALM...
WOOO!!
...AND TAKE A ROAD TRIP WITH HIS BEST BUDDY ACROSS THE ENTIRE WEST VASHI DOMAIN.
IT SOUNDS FUN.
I WISH HE'D TAKE ME...
SIGH♡
ugh. Ailis. NO. stoppeeet.
jasper. we're losing her.
CRUSHES ARE SO DUMB. WHY DO PEOPLE GET THEM?!
HEY...!
u-um...
well...
it's-

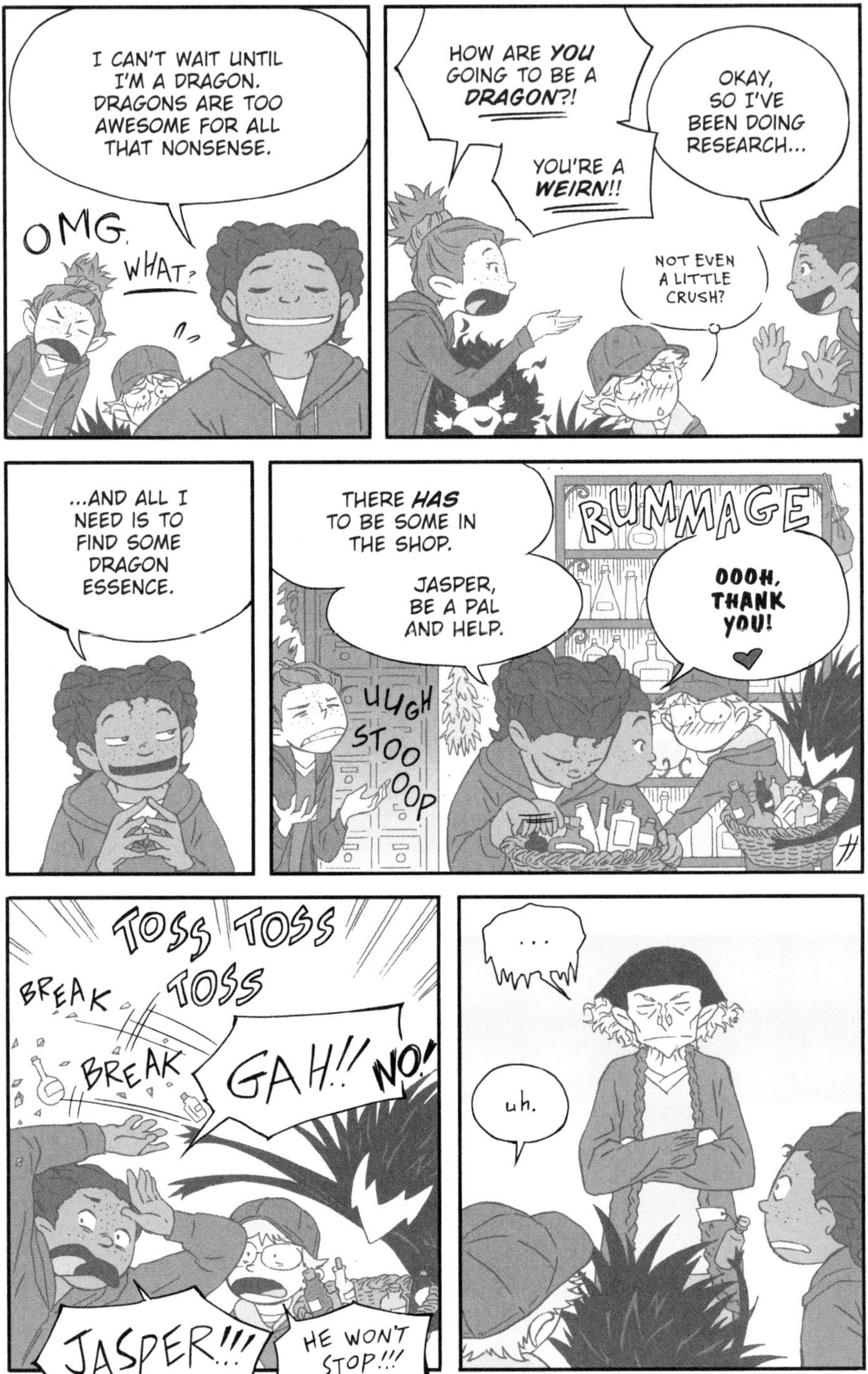
I CAN'T WAIT UNTIL I'M A DRAGON. DRAGONS ARE TOO AWESOME FOR ALL THAT NONSENSE.
OMG.
WHAT?
HOW ARE YOU GOING TO BE A DRAGON?!
YOU'RE A WEIRN!!
OKAY, SO I'VE BEEN DOING RESEARCH...
NOT EVEN A LITTLE CRUSH?
...AND ALL I NEED IS TO FIND SOME DRAGON ESSENCE.
THERE HAS TO BE SOME IN THE SHOP.
JASPER, BE A PAL AND HELP.
RUMMAGE
OOOH, THANK YOU!
UUGH
STOOOOOP
TOSS TOSS
TOSS
BREAK
BREAK
GAH!!
NO!
JASPER!!!
HE WON'T STOP!!!
...
uh.

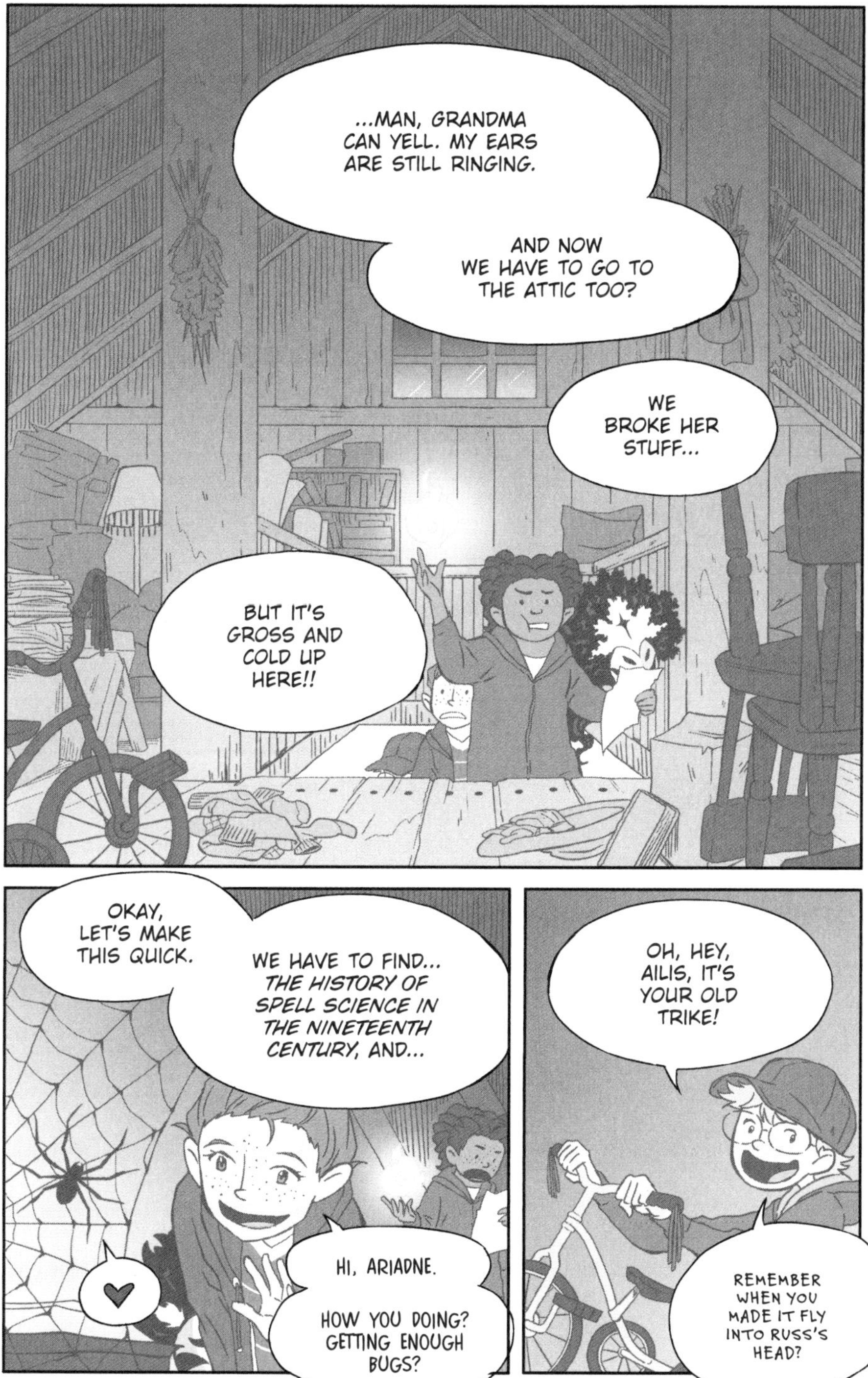
...MAN, GRANDMA CAN YELL. MY EARS ARE STILL RINGING.
AND NOW WE HAVE TO GO TO THE ATTIC TOO?
WE BROKE HER STUFF...
BUT IT'S GROSS AND COLD UP HERE!!
OKAY, LET'S MAKE THIS QUICK.
WE HAVE TO FIND... *THE HISTORY OF SPELL SCIENCE IN THE NINETEENTH CENTURY,* AND...
HI, ARIADNE.
HOW YOU DOING? GETTING ENOUGH BUGS?
OH, HEY, AILIS, IT'S YOUR OLD TRIKE!
REMEMBER WHEN YOU MADE IT FLY INTO RUSS'S HEAD?

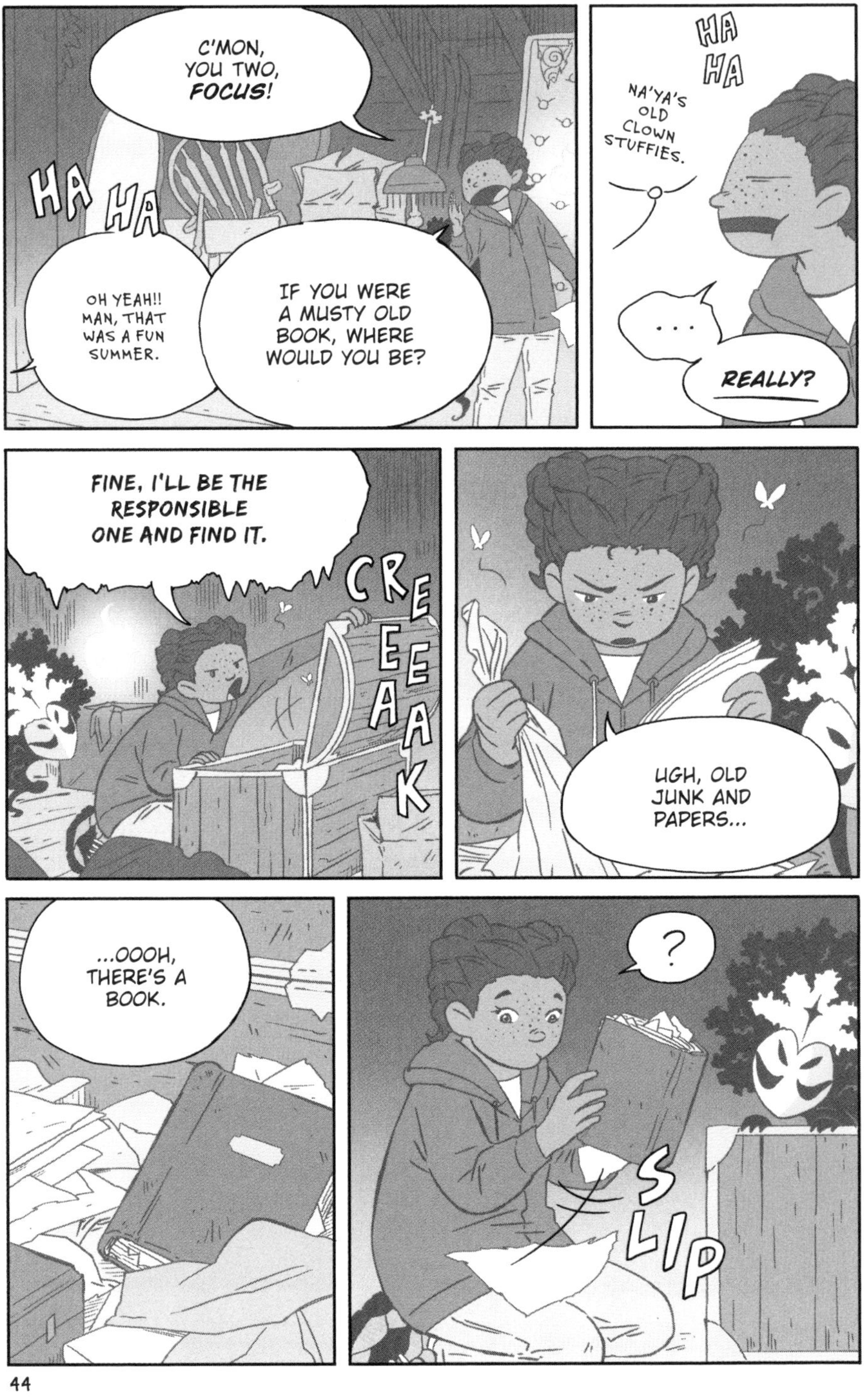
C'MON, YOU TWO, *FOCUS*!
HA HA
OH YEAH!! MAN, THAT WAS A FUN SUMMER.
IF YOU WERE A MUSTY OLD BOOK, WHERE WOULD YOU BE?
HA HA
NA'YA'S OLD CLOWN STUFFIES.
...
REALLY?
FINE, I'LL BE THE RESPONSIBLE ONE AND FIND IT.
CREEEAK
UGH, OLD JUNK AND PAPERS...
...OOOH, THERE'S A BOOK.
?
SLIP

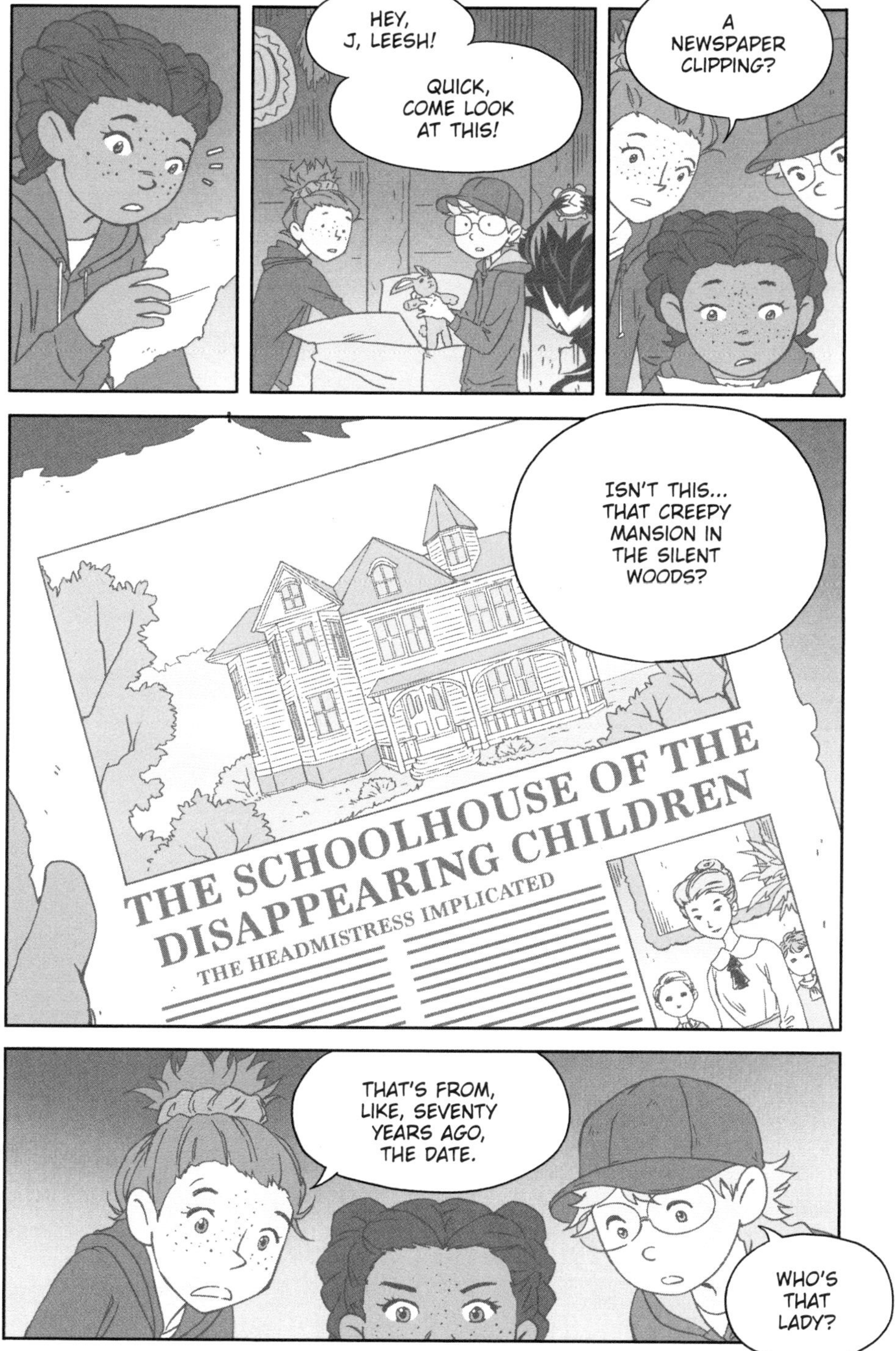
HEY, J, LEESH!
QUICK, COME LOOK AT THIS!
A NEWSPAPER CLIPPING?
ISN'T THIS... THAT CREEPY MANSION IN THE SILENT WOODS?
THE SCHOOLHOUSE OF THE DISAPPEARING CHILDREN
THE HEADMISTRESS IMPLICATED
THAT'S FROM, LIKE, SEVENTY YEARS AGO, THE DATE.
WHO'S THAT LADY?

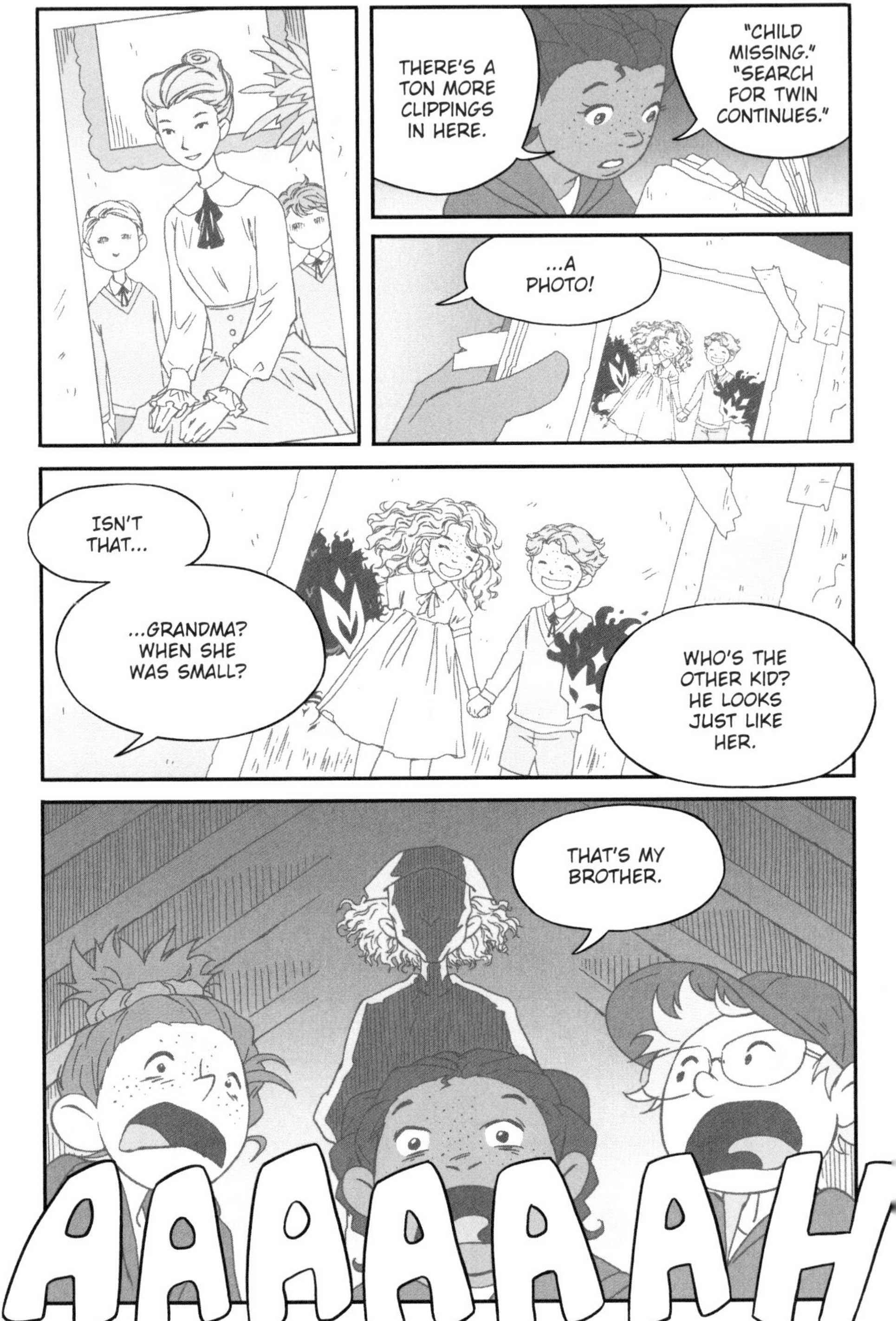
THERE'S A TON MORE CLIPPINGS IN HERE.
"CHILD MISSING." "SEARCH FOR TWIN CONTINUES."
...A PHOTO!
ISN'T THAT...
...GRANDMA? WHEN SHE WAS SMALL?
WHO'S THE OTHER KID? HE LOOKS JUST LIKE HER.
THAT'S MY BROTHER.
AAAAAAAH

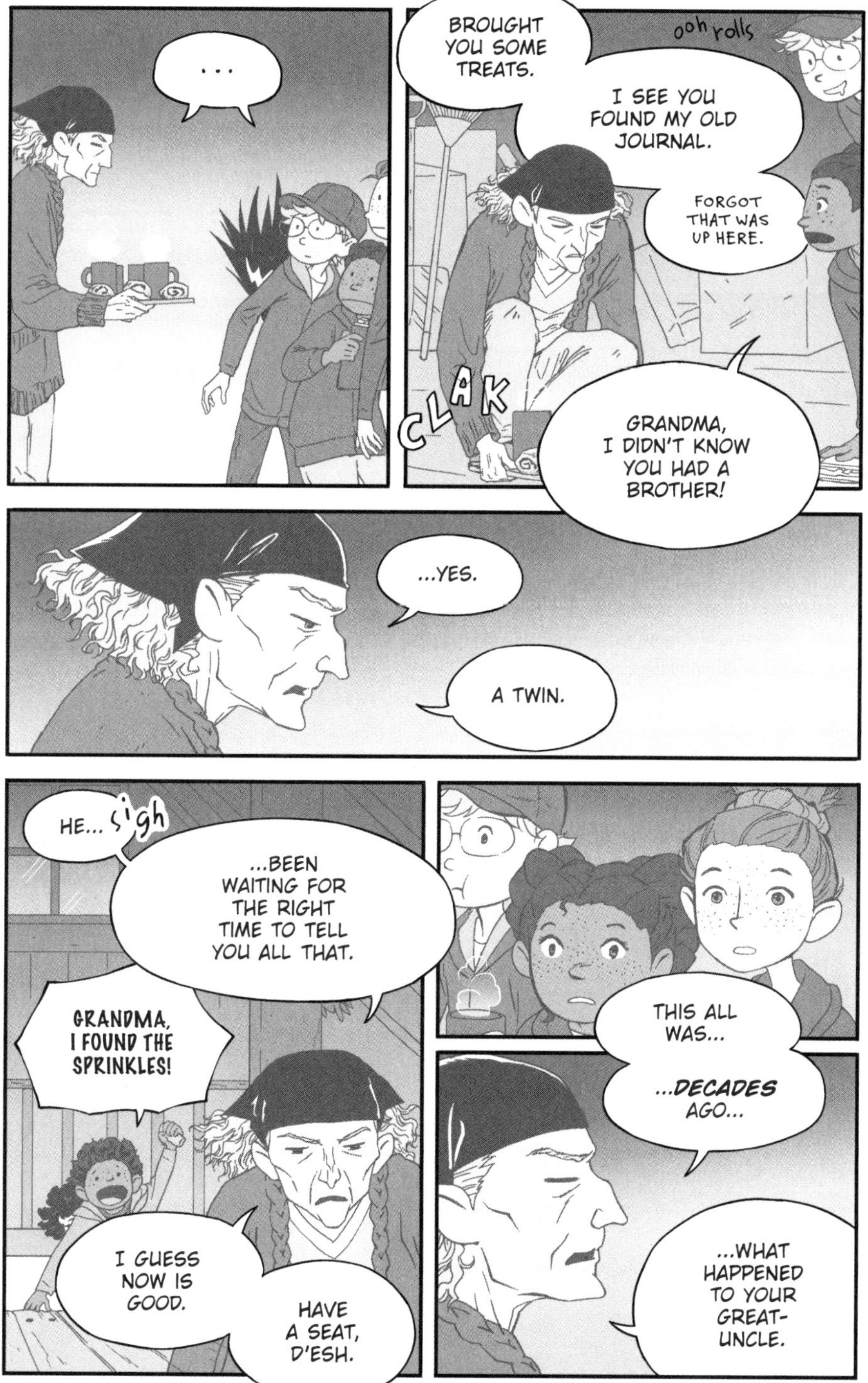
. . .
BROUGHT YOU SOME TREATS.
ooh rolls
I SEE YOU FOUND MY OLD JOURNAL.
FORGOT THAT WAS UP HERE.
CLAK
GRANDMA, I DIDN'T KNOW YOU HAD A BROTHER!
...YES.
A TWIN.
HE... sigh
...BEEN WAITING FOR THE RIGHT TIME TO TELL YOU ALL THAT.
GRANDMA, I FOUND THE SPRINKLES!
I GUESS NOW IS GOOD.
HAVE A SEAT, D'ESH.
THIS ALL WAS...
...DECADES AGO...
...WHAT HAPPENED TO YOUR GREAT-UNCLE.

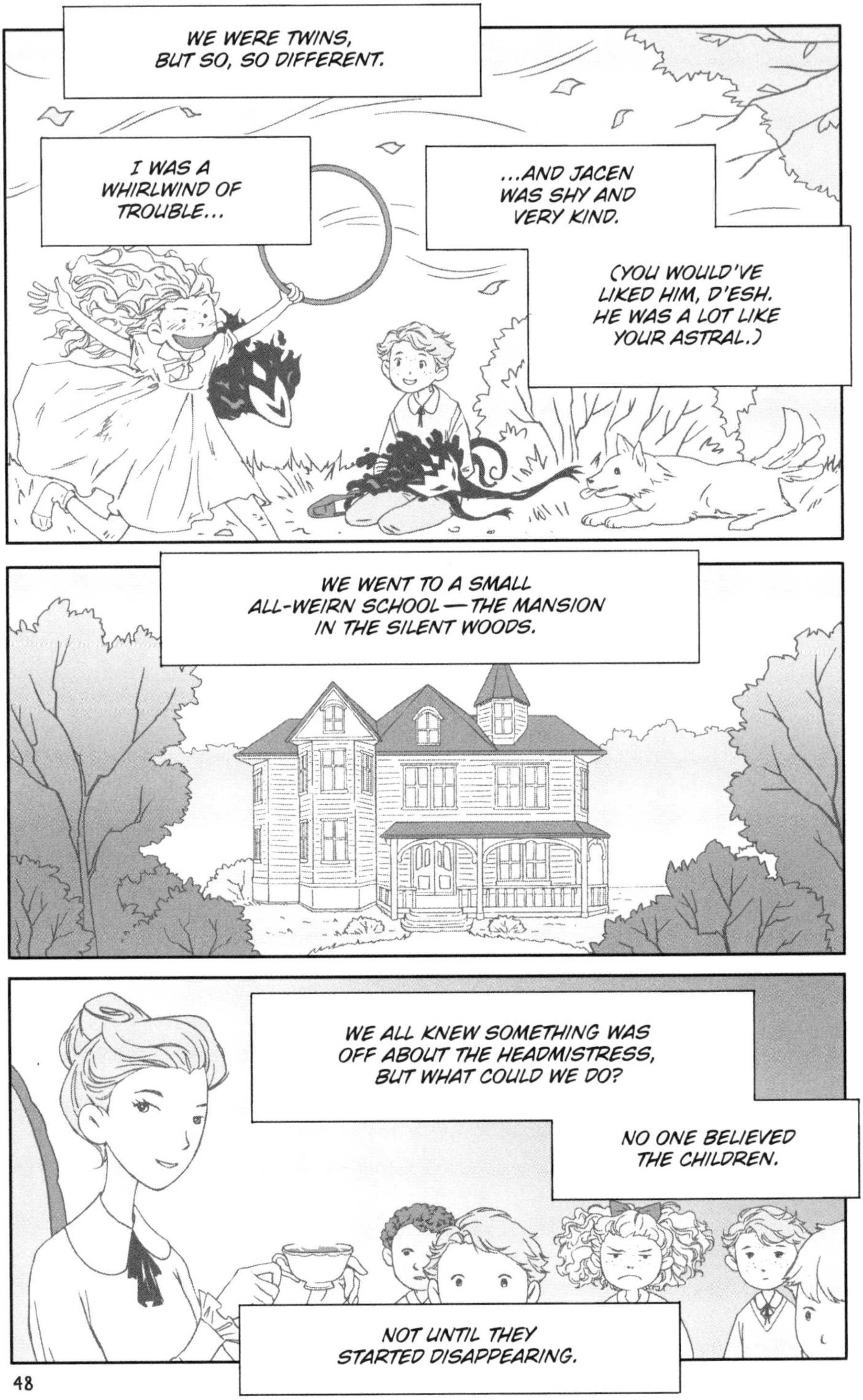
WE WERE TWINS, BUT SO, SO DIFFERENT.
I WAS A WHIRLWIND OF TROUBLE...
...AND JACEN WAS SHY AND VERY KIND.
(YOU WOULD'VE LIKED HIM, D'ESH. HE WAS A LOT LIKE YOUR ASTRAL.)
WE WENT TO A SMALL ALL-WEIRN SCHOOL—THE MANSION IN THE SILENT WOODS.
WE ALL KNEW SOMETHING WAS OFF ABOUT THE HEADMISTRESS, BUT WHAT COULD WE DO?
NO ONE BELIEVED THE CHILDREN.
NOT UNTIL THEY STARTED DISAPPEARING.

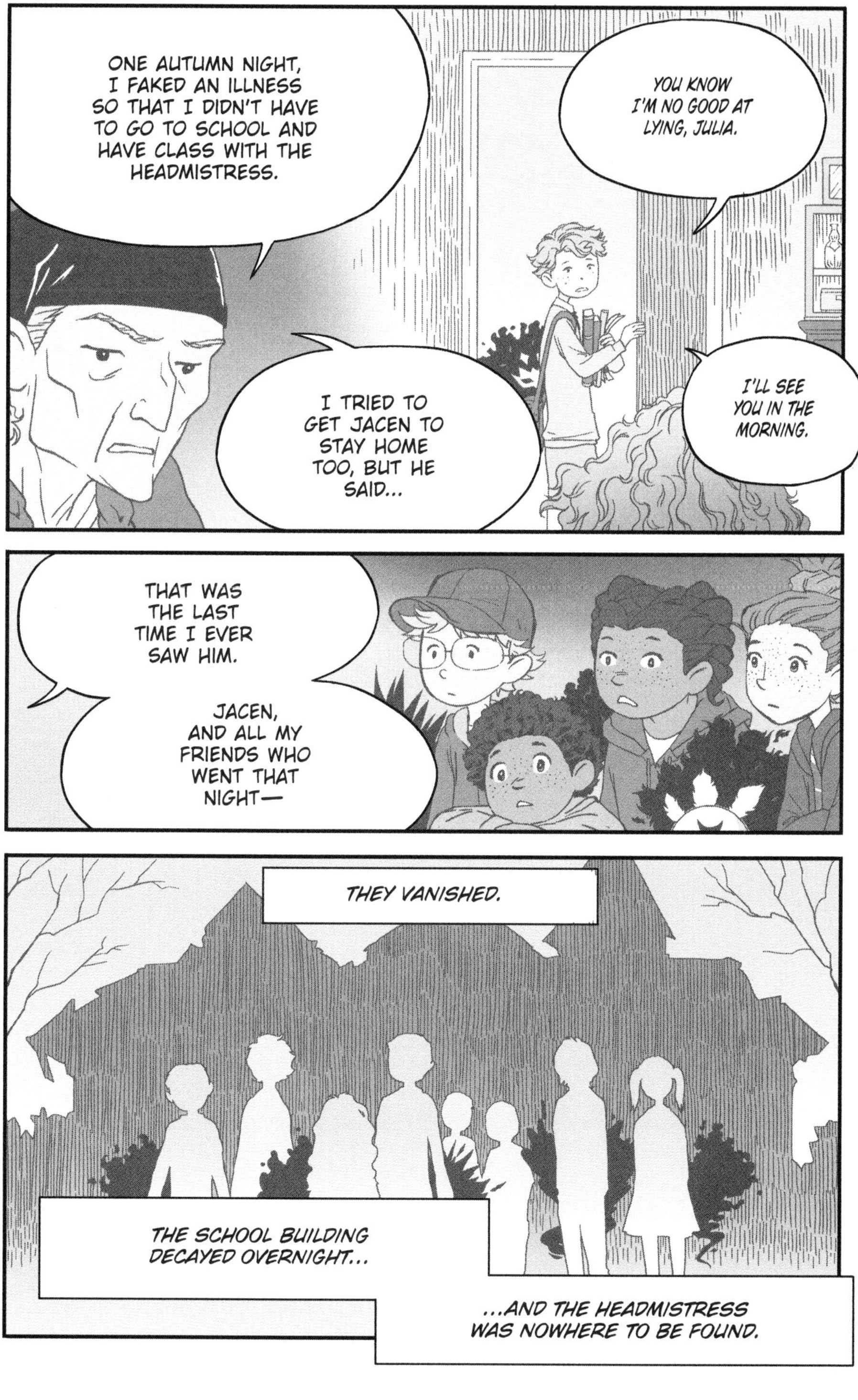
ONE AUTUMN NIGHT, I FAKED AN ILLNESS SO THAT I DIDN'T HAVE TO GO TO SCHOOL AND HAVE CLASS WITH THE HEADMISTRESS.
YOU KNOW I'M NO GOOD AT LYING, JULIA.
I TRIED TO GET JACEN TO STAY HOME TOO, BUT HE SAID...
I'LL SEE YOU IN THE MORNING.
THAT WAS THE LAST TIME I EVER SAW HIM.
JACEN, AND ALL MY FRIENDS WHO WENT THAT NIGHT—
THEY VANISHED.
THE SCHOOL BUILDING DECAYED OVERNIGHT...
...AND THE HEADMISTRESS WAS NOWHERE TO BE FOUND.

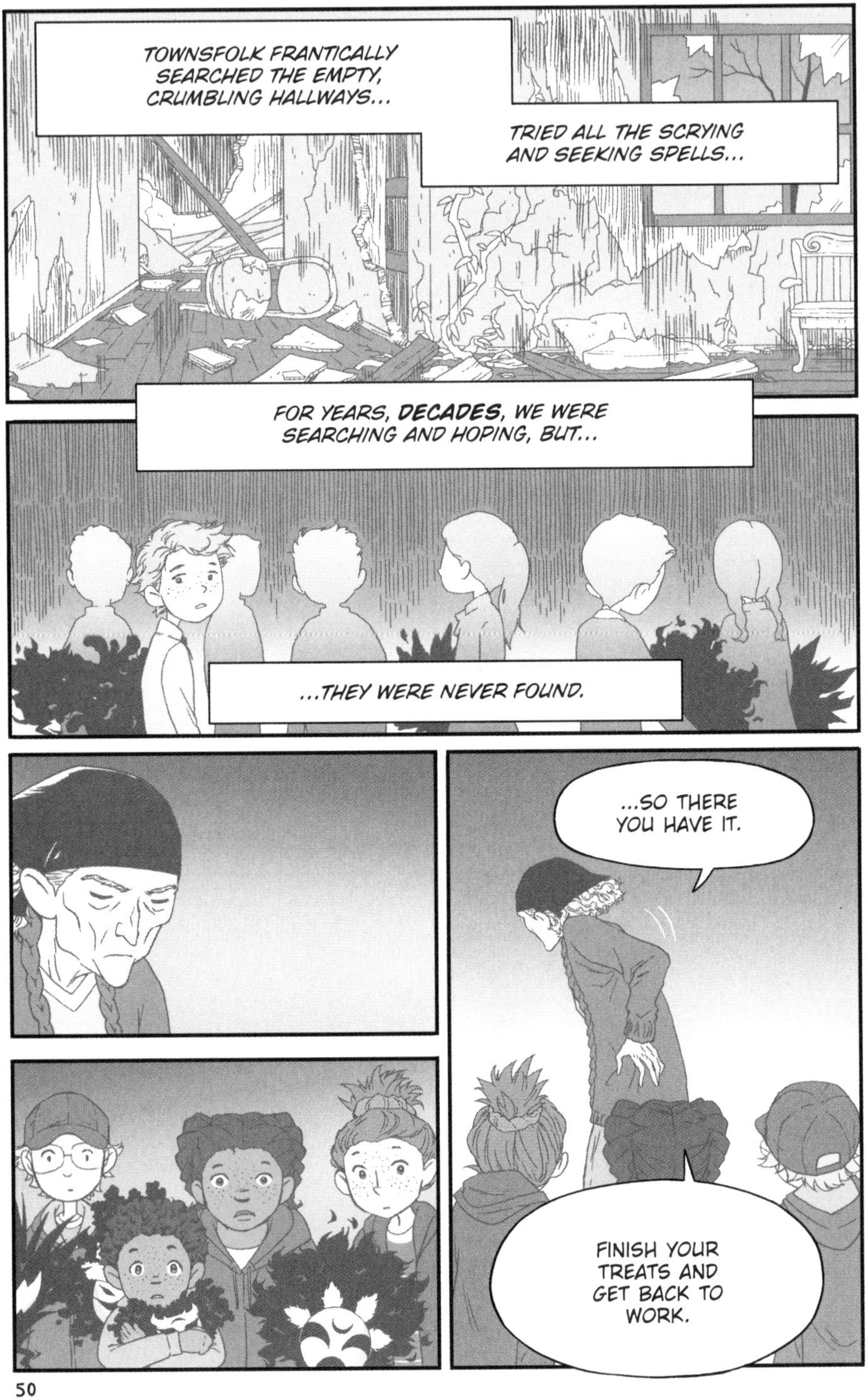
TOWNSFOLK FRANTICALLY SEARCHED THE EMPTY, CRUMBLING HALLWAYS...
TRIED ALL THE SCRYING AND SEEKING SPELLS...
FOR YEARS, **DECADES**, WE WERE SEARCHING AND HOPING, BUT...
...THEY WERE NEVER FOUND.
...SO THERE YOU HAVE IT.
FINISH YOUR TREATS AND GET BACK TO WORK.

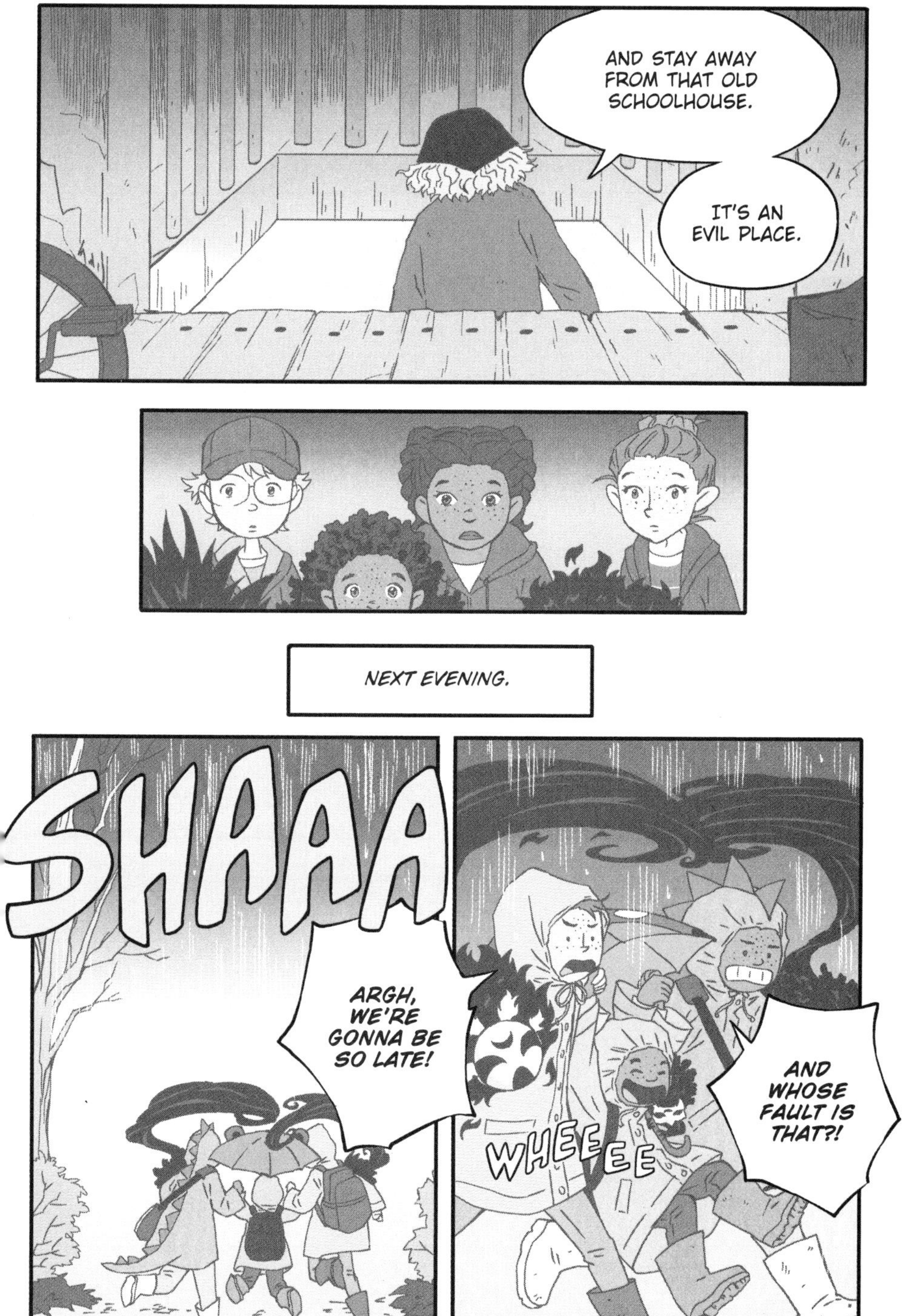
AND STAY AWAY FROM THAT OLD SCHOOLHOUSE.
IT'S AN EVIL PLACE.
NEXT EVENING.
SHAAA
ARGH, WE'RE GONNA BE SO LATE!
WHEEEEE
AND WHOSE FAULT IS THAT?!

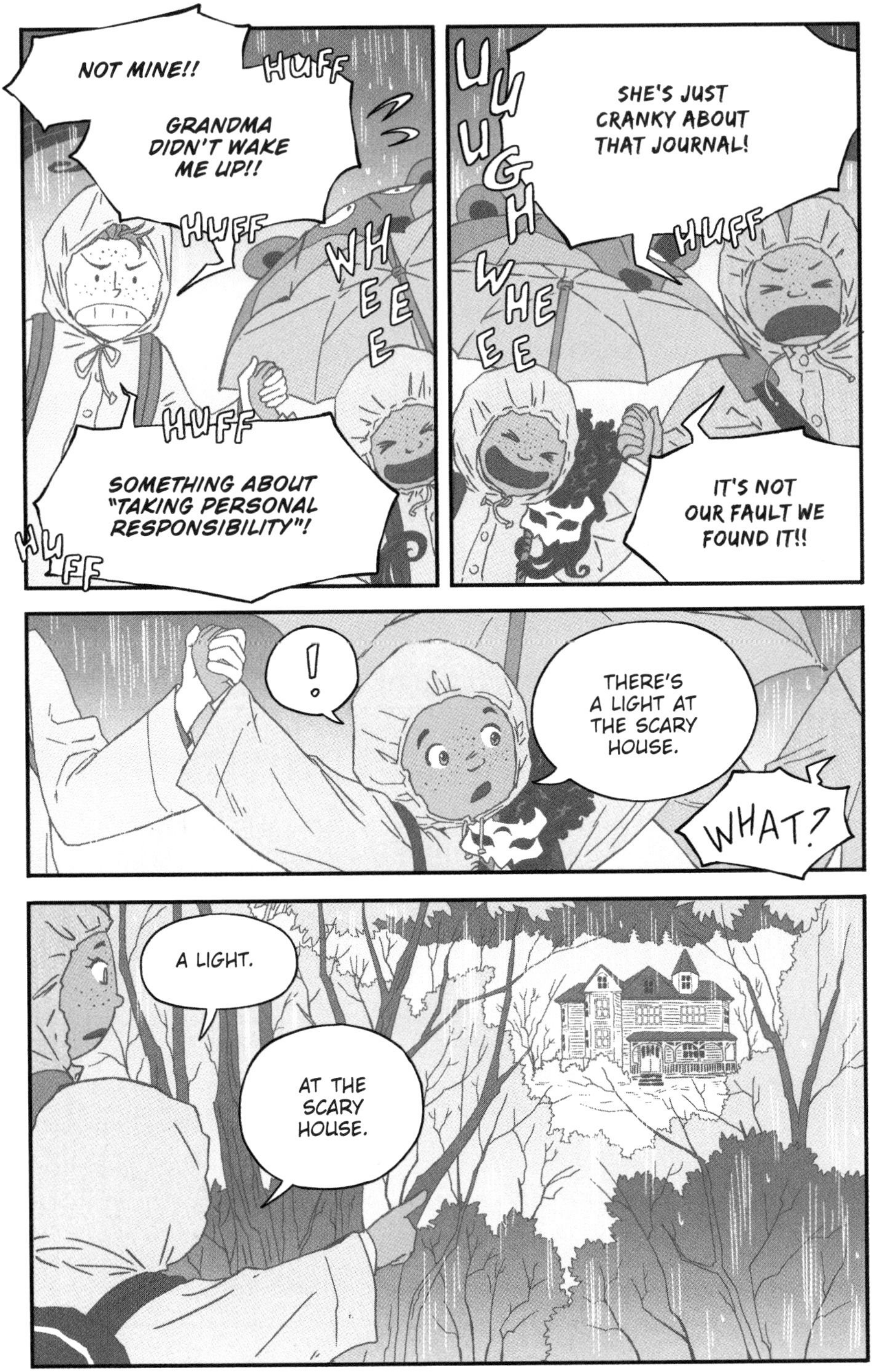
NOT MINE!!
GRANDMA DIDN'T WAKE ME UP!!
HUFF
HUFF
HUFF
SOMETHING ABOUT "TAKING PERSONAL RESPONSIBILITY"!
HUFF
WHEEE
UUUGH
SHE'S JUST CRANKY ABOUT THAT JOURNAL!
HUFF
WHEEE
IT'S NOT OUR FAULT WE FOUND IT!!
!
THERE'S A LIGHT AT THE SCARY HOUSE.
WHAT?
A LIGHT.
AT THE SCARY HOUSE.

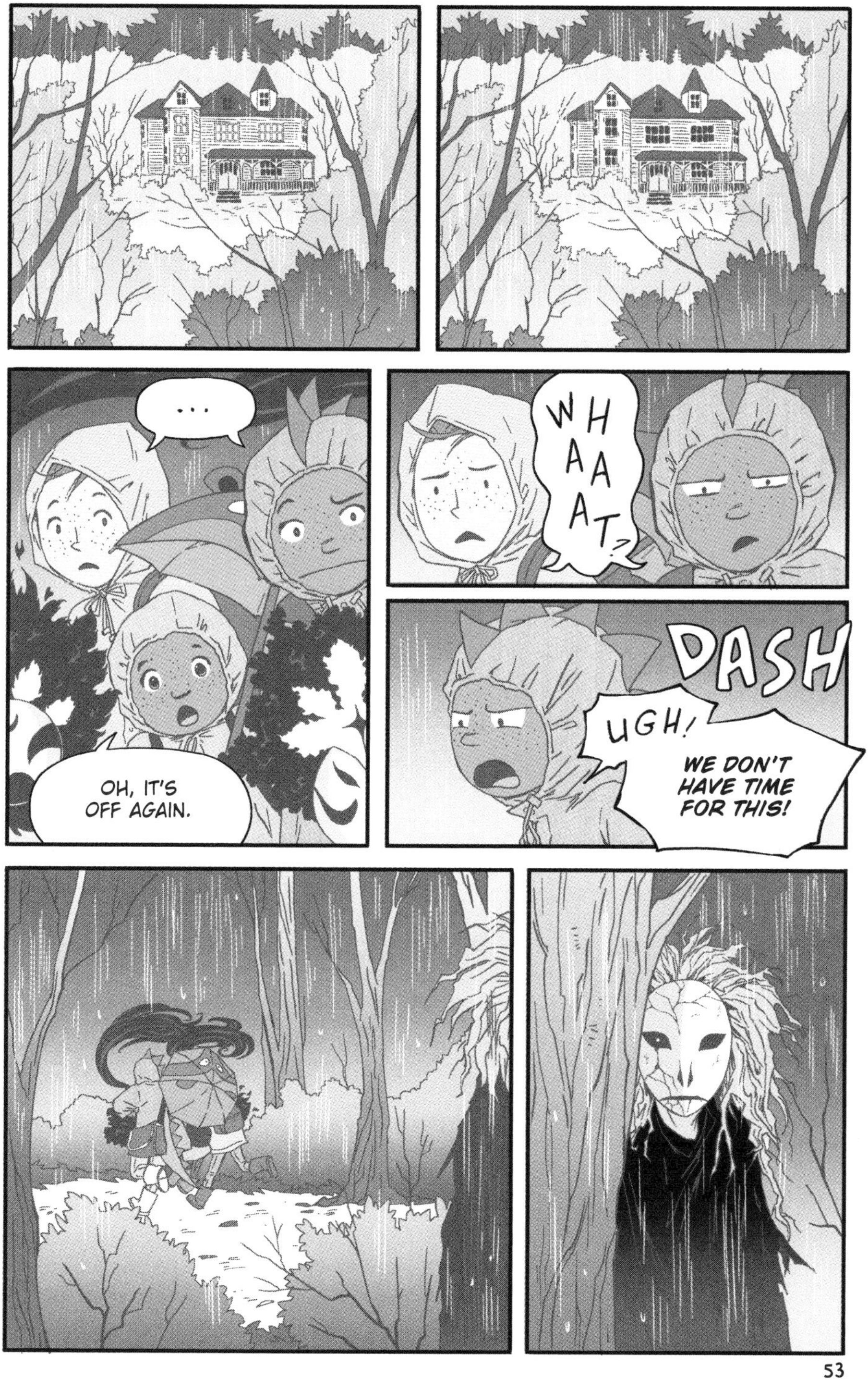
...
OH, IT'S OFF AGAIN.
WHAAAT?
DASH
UGH!
WE DON'T HAVE TIME FOR THIS!

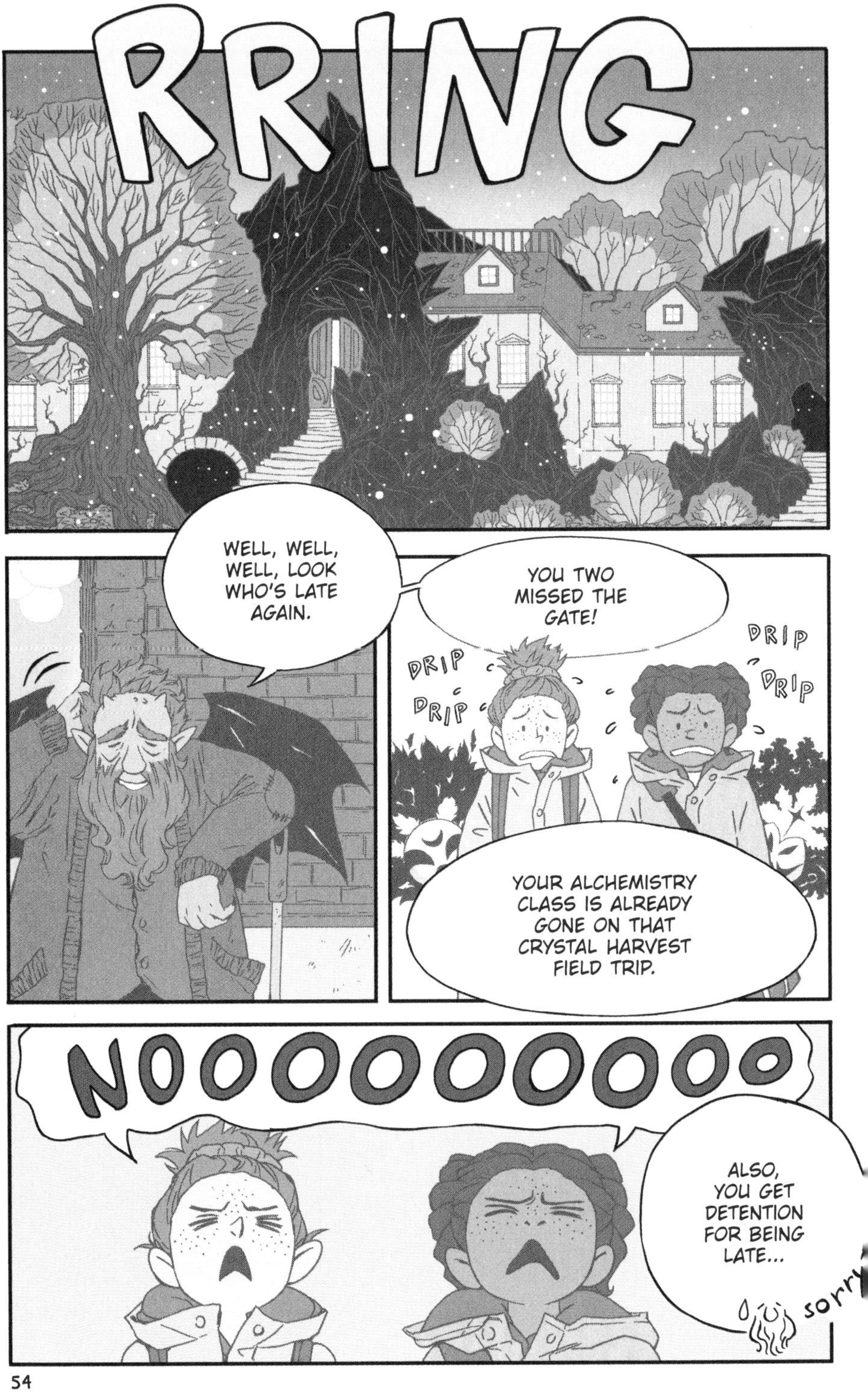
RRING
WELL, WELL, WELL, LOOK WHO'S LATE AGAIN.
YOU TWO MISSED THE GATE!
DRIP DRIP
DRIP DRIP
YOUR ALCHEMISTRY CLASS IS ALREADY GONE ON THAT CRYSTAL HARVEST FIELD TRIP.
NOOOOOOOOO
ALSO, YOU GET DETENTION FOR BEING LATE...
sorry

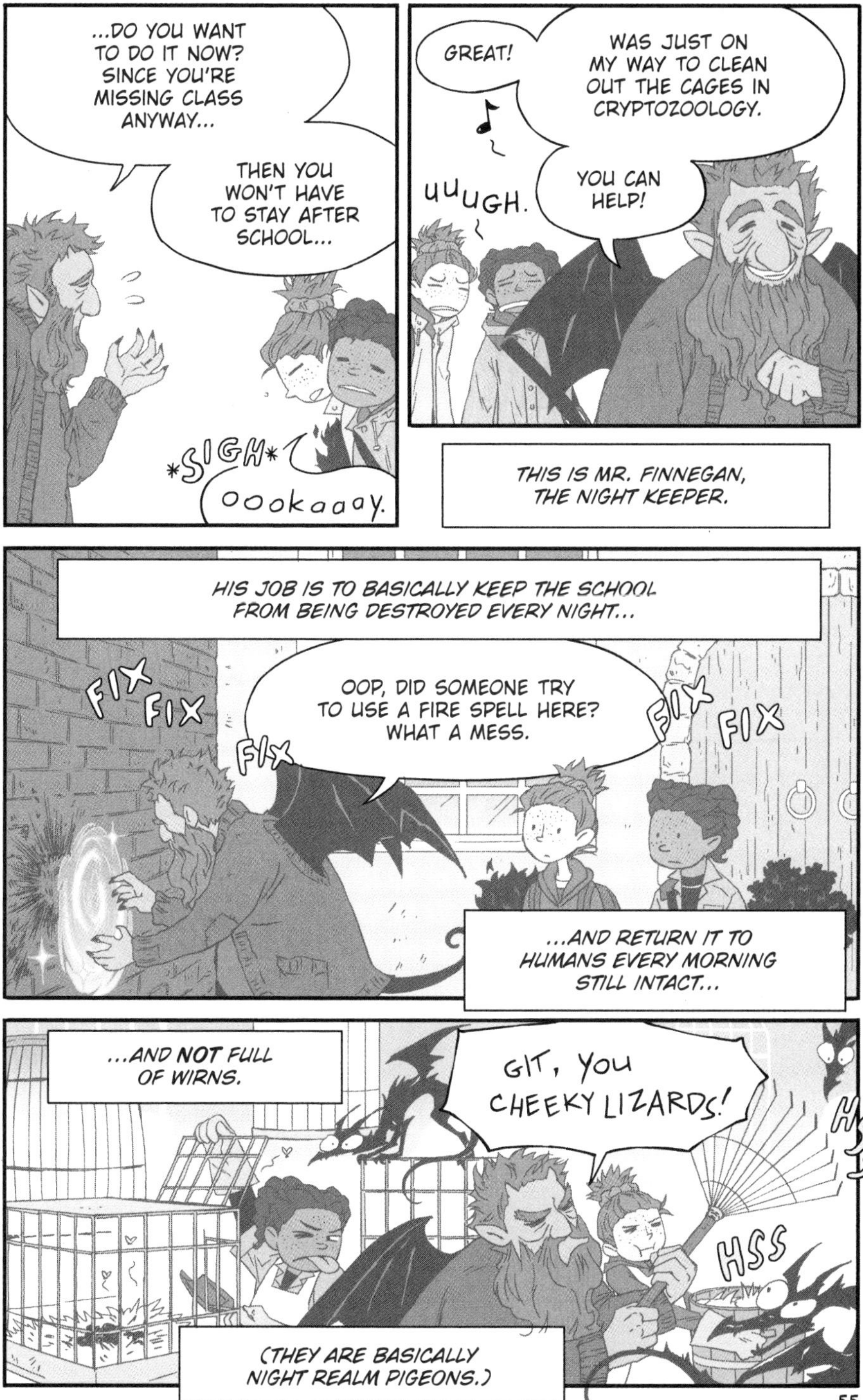
...DO YOU WANT TO DO IT NOW? SINCE YOU'RE MISSING CLASS ANYWAY...
THEN YOU WON'T HAVE TO STAY AFTER SCHOOL...
SIGH
oookaaay.
GREAT!
WAS JUST ON MY WAY TO CLEAN OUT THE CAGES IN CRYPTOZOOLOGY.
YOU CAN HELP!
uuUGH.
THIS IS MR. FINNEGAN, THE NIGHT KEEPER.
HIS JOB IS TO BASICALLY KEEP THE SCHOOL FROM BEING DESTROYED EVERY NIGHT...
OOP, DID SOMEONE TRY TO USE A FIRE SPELL HERE? WHAT A MESS.
FIX FIX
FIX
FIX
FIX
...AND RETURN IT TO HUMANS EVERY MORNING STILL INTACT...
...AND NOT FULL OF WIRNS.
GIT, YOU CHEEKY LIZARDS!
HSS
HSS
(THEY ARE BASICALLY NIGHT REALM PIGEONS.)

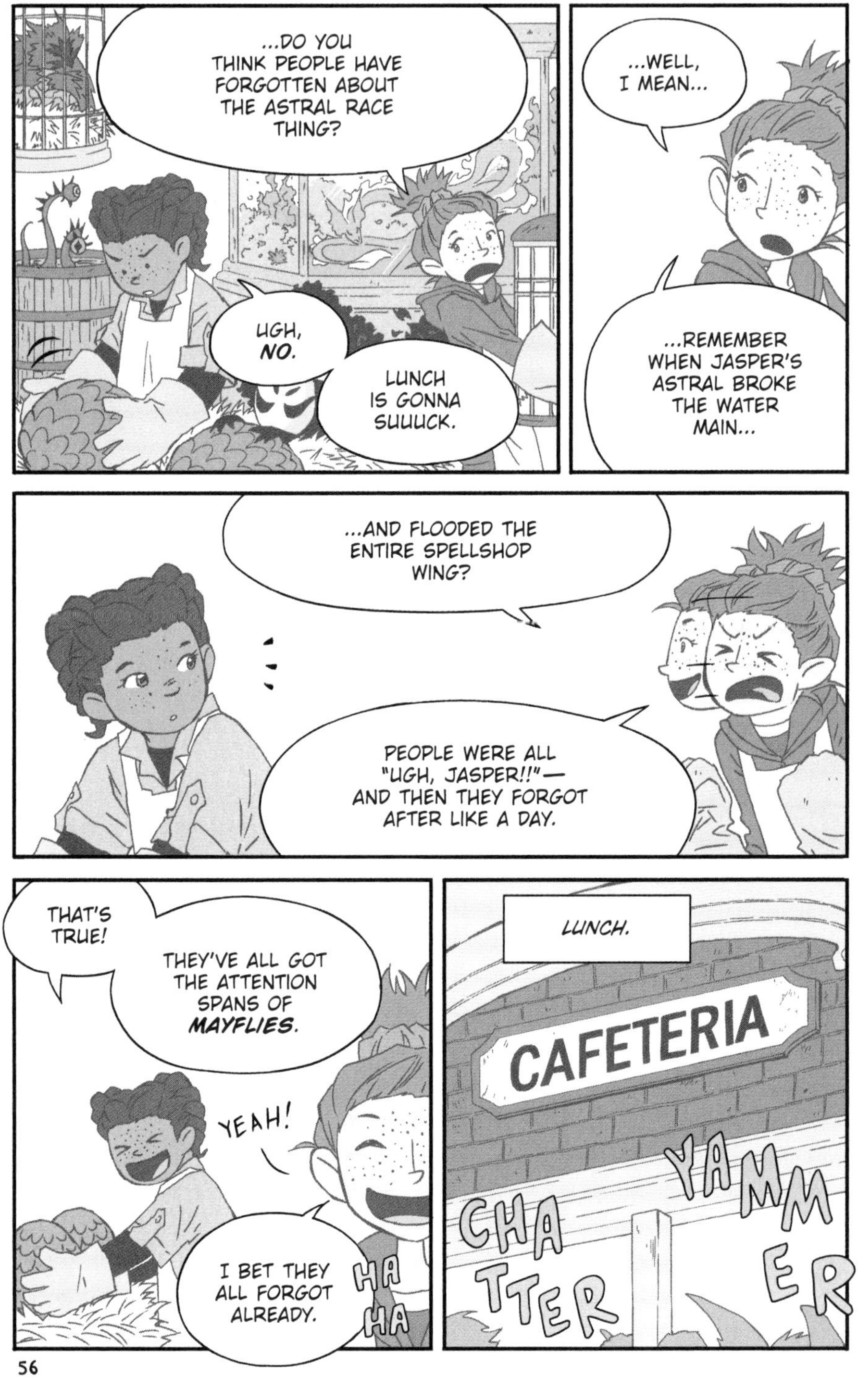

...DO YOU THINK PEOPLE HAVE FORGOTTEN ABOUT THE ASTRAL RACE THING?
UGH, **NO.**
LUNCH IS GONNA SUUUCK.
...WELL, I MEAN...
...REMEMBER WHEN JASPER'S ASTRAL BROKE THE WATER MAIN...
...AND FLOODED THE ENTIRE SPELLSHOP WING?
PEOPLE WERE ALL "UGH, JASPER!!"— AND THEN THEY FORGOT AFTER LIKE A DAY.
THAT'S TRUE!
THEY'VE ALL GOT THE ATTENTION SPANS OF ***MAYFLIES***.
YEAH!
I BET THEY ALL FORGOT ALREADY.
HA HA
LUNCH.
CAFETERIA
CHA TTER
YAMM ER

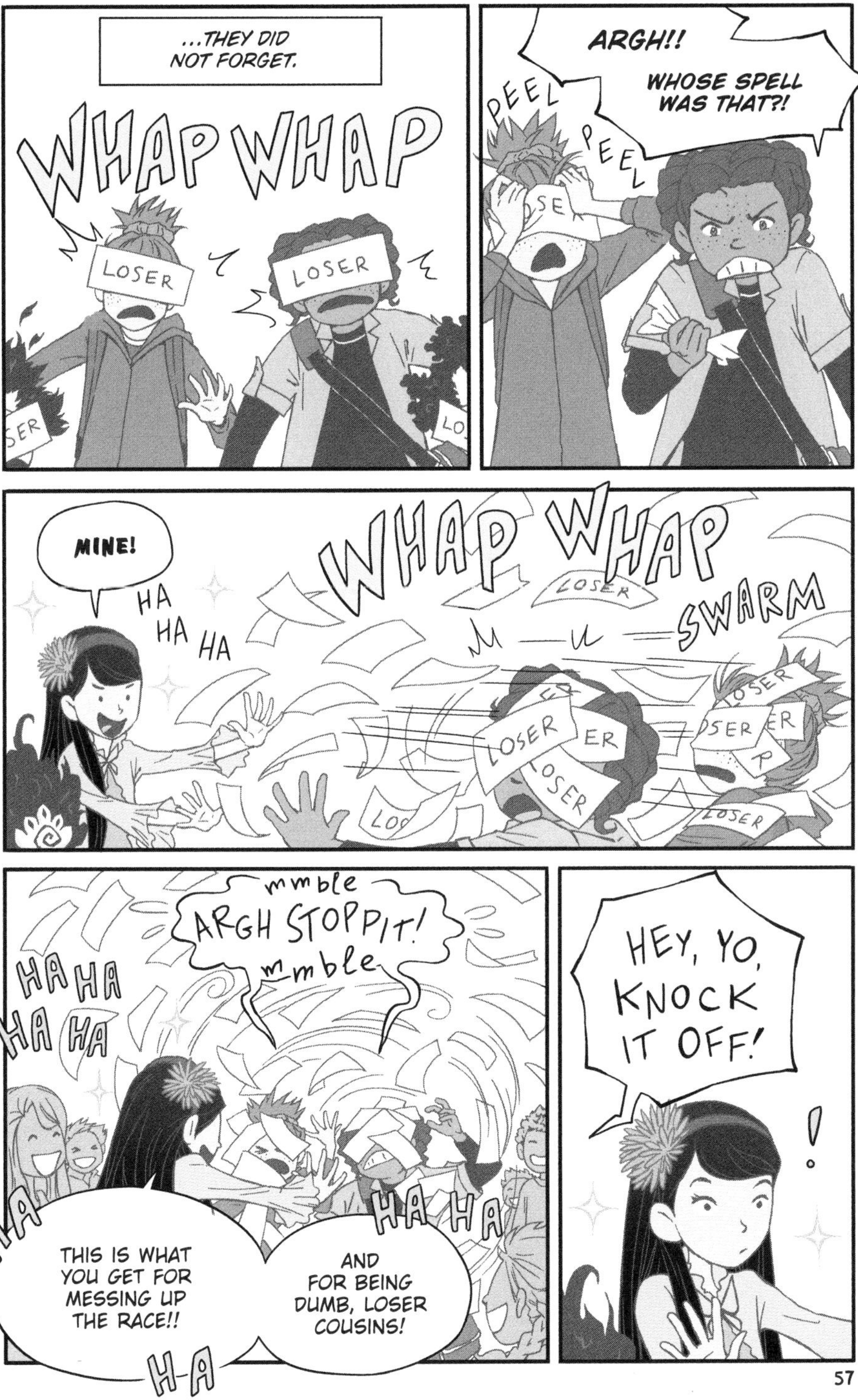
...THEY DID NOT FORGET.
WHAP WHAP
LOSER
LOSER
ARGH!!
WHOSE SPELL WAS THAT?!
PEEL
PEEL
MINE!
HA HA HA
WHAP WHAP
SWARM
LOSER
mmble
ARGH STOPPIT!
mmble
HA HA HA HA HA
HA
THIS IS WHAT YOU GET FOR MESSING UP THE RACE!!
AND FOR BEING DUMB, LOSER COUSINS!
HA HA HA
HA
HEY, YO, KNOCK IT OFF!
!

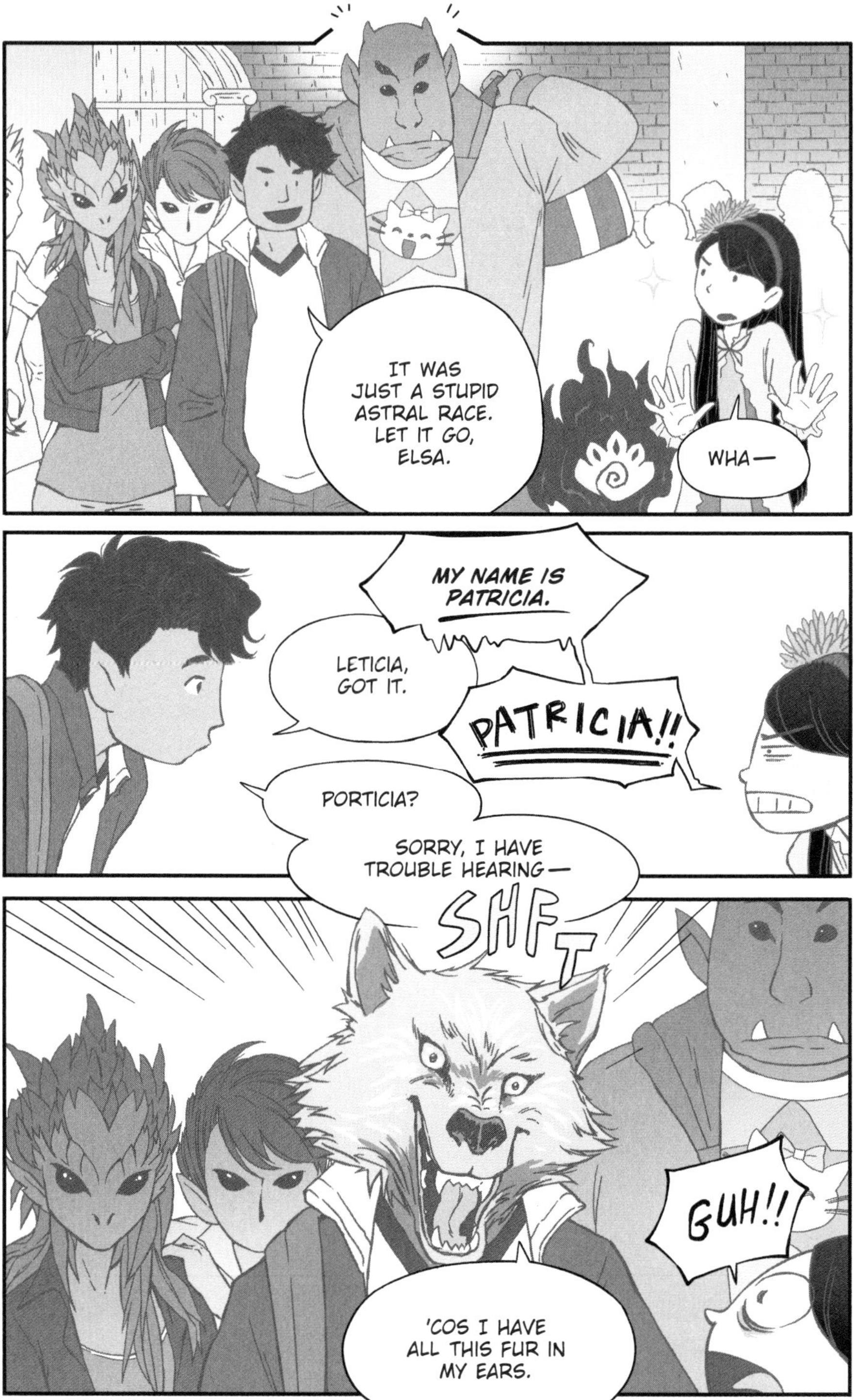
IT WAS JUST A STUPID ASTRAL RACE. LET IT GO, ELSA.
WHA—
MY NAME IS PATRICIA.
LETICIA, GOT IT.
PATRICIA!!
PORTICIA?
SORRY, I HAVE TROUBLE HEARING—
SHFT
GUH!!
'COS I HAVE ALL THIS FUR IN MY EARS.

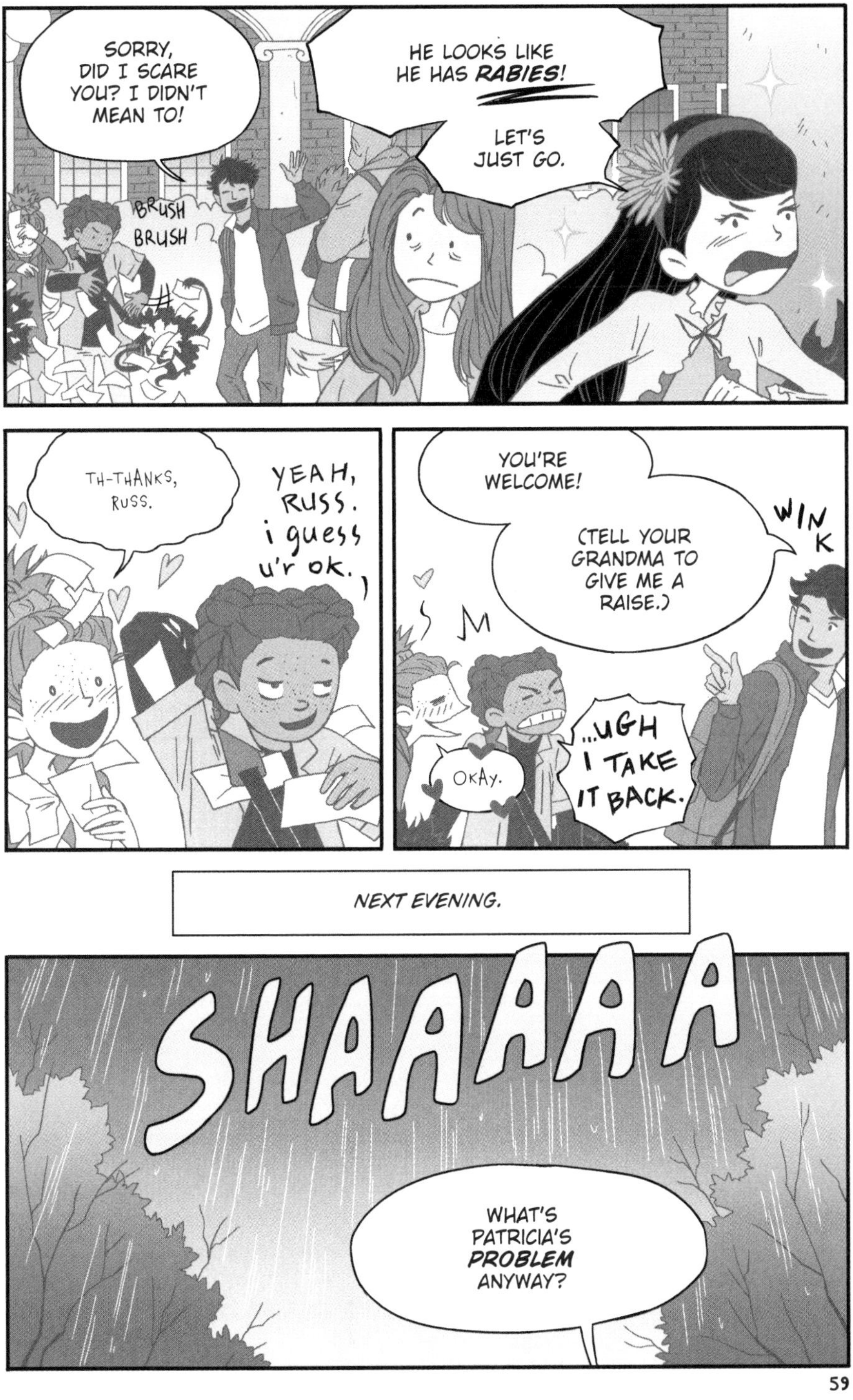
SORRY, DID I SCARE YOU? I DIDN'T MEAN TO!
BRUSH BRUSH
HE LOOKS LIKE HE HAS RABIES!
LET'S JUST GO.
TH-THANKS, RUSS.
YEAH, RUSS. i guess u'r ok.
YOU'RE WELCOME!
(TELL YOUR GRANDMA TO GIVE ME A RAISE.)
WINK
OKAy.
...UGH I TAKE IT BACK.
NEXT EVENING.
SHAAAAA
WHAT'S PATRICIA'S PROBLEM ANYWAY?

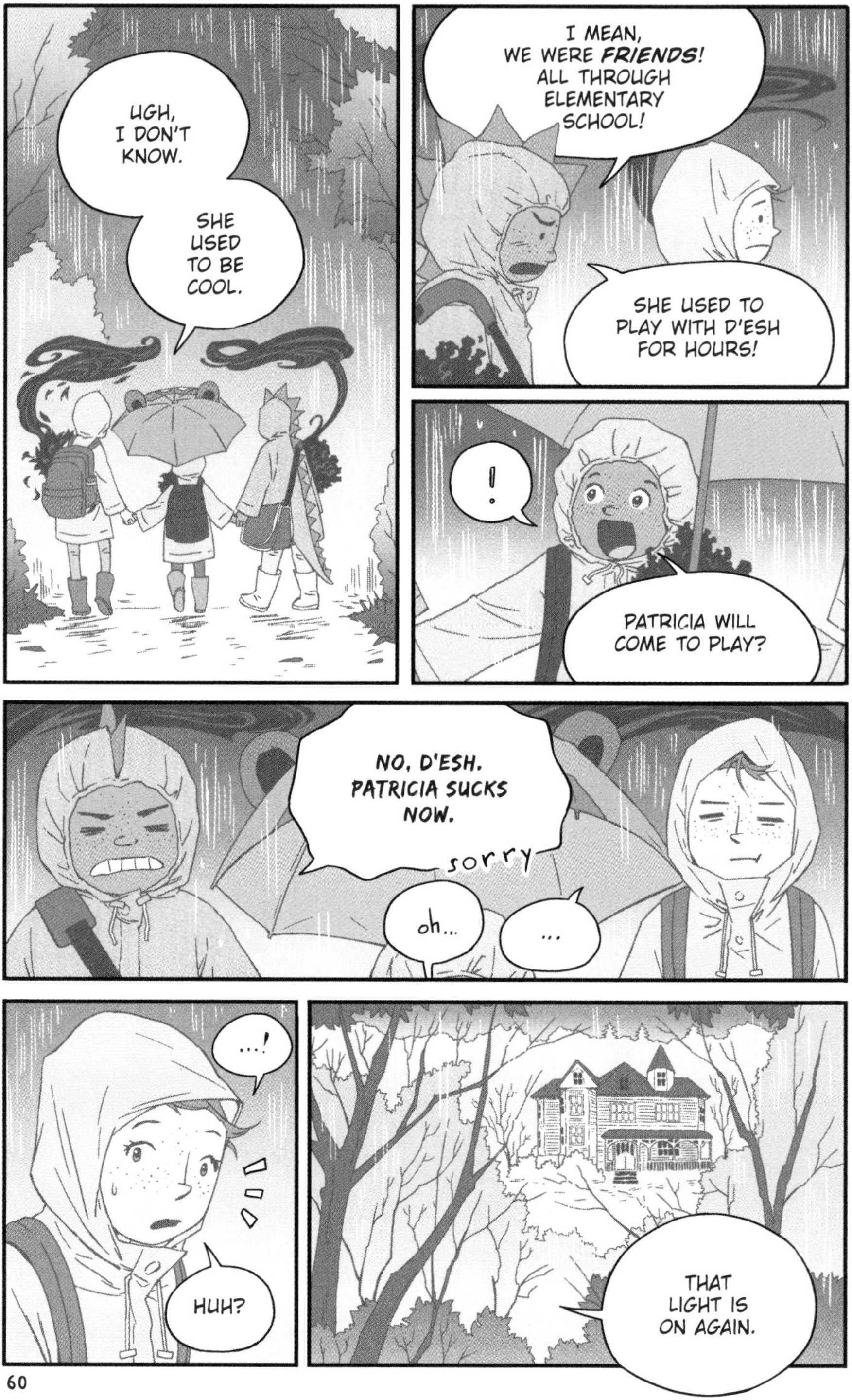
UGH, I DON'T KNOW.
SHE USED TO BE COOL.
I MEAN, WE WERE FRIENDS! ALL THROUGH ELEMENTARY SCHOOL!
SHE USED TO PLAY WITH D'ESH FOR HOURS!
!
PATRICIA WILL COME TO PLAY?
NO, D'ESH. PATRICIA SUCKS NOW.
sorry
oh...
...
...!
HUH?
THAT LIGHT IS ON AGAIN.

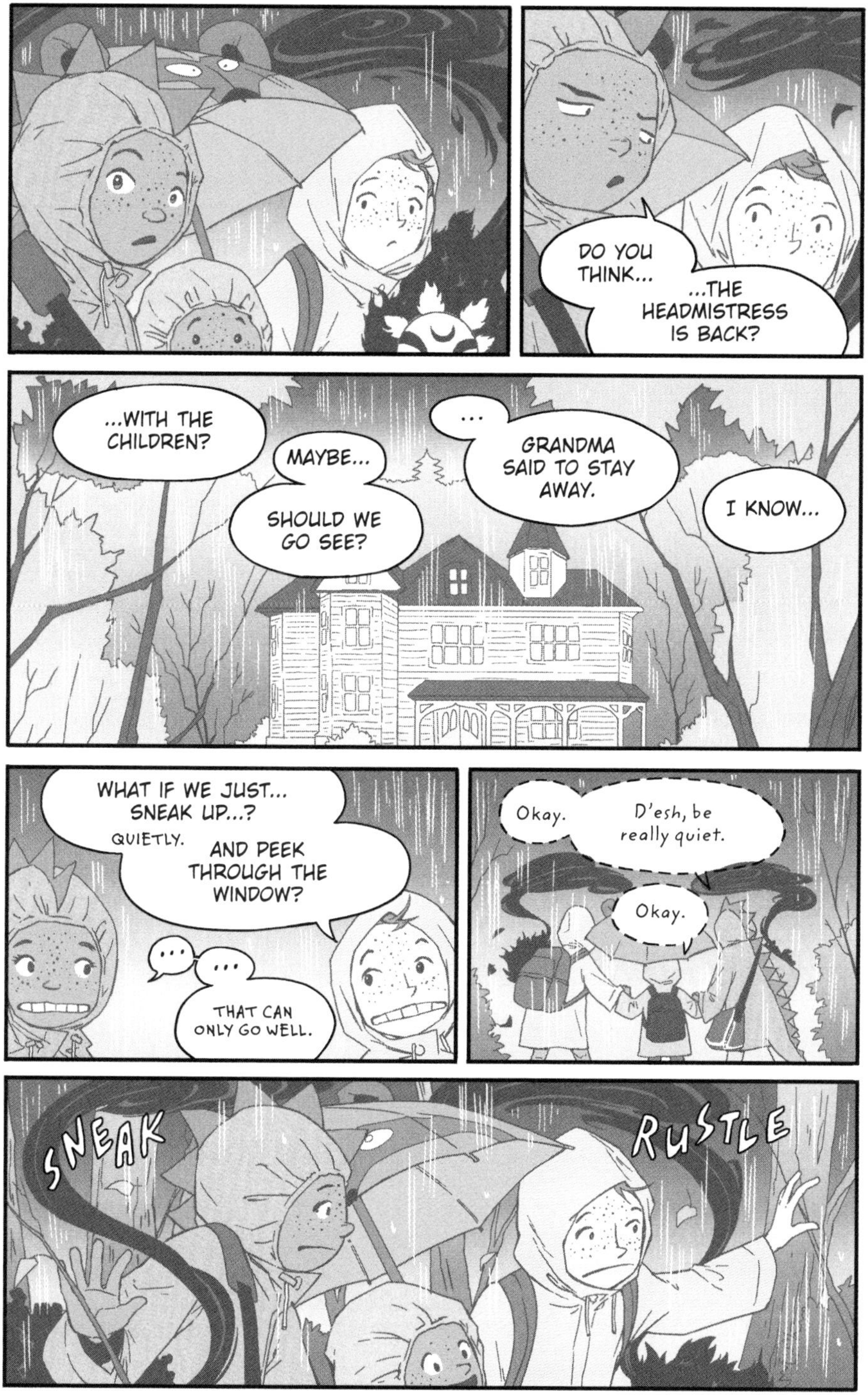
DO YOU THINK...
...THE HEADMISTRESS IS BACK?
...WITH THE CHILDREN?
MAYBE...
SHOULD WE GO SEE?
...
GRANDMA SAID TO STAY AWAY.
I KNOW...
WHAT IF WE JUST... SNEAK UP...?
QUIETLY.
AND PEEK THROUGH THE WINDOW?
...
...
THAT CAN ONLY GO WELL.
Okay.
D'esh, be really quiet.
Okay.
SNEAK
RUSTLE

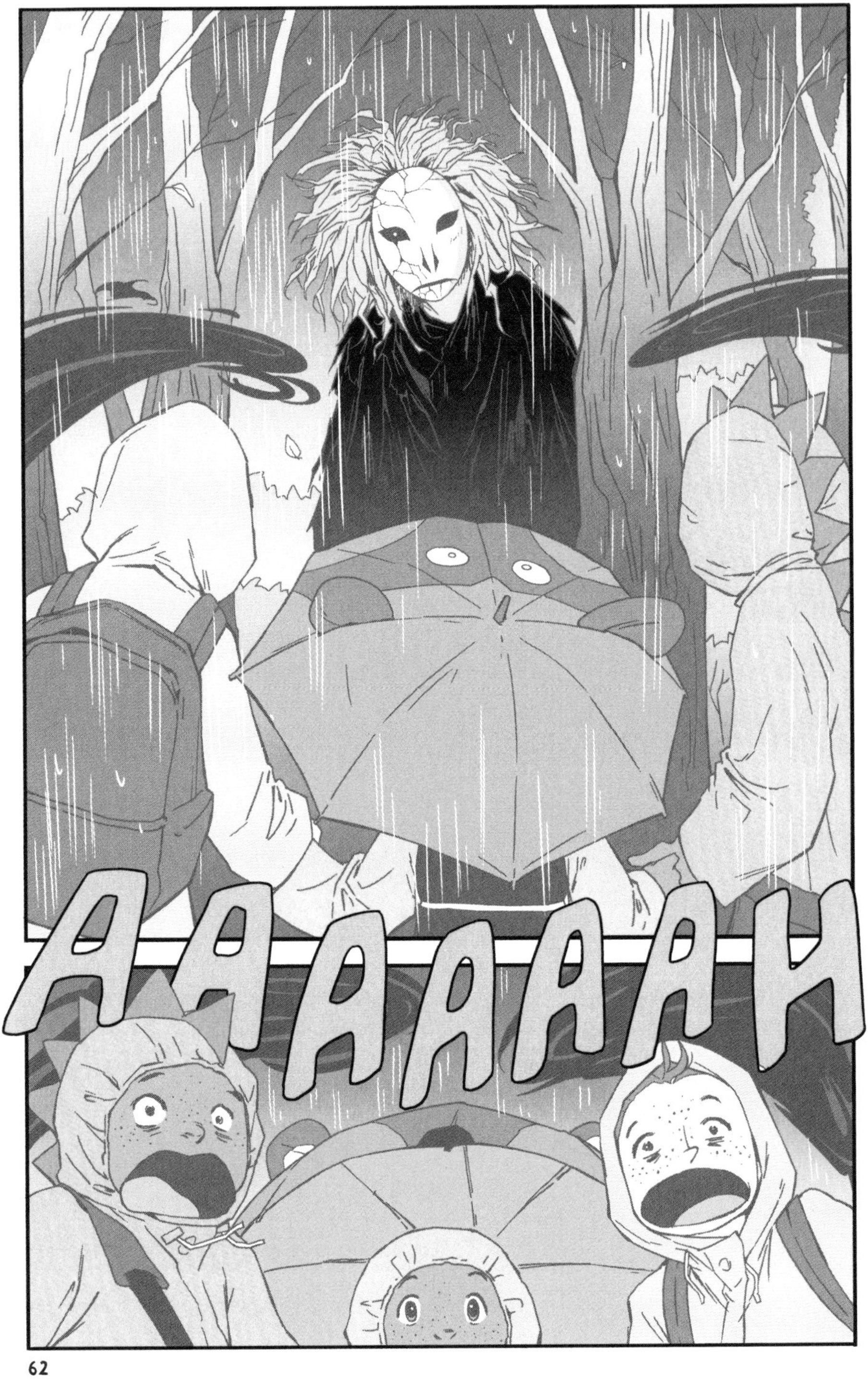
AAAAAAAH

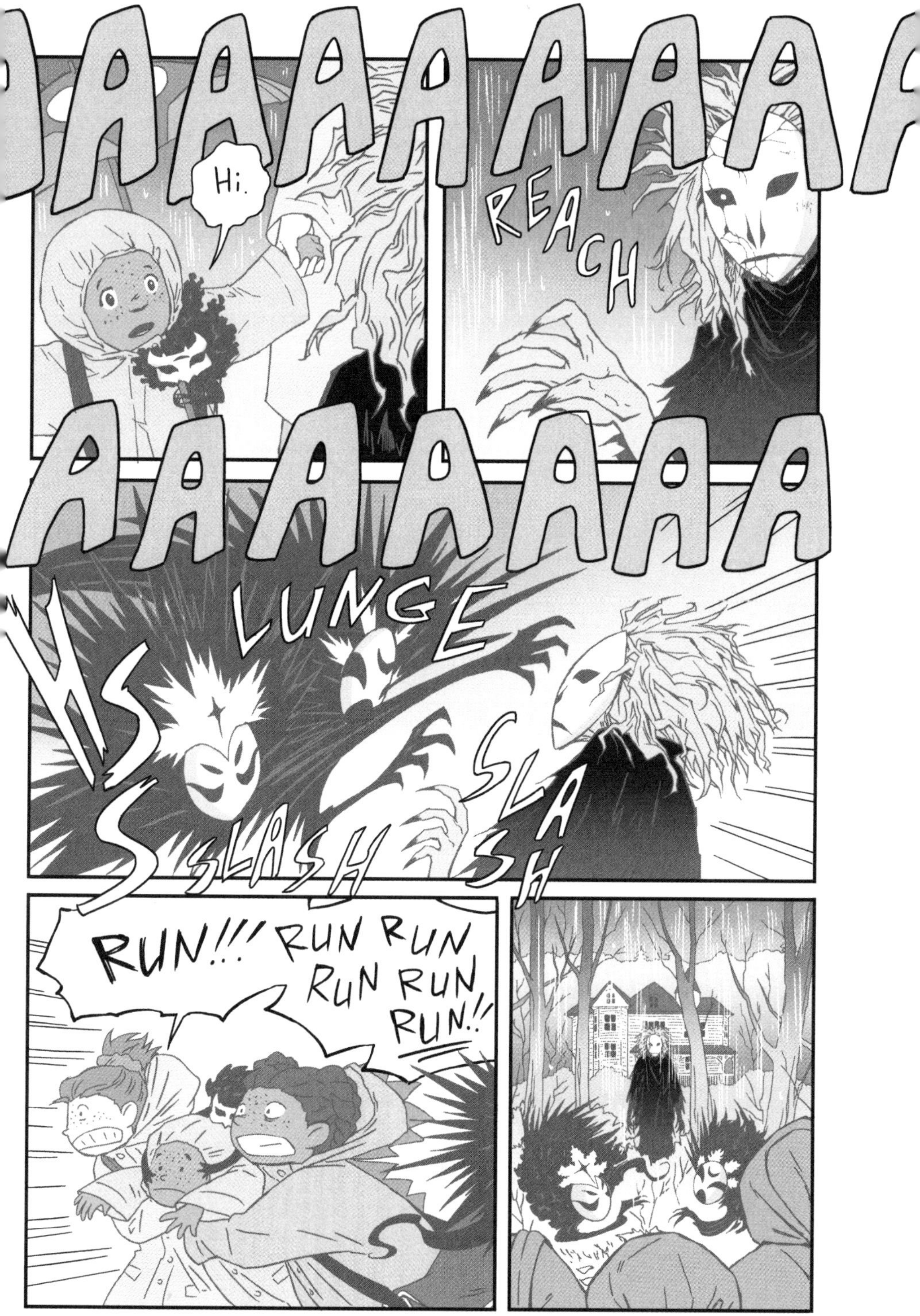
AAAAAAAAAAA
Hi.
REACH
AAAAAAAAA
HS
LUNGE
SLASH
SLASH
S
RUN!!! RUN RUN
RUN RUN
RUN!!

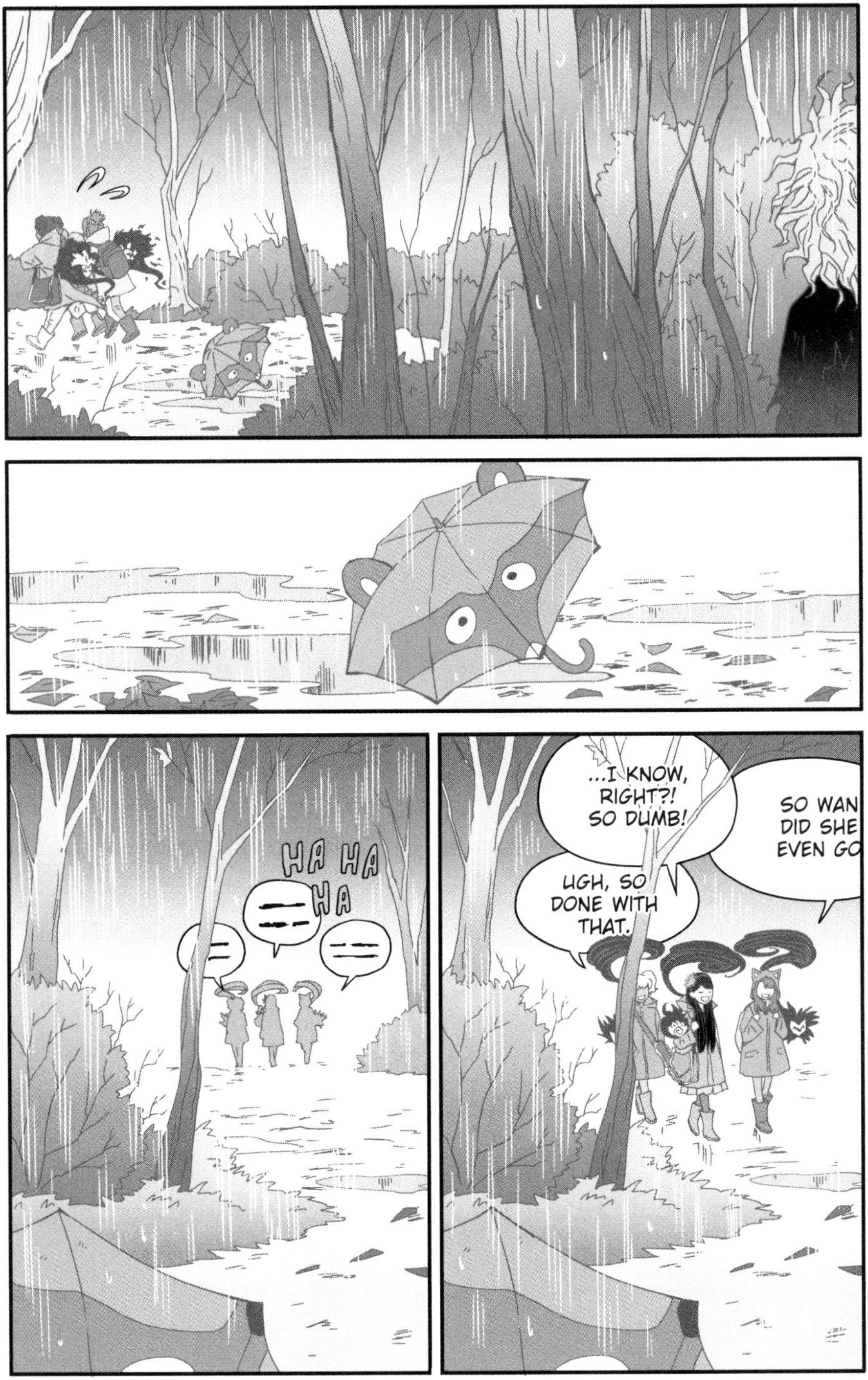
SO WAN
DID SHE
EVEN GO
...I KNOW, RIGHT?! SO DUMB!
UGH, SO DONE WITH THAT.
HA HA HA

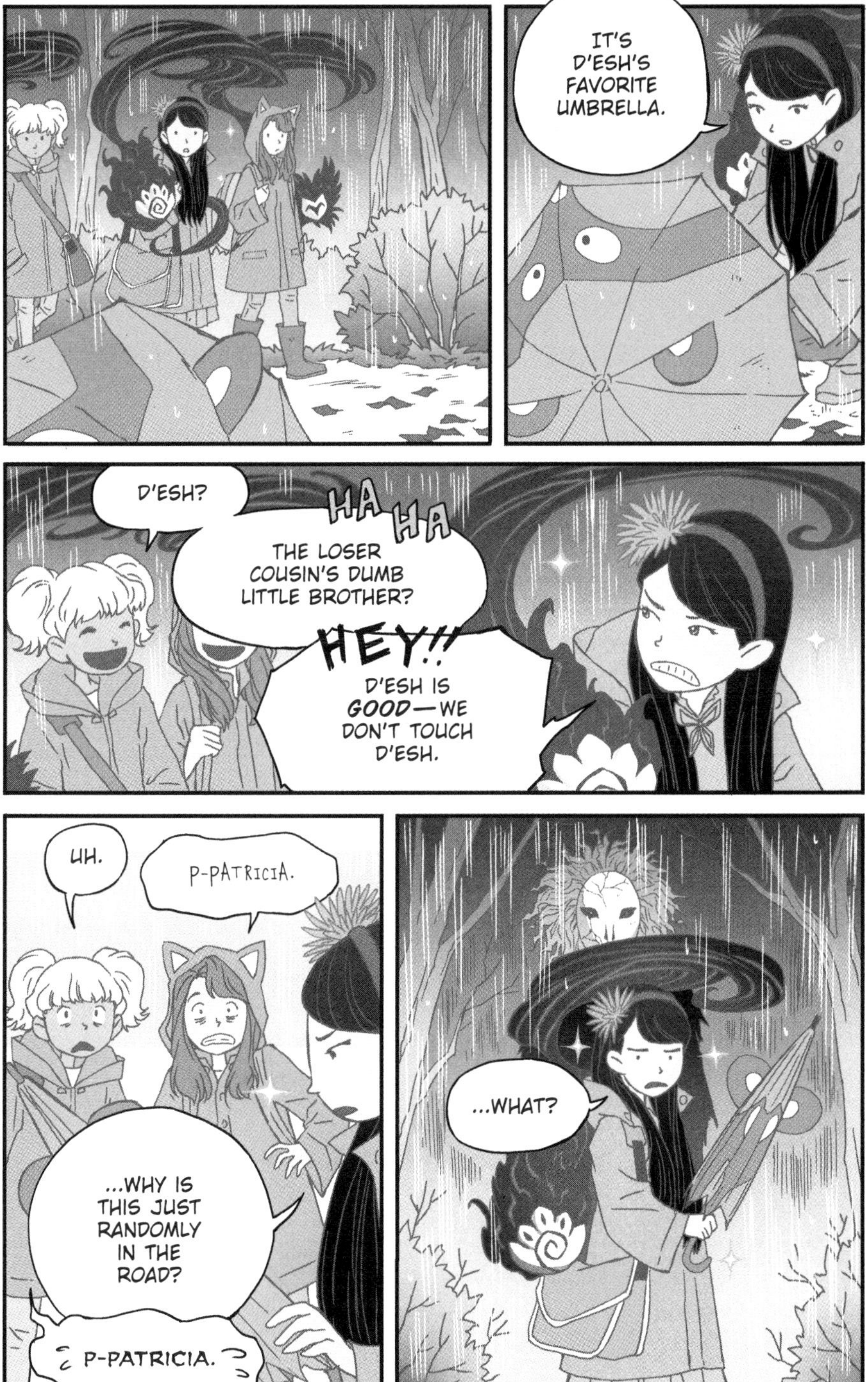
IT'S D'ESH'S FAVORITE UMBRELLA.
D'ESH?
HA HA
THE LOSER COUSIN'S DUMB LITTLE BROTHER?
HEY!!
D'ESH IS GOOD—WE DON'T TOUCH D'ESH.
UH.
P-PATRICIA.
...WHY IS THIS JUST RANDOMLY IN THE ROAD?
P-PATRICIA.
...WHAT?

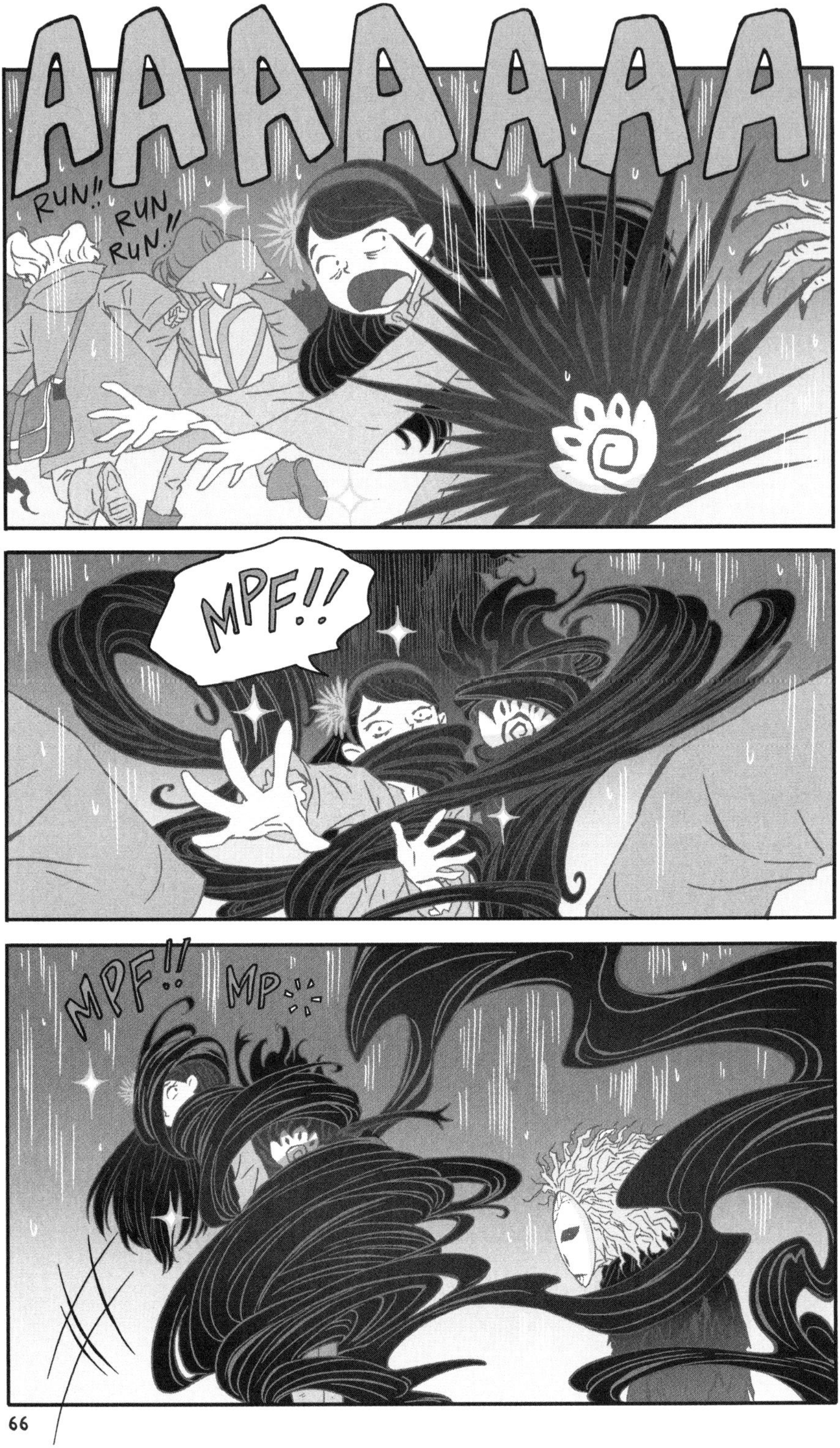
AAAAAAA
RUN!!
RUN RUN!!
MPF!!
MPF!!
MP

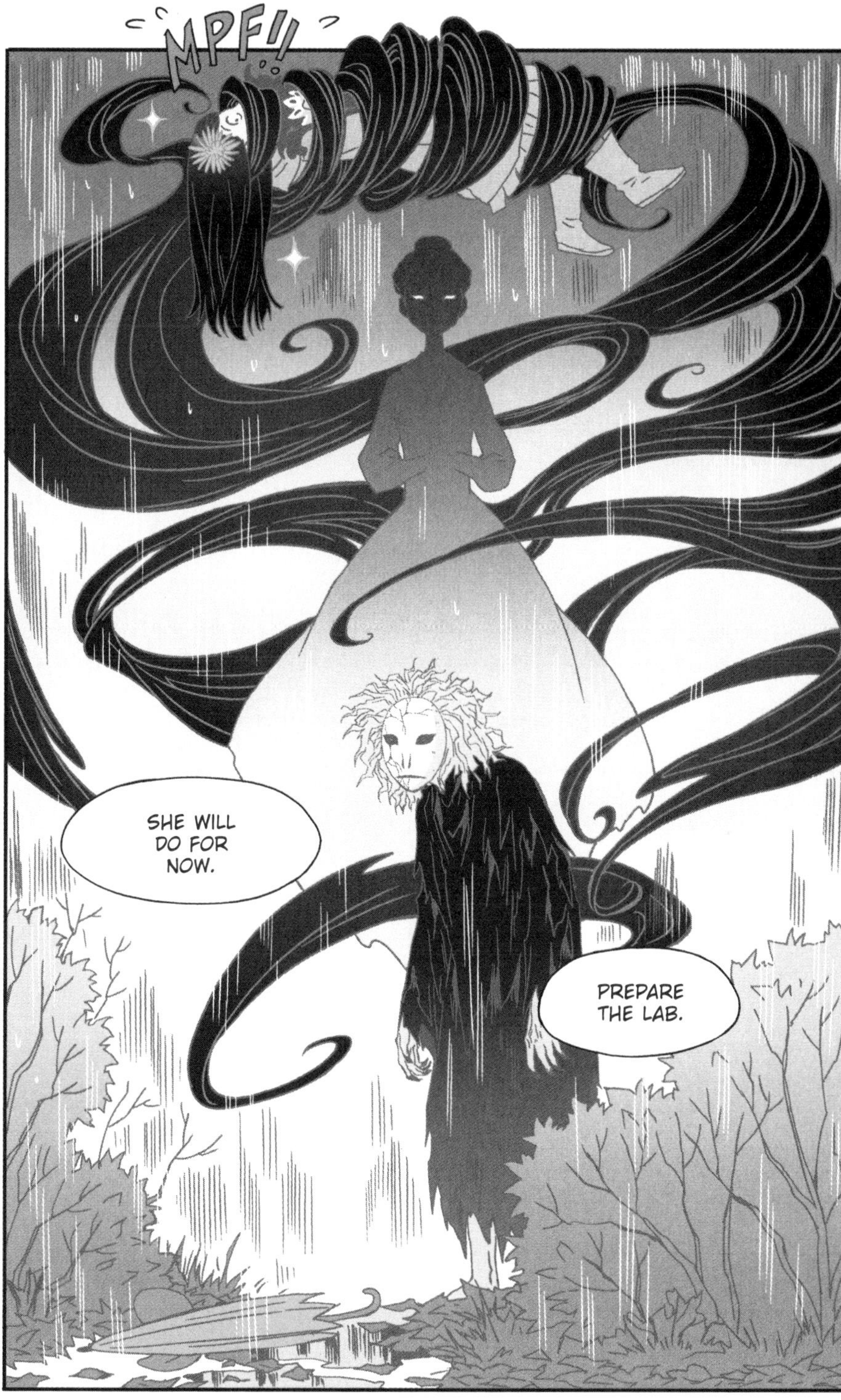
MPF!!
SHE WILL DO FOR NOW.
PREPARE THE LAB.

Chapter 3

NEXT EVENING.

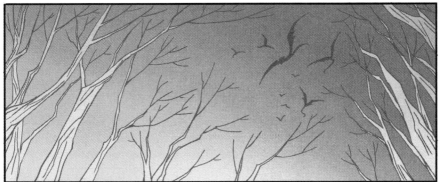

RRUMBLE

RRRING

...DID YOU TELL YOUR PARENTS?

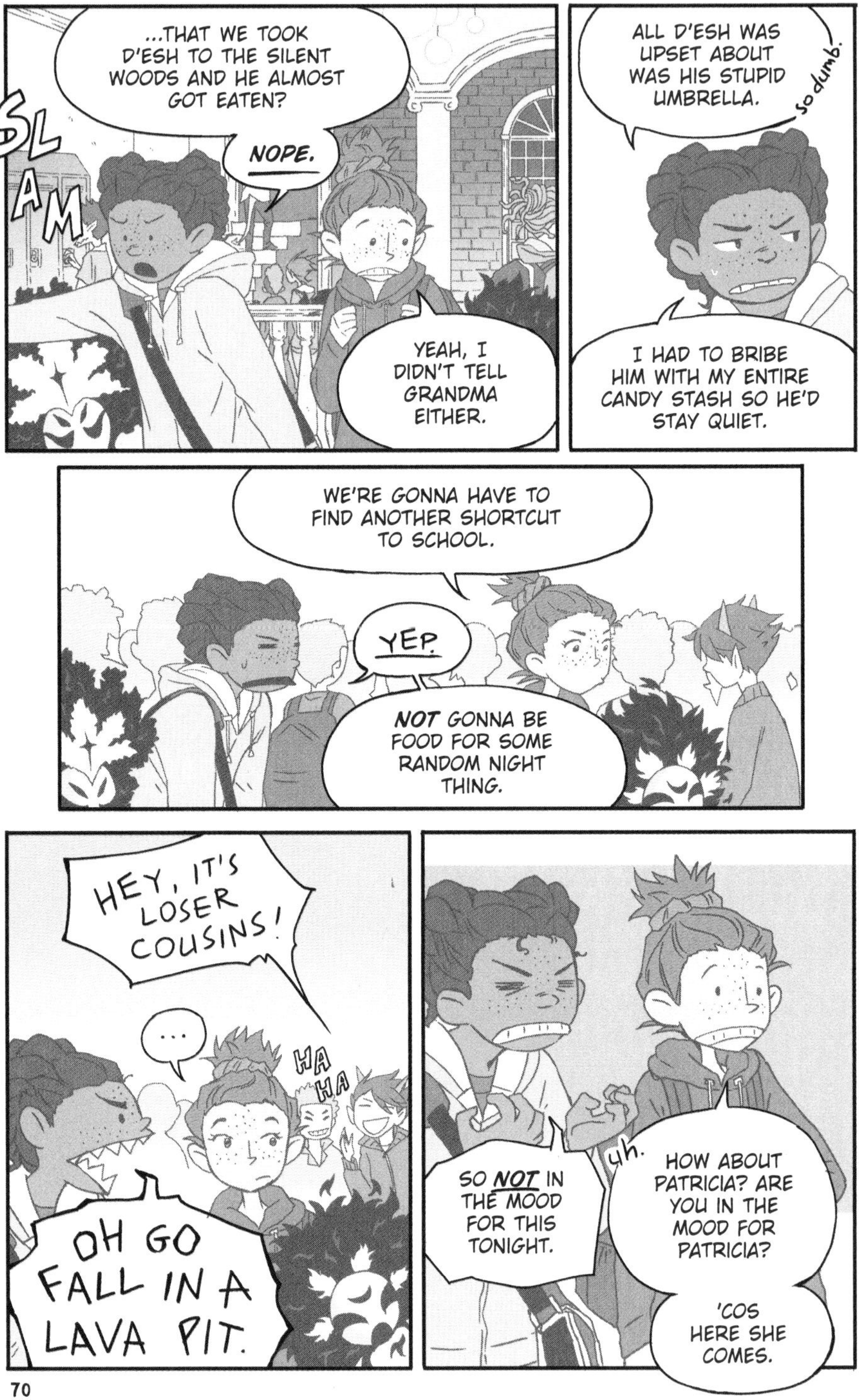
...THAT WE TOOK D'ESH TO THE SILENT WOODS AND HE ALMOST GOT EATEN?
SLAM
NOPE.
YEAH, I DIDN'T TELL GRANDMA EITHER.
ALL D'ESH WAS UPSET ABOUT WAS HIS STUPID UMBRELLA.
so dumb.
I HAD TO BRIBE HIM WITH MY ENTIRE CANDY STASH SO HE'D STAY QUIET.
WE'RE GONNA HAVE TO FIND ANOTHER SHORTCUT TO SCHOOL.
YEP.
NOT GONNA BE FOOD FOR SOME RANDOM NIGHT THING.
HEY, IT'S LOSER COUSINS!
...
HA HA
OH GO FALL IN A LAVA PIT.
SO NOT IN THE MOOD FOR THIS TONIGHT.
uh.
HOW ABOUT PATRICIA? ARE YOU IN THE MOOD FOR PATRICIA?
'COS HERE SHE COMES.

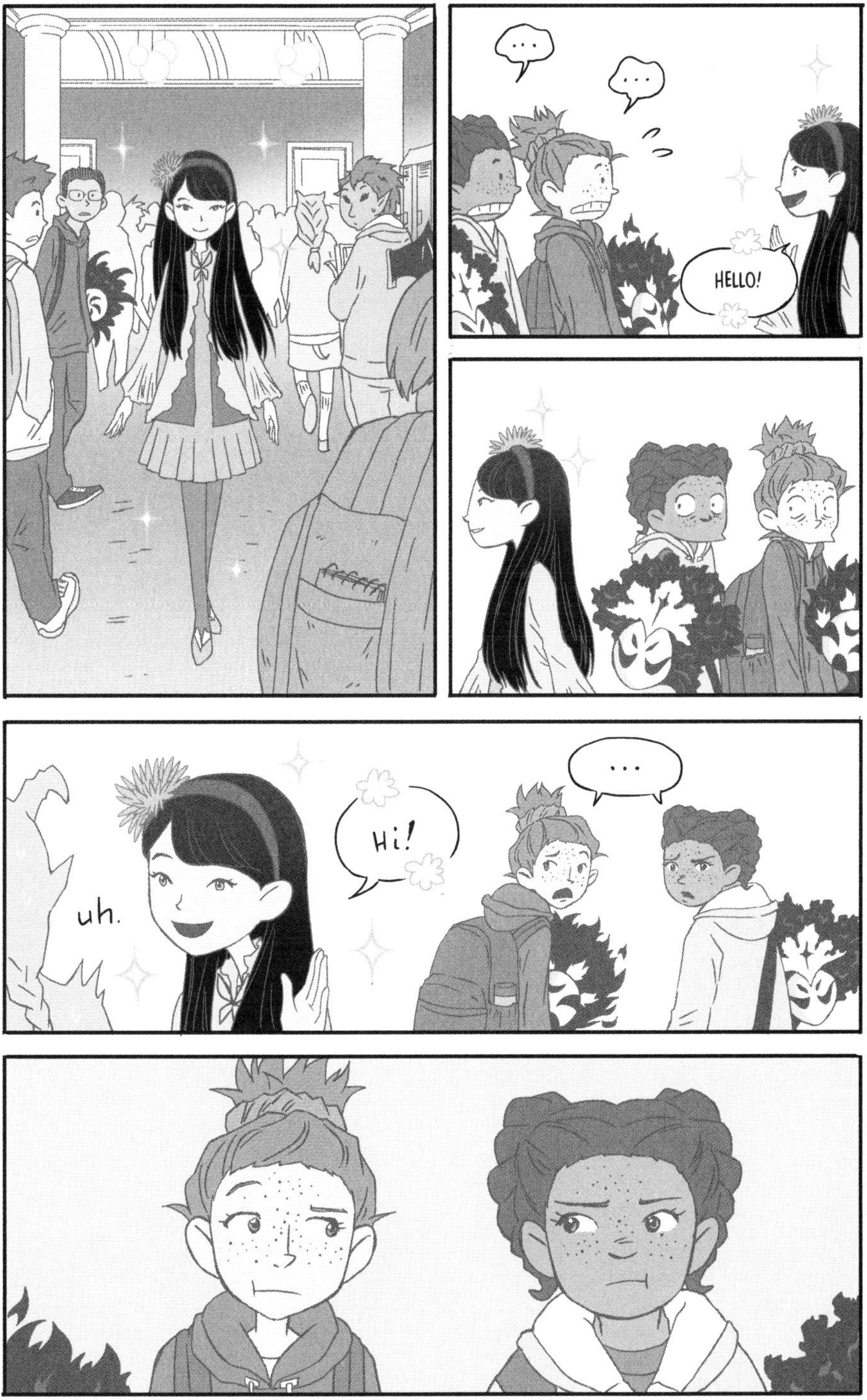
...
...
HELLO!
uh.
Hi!
...

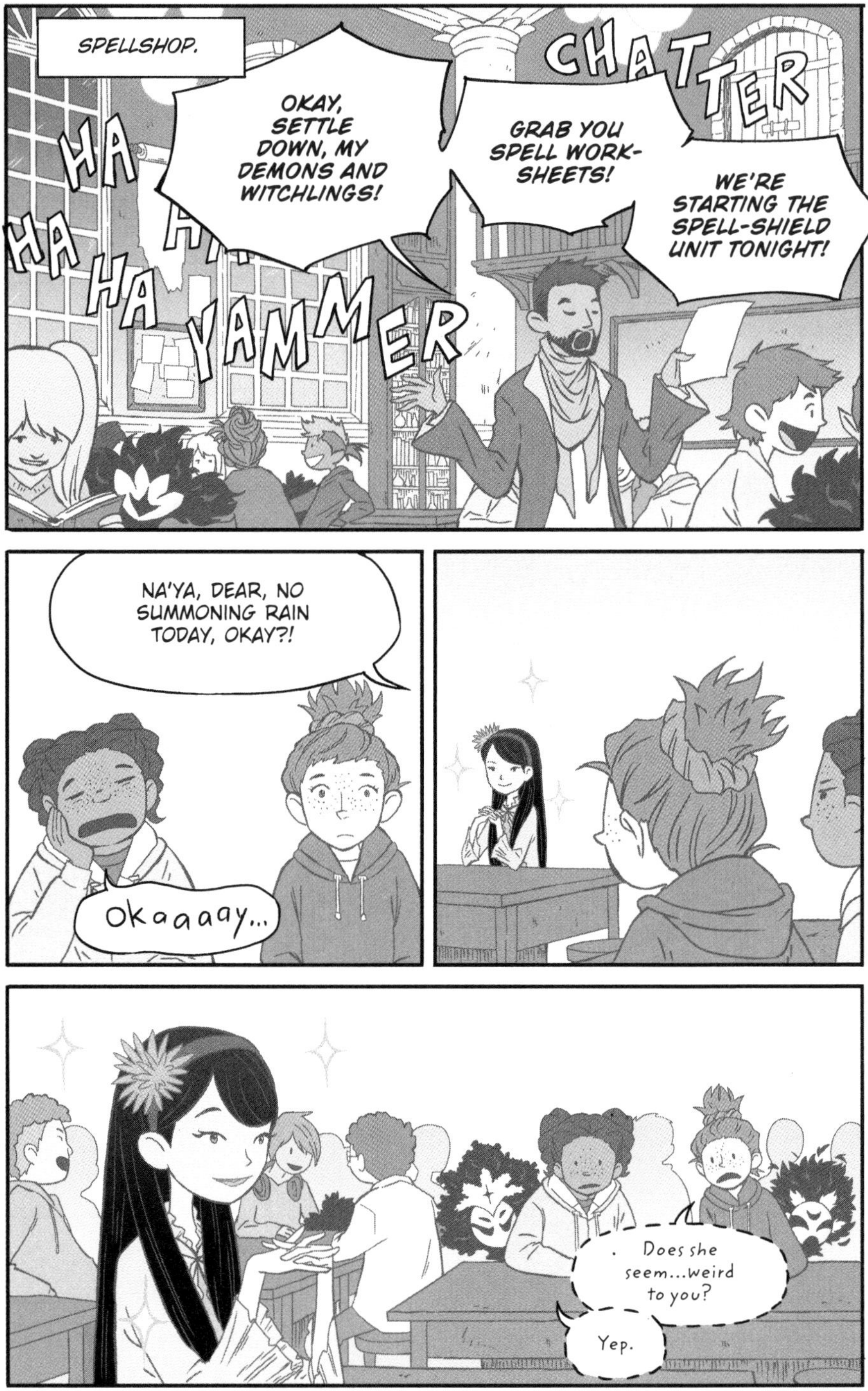
SPELLSHOP.
CHATTER
OKAY, SETTLE DOWN, MY DEMONS AND WITCHLINGS!
GRAB YOU SPELL WORK-SHEETS!
WE'RE STARTING THE SPELL-SHIELD UNIT TONIGHT!
HA HA HA HA
YAMMER
NA'YA, DEAR, NO SUMMONING RAIN TODAY, OKAY?!
Okaaaay...
Does she seem...weird to you?
Yep.

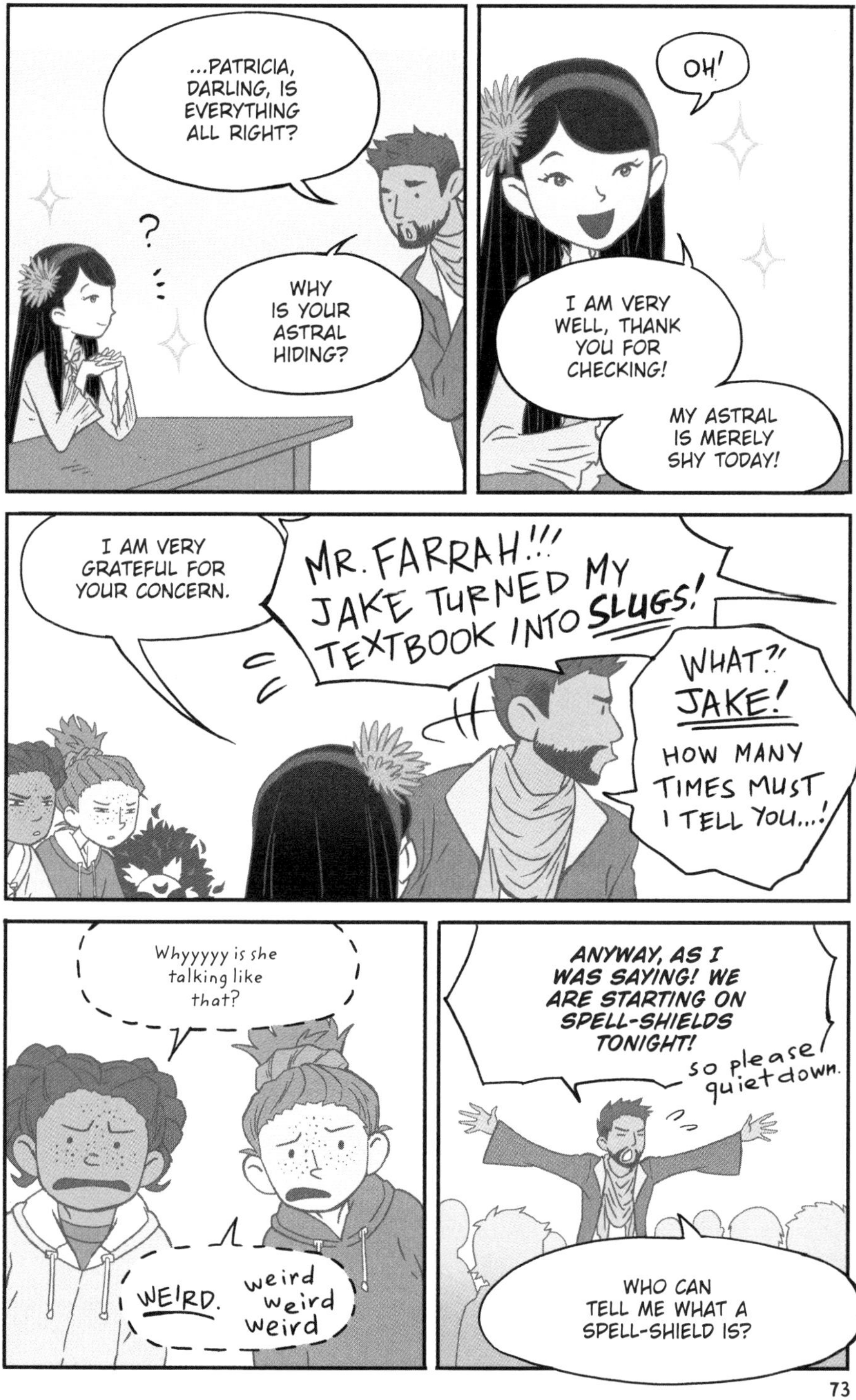
...PATRICIA, DARLING, IS EVERYTHING ALL RIGHT?
?
WHY IS YOUR ASTRAL HIDING?
OH!
I AM VERY WELL, THANK YOU FOR CHECKING!
MY ASTRAL IS MERELY SHY TODAY!
I AM VERY GRATEFUL FOR YOUR CONCERN.
MR. FARRAH!!! JAKE TURNED MY TEXTBOOK INTO SLUGS!
WHAT?! JAKE!
HOW MANY TIMES MUST I TELL YOU...!
Whyyyyy is she talking like that?
WEIRD.
weird weird weird
ANYWAY, AS I WAS SAYING! WE ARE STARTING ON SPELL-SHIELDS TONIGHT!
so please quiet down.
WHO CAN TELL ME WHAT A SPELL-SHIELD IS?

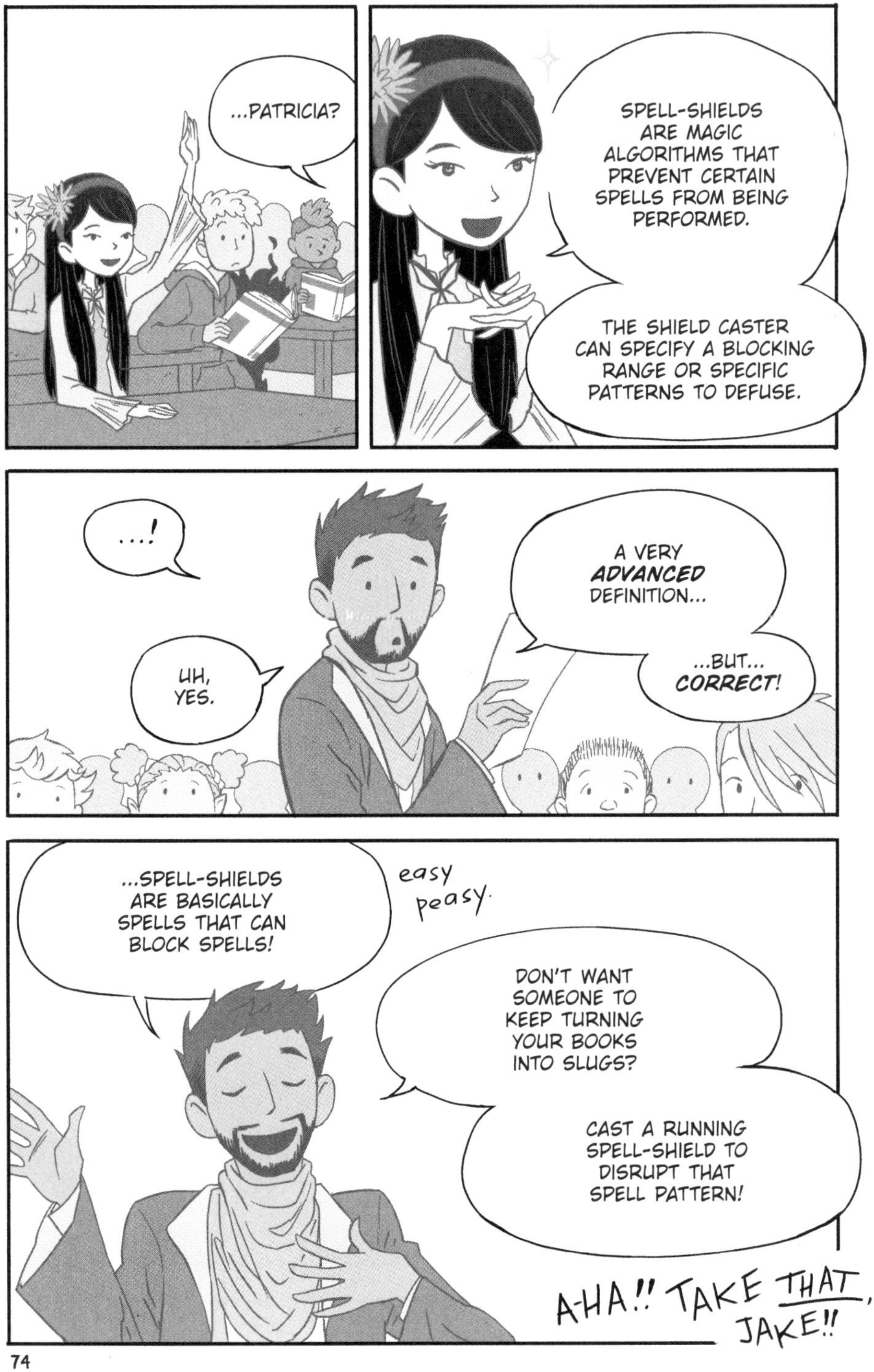
...PATRICIA?
SPELL-SHIELDS ARE MAGIC ALGORITHMS THAT PREVENT CERTAIN SPELLS FROM BEING PERFORMED.
THE SHIELD CASTER CAN SPECIFY A BLOCKING RANGE OR SPECIFIC PATTERNS TO DEFUSE.
...!
A VERY ADVANCED DEFINITION...
...BUT... CORRECT!
UH, YES.
...SPELL-SHIELDS ARE BASICALLY SPELLS THAT CAN BLOCK SPELLS!
easy peasy.
DON'T WANT SOMEONE TO KEEP TURNING YOUR BOOKS INTO SLUGS?
CAST A RUNNING SPELL-SHIELD TO DISRUPT THAT SPELL PATTERN!
A-HA!! TAKE THAT, JAKE!!

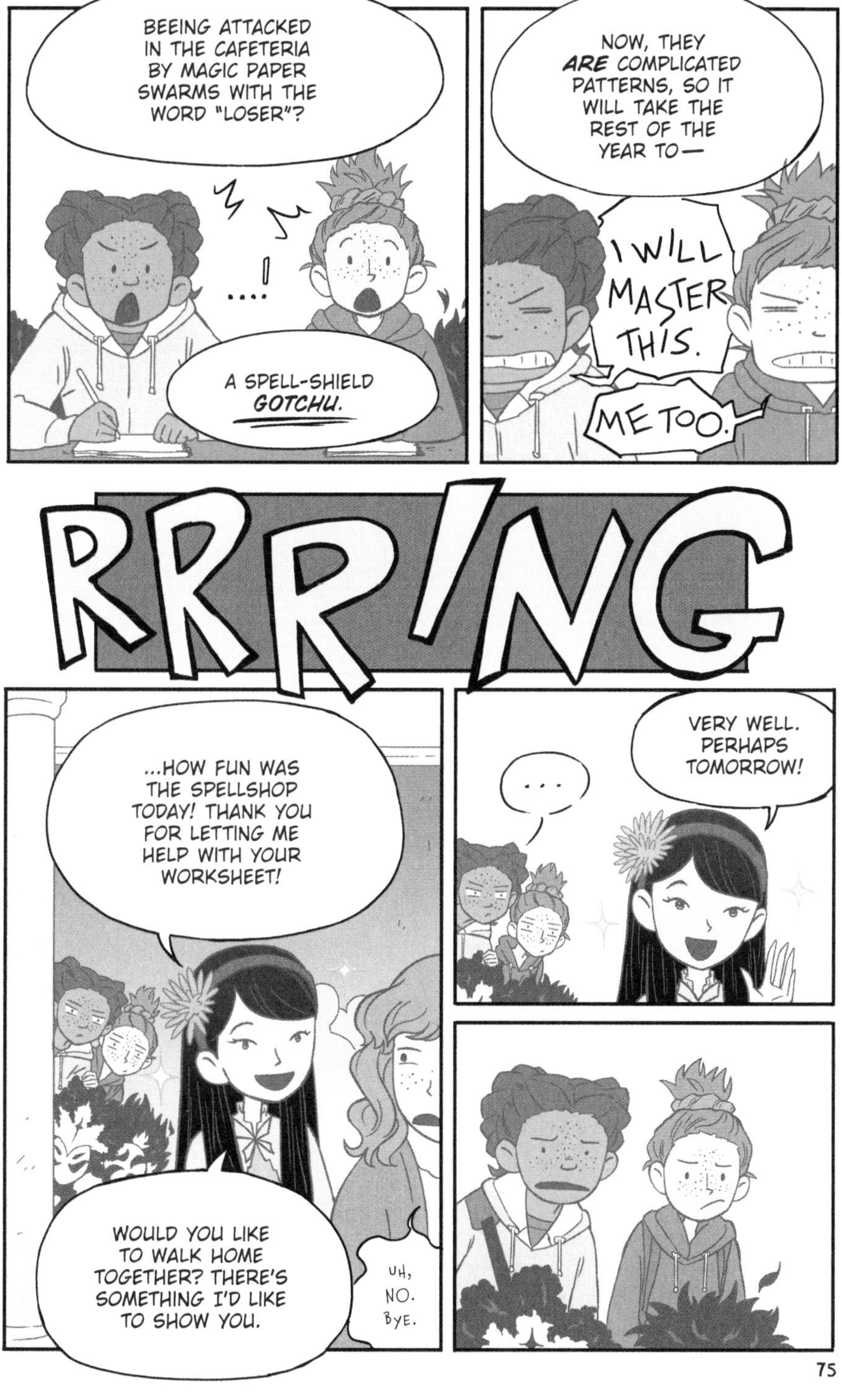
BEEING ATTACKED IN THE CAFETERIA BY MAGIC PAPER SWARMS WITH THE WORD "LOSER"?
...!
A SPELL-SHIELD GOTCHU.
NOW, THEY ARE COMPLICATED PATTERNS, SO IT WILL TAKE THE REST OF THE YEAR TO—
I WILL MASTER THIS.
ME TOO.
RRRING
...HOW FUN WAS THE SPELLSHOP TODAY! THANK YOU FOR LETTING ME HELP WITH YOUR WORKSHEET!
WOULD YOU LIKE TO WALK HOME TOGETHER? THERE'S SOMETHING I'D LIKE TO SHOW YOU.
UH, NO. BYE.
...
VERY WELL. PERHAPS TOMORROW!

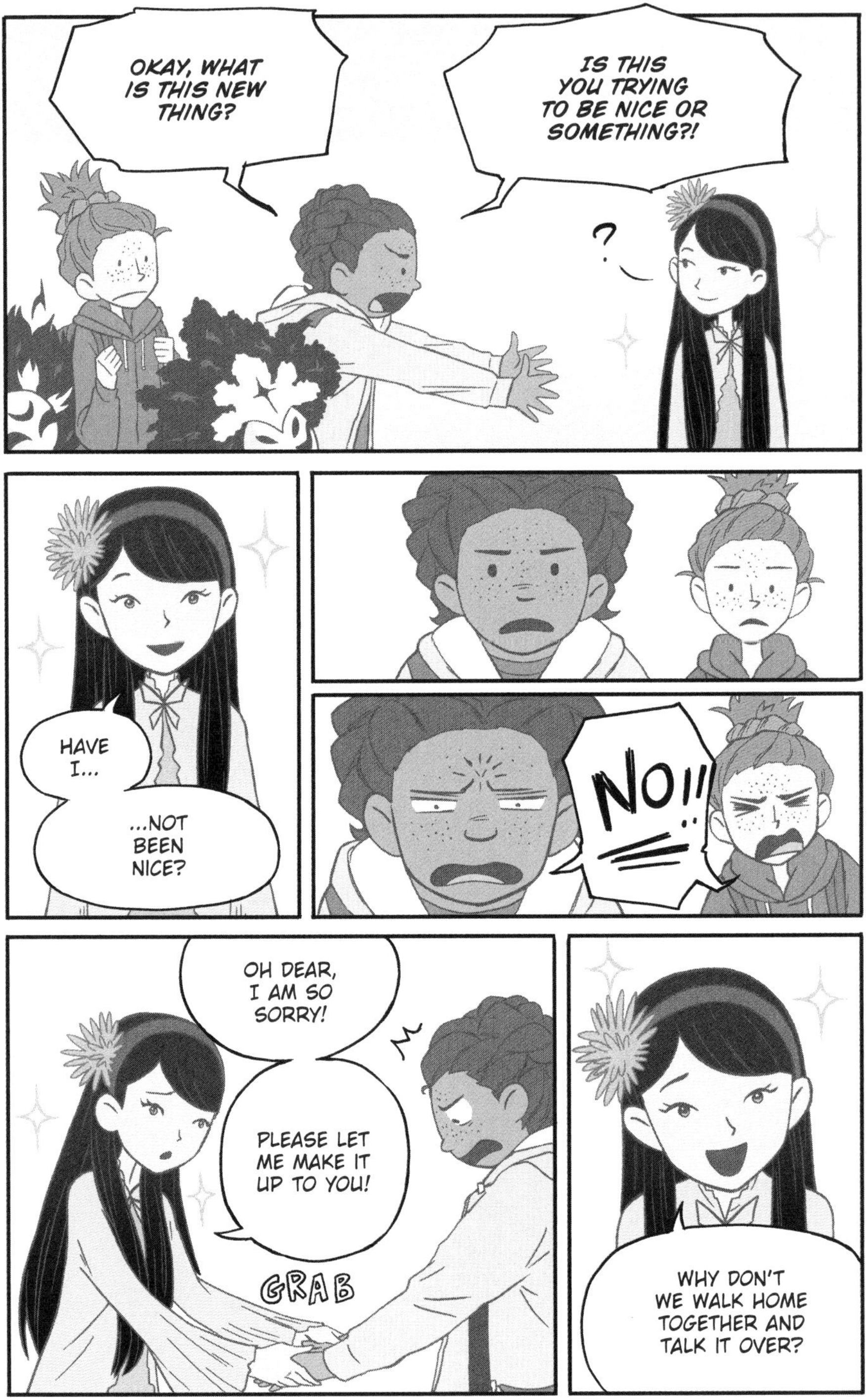
OKAY, WHAT IS THIS NEW THING?
IS THIS YOU TRYING TO BE NICE OR SOMETHING?!
?
HAVE I...
...NOT BEEN NICE?
NO!!
OH DEAR, I AM SO SORRY!
PLEASE LET ME MAKE IT UP TO YOU!
GRAB
WHY DON'T WE WALK HOME TOGETHER AND TALK IT OVER?

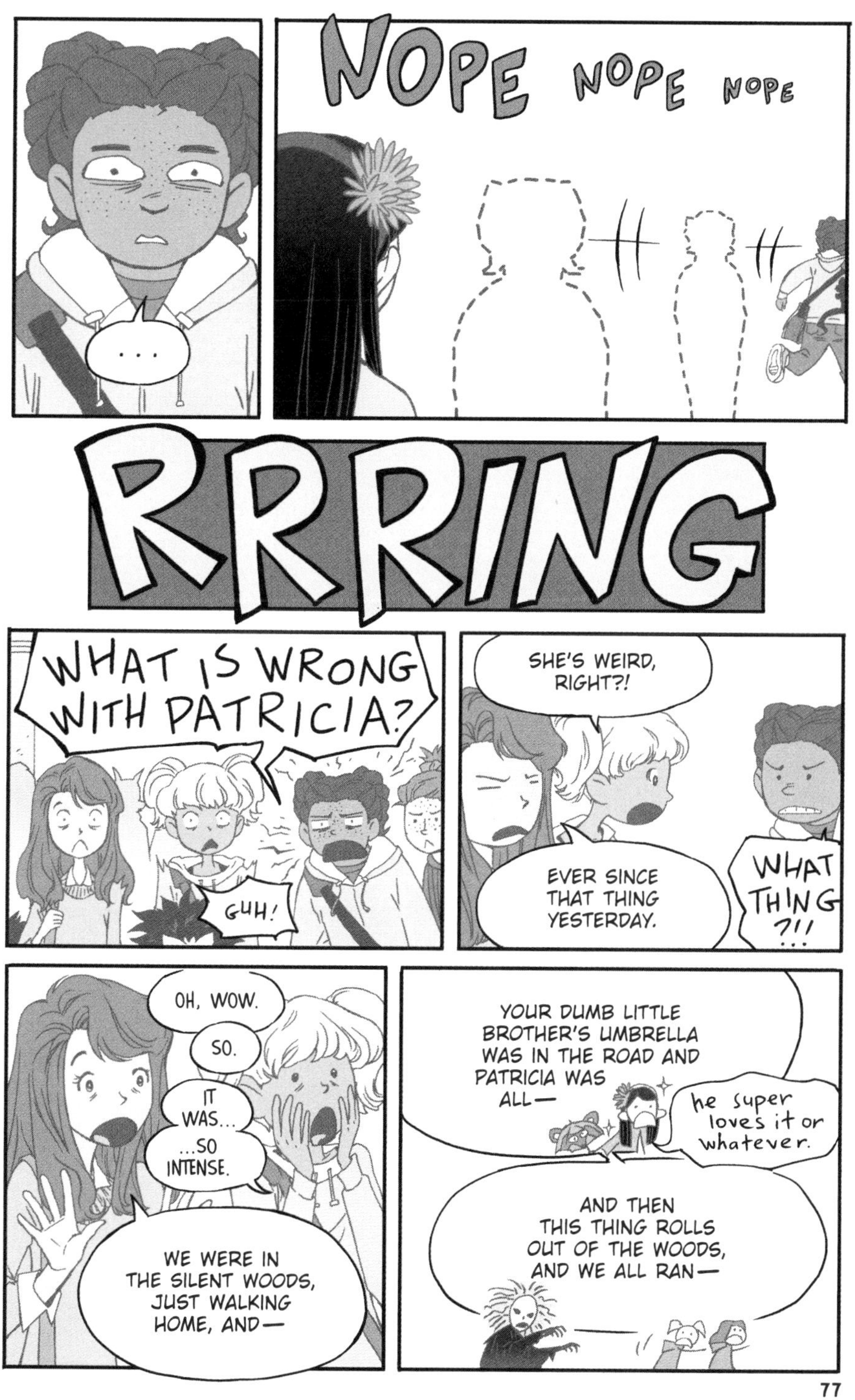
. . .
NOPE NOPE NOPE
RRRING
WHAT IS WRONG WITH PATRICIA?
GUH!
SHE'S WEIRD, RIGHT?!
EVER SINCE THAT THING YESTERDAY.
WHAT THING ?!!
OH, WOW.
SO.
IT WAS...
...SO INTENSE.
WE WERE IN THE SILENT WOODS, JUST WALKING HOME, AND—
YOUR DUMB LITTLE BROTHER'S UMBRELLA WAS IN THE ROAD AND PATRICIA WAS ALL—
he super loves it or whatever.
AND THEN THIS THING ROLLS OUT OF THE WOODS, AND WE ALL RAN—

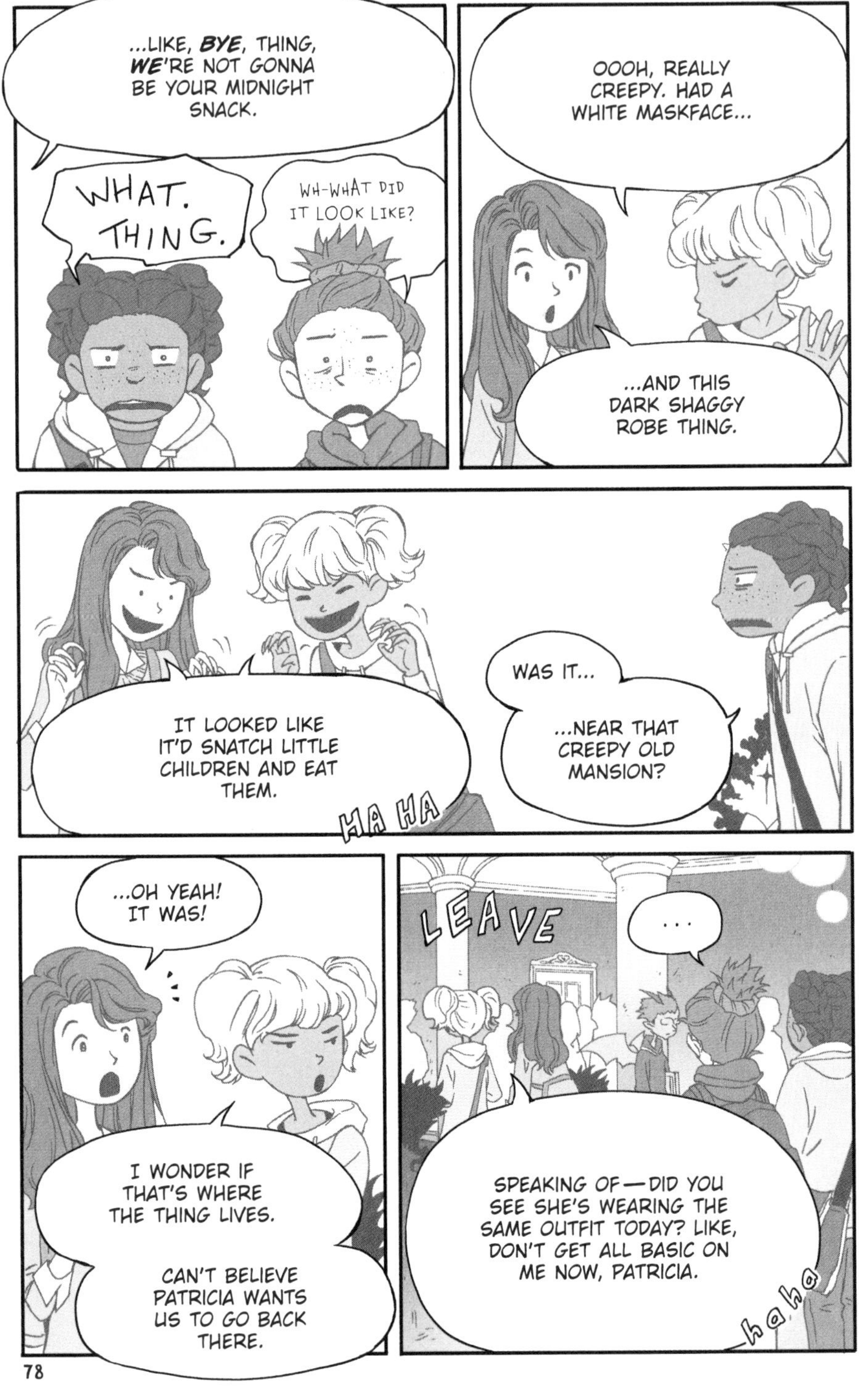
...LIKE, BYE, THING, WE'RE NOT GONNA BE YOUR MIDNIGHT SNACK.
WHAT. THING.
WH-WHAT DID IT LOOK LIKE?
OOOH, REALLY CREEPY. HAD A WHITE MASKFACE...
...AND THIS DARK SHAGGY ROBE THING.
IT LOOKED LIKE IT'D SNATCH LITTLE CHILDREN AND EAT THEM.
HA HA
WAS IT...
...NEAR THAT CREEPY OLD MANSION?
...OH YEAH! IT WAS!
I WONDER IF THAT'S WHERE THE THING LIVES.
CAN'T BELIEVE PATRICIA WANTS US TO GO BACK THERE.
LEAVE
...
SPEAKING OF—DID YOU SEE SHE'S WEARING THE SAME OUTFIT TODAY? LIKE, DON'T GET ALL BASIC ON ME NOW, PATRICIA.
haha

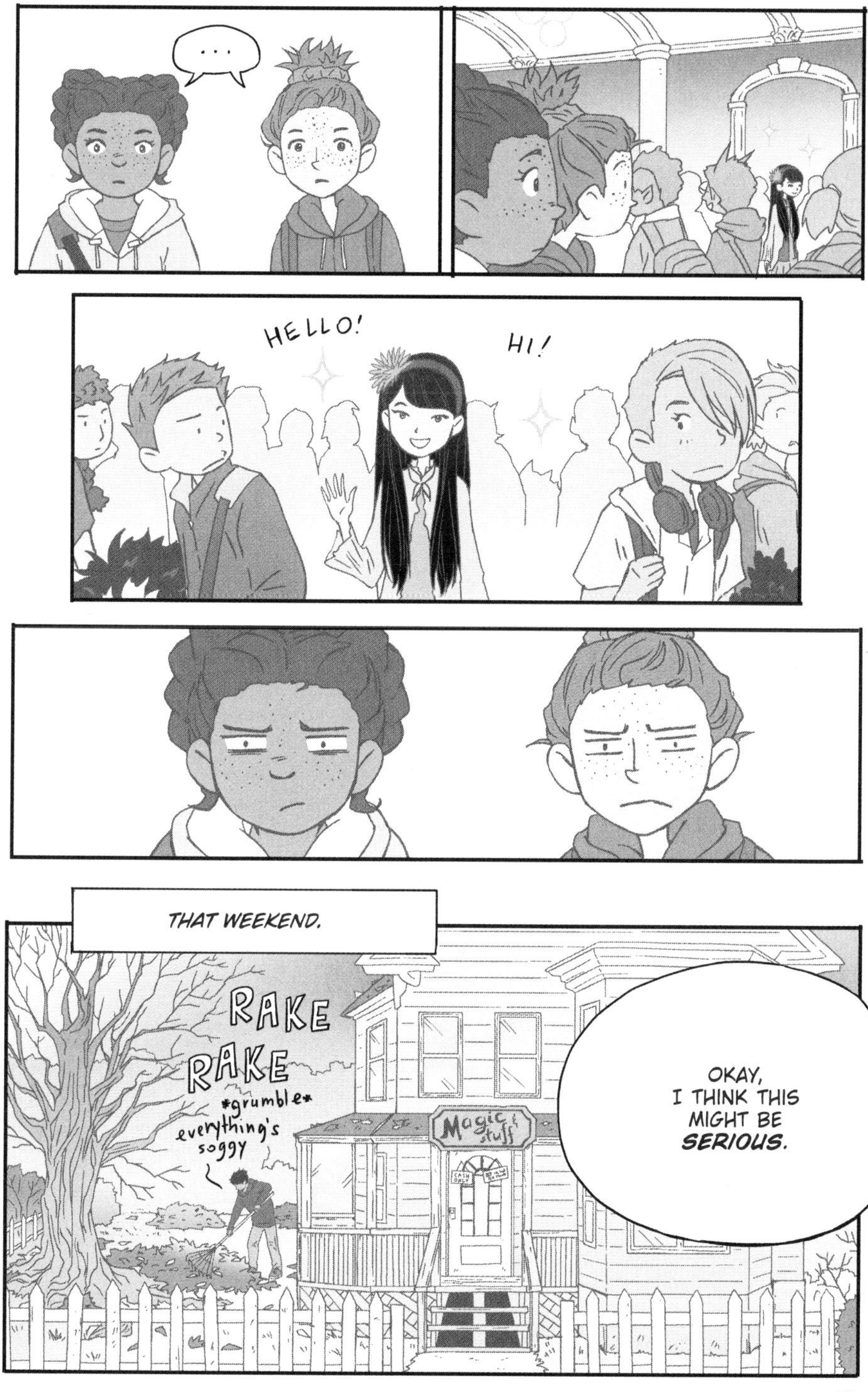
. . .
HELLO!
HI!
THAT WEEKEND.
RAKE
RAKE
grumble
everything's soggy
Magic & stuff
CASH ONLY
OKAY, I THINK THIS MIGHT BE **SERIOUS**.

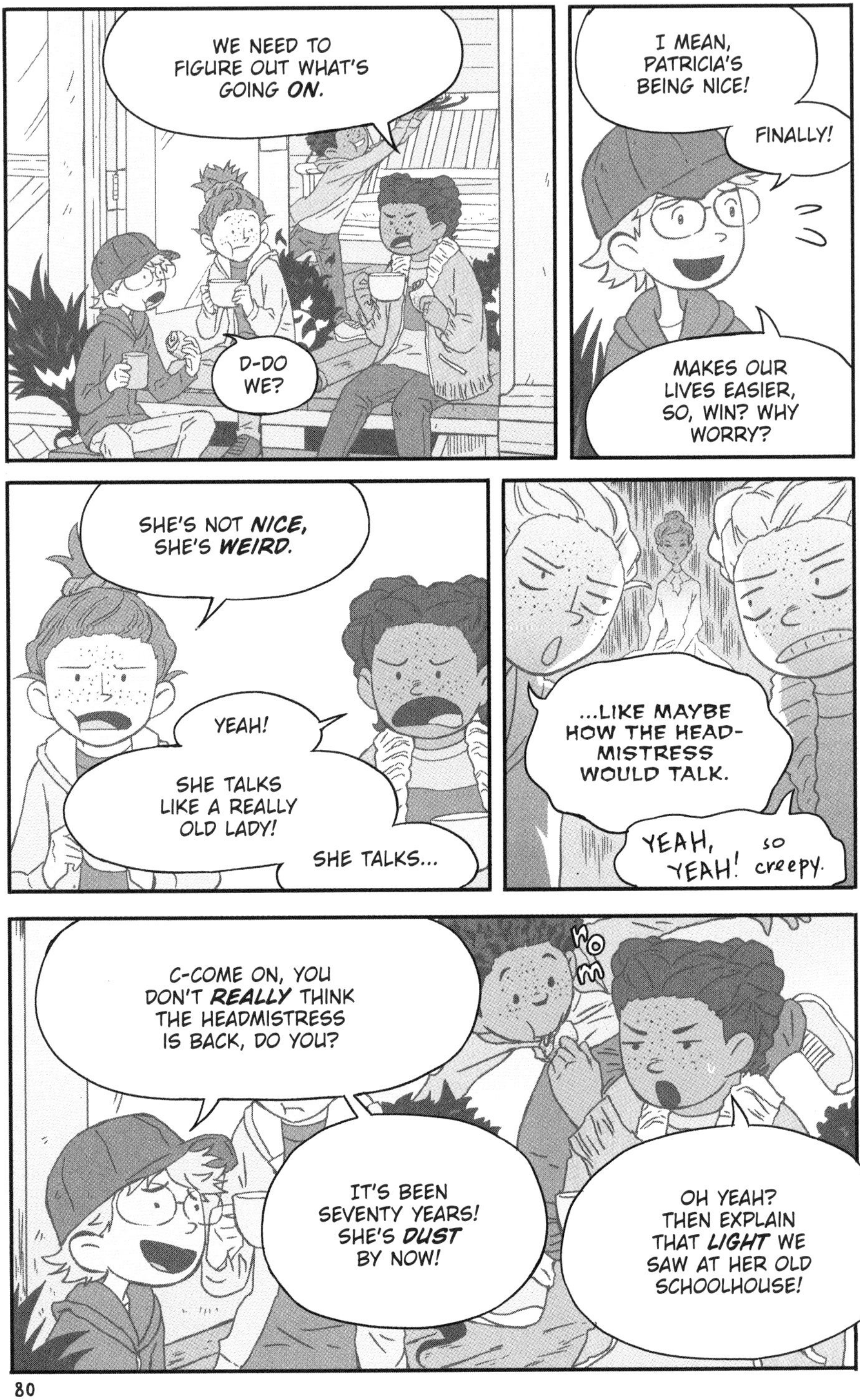
WE NEED TO FIGURE OUT WHAT'S GOING ON.
D-DO WE?
I MEAN, PATRICIA'S BEING NICE!
FINALLY!
MAKES OUR LIVES EASIER, SO, WIN? WHY WORRY?
SHE'S NOT NICE, SHE'S WEIRD.
YEAH!
SHE TALKS LIKE A REALLY OLD LADY!
SHE TALKS...
...LIKE MAYBE HOW THE HEAD-MISTRESS WOULD TALK.
YEAH, YEAH! so creepy.
C-COME ON, YOU DON'T REALLY THINK THE HEADMISTRESS IS BACK, DO YOU?
IT'S BEEN SEVENTY YEARS! SHE'S DUST BY NOW!
OH YEAH? THEN EXPLAIN THAT LIGHT WE SAW AT HER OLD SCHOOLHOUSE!

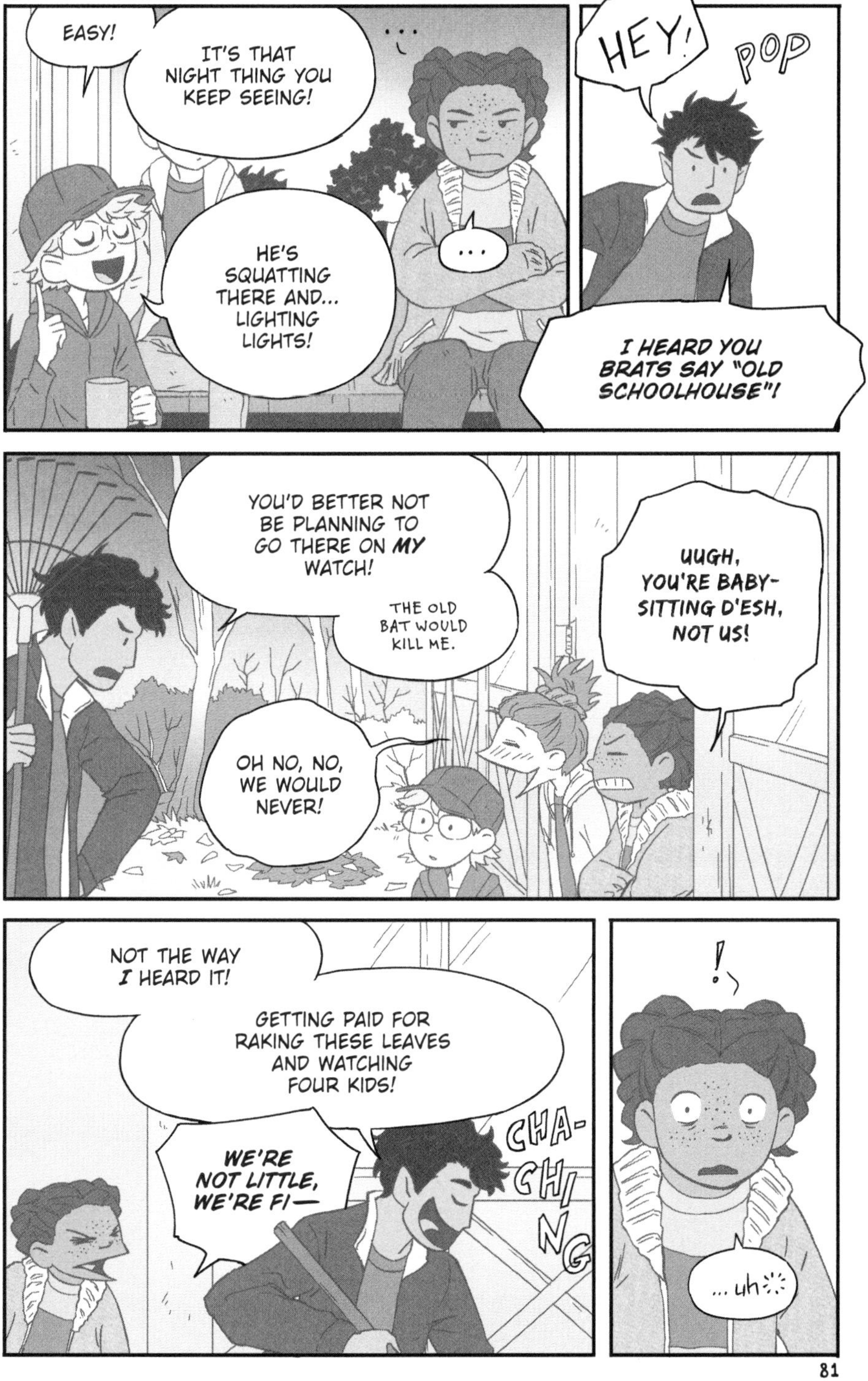
EASY!
IT'S THAT NIGHT THING YOU KEEP SEEING!
...
HE'S SQUATTING THERE AND... LIGHTING LIGHTS!
...
HEY!
POP
I HEARD YOU BRATS SAY "OLD SCHOOLHOUSE"!
YOU'D BETTER NOT BE PLANNING TO GO THERE ON MY WATCH!
THE OLD BAT WOULD KILL ME.
UUGH, YOU'RE BABY-SITTING D'ESH, NOT US!
OH NO, NO, WE WOULD NEVER!
NOT THE WAY I HEARD IT!
GETTING PAID FOR RAKING THESE LEAVES AND WATCHING FOUR KIDS!
WE'RE NOT LITTLE, WE'RE FI—
CHA-CHING
!
...uh

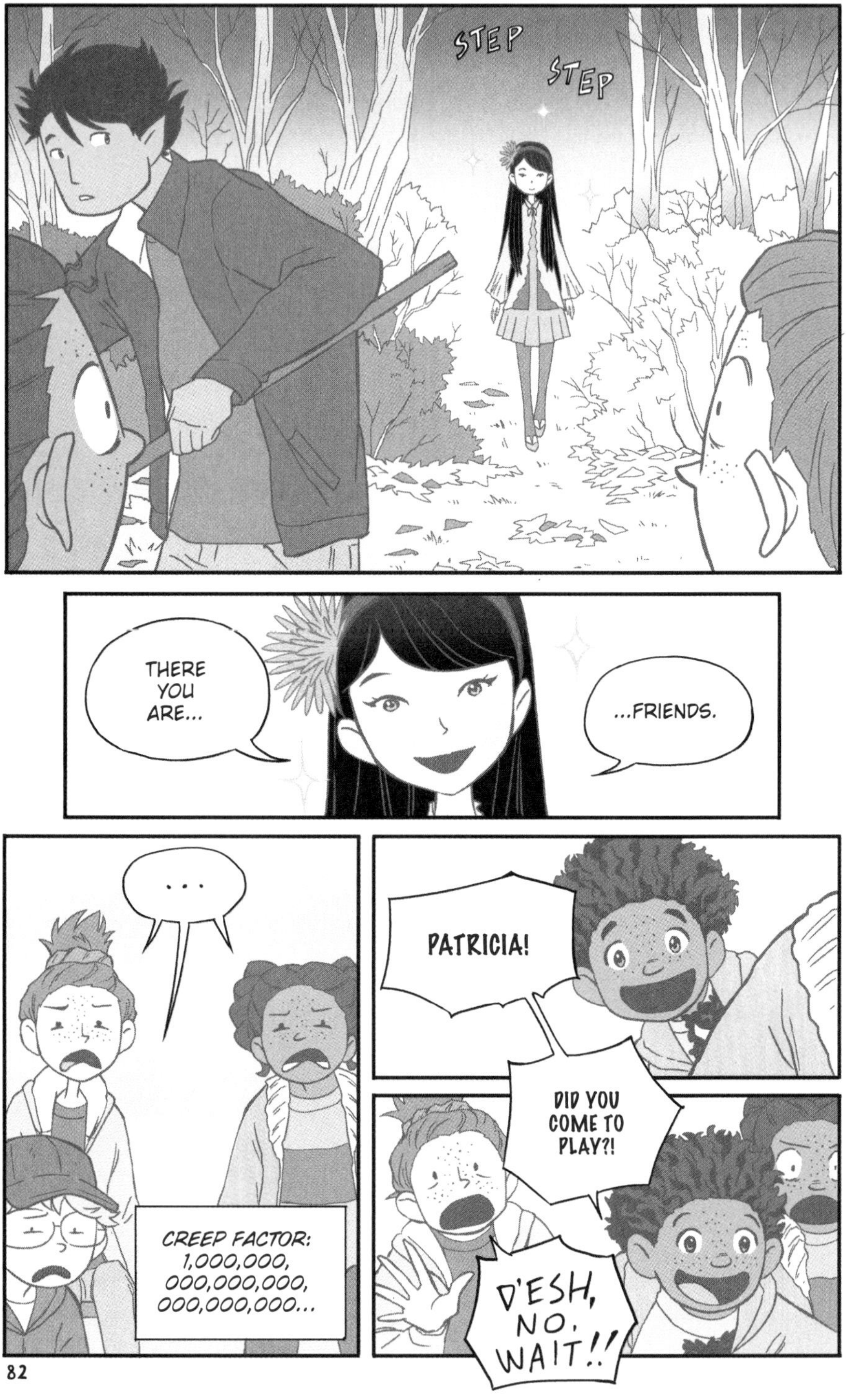
STEP
STEP
THERE YOU ARE...
...FRIENDS.
. . .
CREEP FACTOR: 1,000,000, 000,000,000, 000,000,000...
PATRICIA!
DID YOU COME TO PLAY?!
D'ESH, NO, WAIT!!

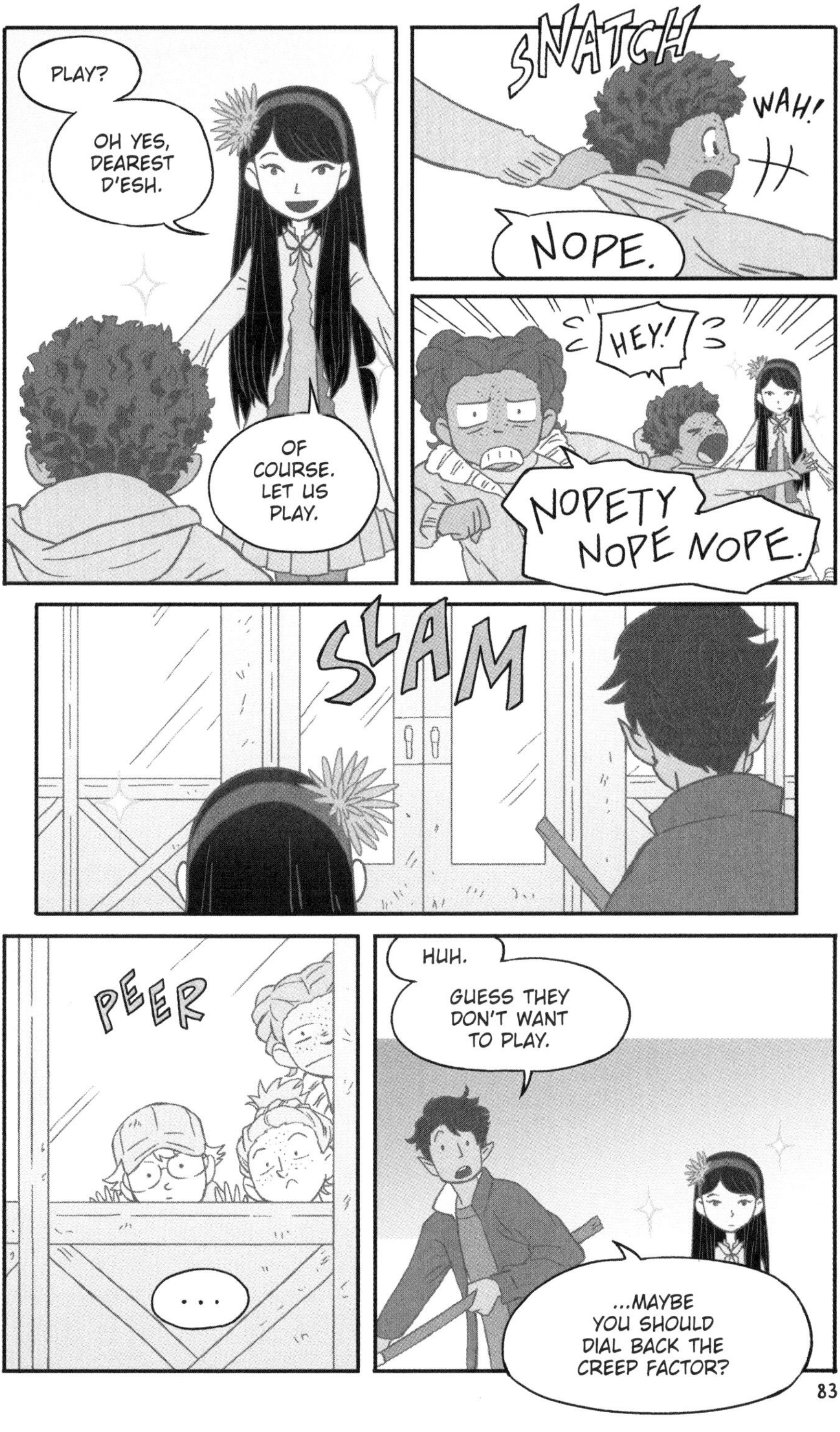
PLAY?
OH YES, DEAREST D'ESH.
OF COURSE. LET US PLAY.
SNATCH
WAH!
NOPE.
HEY!
NOPETY NOPE NOPE.
SLAM
PEER
...
HUH.
GUESS THEY DON'T WANT TO PLAY.
...MAYBE YOU SHOULD DIAL BACK THE CREEP FACTOR?

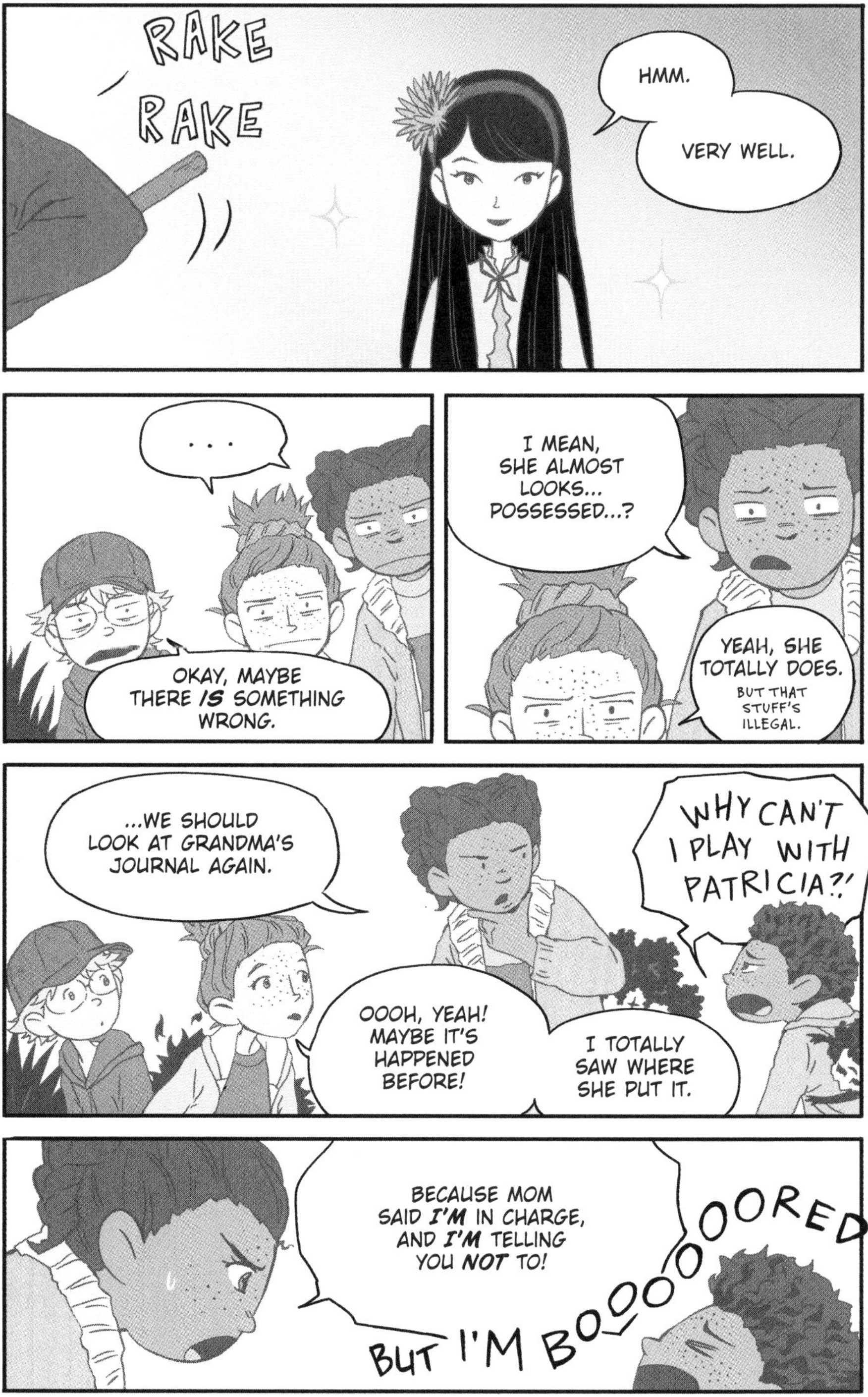
RAKE
RAKE
HMM.
VERY WELL.
. . .
OKAY, MAYBE THERE IS SOMETHING WRONG.
I MEAN, SHE ALMOST LOOKS... POSSESSED...?
YEAH, SHE TOTALLY DOES.
BUT THAT STUFF'S ILLEGAL.
...WE SHOULD LOOK AT GRANDMA'S JOURNAL AGAIN.
WHY CAN'T I PLAY WITH PATRICIA?!
OOOH, YEAH! MAYBE IT'S HAPPENED BEFORE!
I TOTALLY SAW WHERE SHE PUT IT.
BECAUSE MOM SAID I'M IN CHARGE, AND I'M TELLING YOU NOT TO!
BUT I'M BOOOOOOORED

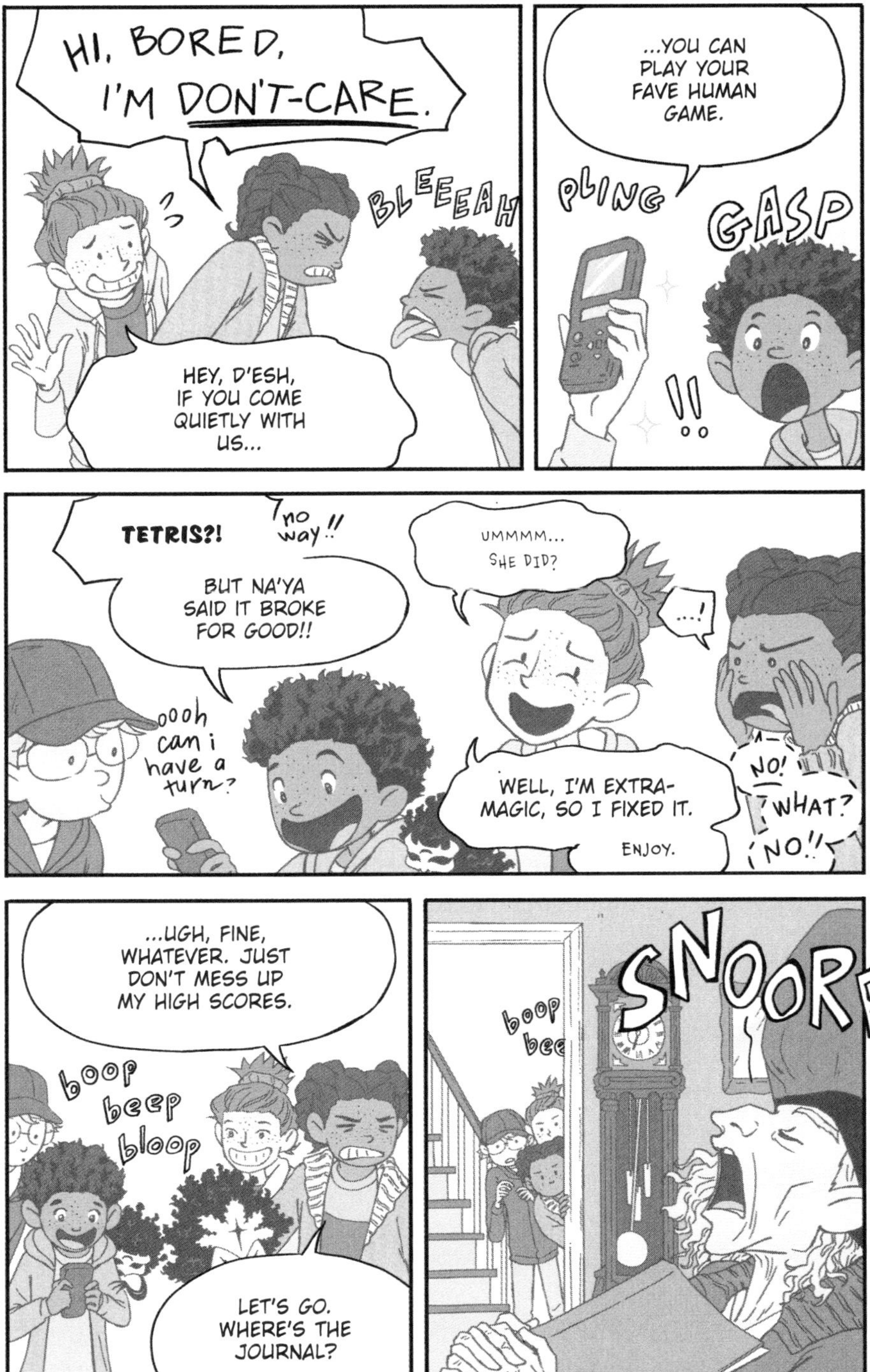
HI, BORED, I'M DON'T-CARE.
BLEEEAH
HEY, D'ESH, IF YOU COME QUIETLY WITH US...
...YOU CAN PLAY YOUR FAVE HUMAN GAME.
PLING
GASP
!!
TETRIS?!
no way!!
BUT NA'YA SAID IT BROKE FOR GOOD!!
UMMMM... SHE DID?
...!
oooh can i have a turn?
WELL, I'M EXTRA-MAGIC, SO I FIXED IT.
ENJOY.
NO!
WHAT?
NO!!
...UGH, FINE, WHATEVER. JUST DON'T MESS UP MY HIGH SCORES.
boop beep bloop
LET'S GO. WHERE'S THE JOURNAL?
SNOORE

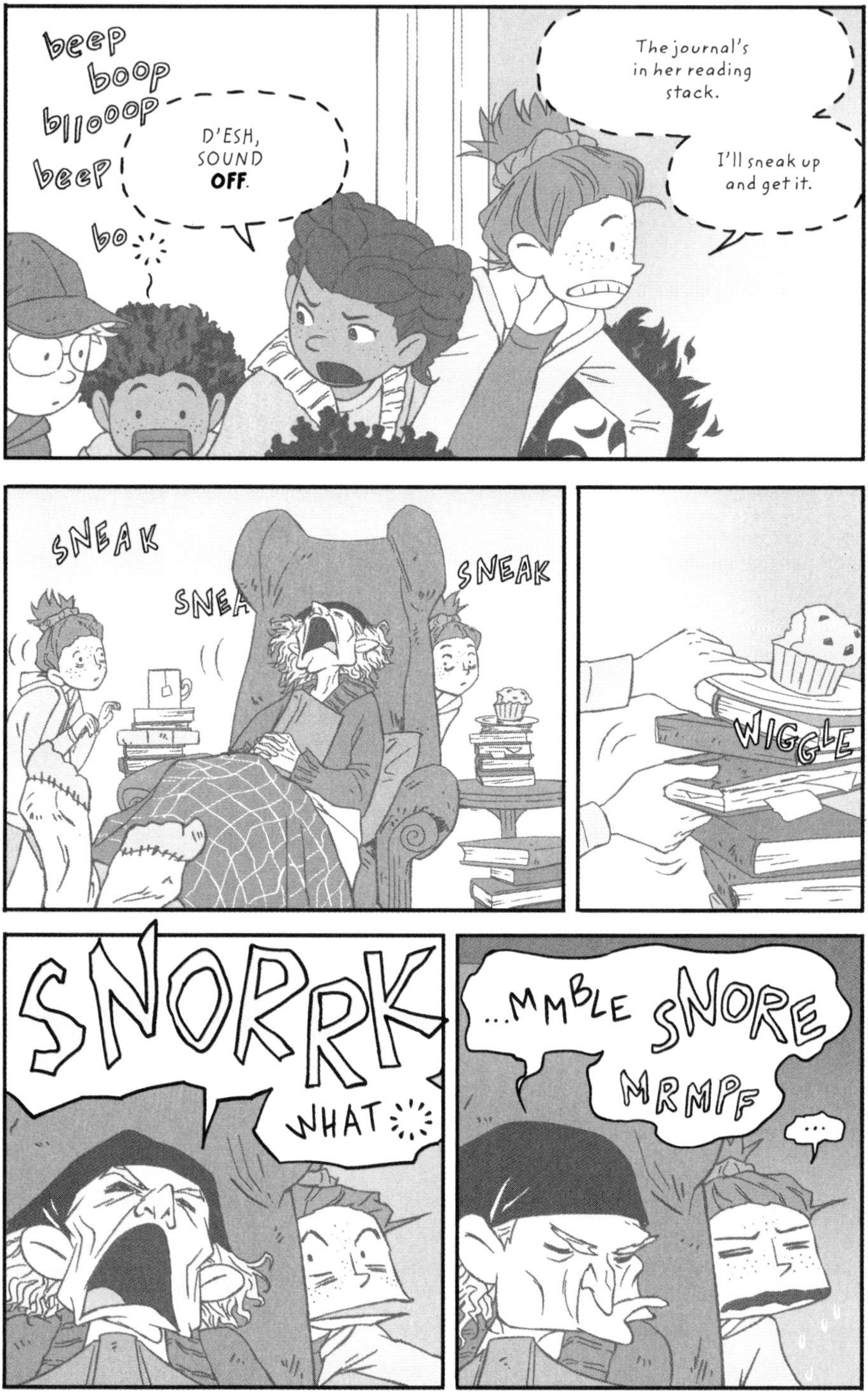
beep
boop
bllooop
beep
bo
D'ESH, SOUND OFF.
The journal's in her reading stack.
I'll sneak up and get it.
SNEAK
SNEA
SNEAK
WIGGLE
SNORRK
WHAT
...MMBLE SNORE
MRMPF
...

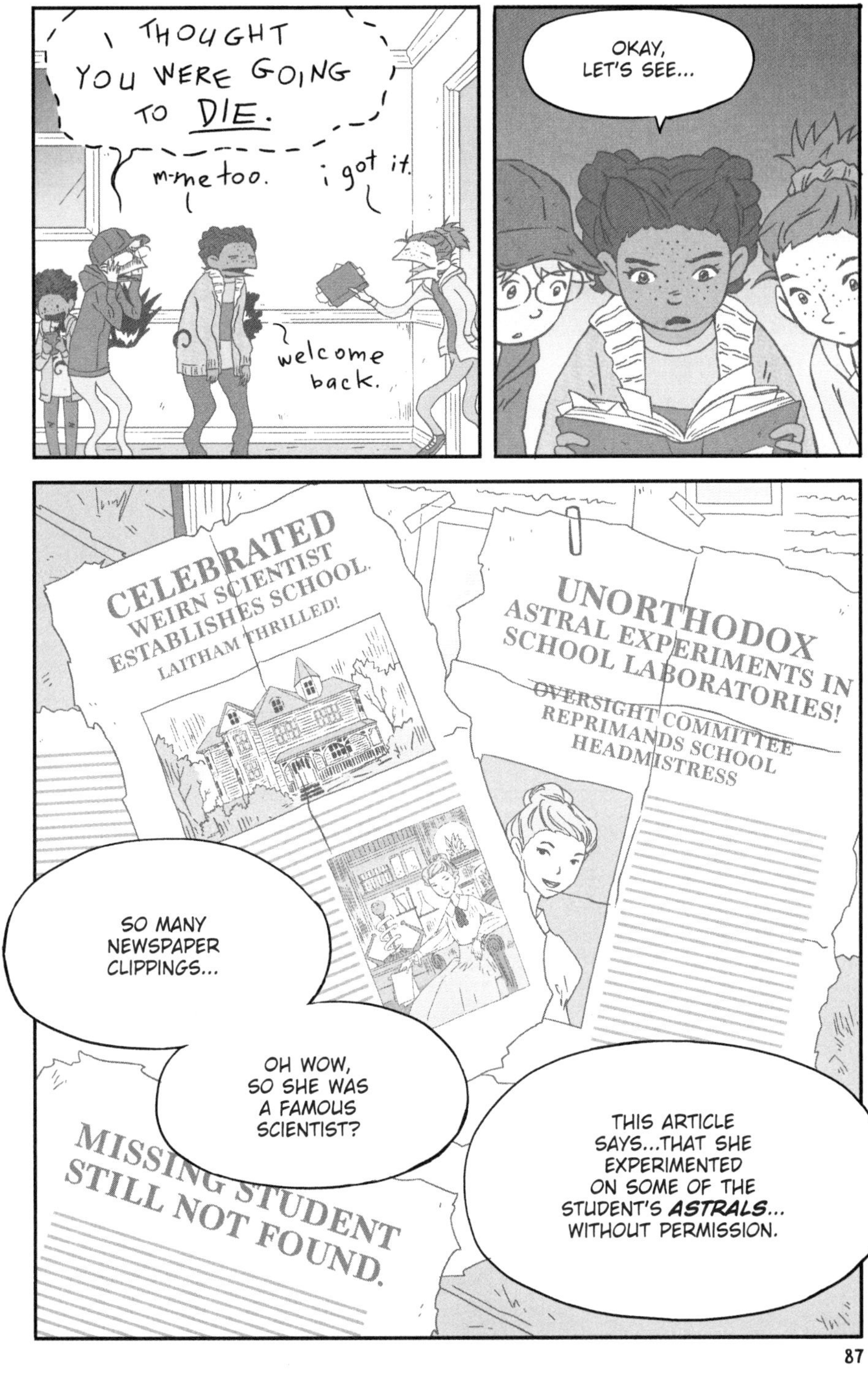
THOUGHT YOU WERE GOING TO DIE.
m-me too.
i got it.
welcome back.
OKAY, LET'S SEE...
CELEBRATED WEIRN SCIENTIST ESTABLISHES SCHOOL.
LAITHAM THRILLED!
UNORTHODOX ASTRAL EXPERIMENTS IN SCHOOL LABORATORIES!
OVERSIGHT COMMITTEE REPRIMANDS SCHOOL HEADMISTRESS
SO MANY NEWSPAPER CLIPPINGS...
OH WOW, SO SHE WAS A FAMOUS SCIENTIST?
MISSING STUDENT STILL NOT FOUND.
THIS ARTICLE SAYS...THAT SHE EXPERIMENTED ON SOME OF THE STUDENT'S ASTRALS... WITHOUT PERMISSION.

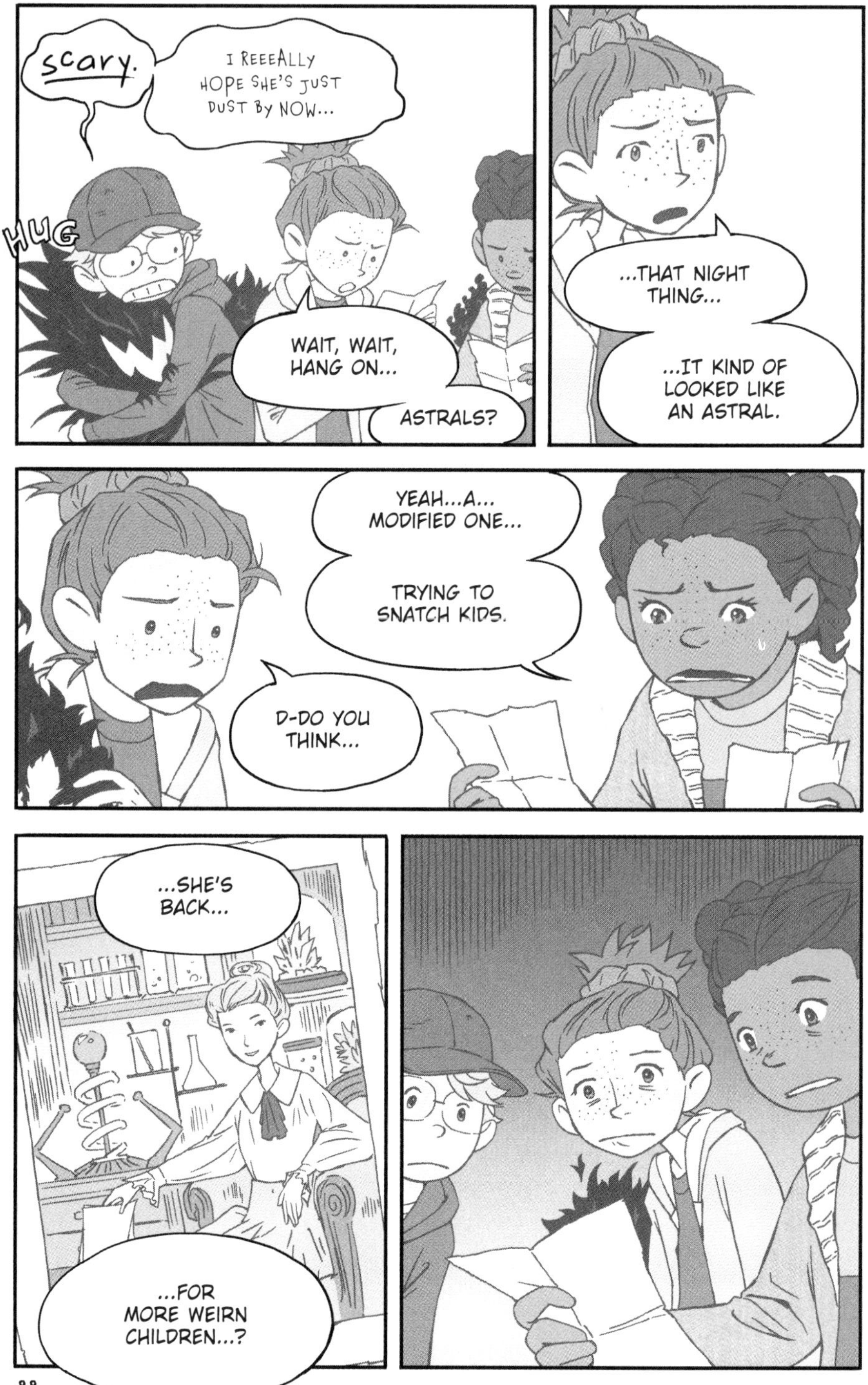
scary.
I REEEALLY HOPE SHE'S JUST DUST BY NOW...
HUG
WAIT, WAIT, HANG ON...
ASTRALS?
...THAT NIGHT THING...
...IT KIND OF LOOKED LIKE AN ASTRAL.
YEAH...A... MODIFIED ONE...
TRYING TO SNATCH KIDS.
D-DO YOU THINK...
...SHE'S BACK...
...FOR MORE WEIRN CHILDREN...?

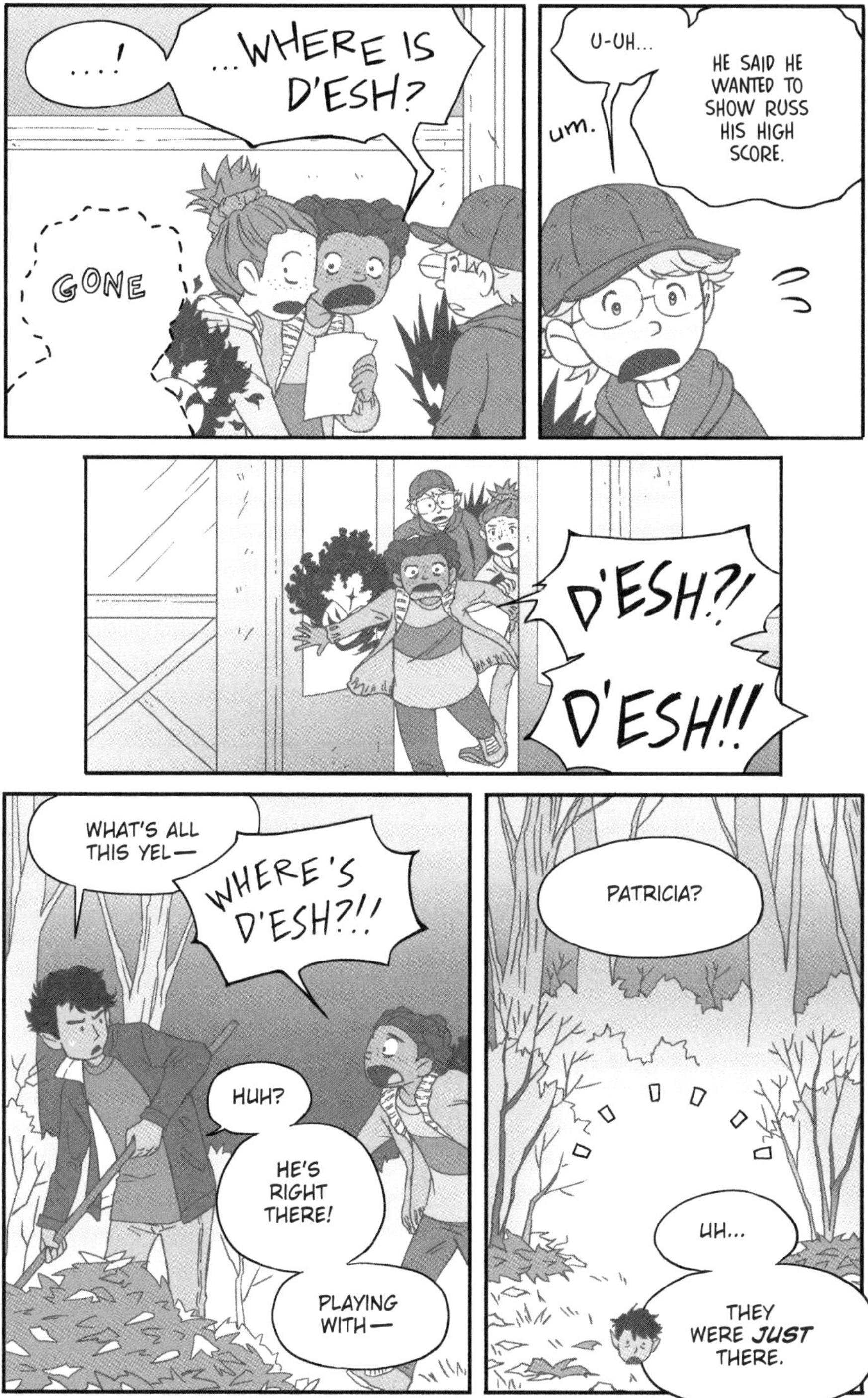
...!
...WHERE IS D'ESH?
GONE
U-UH...
um.
HE SAID HE WANTED TO SHOW RUSS HIS HIGH SCORE.
D'ESH?!
D'ESH!!
WHAT'S ALL THIS YEL—
WHERE'S D'ESH?!!
HUH?
HE'S RIGHT THERE!
PLAYING WITH—
PATRICIA?
UH...
THEY WERE *JUST* THERE.

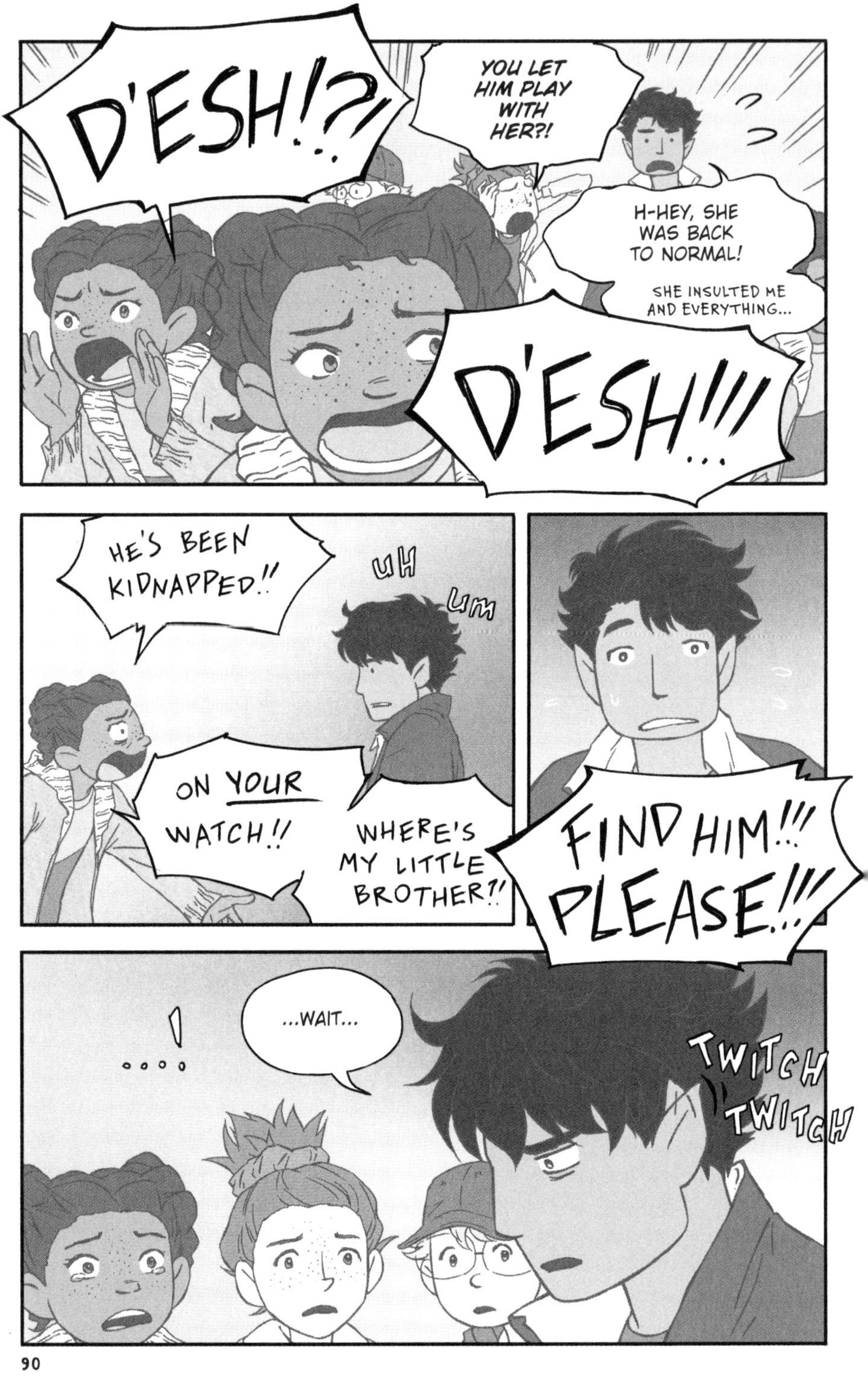
D'ESH!?!...
YOU LET HIM PLAY WITH HER?!
H-HEY, SHE WAS BACK TO NORMAL!
SHE INSULTED ME AND EVERYTHING...
D'ESH!!!!...
HE'S BEEN KIDNAPPED!!
UH
UM
ON YOUR WATCH!!
WHERE'S MY LITTLE BROTHER?!
FIND HIM!!!...
PLEASE!!!...
!
....
...WAIT...
TWITCH
TWITCH

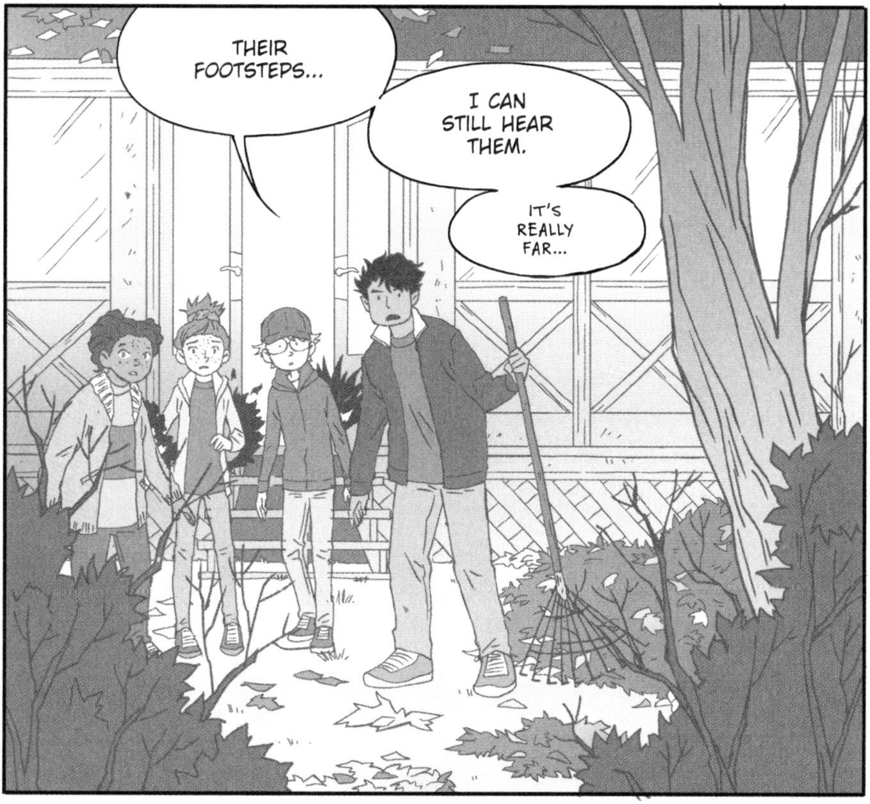
THEIR FOOTSTEPS...
I CAN STILL HEAR THEM.
IT'S REALLY FAR...

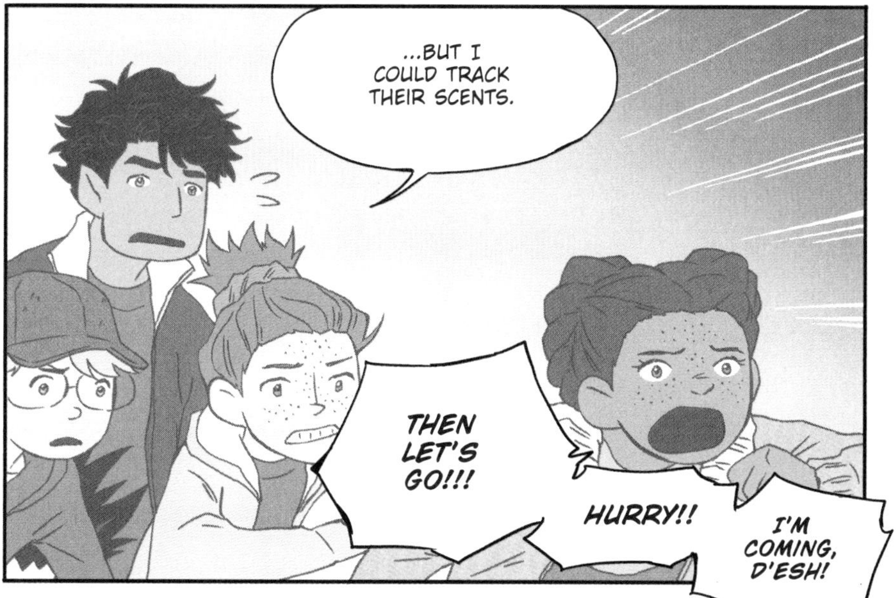
...BUT I COULD TRACK THEIR SCENTS.
THEN LET'S GO!!!
HURRY!!
I'M COMING, D'ESH!

Chapter 4

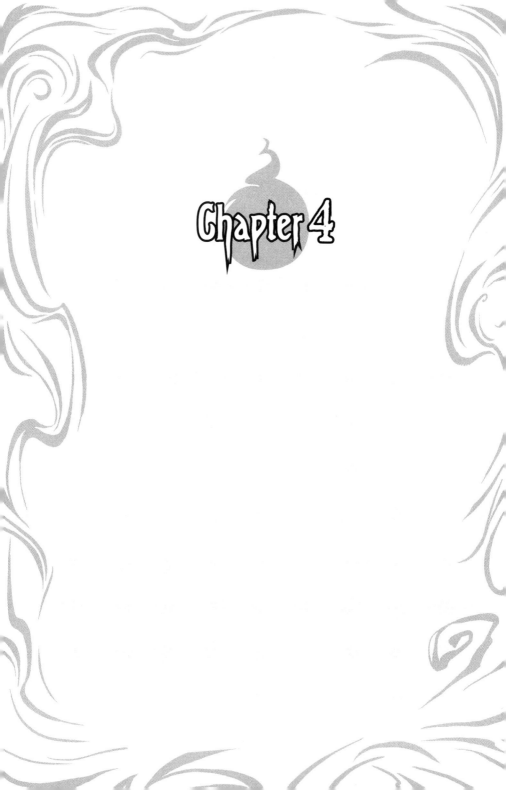

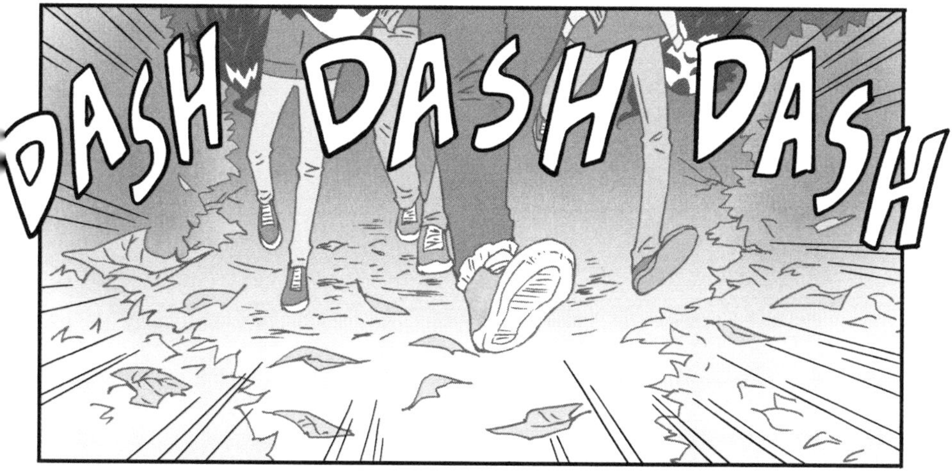
DASH DASH DASH

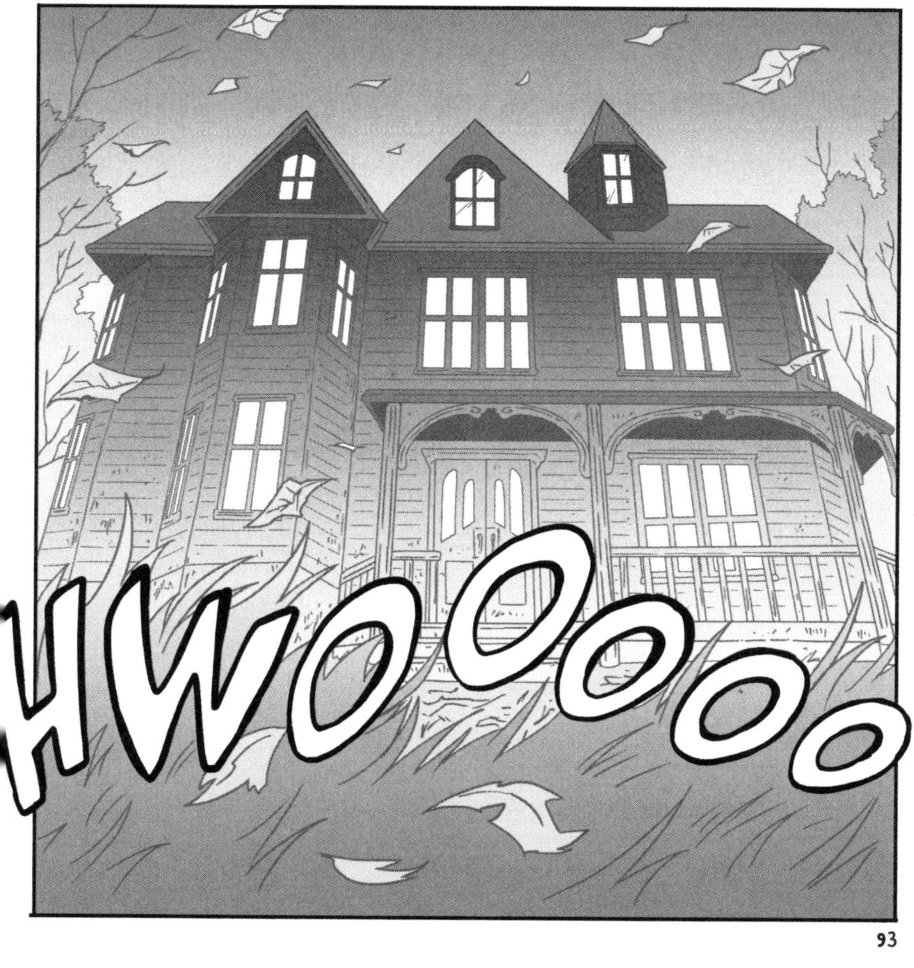
HWOOOOOO

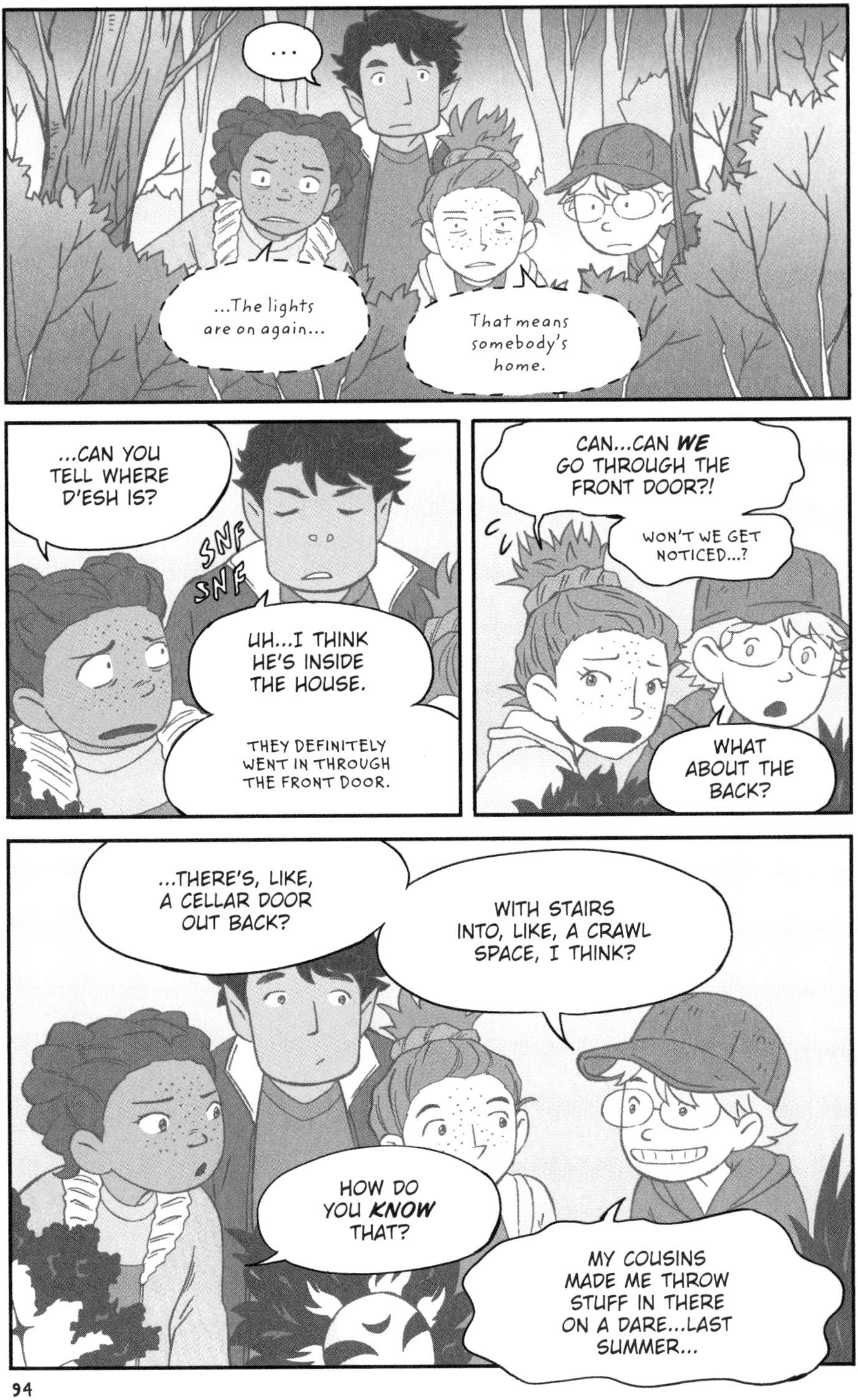
...
...The lights are on again...
That means somebody's home.
...CAN YOU TELL WHERE D'ESH IS?
SNF SNF
UH...I THINK HE'S INSIDE THE HOUSE.
THEY DEFINITELY WENT IN THROUGH THE FRONT DOOR.
CAN...CAN WE GO THROUGH THE FRONT DOOR?!
WON'T WE GET NOTICED...?
WHAT ABOUT THE BACK?
...THERE'S, LIKE, A CELLAR DOOR OUT BACK?
WITH STAIRS INTO, LIKE, A CRAWL SPACE, I THINK?
HOW DO YOU KNOW THAT?
MY COUSINS MADE ME THROW STUFF IN THERE ON A DARE...LAST SUMMER...

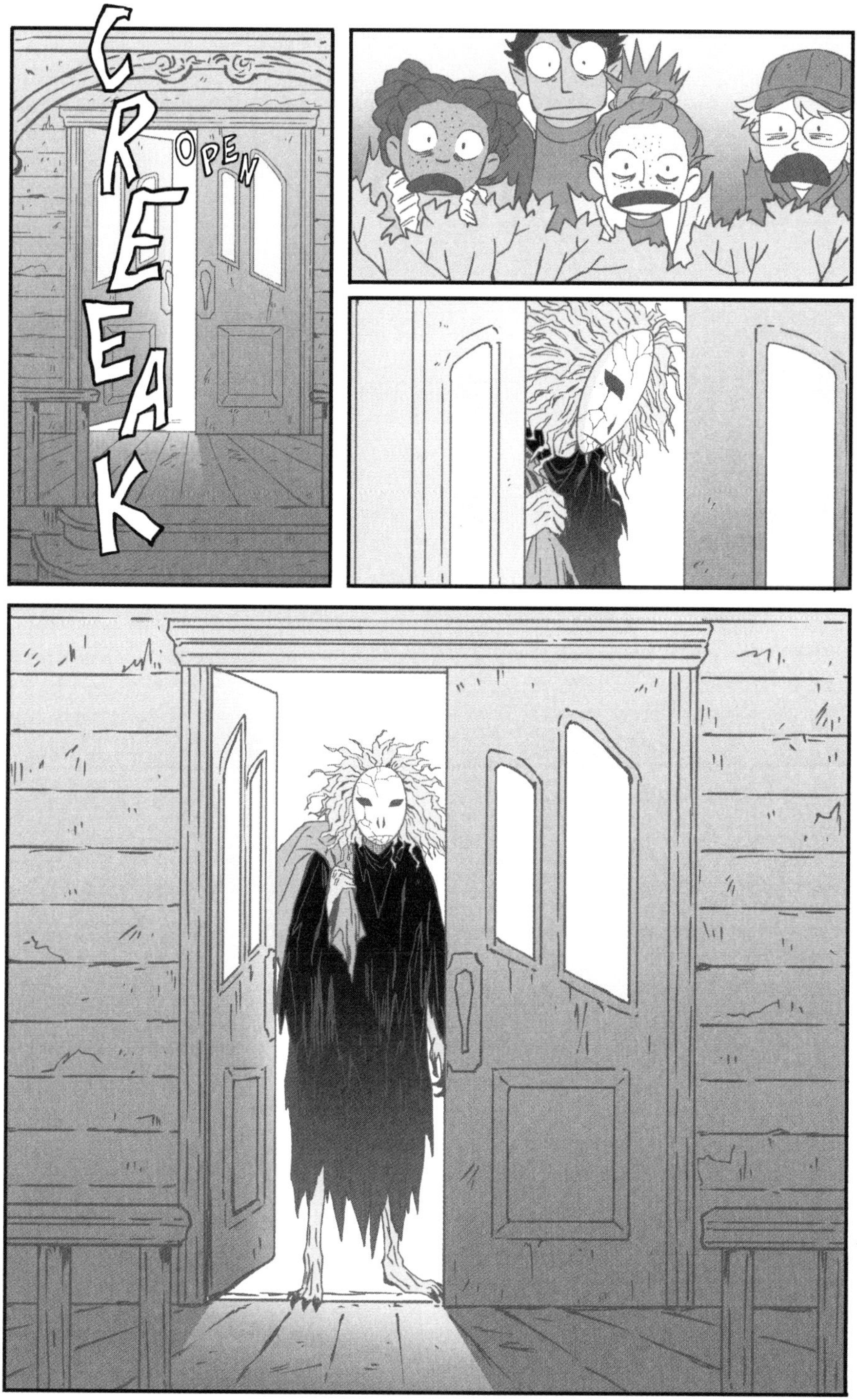
CREEAK
OPEN

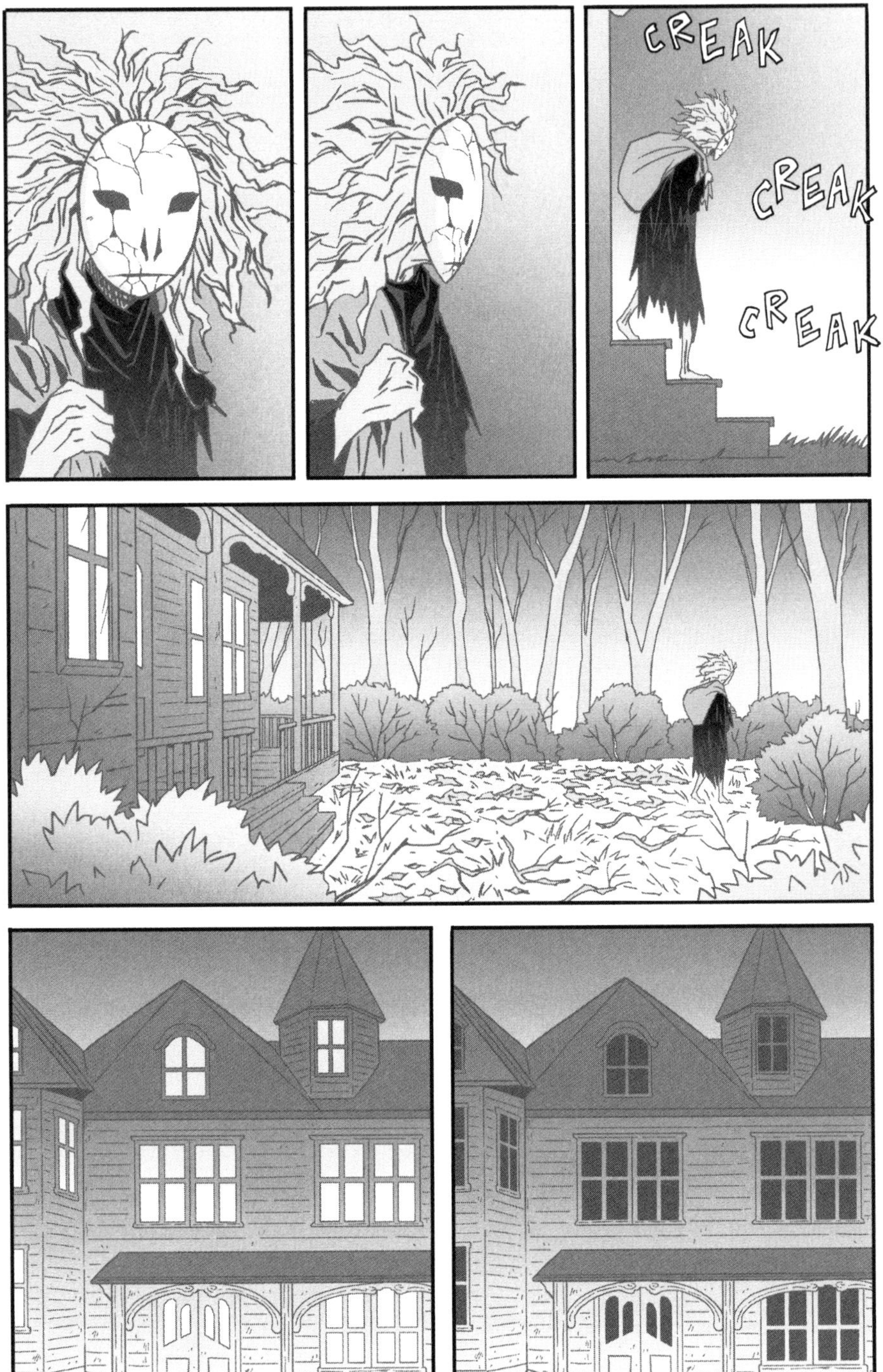
CREAK
CREAK
CREAK

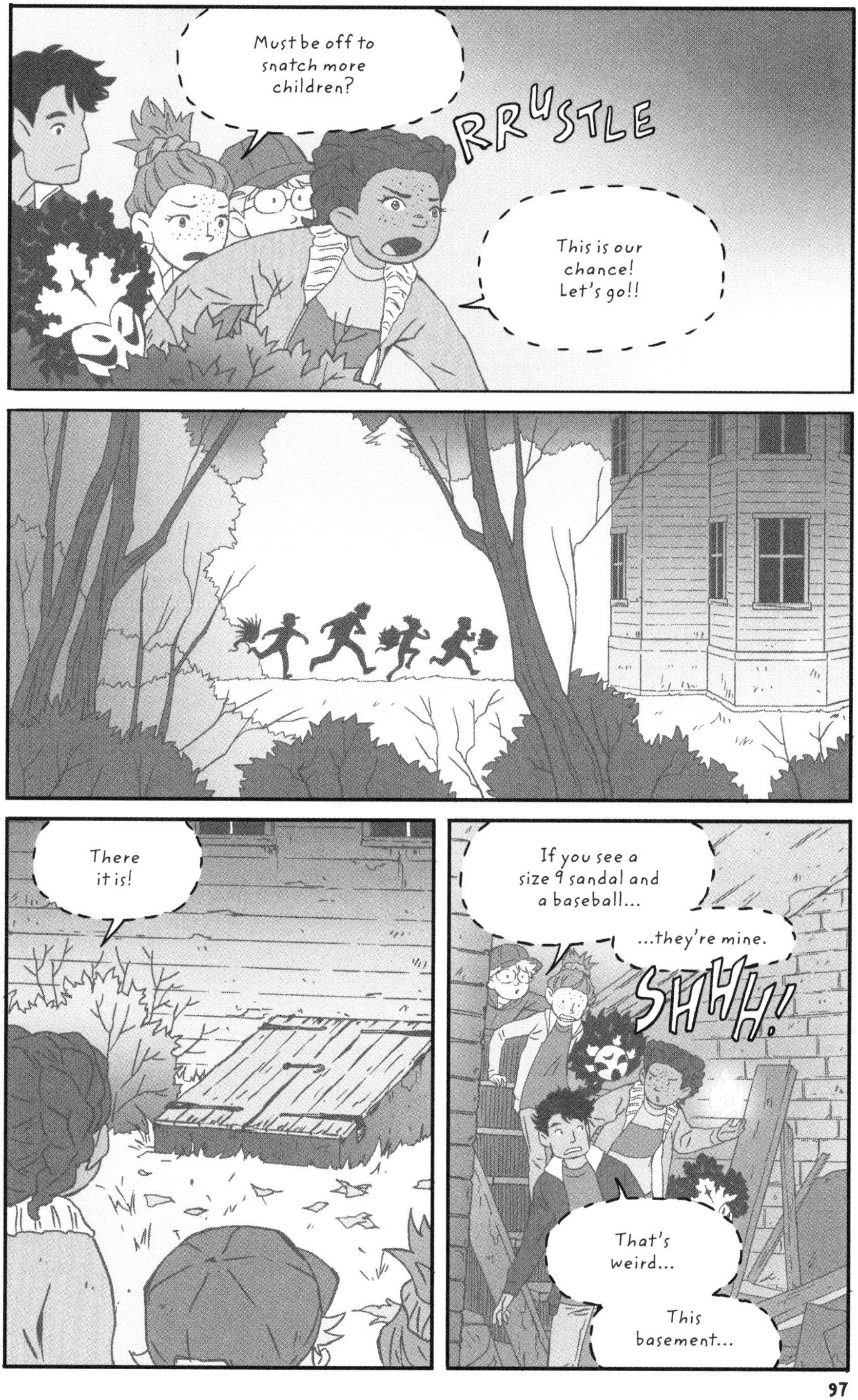
Must be off to snatch more children?
RRUSTLE
This is our chance! Let's go!!
There it is!
If you see a size 9 sandal and a baseball...
...they're mine.
SHHH!
That's weird...
This basement...

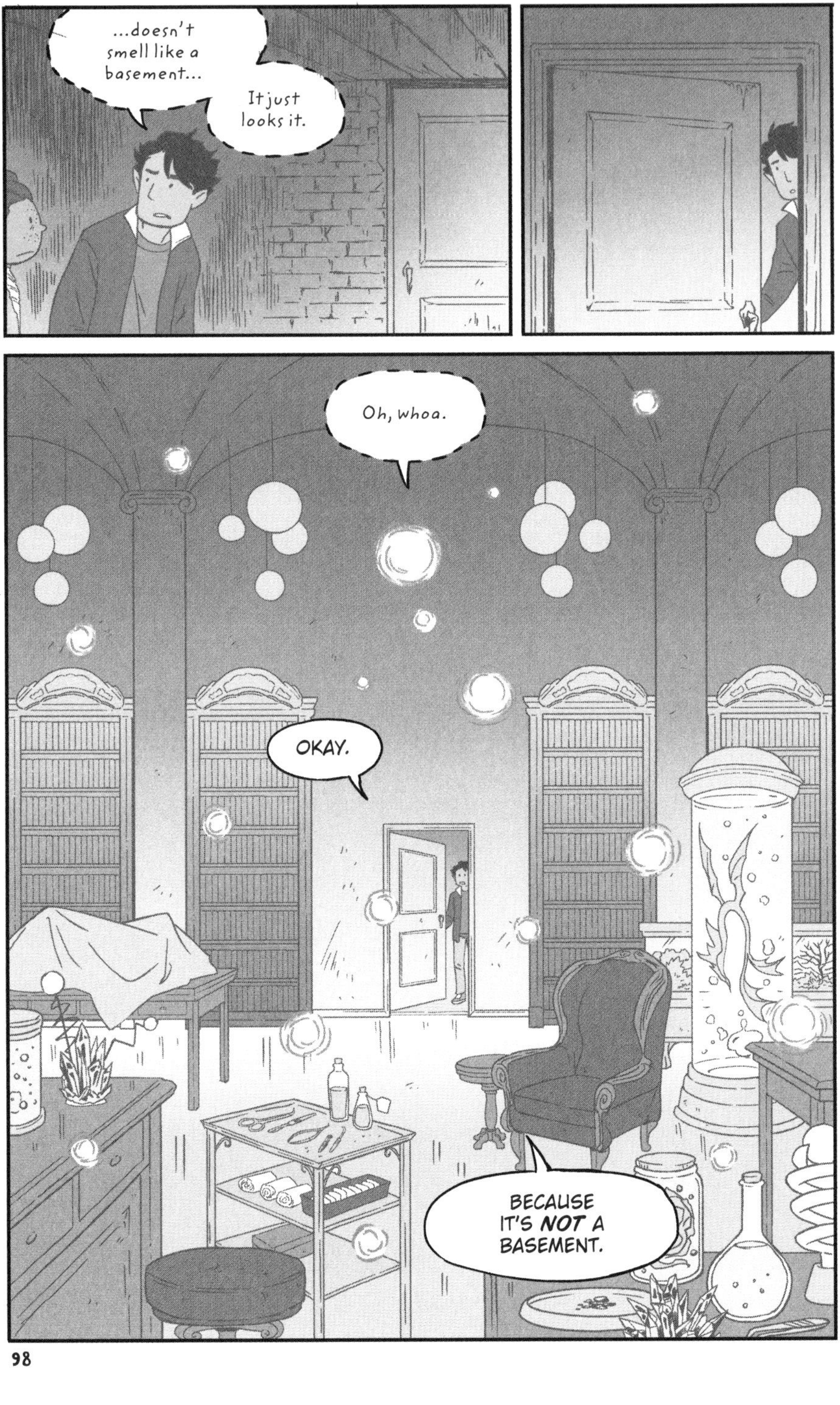
...doesn't smell like a basement...
It just looks it.
Oh, whoa.
OKAY.
BECAUSE IT'S *NOT* A BASEMENT.

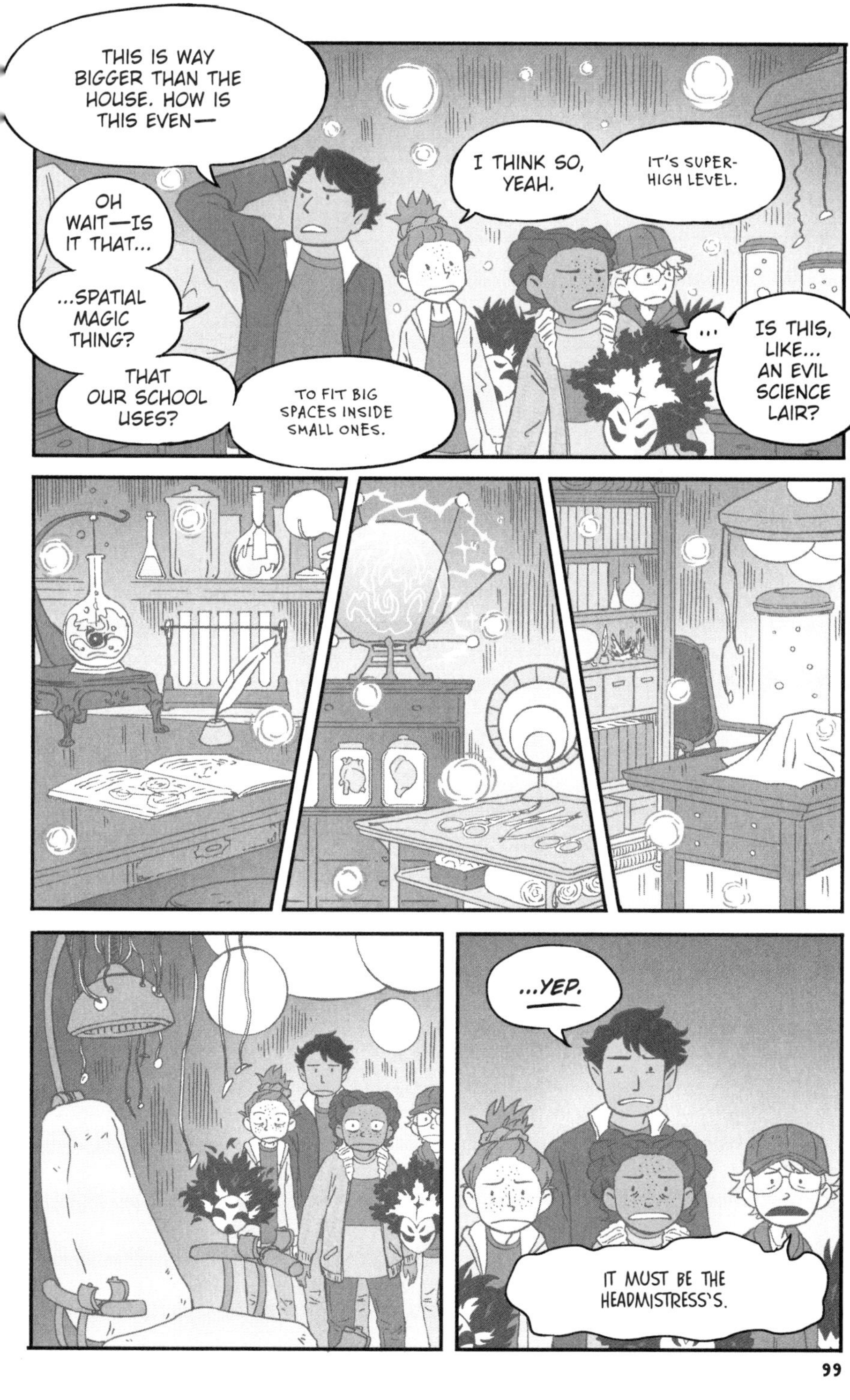
THIS IS WAY BIGGER THAN THE HOUSE. HOW IS THIS EVEN—
OH WAIT—IS IT THAT...
...SPATIAL MAGIC THING?
THAT OUR SCHOOL USES?
TO FIT BIG SPACES INSIDE SMALL ONES.
I THINK SO, YEAH.
IT'S SUPER-HIGH LEVEL.
...
IS THIS, LIKE... AN EVIL SCIENCE LAIR?
...YEP.
IT MUST BE THE HEADMISTRESS'S.

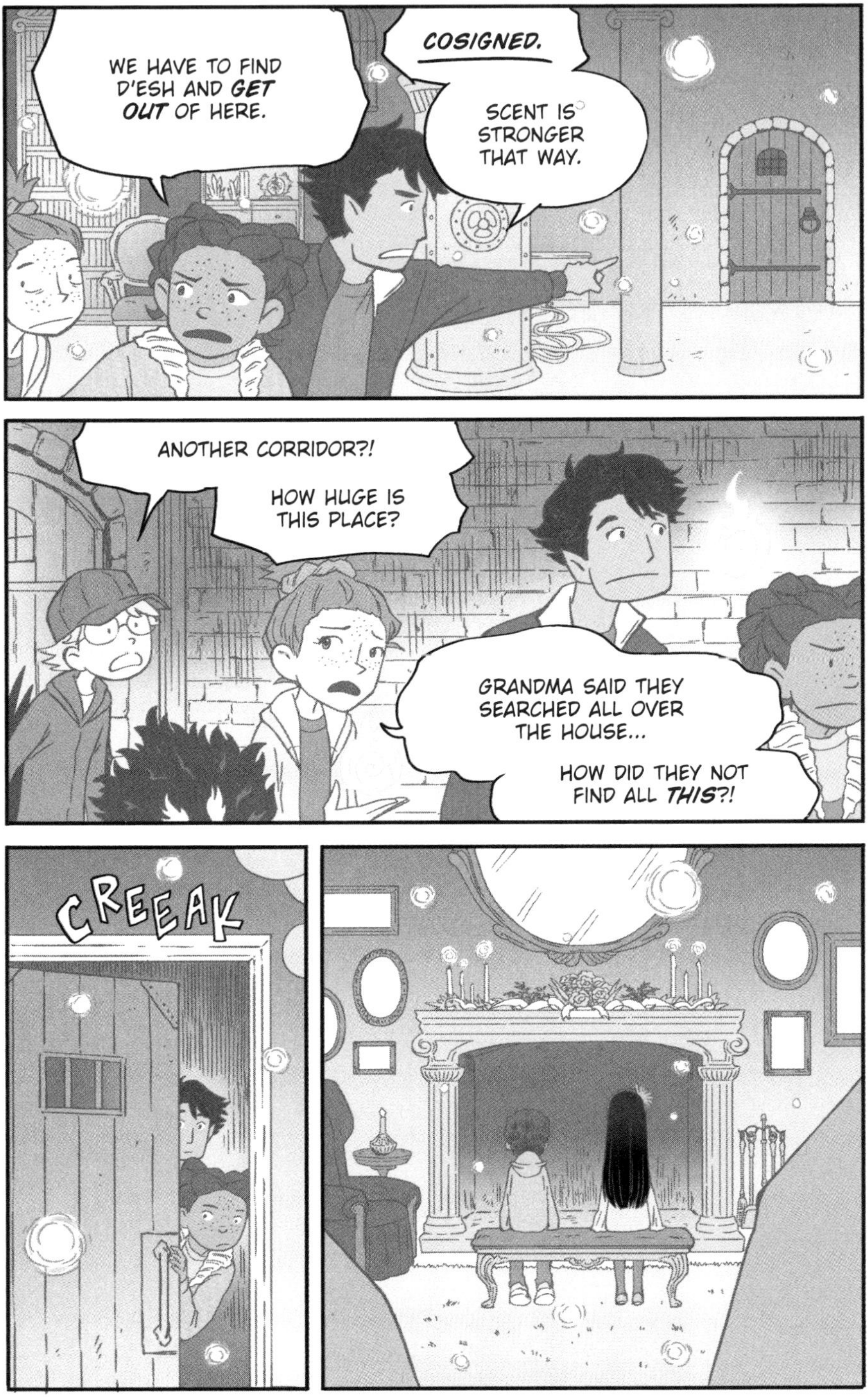
WE HAVE TO FIND D'ESH AND **GET OUT** OF HERE.
COSIGNED.
SCENT IS STRONGER THAT WAY.
ANOTHER CORRIDOR?!
HOW HUGE IS THIS PLACE?
GRANDMA SAID THEY SEARCHED ALL OVER THE HOUSE...
HOW DID THEY NOT FIND ALL **THIS**?!
CREEAK

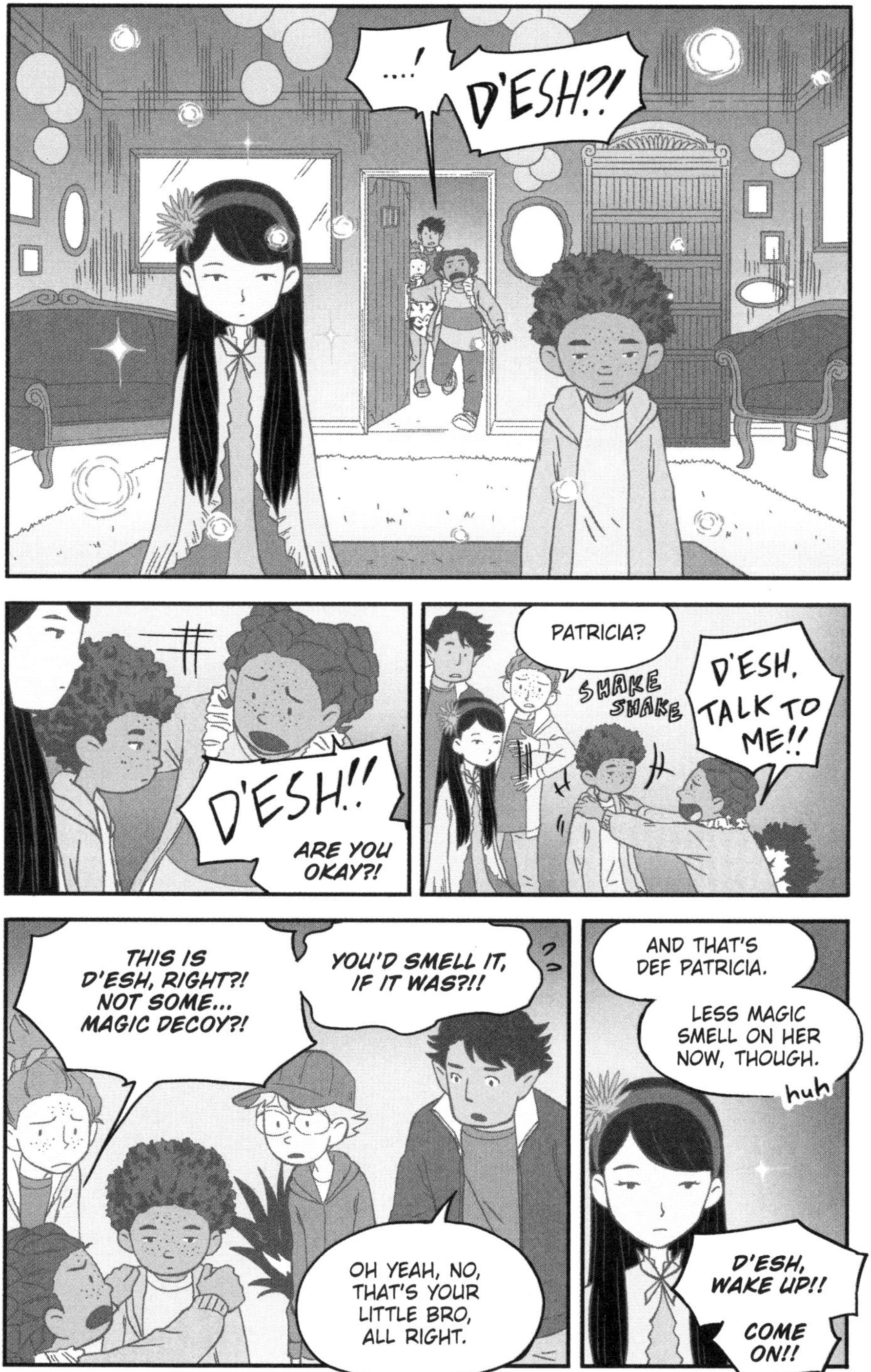
...!
D'ESH?!
D'ESH!!
ARE YOU OKAY?!
PATRICIA?
SHAKE SHAKE
D'ESH, TALK TO ME!!
THIS IS D'ESH, RIGHT?! NOT SOME... MAGIC DECOY?!
YOU'D SMELL IT, IF IT WAS?!!
??
OH YEAH, NO, THAT'S YOUR LITTLE BRO, ALL RIGHT.
AND THAT'S DEF PATRICIA.
LESS MAGIC SMELL ON HER NOW, THOUGH.
huh
D'ESH, WAKE UP!!
COME ON!!

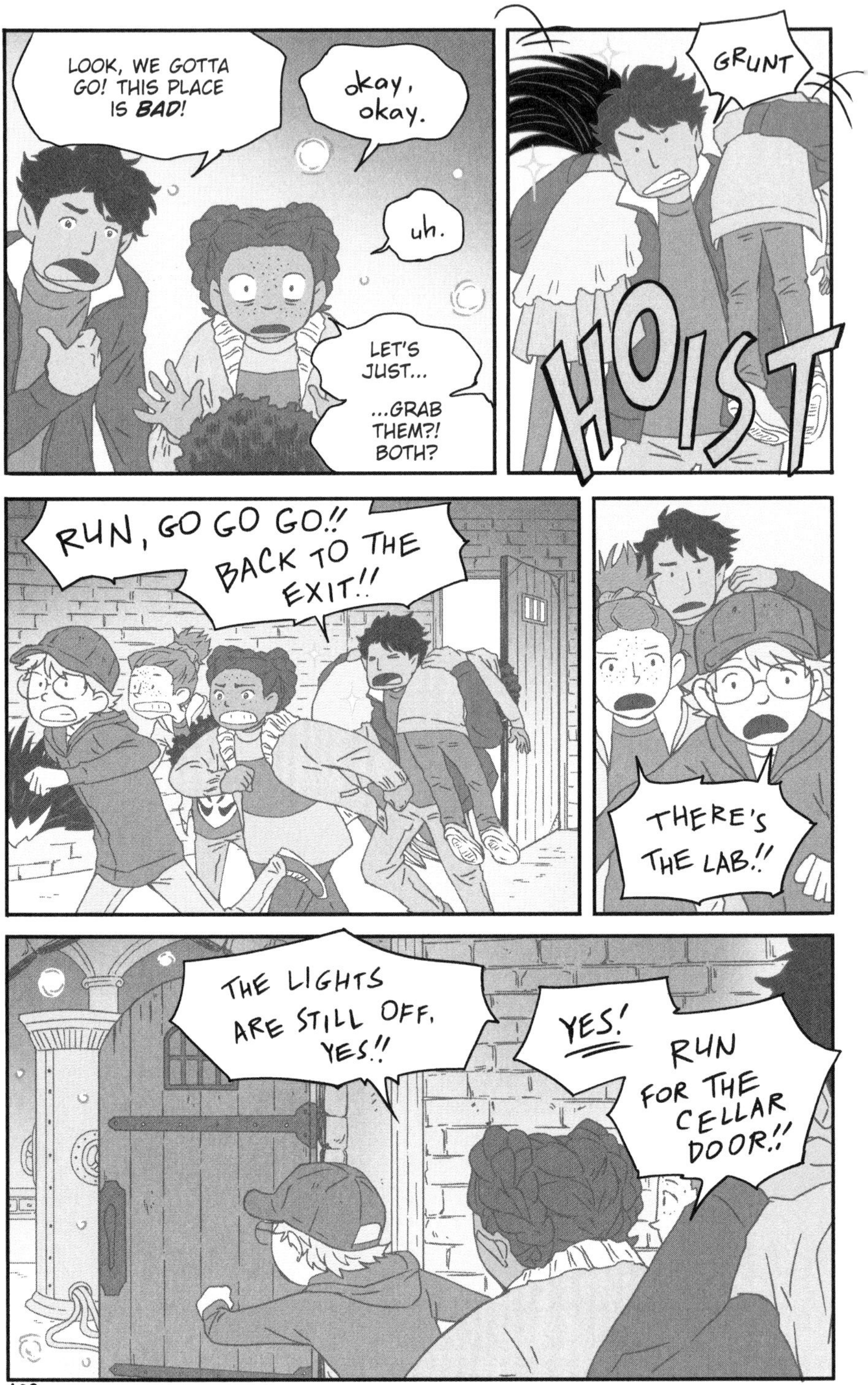

LOOK, WE GOTTA GO! THIS PLACE IS BAD!
okay, okay.
uh.
LET'S JUST...
...GRAB THEM?! BOTH?
GRUNT
HOIST
RUN, GO GO GO!! BACK TO THE EXIT!!
THERE'S THE LAB!!
THE LIGHTS ARE STILL OFF. YES!!
YES!
RUN FOR THE CELLAR DOOR!!

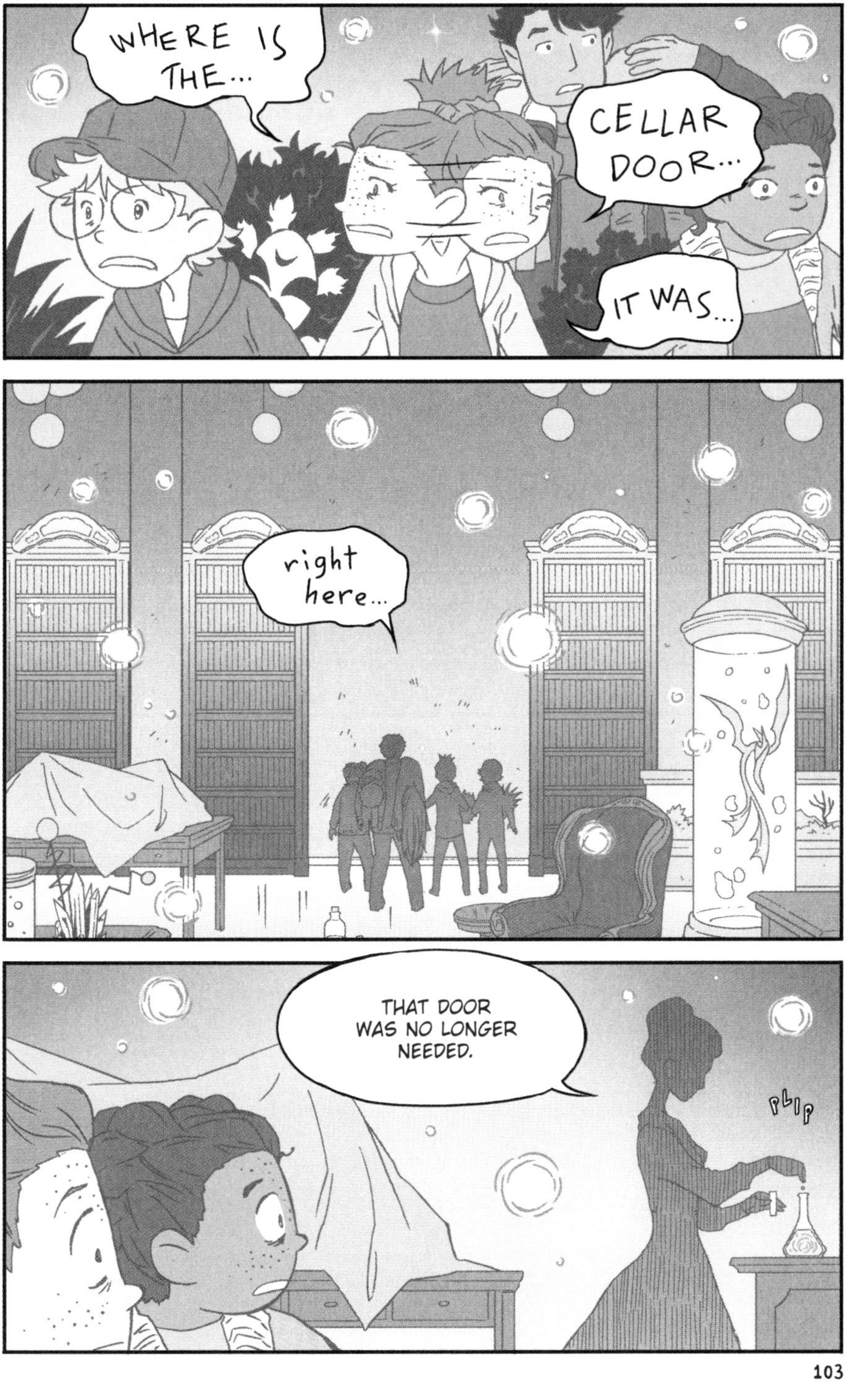
WHERE IS THE...
CELLAR DOOR...
IT WAS...
right here...
THAT DOOR WAS NO LONGER NEEDED.
PLIP

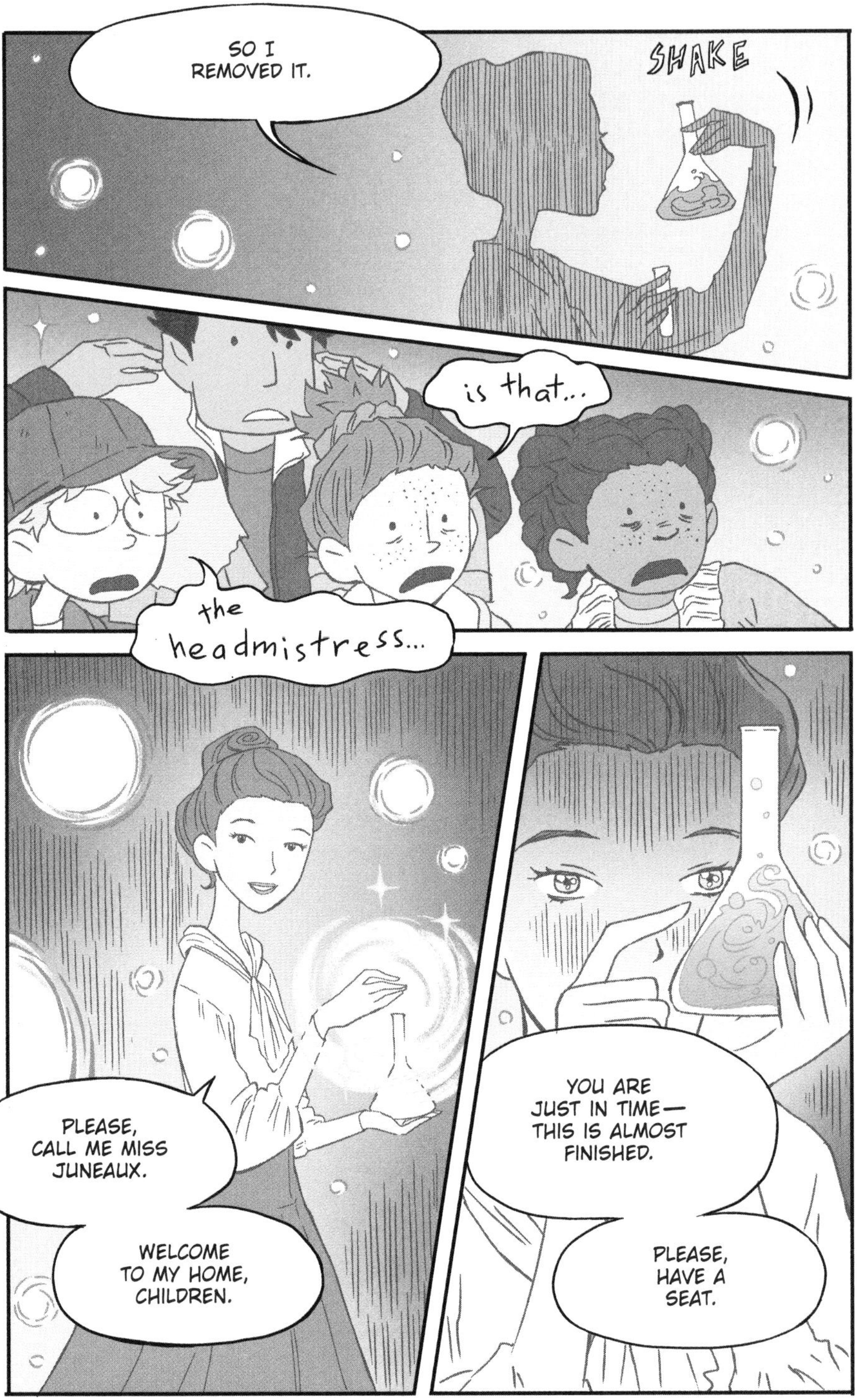
SO I REMOVED IT.
SHAKE
is that...
the headmistress...
PLEASE, CALL ME MISS JUNEAUX.
WELCOME TO MY HOME, CHILDREN.
YOU ARE JUST IN TIME— THIS IS ALMOST FINISHED.
PLEASE, HAVE A SEAT.

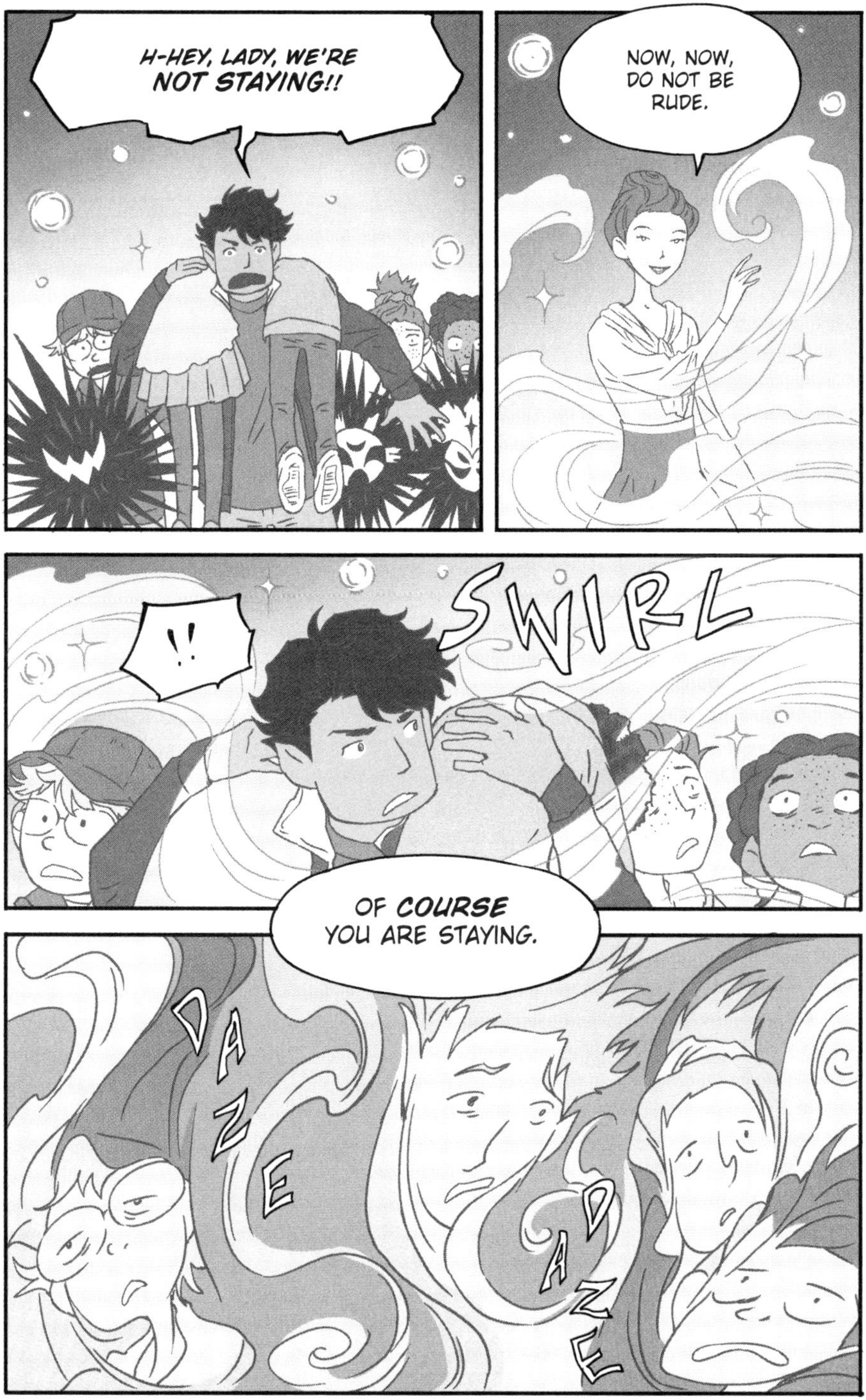
H-HEY, LADY, WE'RE **NOT STAYING!!**
NOW, NOW, DO NOT BE RUDE.
!!
SWIRL
OF **COURSE** YOU ARE STAYING.
DAZE
DAZE
DAZE

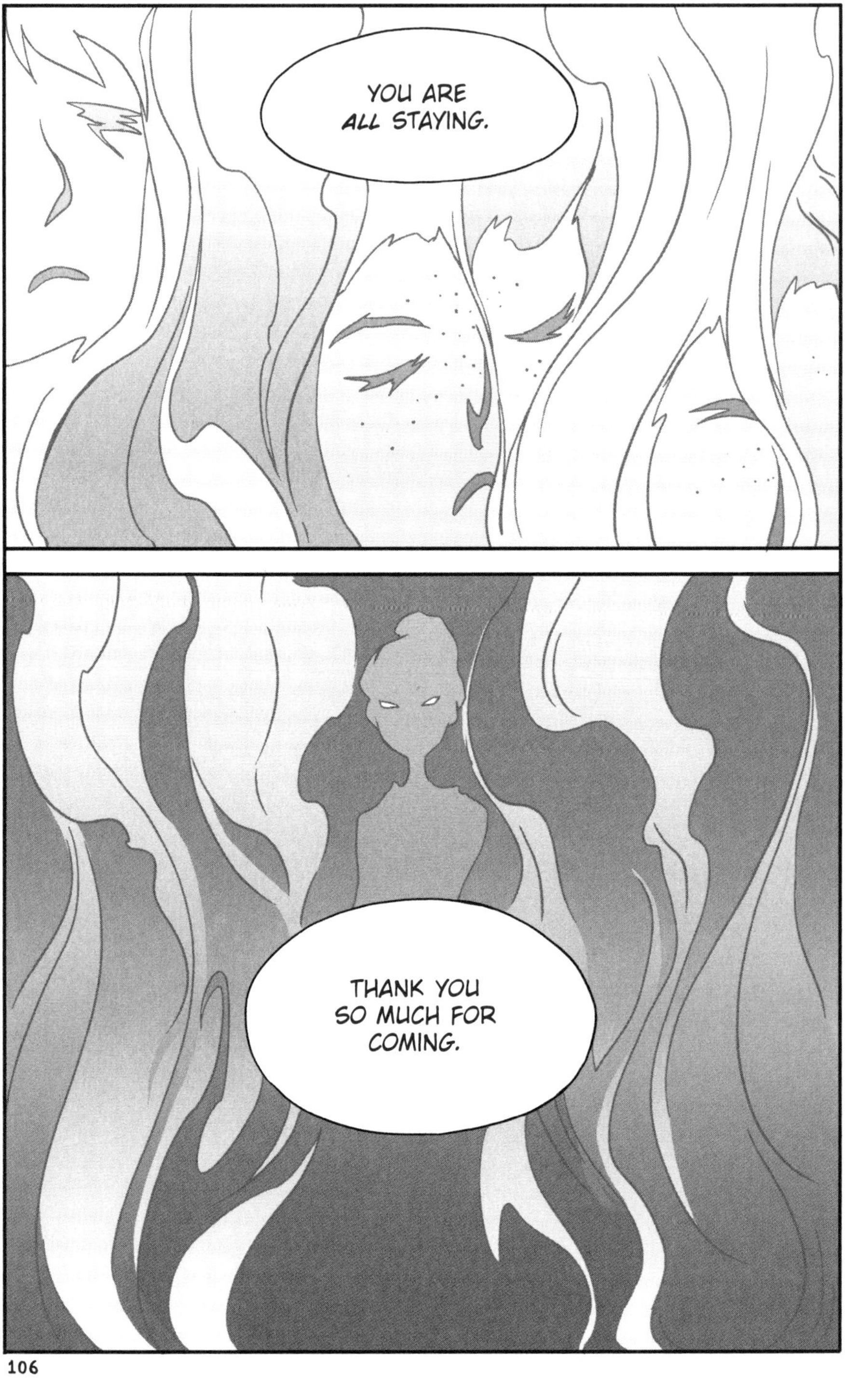
YOU ARE ALL STAYING.
THANK YOU SO MUCH FOR COMING.

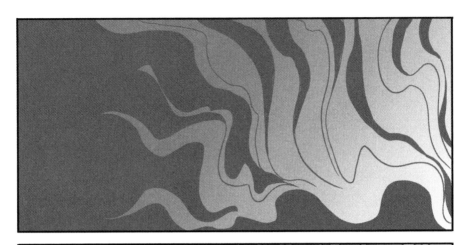

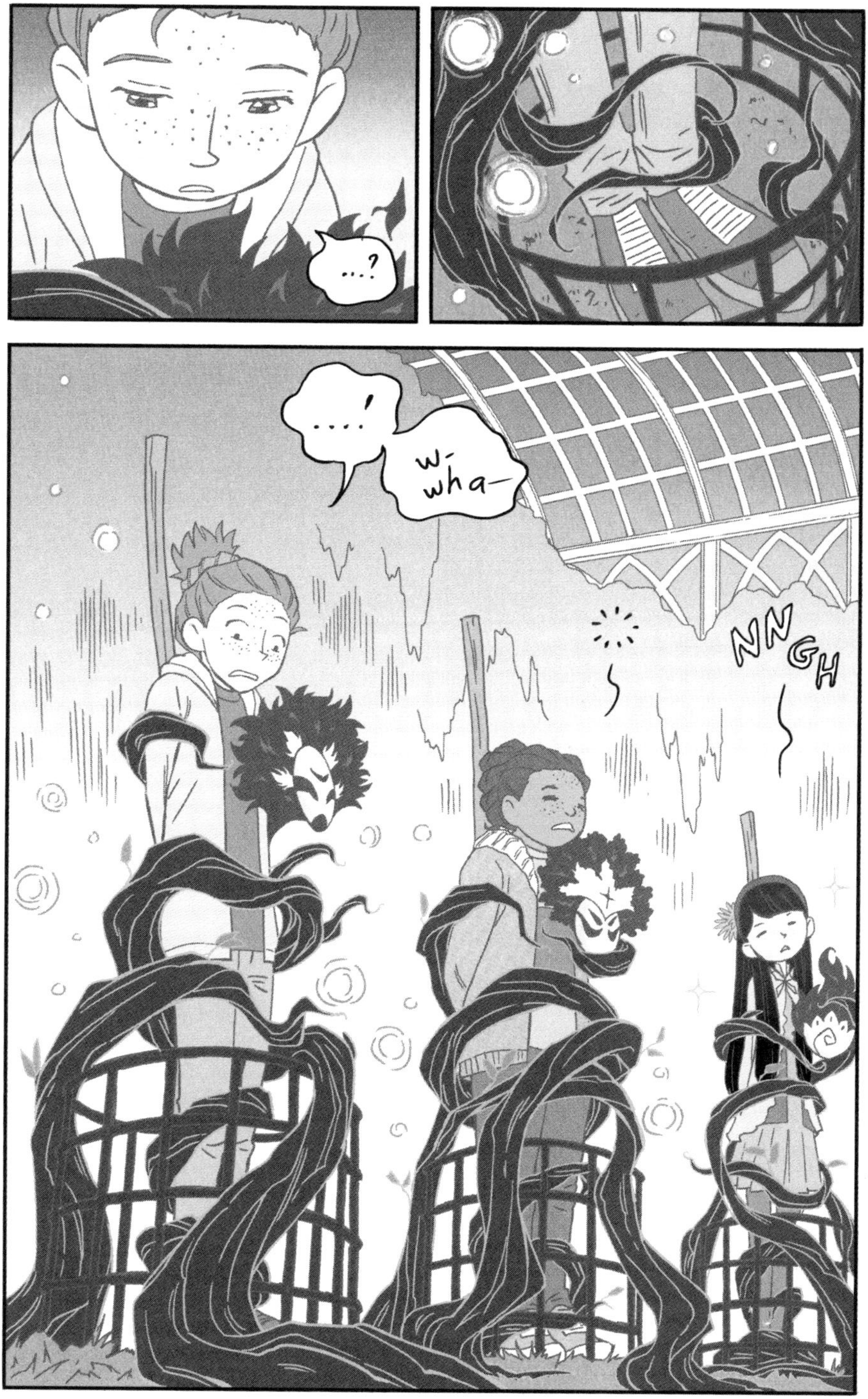
...?
...!
w-wha—
NNGH

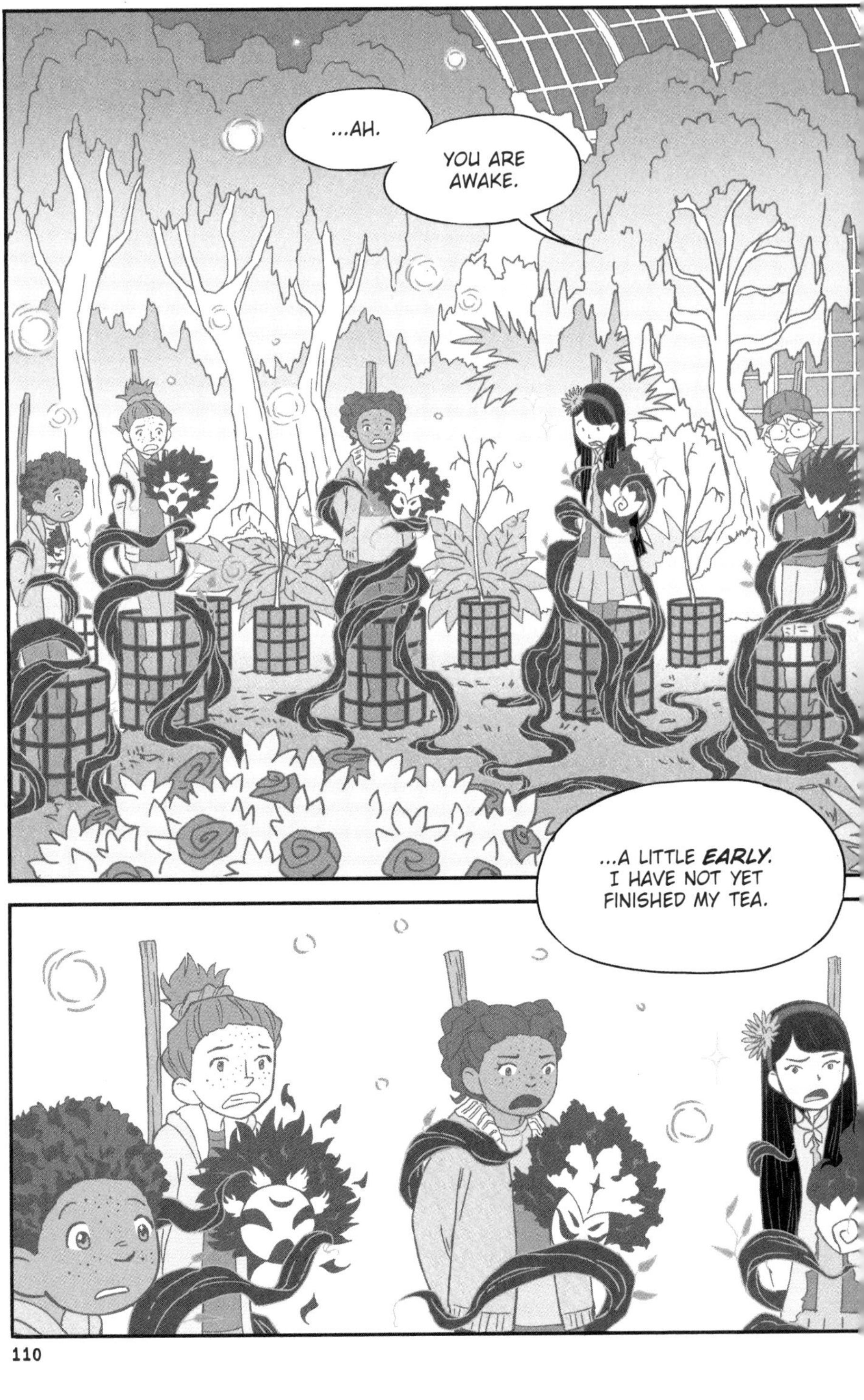
...AH.
YOU ARE AWAKE.
...A LITTLE EARLY. I HAVE NOT YET FINISHED MY TEA.

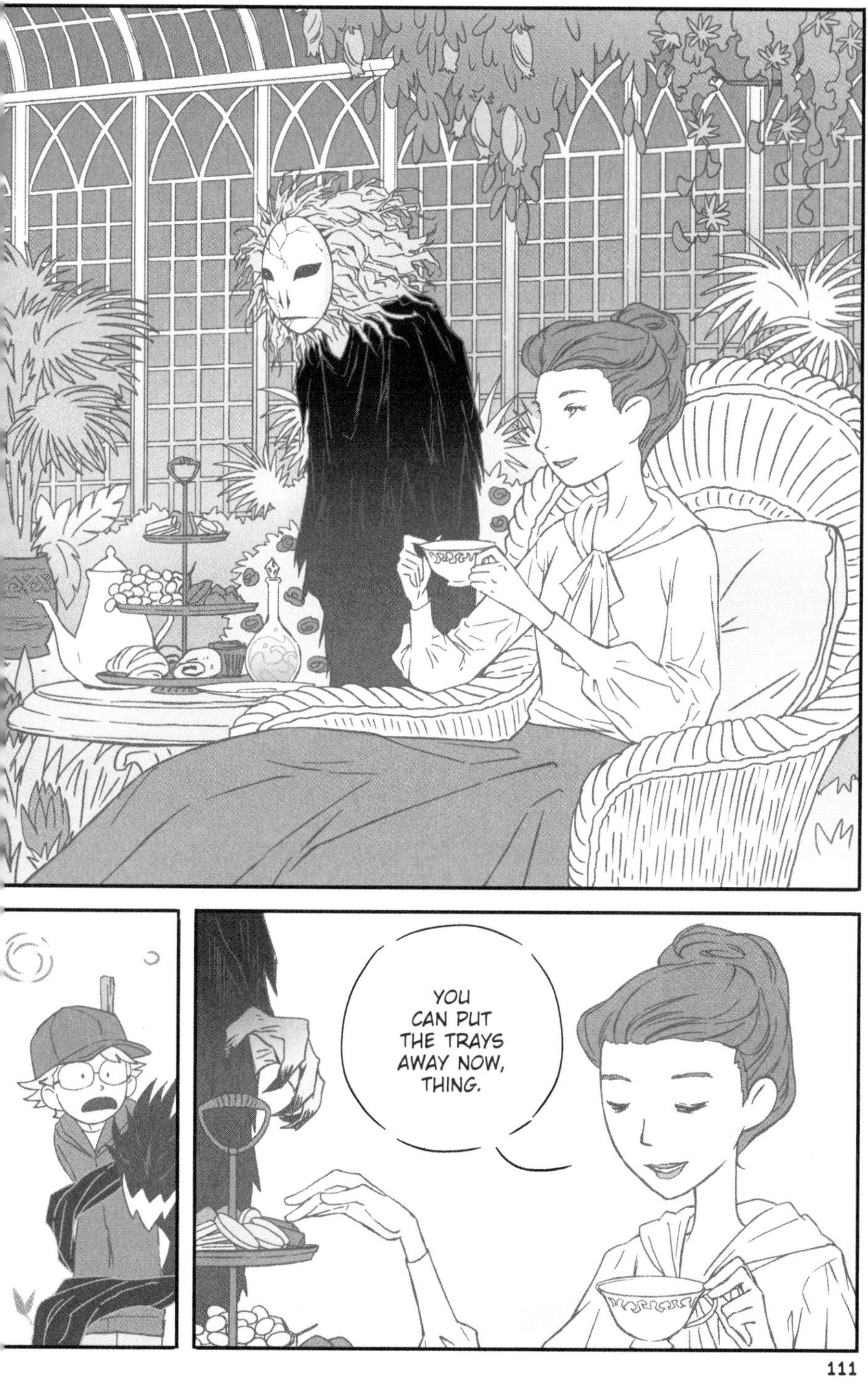
YOU CAN PUT THE TRAYS AWAY NOW, THING.

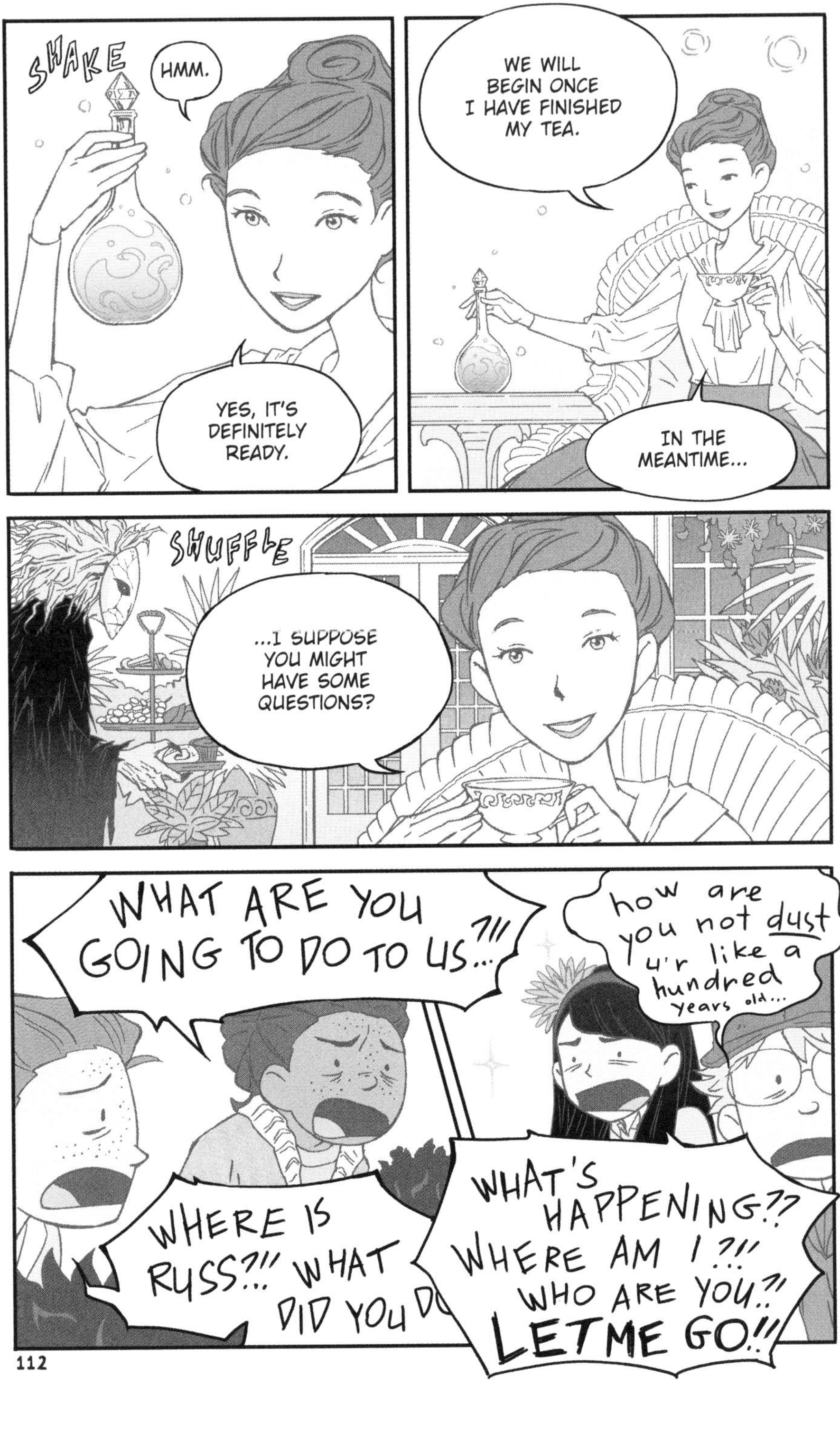
SHAKE
HMM.
YES, IT'S DEFINITELY READY.
WE WILL BEGIN ONCE I HAVE FINISHED MY TEA.
IN THE MEANTIME...
SHUFFLE
...I SUPPOSE YOU MIGHT HAVE SOME QUESTIONS?
WHAT ARE YOU GOING TO DO TO US?!!...
how are you not dust u'r like a hundred years old...
WHERE IS RUSS?!!... WHAT DID YOU DO
WHAT'S HAPPENING?? WHERE AM I?!!... WHO ARE YOU?!.. LETME GO!!

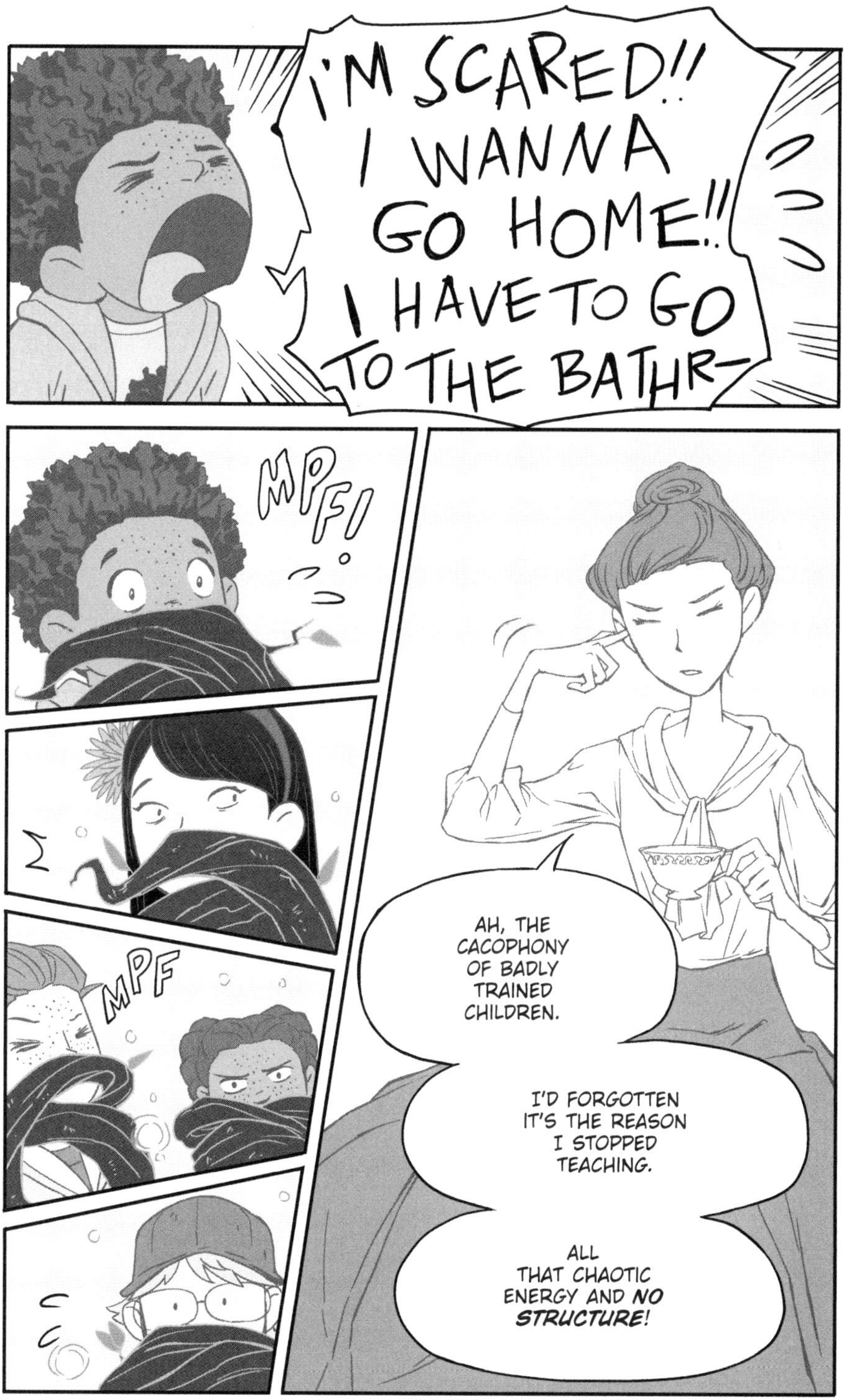
I'M SCARED!! I WANNA GO HOME!! I HAVE TO GO TO THE BATHR—
MPFF!
MPF
AH, THE CACOPHONY OF BADLY TRAINED CHILDREN.
I'D FORGOTTEN IT'S THE REASON I STOPPED TEACHING.
ALL THAT CHAOTIC ENERGY AND ***NO STRUCTURE***!

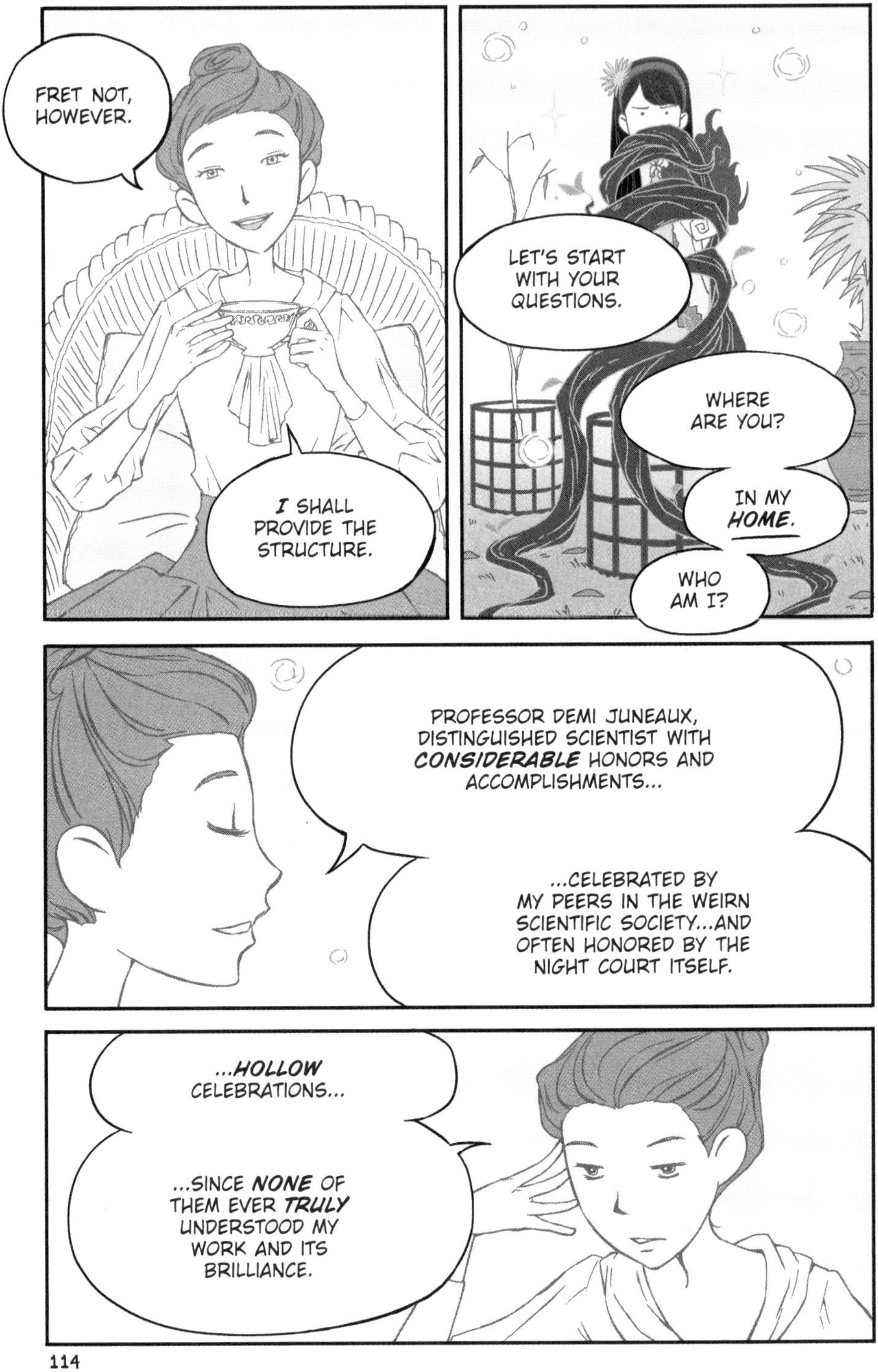

FRET NOT, HOWEVER.
I SHALL PROVIDE THE STRUCTURE.
LET'S START WITH YOUR QUESTIONS.
WHERE ARE YOU?
IN MY HOME.
WHO AM I?
PROFESSOR DEMI JUNEAUX, DISTINGUISHED SCIENTIST WITH CONSIDERABLE HONORS AND ACCOMPLISHMENTS...
...CELEBRATED BY MY PEERS IN THE WEIRN SCIENTIFIC SOCIETY...AND OFTEN HONORED BY THE NIGHT COURT ITSELF.
...HOLLOW CELEBRATIONS...
...SINCE NONE OF THEM EVER TRULY UNDERSTOOD MY WORK AND ITS BRILLIANCE.

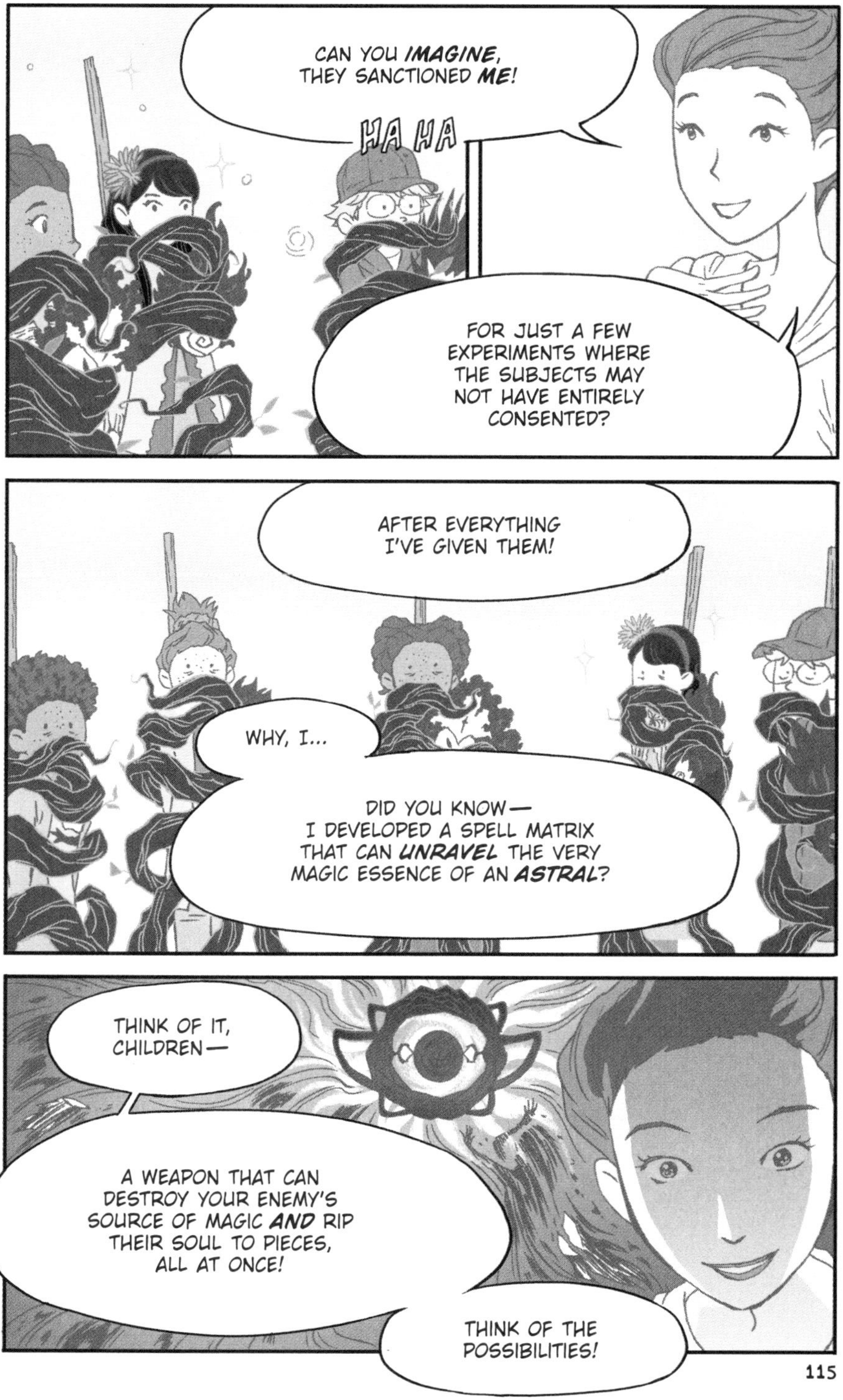
CAN YOU IMAGINE, THEY SANCTIONED ME!
HA HA
FOR JUST A FEW EXPERIMENTS WHERE THE SUBJECTS MAY NOT HAVE ENTIRELY CONSENTED?
AFTER EVERYTHING I'VE GIVEN THEM!
WHY, I...
DID YOU KNOW— I DEVELOPED A SPELL MATRIX THAT CAN UNRAVEL THE VERY MAGIC ESSENCE OF AN ASTRAL?
THINK OF IT, CHILDREN—
A WEAPON THAT CAN DESTROY YOUR ENEMY'S SOURCE OF MAGIC AND RIP THEIR SOUL TO PIECES, ALL AT ONCE!
THINK OF THE POSSIBILITIES!

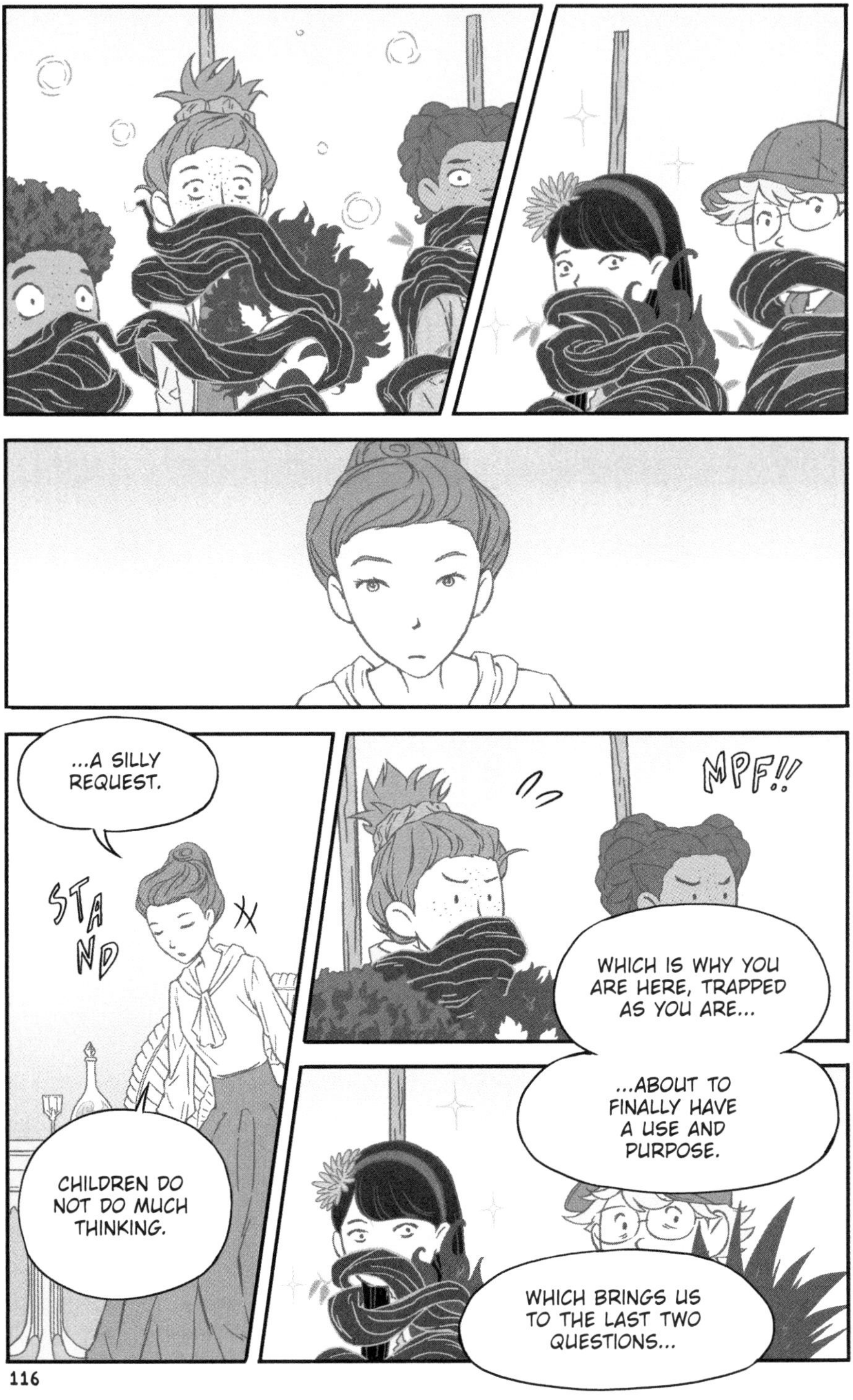
...A SILLY REQUEST.
STAND
CHILDREN DO NOT DO MUCH THINKING.
MPF!!
WHICH IS WHY YOU ARE HERE, TRAPPED AS YOU ARE...
...ABOUT TO FINALLY HAVE A USE AND PURPOSE.
WHICH BRINGS US TO THE LAST TWO QUESTIONS...

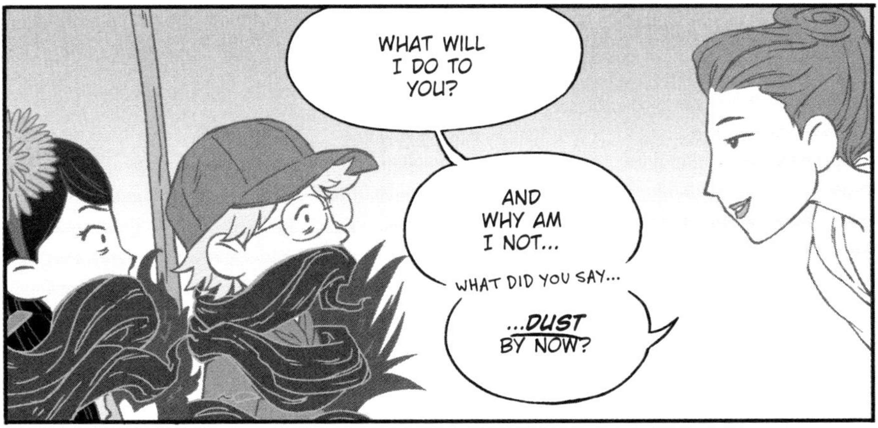
WHAT WILL I DO TO YOU?
AND WHY AM I NOT...
WHAT DID YOU SAY...
...DUST BY NOW?

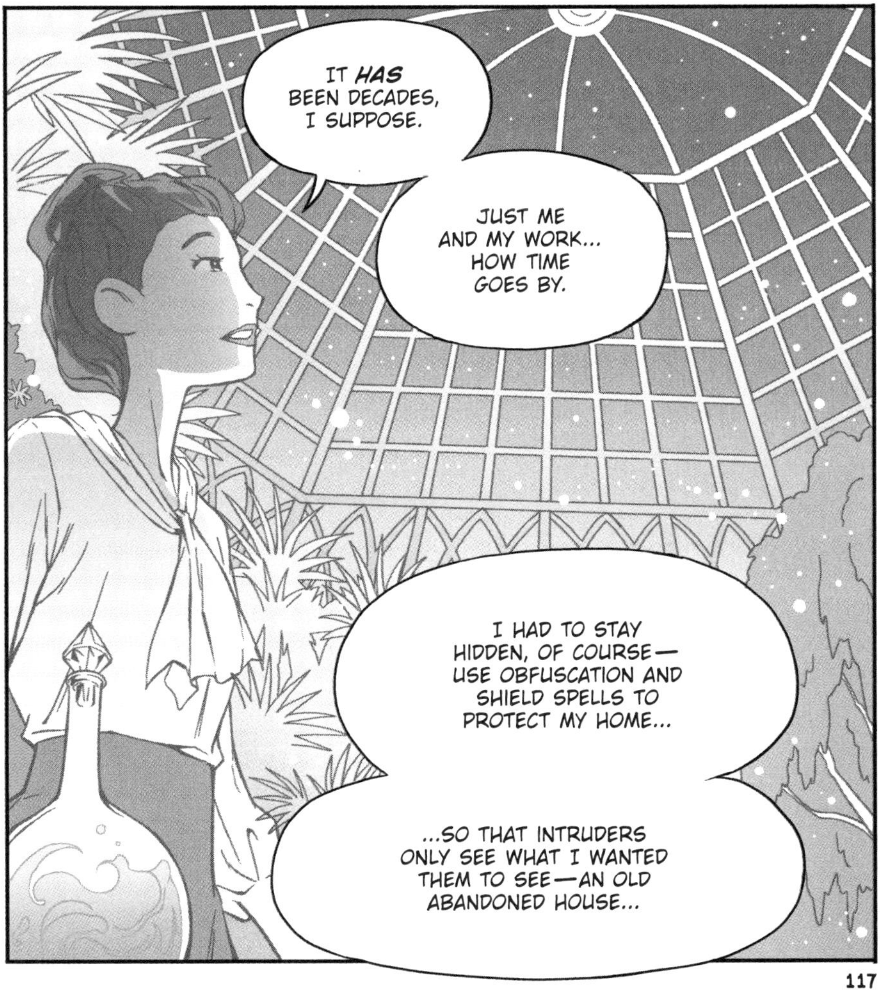
IT HAS BEEN DECADES, I SUPPOSE.
JUST ME AND MY WORK... HOW TIME GOES BY.
I HAD TO STAY HIDDEN, OF COURSE—USE OBFUSCATION AND SHIELD SPELLS TO PROTECT MY HOME...
...SO THAT INTRUDERS ONLY SEE WHAT I WANTED THEM TO SEE—AN OLD ABANDONED HOUSE...

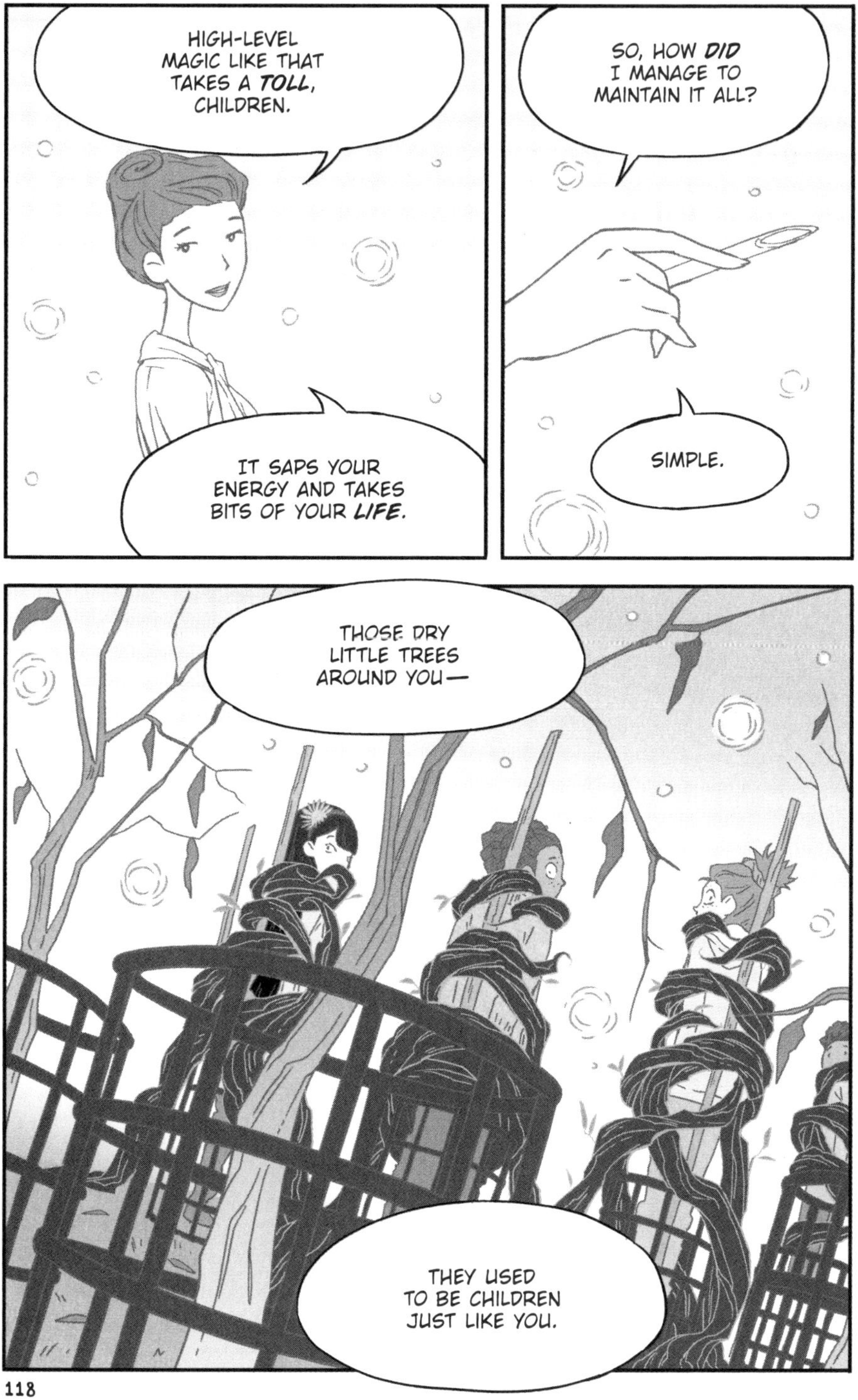
HIGH-LEVEL MAGIC LIKE THAT TAKES A **TOLL**, CHILDREN.
IT SAPS YOUR ENERGY AND TAKES BITS OF YOUR **LIFE**.
SO, HOW **DID** I MANAGE TO MAINTAIN IT ALL?
SIMPLE.
THOSE DRY LITTLE TREES AROUND YOU—
THEY USED TO BE CHILDREN JUST LIKE YOU.

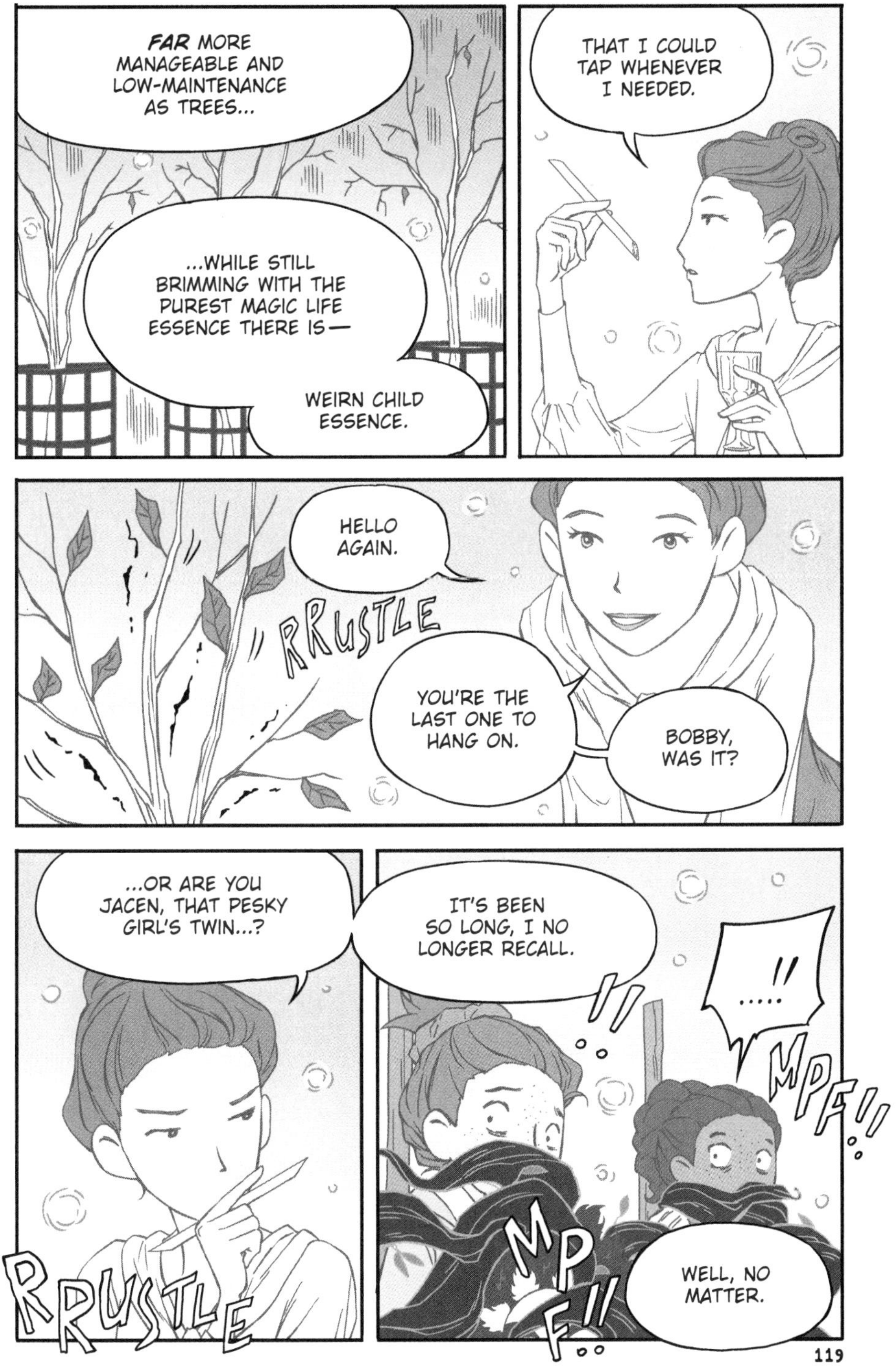

FAR MORE MANAGEABLE AND LOW-MAINTENANCE AS TREES...
...WHILE STILL BRIMMING WITH THE PUREST MAGIC LIFE ESSENCE THERE IS—
WEIRN CHILD ESSENCE.
THAT I COULD TAP WHENEVER I NEEDED.
HELLO AGAIN.
RRUSTLE
YOU'RE THE LAST ONE TO HANG ON.
BOBBY, WAS IT?
...OR ARE YOU JACEN, THAT PESKY GIRL'S TWIN...?
IT'S BEEN SO LONG, I NO LONGER RECALL.
!!
.....!!
MPF!!
RRUSTLE
MPF!!
WELL, NO MATTER.

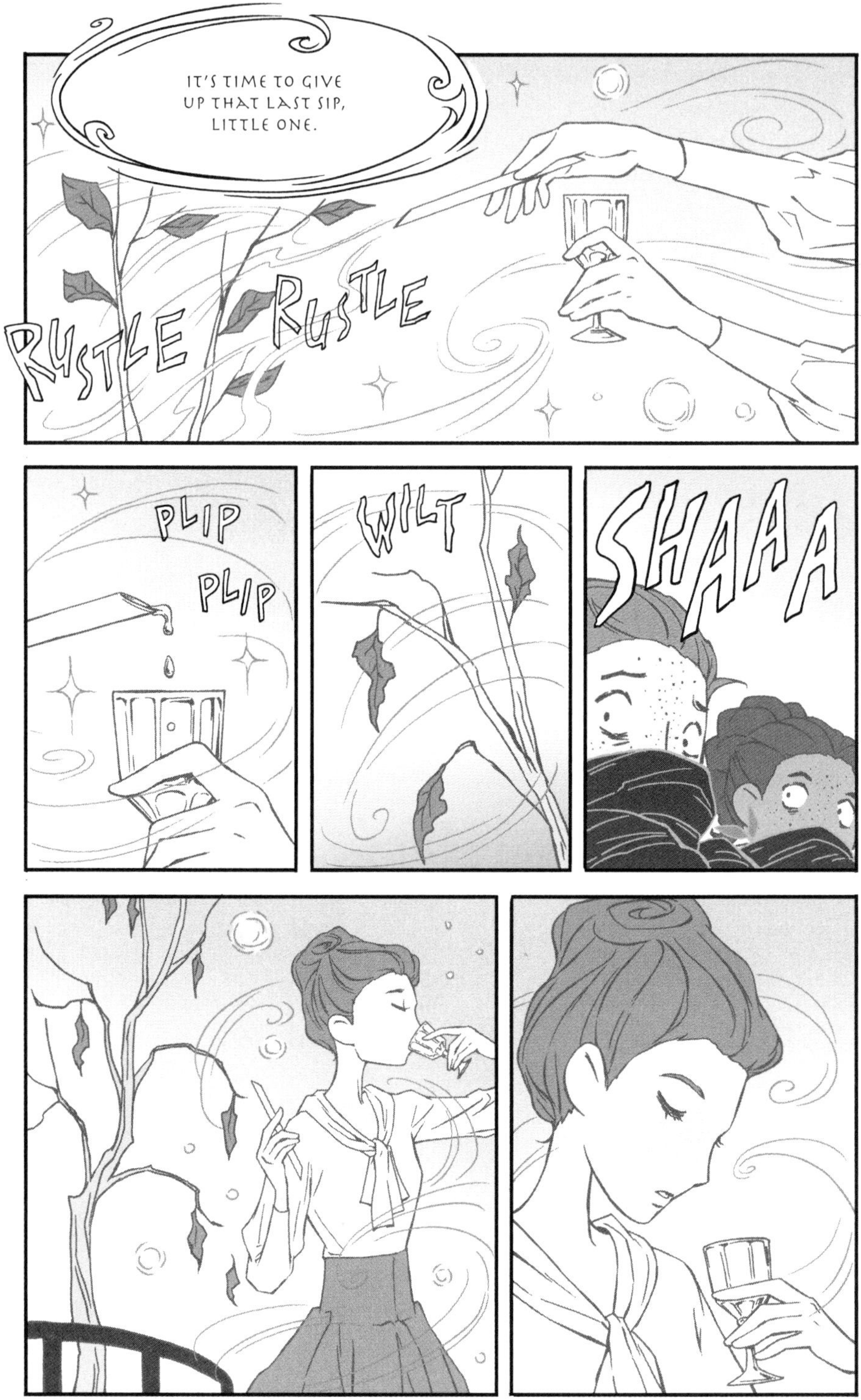
IT'S TIME TO GIVE UP THAT LAST SIP, LITTLE ONE.
RUSTLE RUSTLE
PLIP
PLIP
WILT
SHAAA

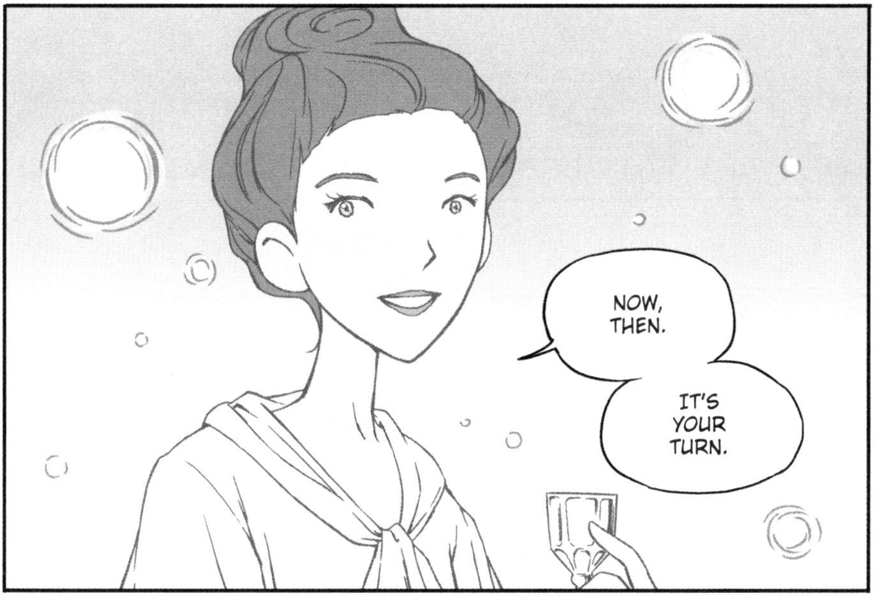
NOW, THEN.
IT'S YOUR TURN.

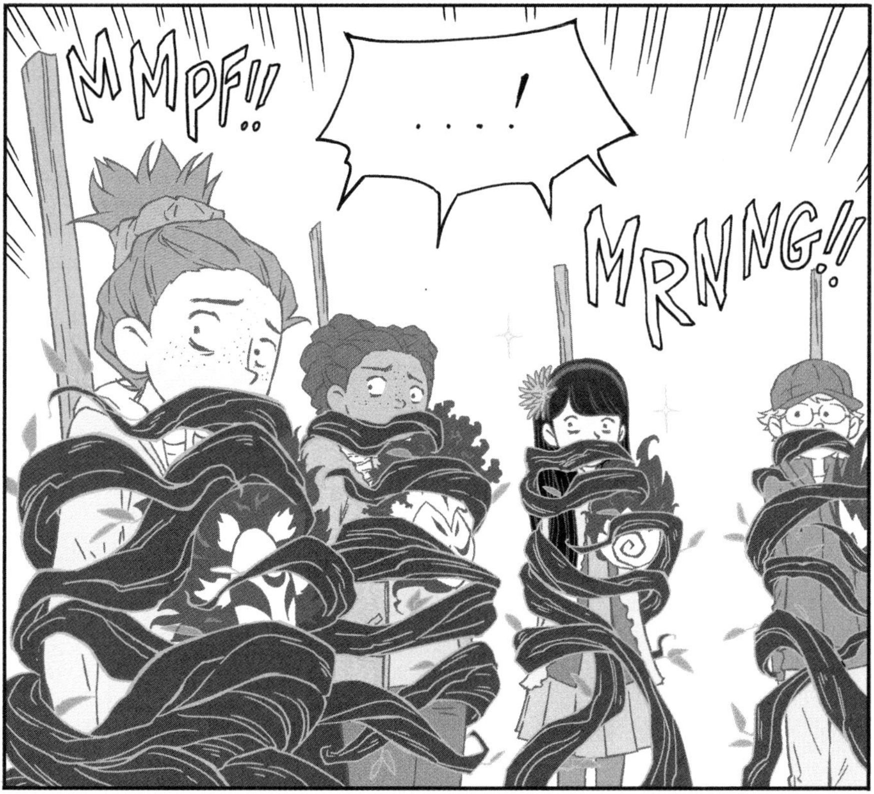
MMPF!!
....!
MRNNG!!

Chapter 5

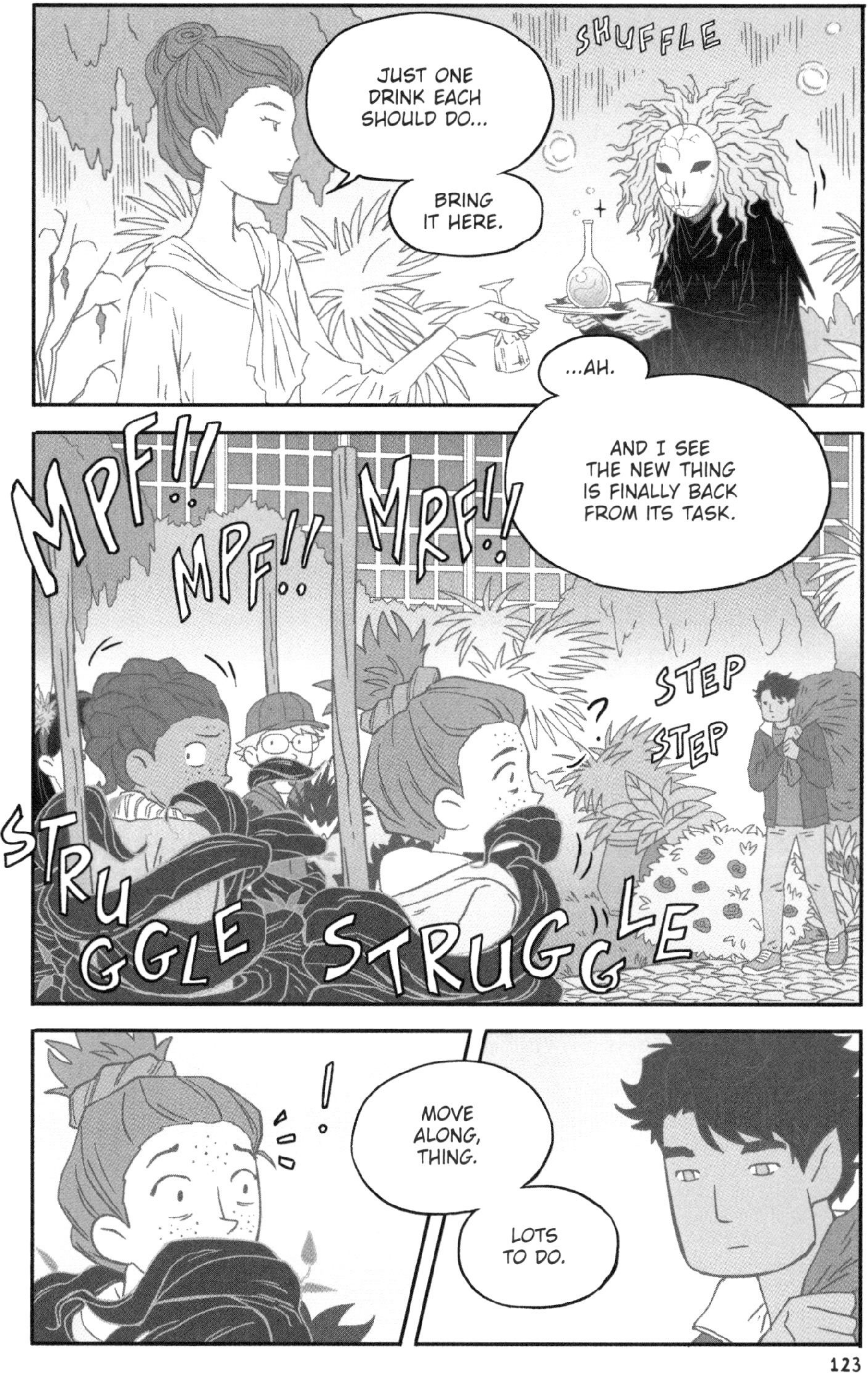

JUST ONE DRINK EACH SHOULD DO...
BRING IT HERE.
SHUFFLE
...AH.
AND I SEE THE NEW THING IS FINALLY BACK FROM ITS TASK.
MPF!!
MPF!!
MRF!!
STEP
STEP
STRUGGLE
STRUGGLE
!
MOVE ALONG, THING.
LOTS TO DO.

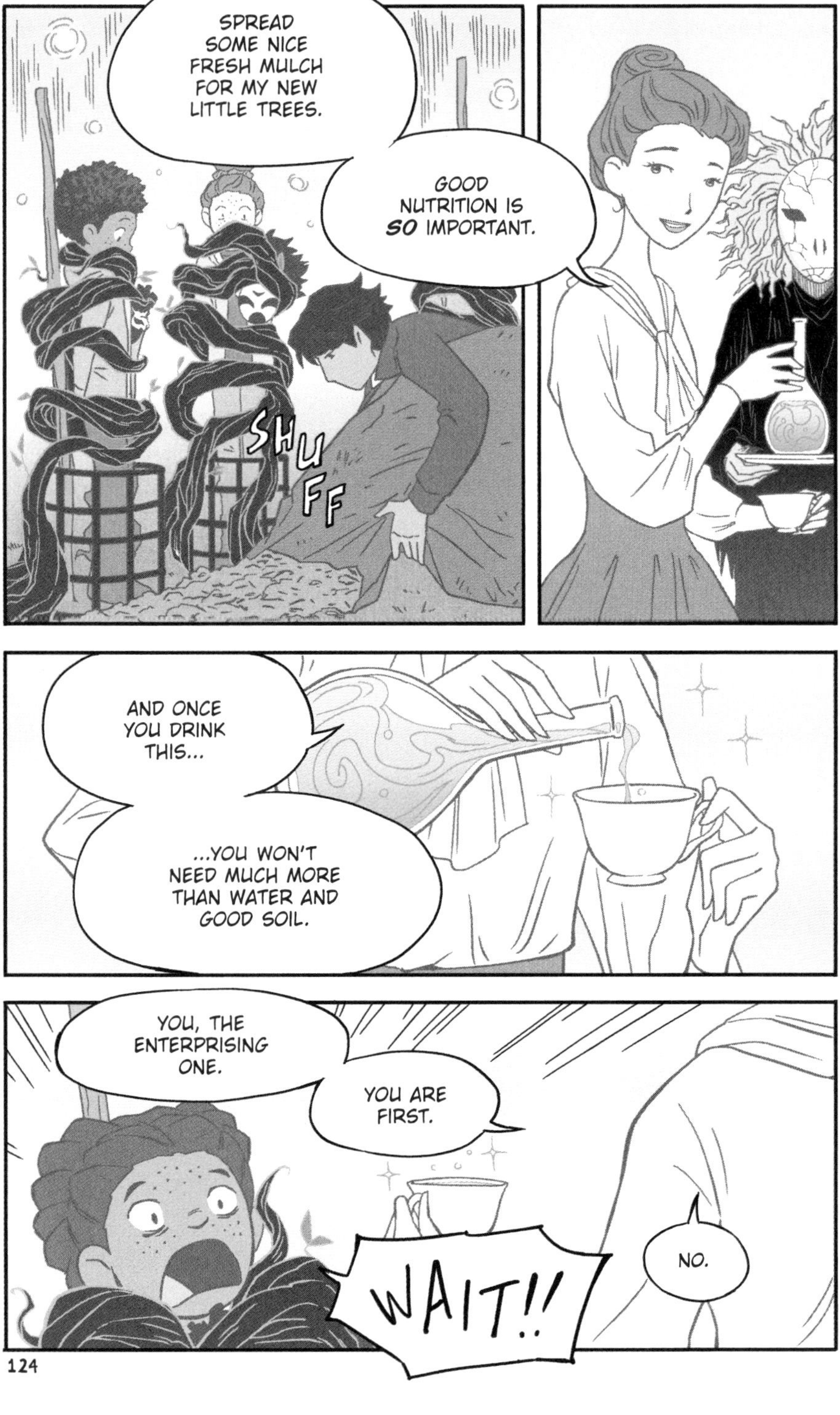
SPREAD SOME NICE FRESH MULCH FOR MY NEW LITTLE TREES.
GOOD NUTRITION IS *SO* IMPORTANT.
SHUFF
AND ONCE YOU DRINK THIS...
...YOU WON'T NEED MUCH MORE THAN WATER AND GOOD SOIL.
YOU, THE ENTERPRISING ONE.
YOU ARE FIRST.
WAIT!!
NO.

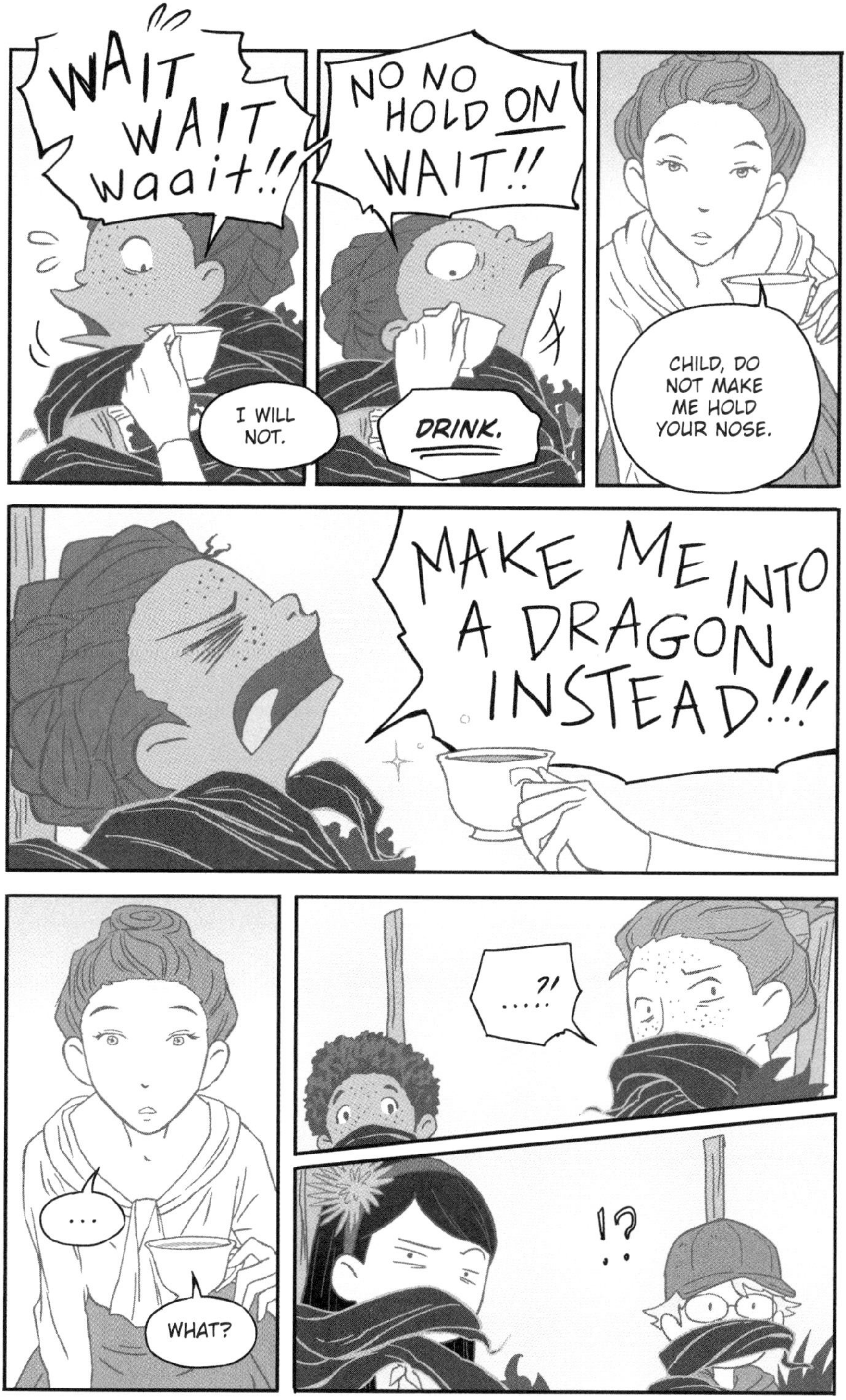
WAIT WAIT waait!!
I WILL NOT.
NO NO HOLD ON WAIT!!
DRINK.
CHILD, DO NOT MAKE ME HOLD YOUR NOSE.
MAKE ME INTO A DRAGON INSTEAD!!!
...
WHAT?
....?!
!?

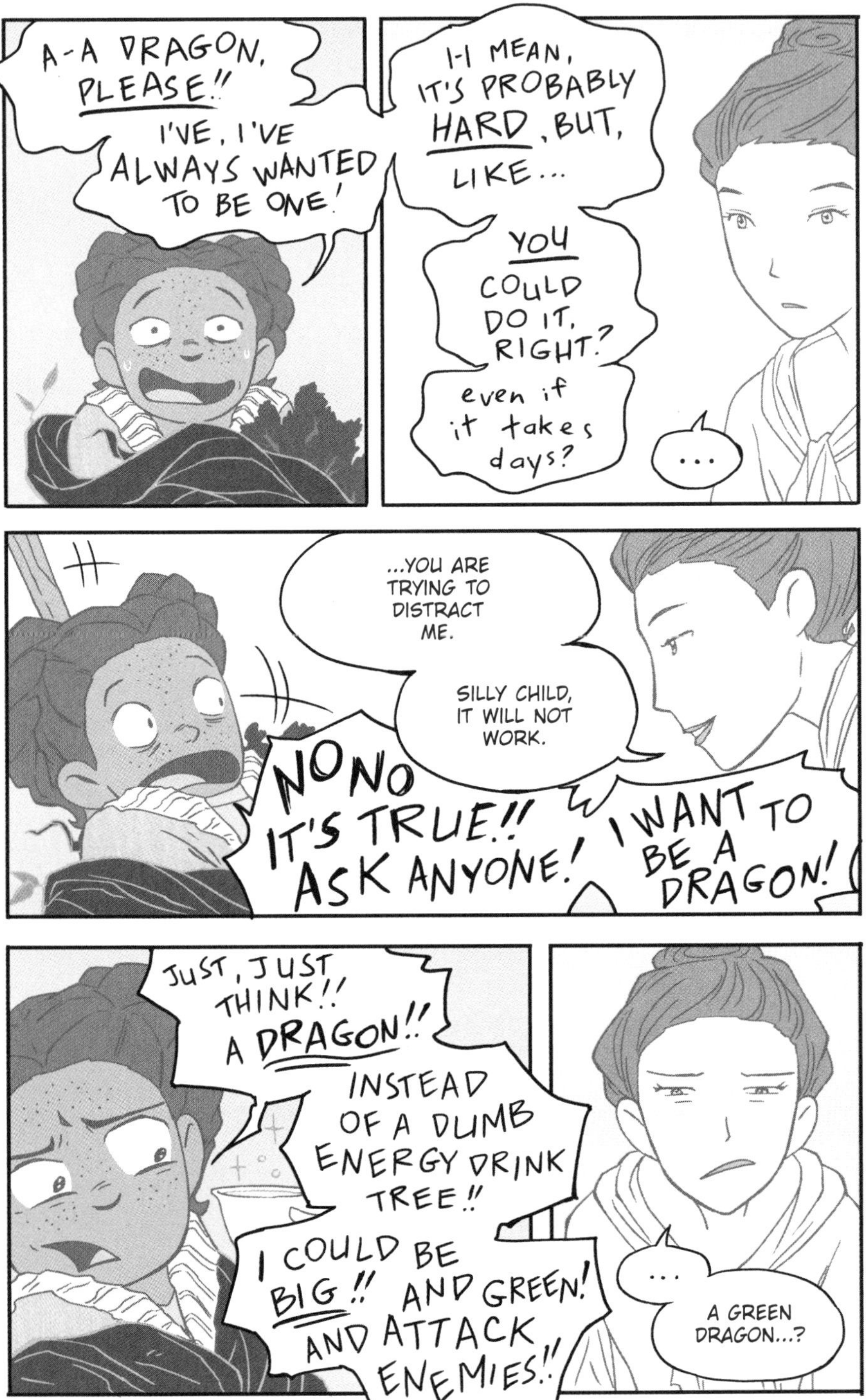
A-A DRAGON, PLEASE!!
I'VE, I'VE ALWAYS WANTED TO BE ONE!
I-I MEAN, IT'S PROBABLY HARD, BUT, LIKE...
YOU COULD DO IT, RIGHT?
even if it takes days?
...
...YOU ARE TRYING TO DISTRACT ME.
SILLY CHILD, IT WILL NOT WORK.
NO NO IT'S TRUE!! ASK ANYONE! I WANT TO BE A DRAGON!
JUST, JUST THINK!! A DRAGON!!
INSTEAD OF A DUMB ENERGY DRINK TREE!!
I COULD BE BIG!! AND GREEN! AND ATTACK ENEMIES!!
...
A GREEN DRAGON...?

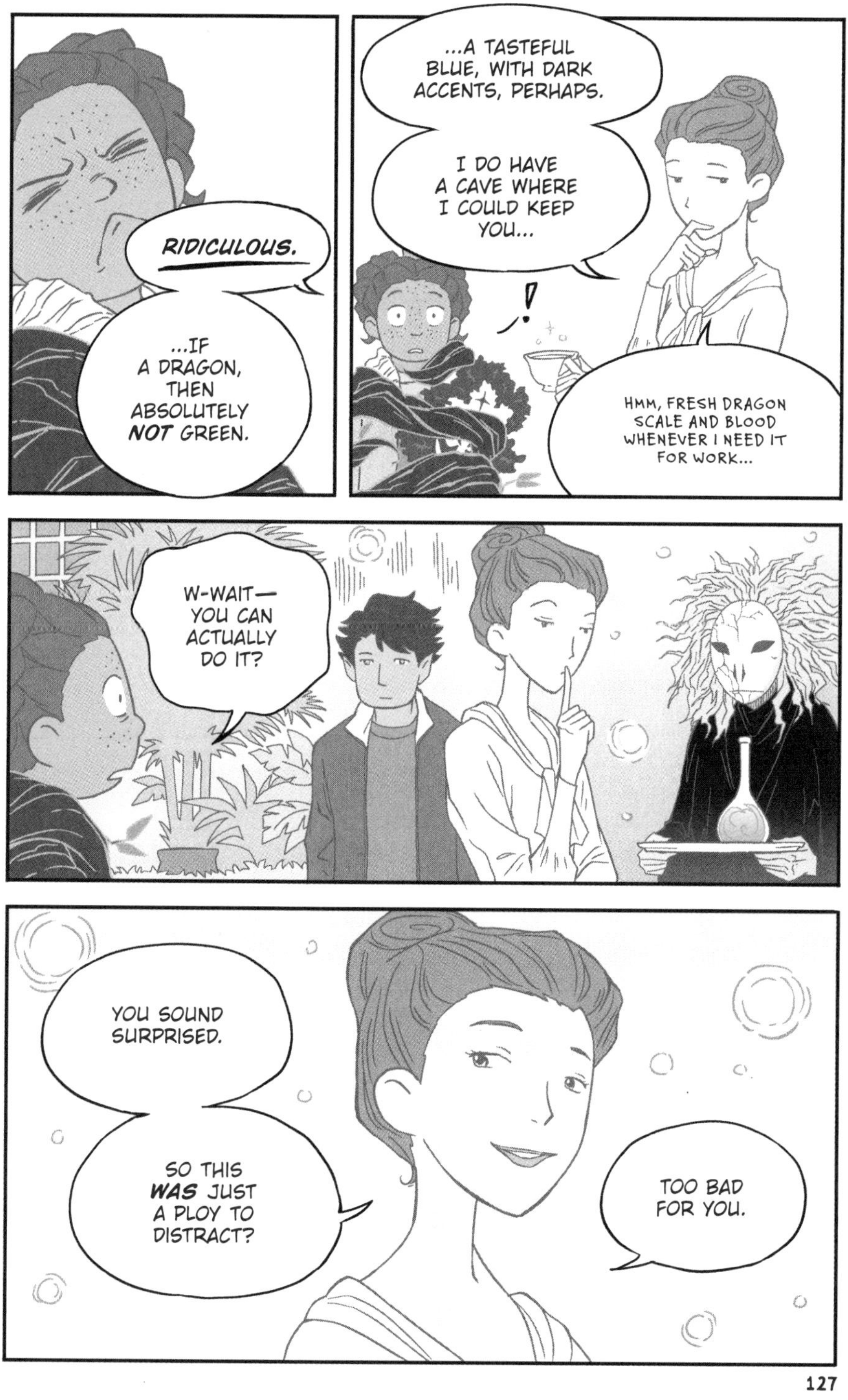
RIDICULOUS.
...IF A DRAGON, THEN ABSOLUTELY NOT GREEN.
...A TASTEFUL BLUE, WITH DARK ACCENTS, PERHAPS.
I DO HAVE A CAVE WHERE I COULD KEEP YOU...
!
HMM, FRESH DRAGON SCALE AND BLOOD WHENEVER I NEED IT FOR WORK...
W-WAIT— YOU CAN ACTUALLY DO IT?
YOU SOUND SURPRISED.
SO THIS WAS JUST A PLOY TO DISTRACT?
TOO BAD FOR YOU.

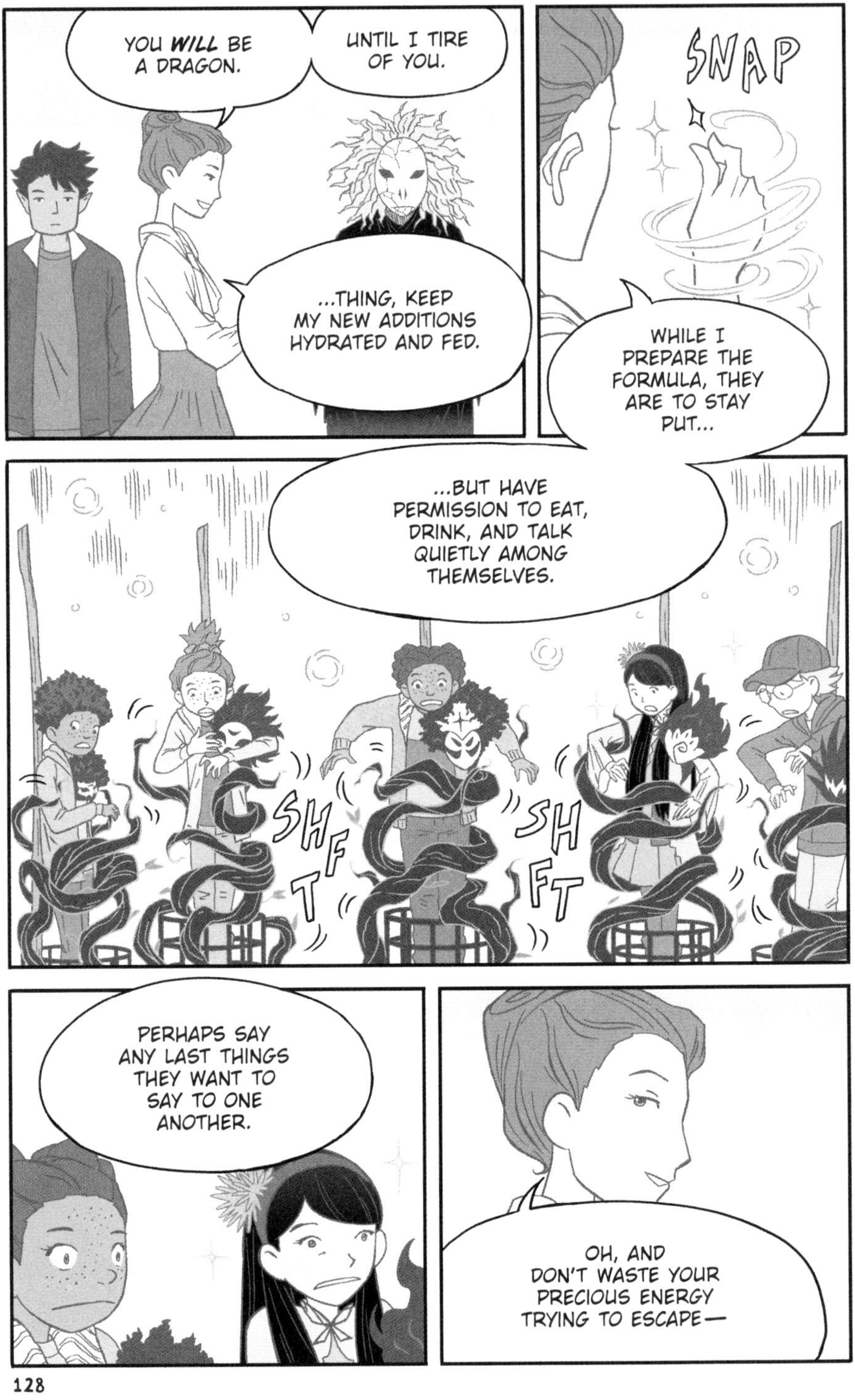
YOU **WILL** BE A DRAGON.
UNTIL I TIRE OF YOU.
...THING, KEEP MY NEW ADDITIONS HYDRATED AND FED.
SNAP
WHILE I PREPARE THE FORMULA, THEY ARE TO STAY PUT...
...BUT HAVE PERMISSION TO EAT, DRINK, AND TALK QUIETLY AMONG THEMSELVES.
SHFT
SHFT
PERHAPS SAY ANY LAST THINGS THEY WANT TO SAY TO ONE ANOTHER.
OH, AND DON'T WASTE YOUR PRECIOUS ENERGY TRYING TO ESCAPE—

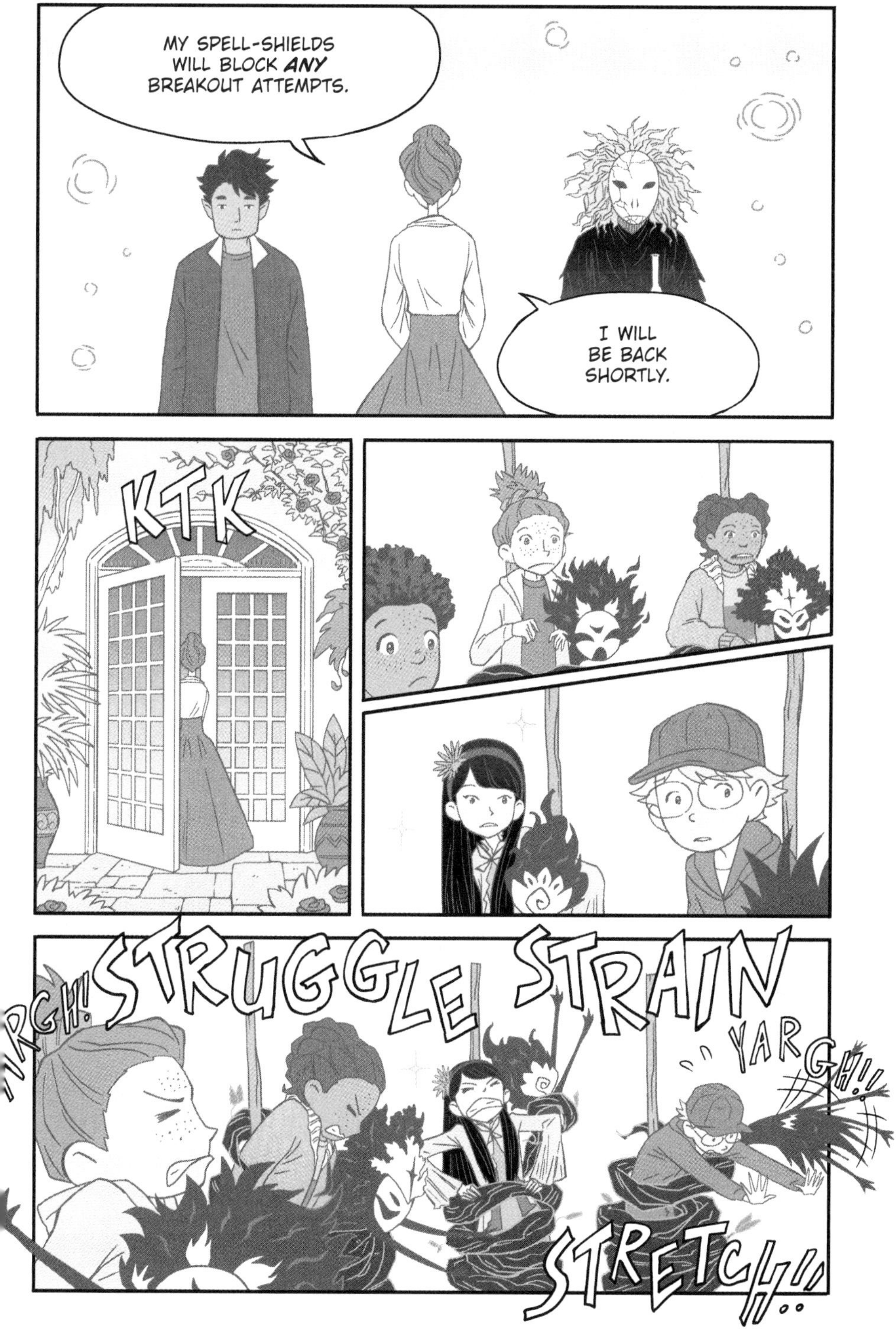
MY SPELL-SHIELDS WILL BLOCK ANY BREAKOUT ATTEMPTS.
I WILL BE BACK SHORTLY.
KTK
RGH!
STRUGGLE
STRAIN
YARGH!!
STRETCH!!

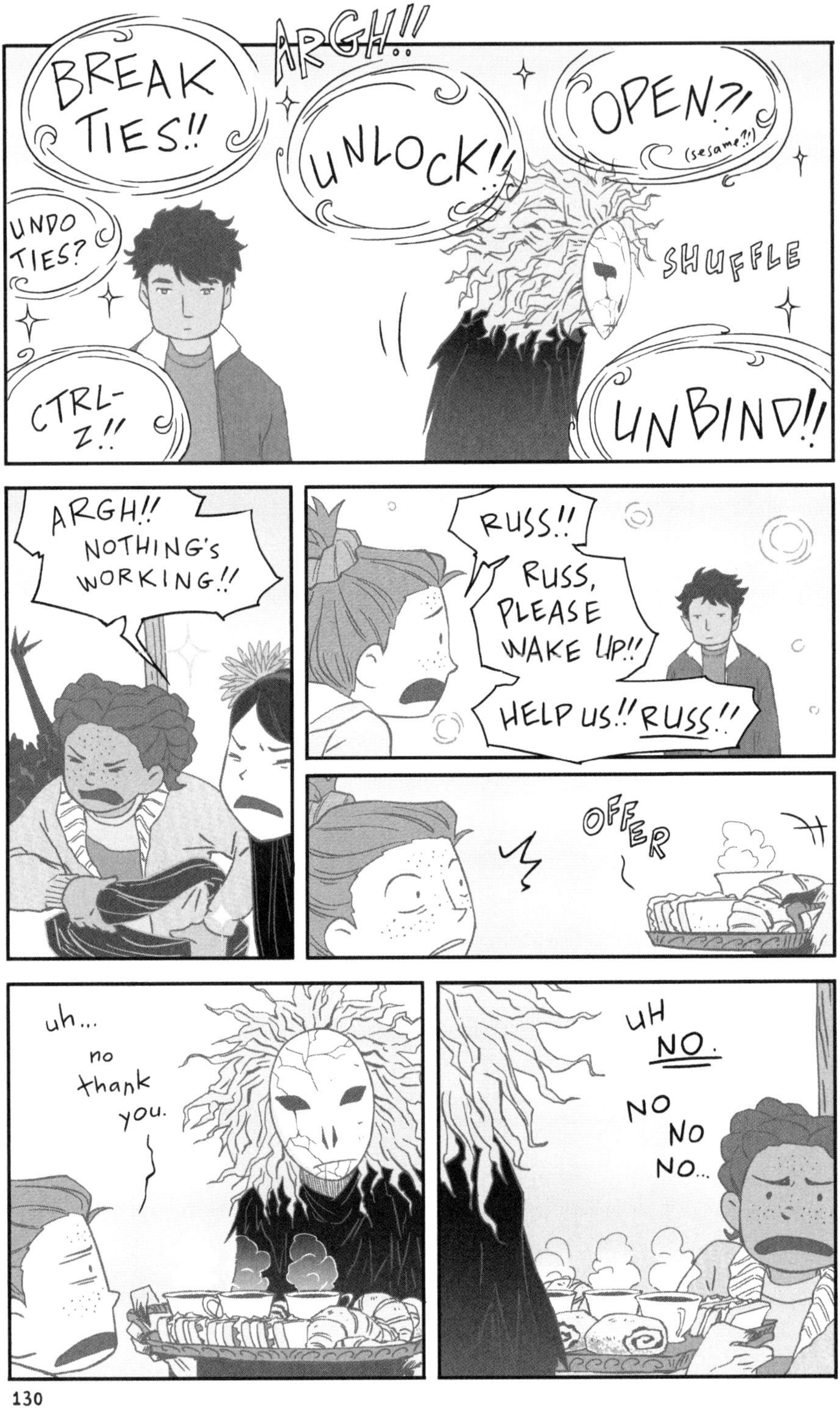

BREAK TIES!!
ARGH!!
UNLOCK!!
OPEN?!
(sesame?!)
UNDO TIES?
SHUFFLE
CTRL-Z!!
UNBIND!!
ARGH!! NOTHING's WORKING!!
RUSS!!
RUSS, PLEASE WAKE UP!!
HELP US!! RUSS!!
OFFER
uh... no thank you.
UH NO.
NO NO NO...

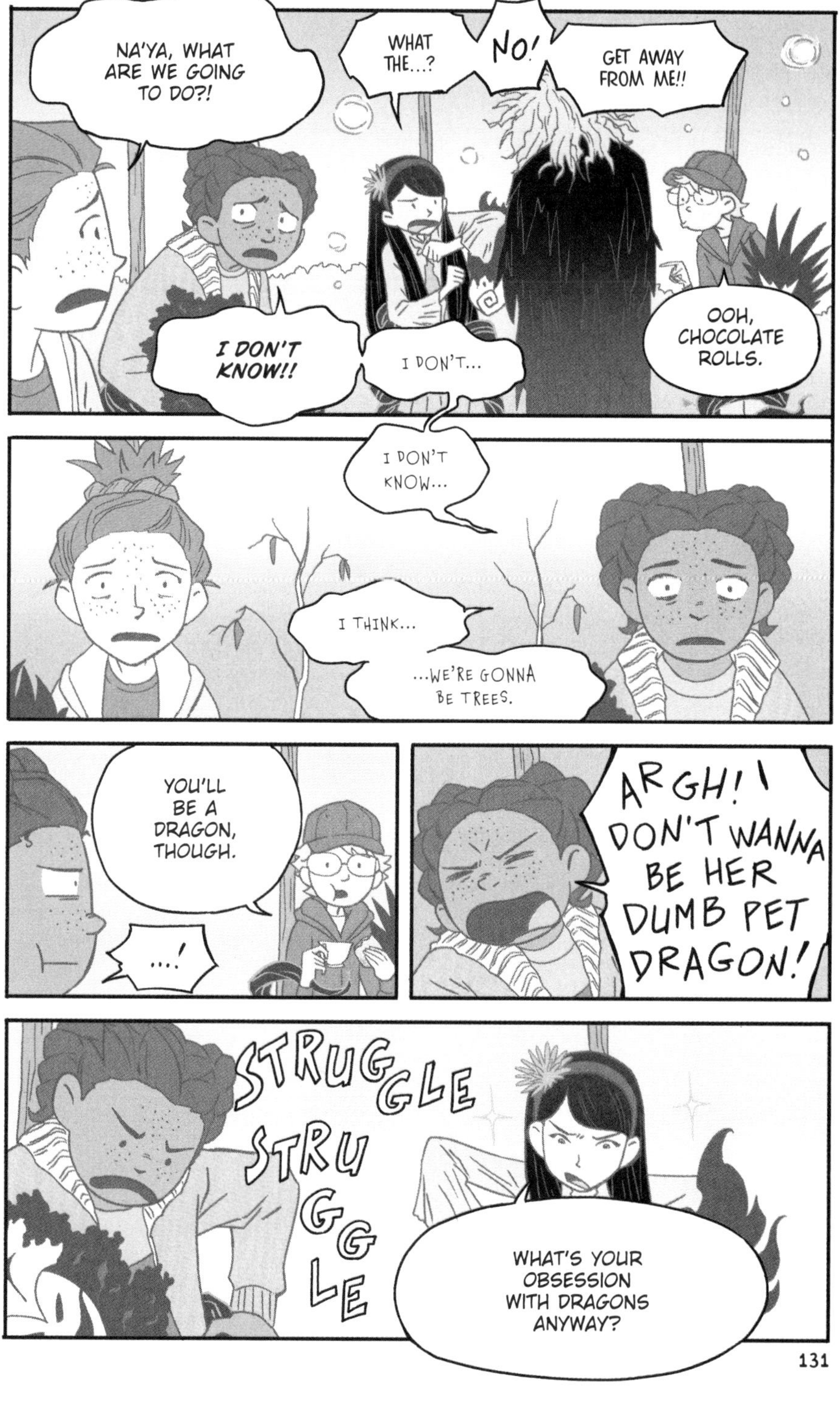
NA'YA, WHAT ARE WE GOING TO DO?!
WHAT THE...?
NO!
GET AWAY FROM ME!!
I DON'T KNOW!!
I DON'T...
OOH, CHOCOLATE ROLLS.
I DON'T KNOW...
I THINK...
...WE'RE GONNA BE TREES.
YOU'LL BE A DRAGON, THOUGH.
...!
ARGH! I DON'T WANNA BE HER DUMB PET DRAGON!
STRUGGLE STRUGGLE
WHAT'S YOUR OBSESSION WITH DRAGONS ANYWAY?

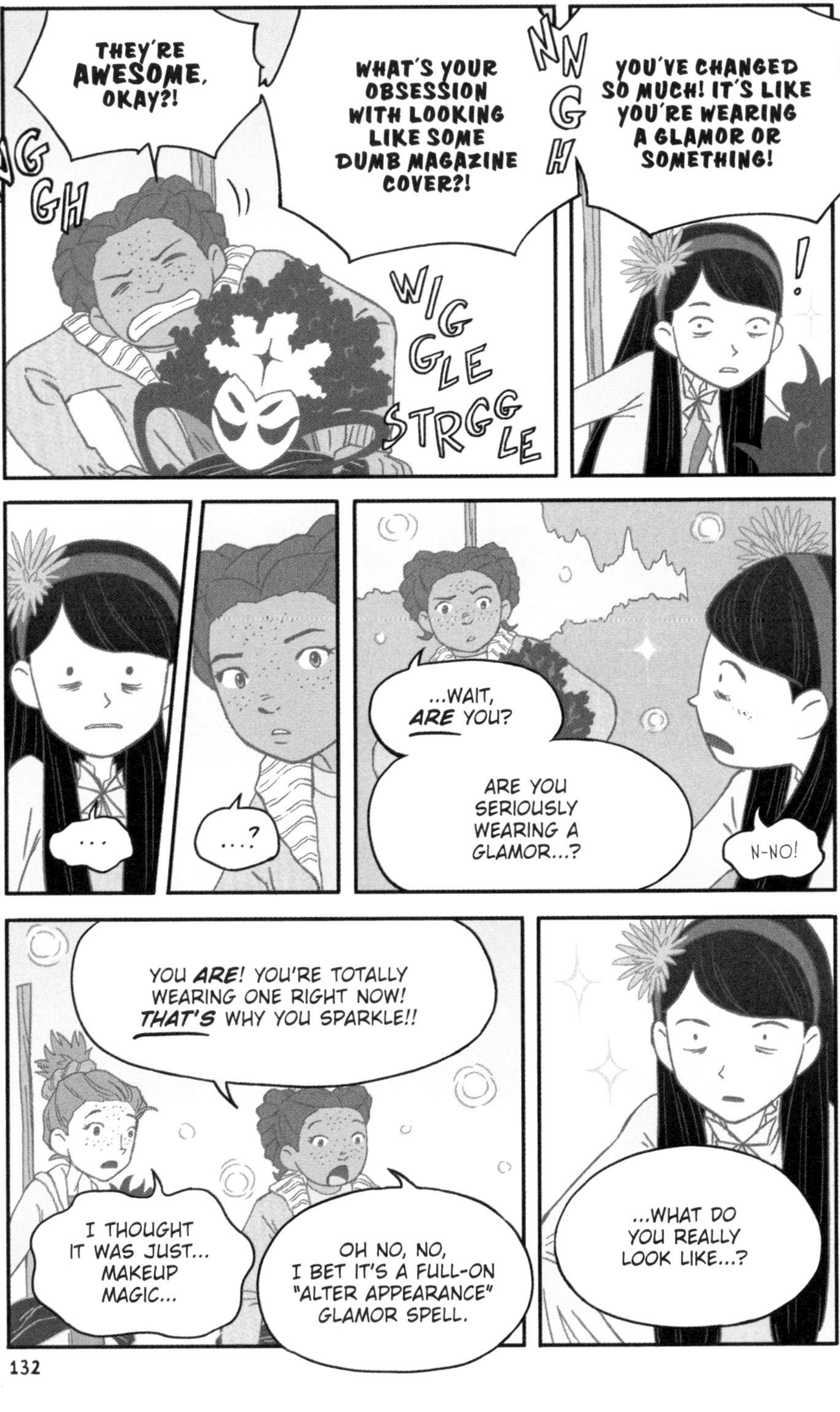

THEY'RE AWESOME, OKAY?!
NGGH
WHAT'S YOUR OBSESSION WITH LOOKING LIKE SOME DUMB MAGAZINE COVER?!
WIGGLE STRGGLE
NNGH
YOU'VE CHANGED SO MUCH! IT'S LIKE YOU'RE WEARING A GLAMOR OR SOMETHING!
!
...
...?
...WAIT, ARE YOU?
ARE YOU SERIOUSLY WEARING A GLAMOR...?
N-NO!
YOU ARE! YOU'RE TOTALLY WEARING ONE RIGHT NOW! THAT'S WHY YOU SPARKLE!!
I THOUGHT IT WAS JUST... MAKEUP MAGIC...
OH NO, NO, I BET IT'S A FULL-ON "ALTER APPEARANCE" GLAMOR SPELL.
...WHAT DO YOU REALLY LOOK LIKE...?

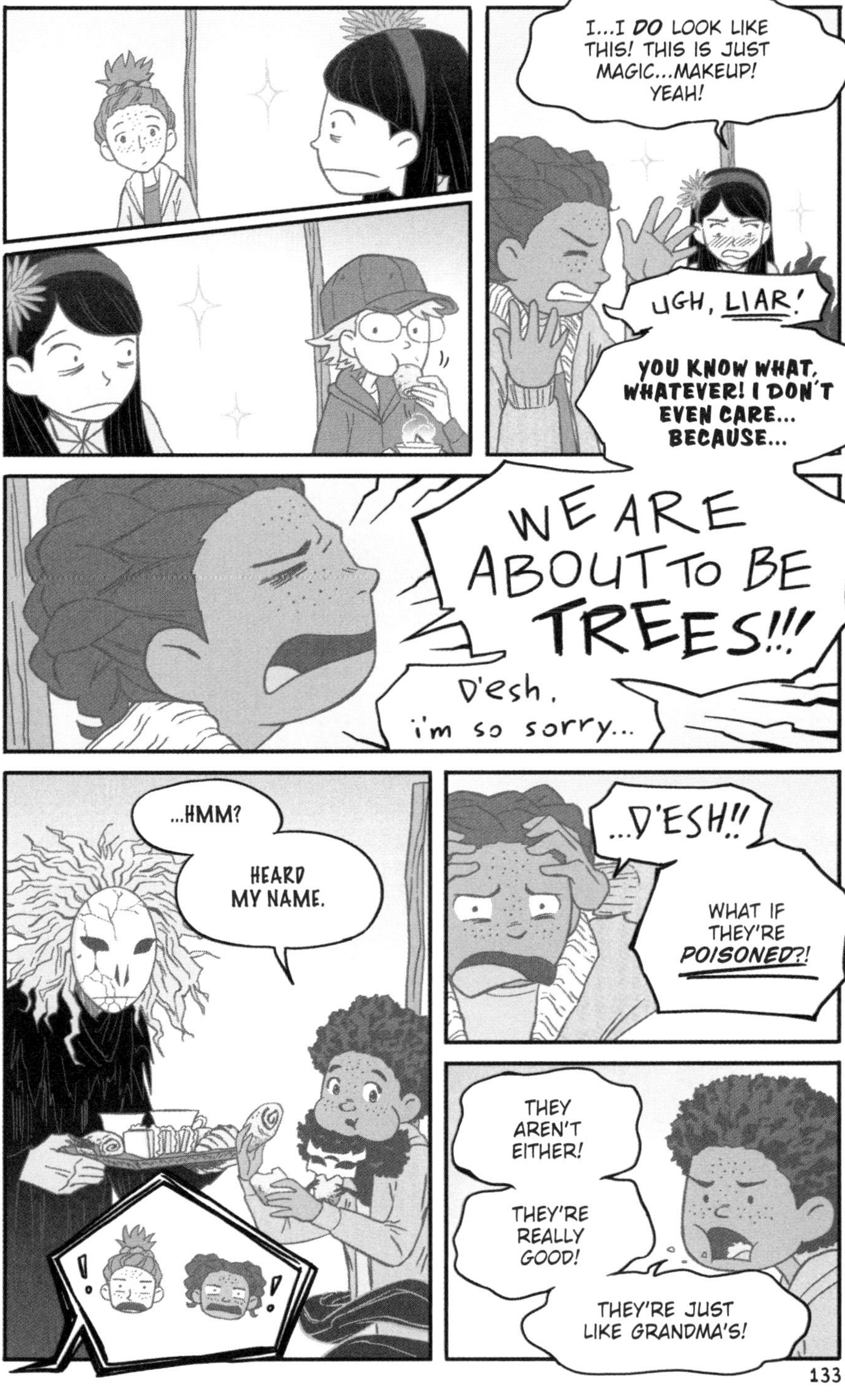

I...I DO LOOK LIKE THIS! THIS IS JUST MAGIC...MAKEUP! YEAH!
UGH, LIAR!
YOU KNOW WHAT, WHATEVER! I DON'T EVEN CARE... BECAUSE...
WE ARE ABOUT TO BE TREES!!!
D'esh, i'm so sorry...
...HMM?
HEARD MY NAME.
...D'ESH!!
WHAT IF THEY'RE POISONED?!
THEY AREN'T EITHER!
THEY'RE REALLY GOOD!
THEY'RE JUST LIKE GRANDMA'S!

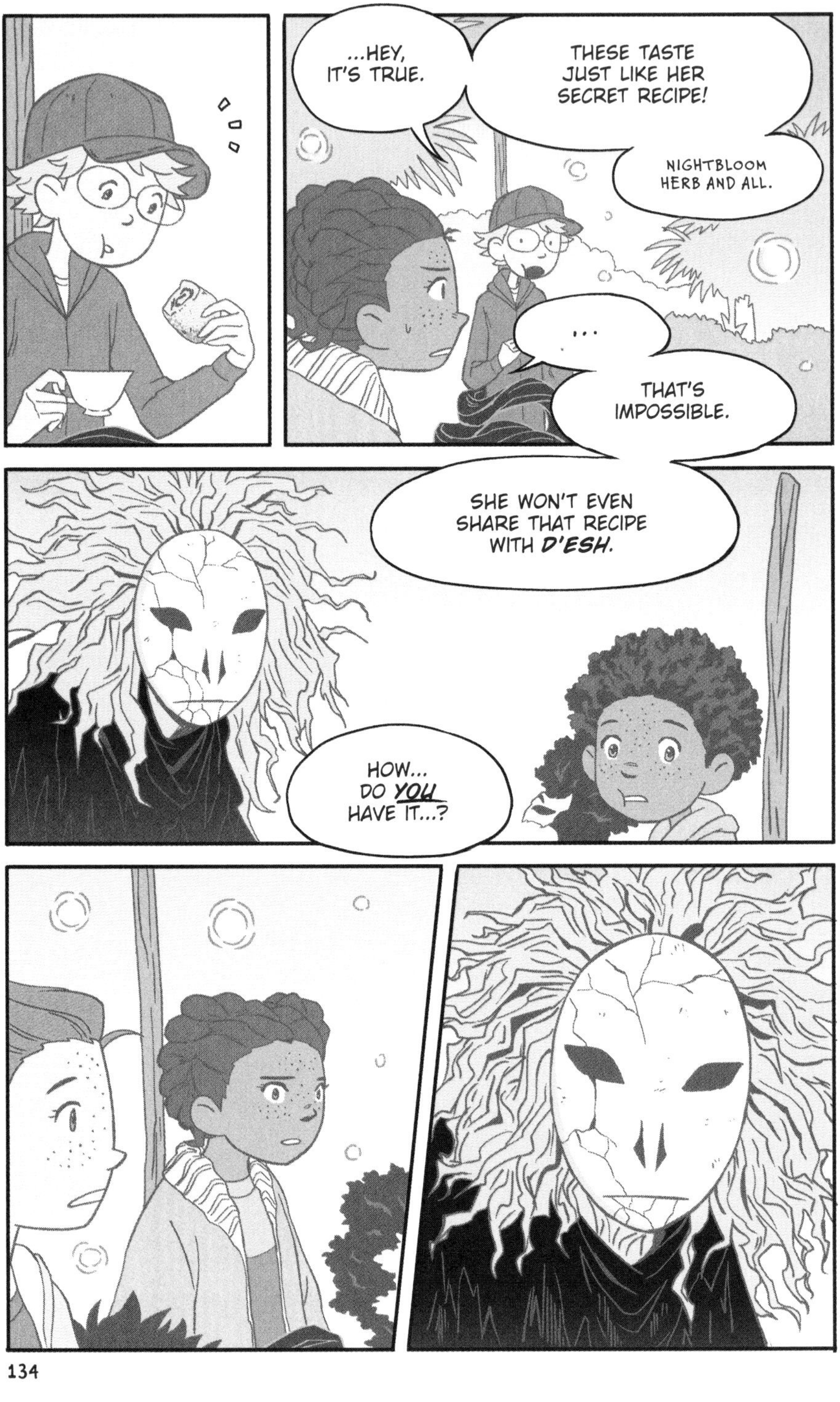
...HEY, IT'S TRUE.
THESE TASTE JUST LIKE HER SECRET RECIPE!
NIGHTBLOOM HERB AND ALL.
...
THAT'S IMPOSSIBLE.
SHE WON'T EVEN SHARE THAT RECIPE WITH D'ESH.
HOW... DO YOU HAVE IT...?

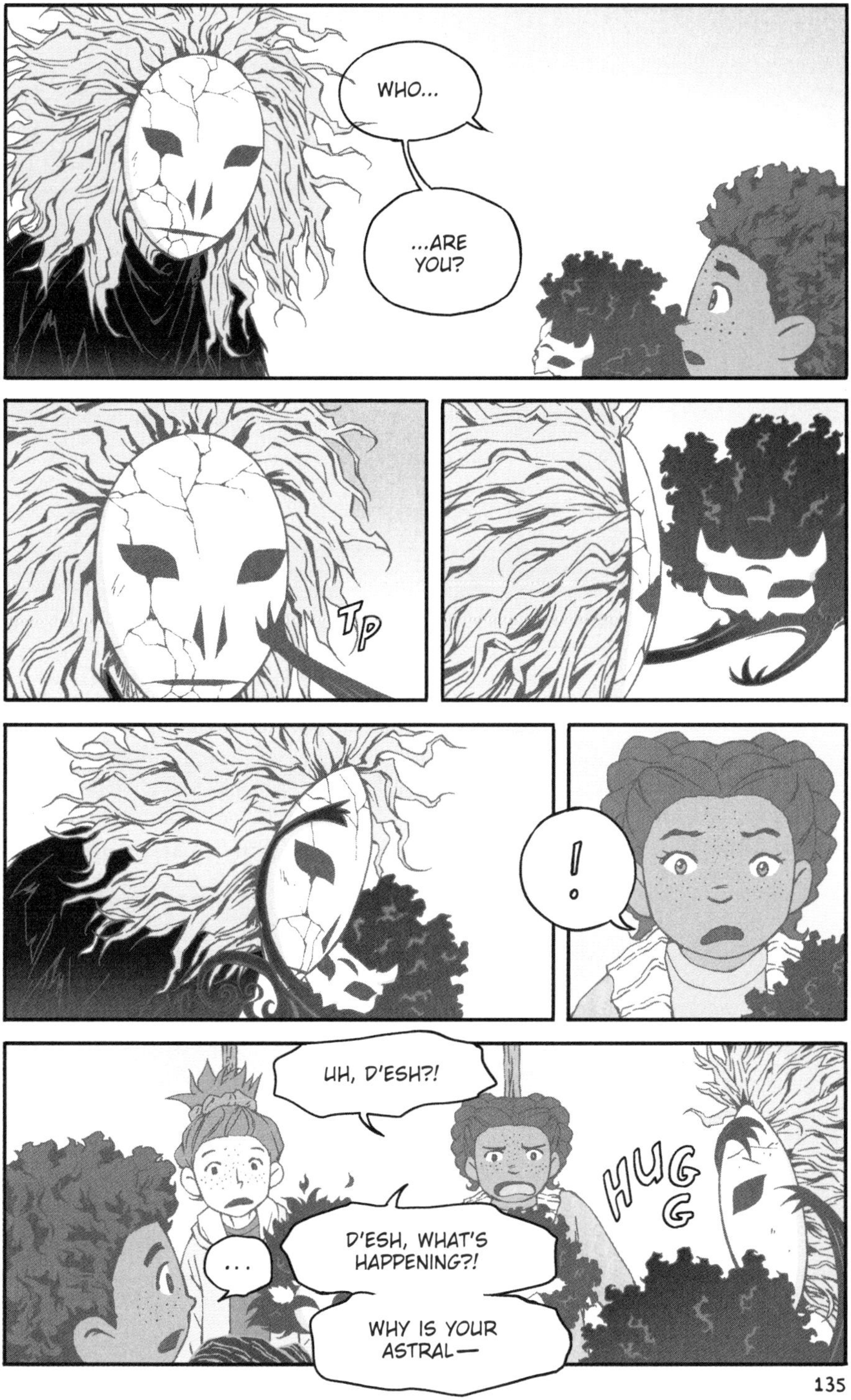
WHO...
...ARE YOU?
TP
!
UH, D'ESH?!
HUGG
...
D'ESH, WHAT'S HAPPENING?!
WHY IS YOUR ASTRAL—

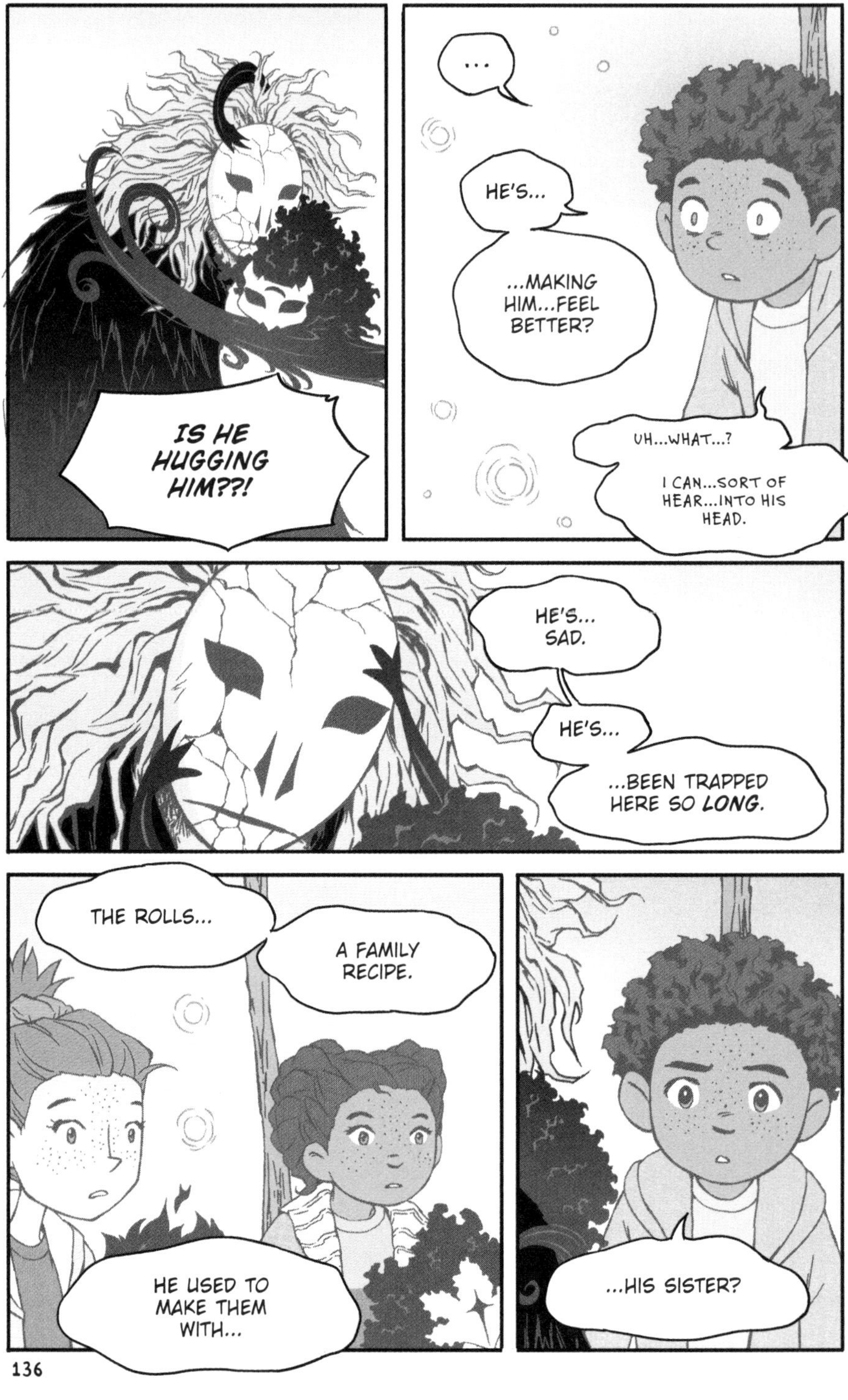
IS HE HUGGING HIM??!
...
HE'S...
...MAKING HIM...FEEL BETTER?
UH...WHAT...?
I CAN...SORT OF HEAR...INTO HIS HEAD.
HE'S... SAD.
HE'S...
...BEEN TRAPPED HERE SO LONG.
THE ROLLS...
A FAMILY RECIPE.
HE USED TO MAKE THEM WITH...
...HIS SISTER?

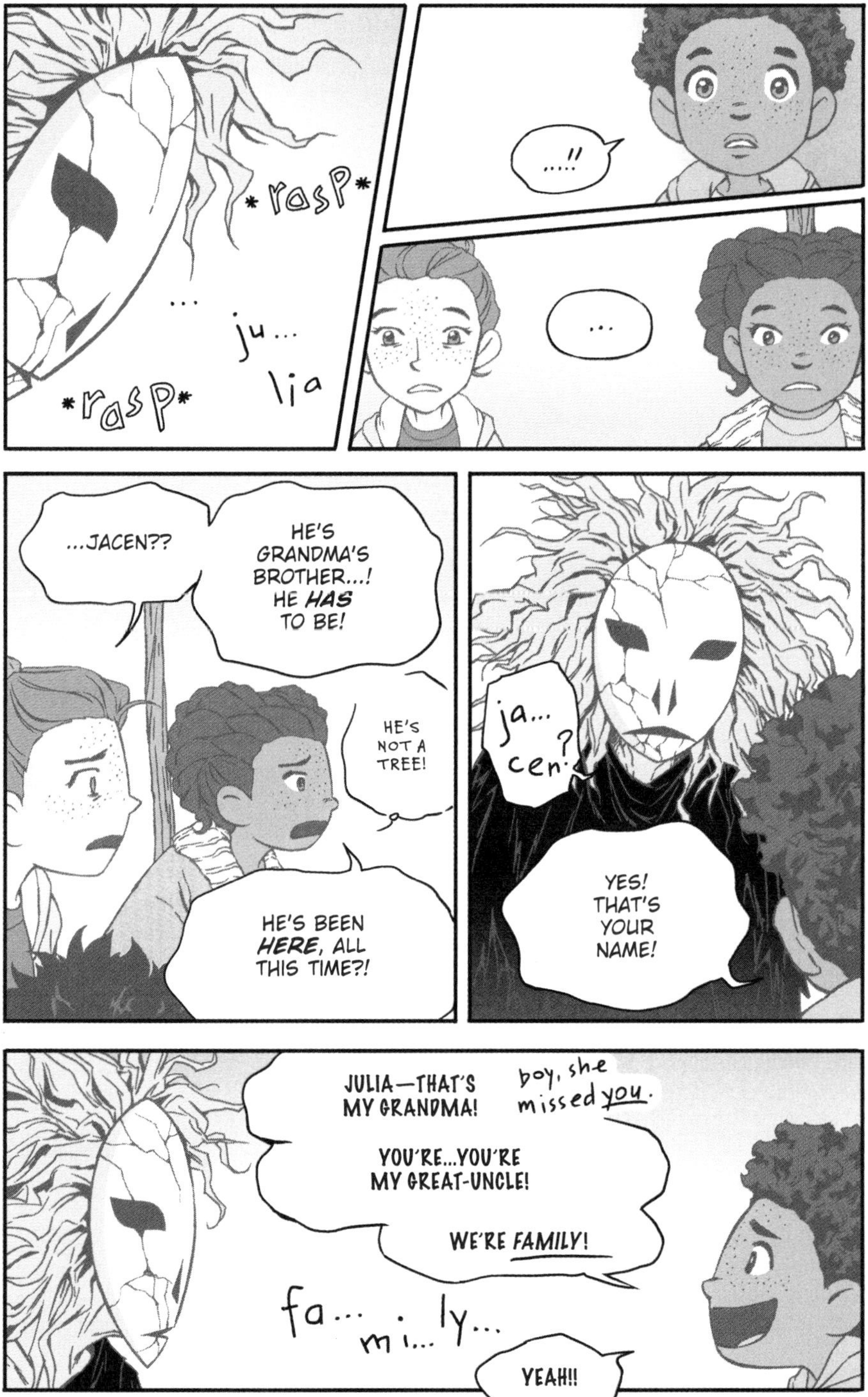

rasp
...
ju...
lia
rasp
....!!
...
...JACEN??
HE'S GRANDMA'S BROTHER...! HE HAS TO BE!
HE'S NOT A TREE!
HE'S BEEN HERE, ALL THIS TIME?!
ja... cen?
YES! THAT'S YOUR NAME!
JULIA—THAT'S MY GRANDMA!
boy, she missed you.
YOU'RE...YOU'RE MY GREAT-UNCLE!
WE'RE FAMILY!
fa... mi... ly...
YEAH!!

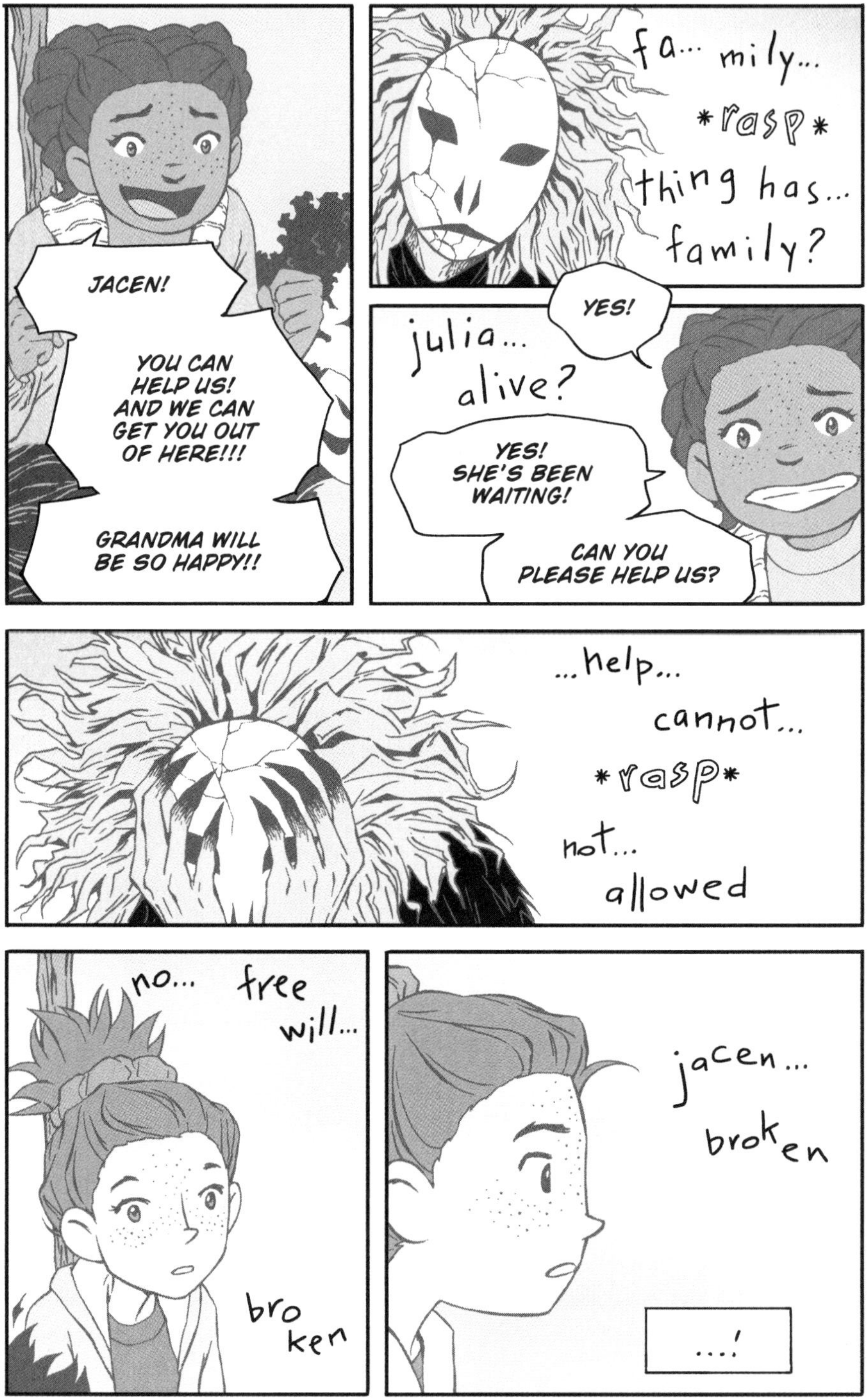
JACEN!
YOU CAN HELP US! AND WE CAN GET YOU OUT OF HERE!!!
GRANDMA WILL BE SO HAPPY!!
fa... mily...
rasp
thing has... family?
julia... alive?
YES!
YES! SHE'S BEEN WAITING!
CAN YOU PLEASE HELP US?
...help... cannot...
rasp
not... allowed
no... free will...
broken
jacen... broken
...!

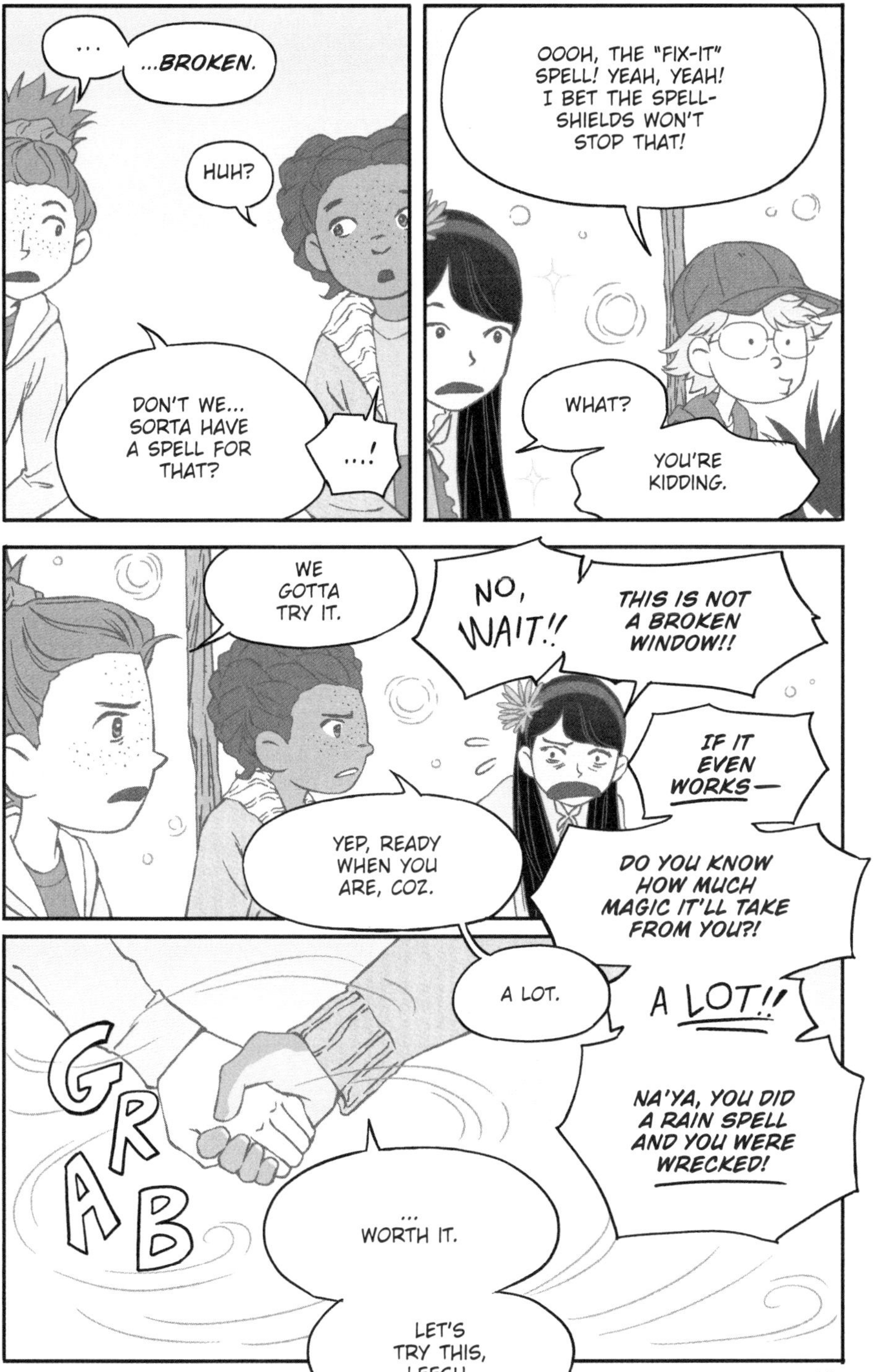
...
...BROKEN.
HUH?
DON'T WE... SORTA HAVE A SPELL FOR THAT?
...!
OOOH, THE "FIX-IT" SPELL! YEAH, YEAH! I BET THE SPELL-SHIELDS WON'T STOP THAT!
WHAT?
YOU'RE KIDDING.
WE GOTTA TRY IT.
NO, WAIT!!
THIS IS NOT A BROKEN WINDOW!!
IF IT EVEN WORKS—
YEP, READY WHEN YOU ARE, COZ.
DO YOU KNOW HOW MUCH MAGIC IT'LL TAKE FROM YOU?!
A LOT.
A LOT!!
NA'YA, YOU DID A RAIN SPELL AND YOU WERE WRECKED!
GRAB
... WORTH IT.
LET'S TRY THIS, LEESH.

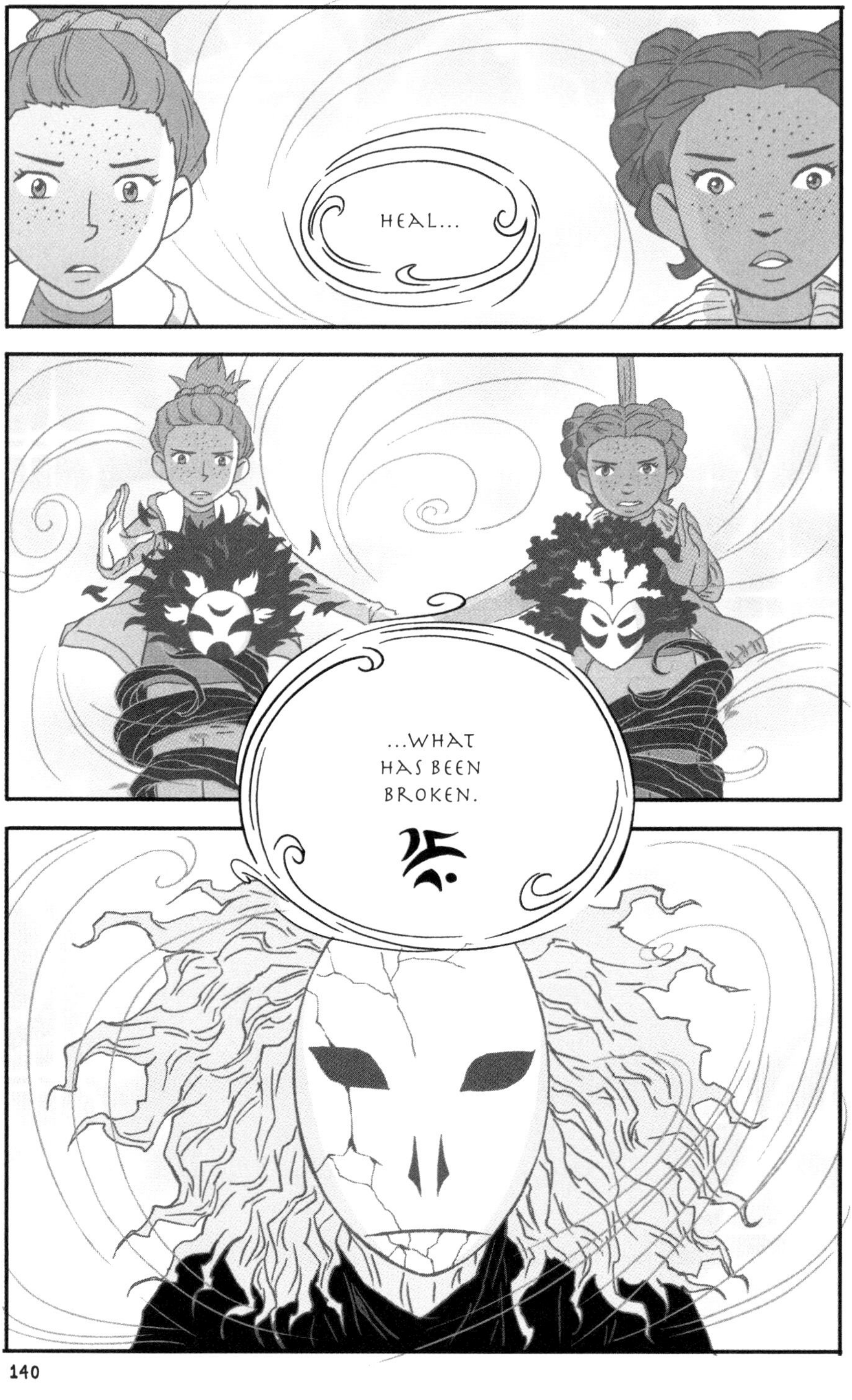
HEAL...
...WHAT HAS BEEN BROKEN.

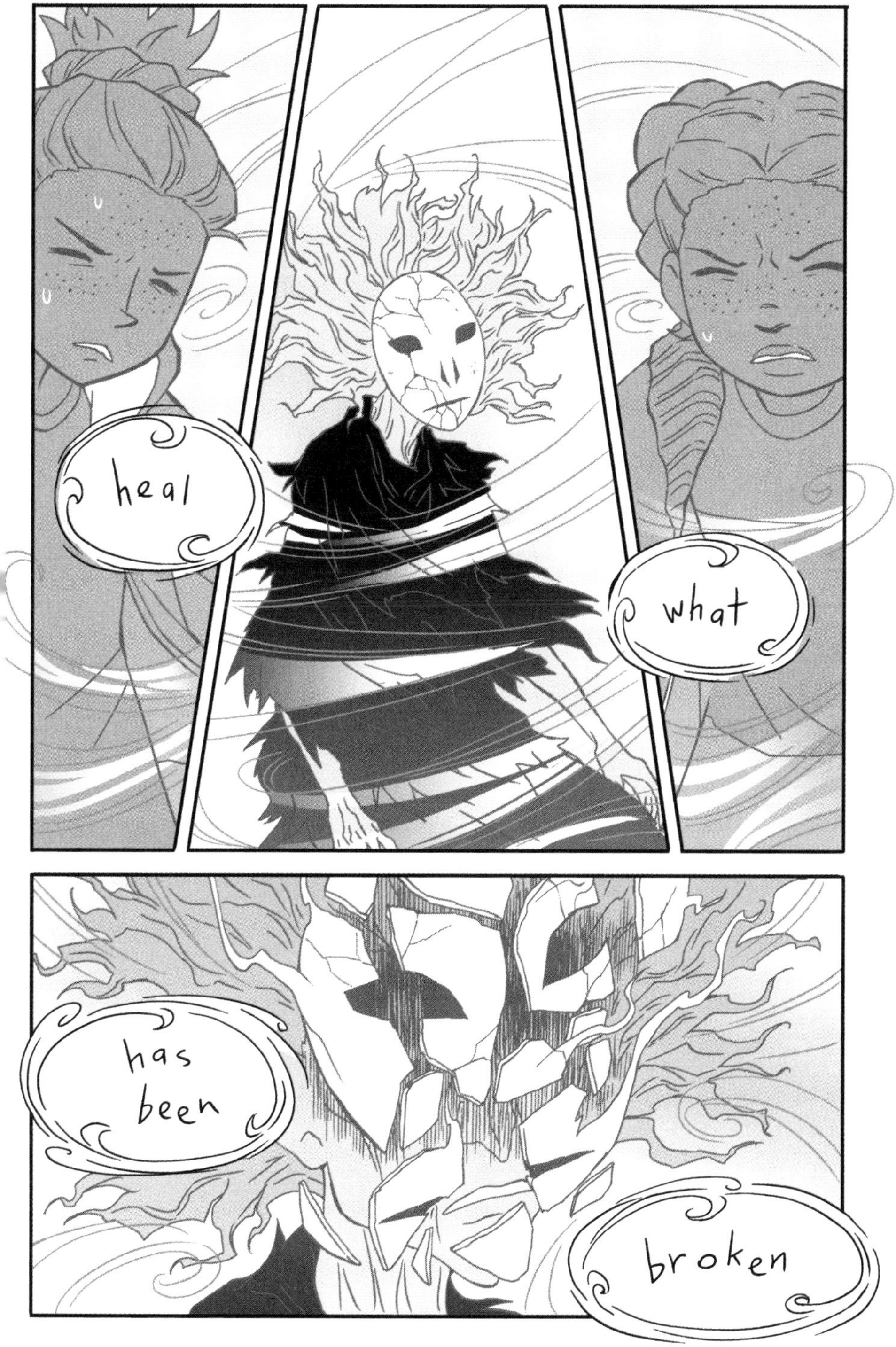
heal
what
has been
broken

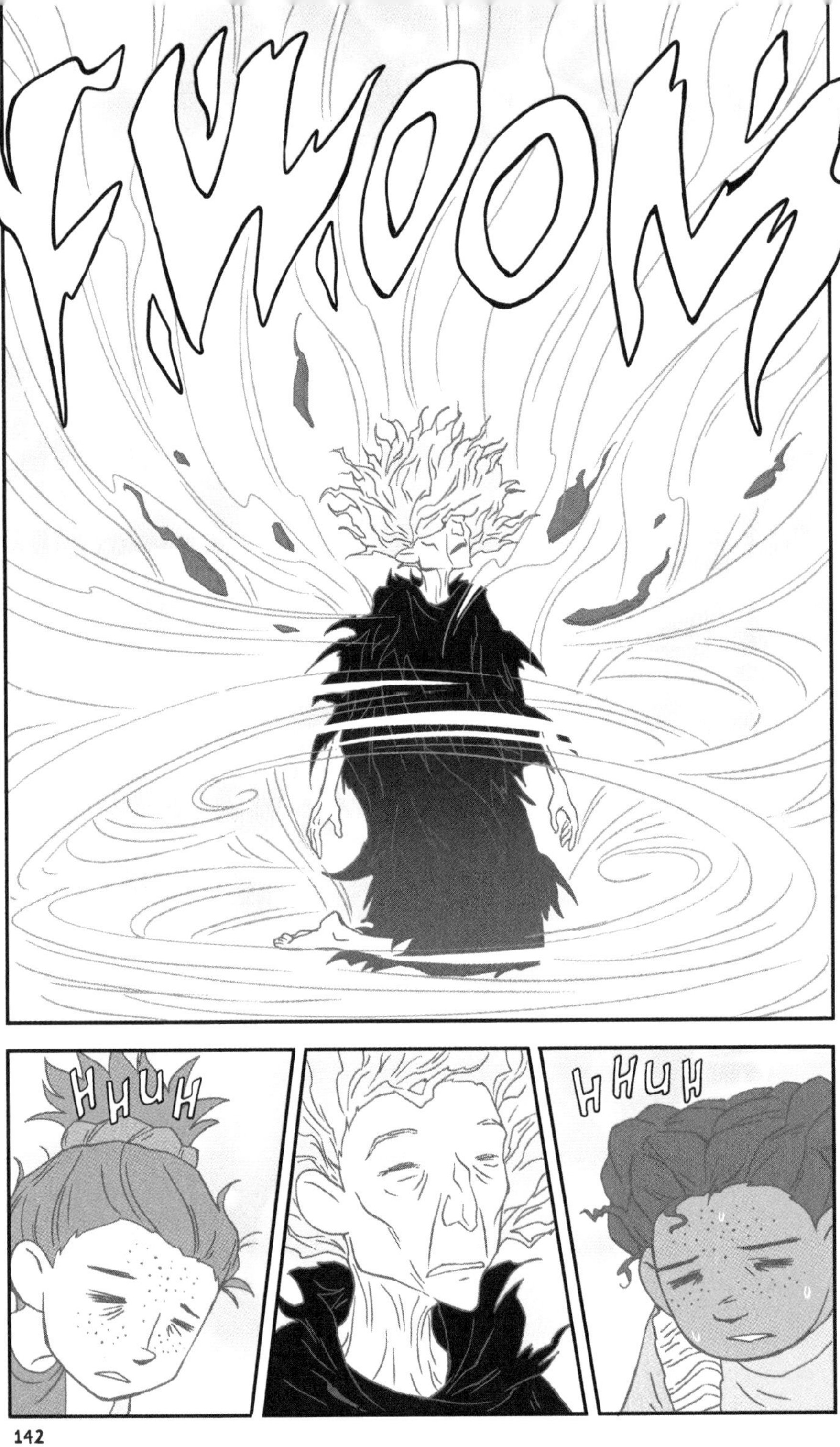
FWOOM
HHUH
HHUH

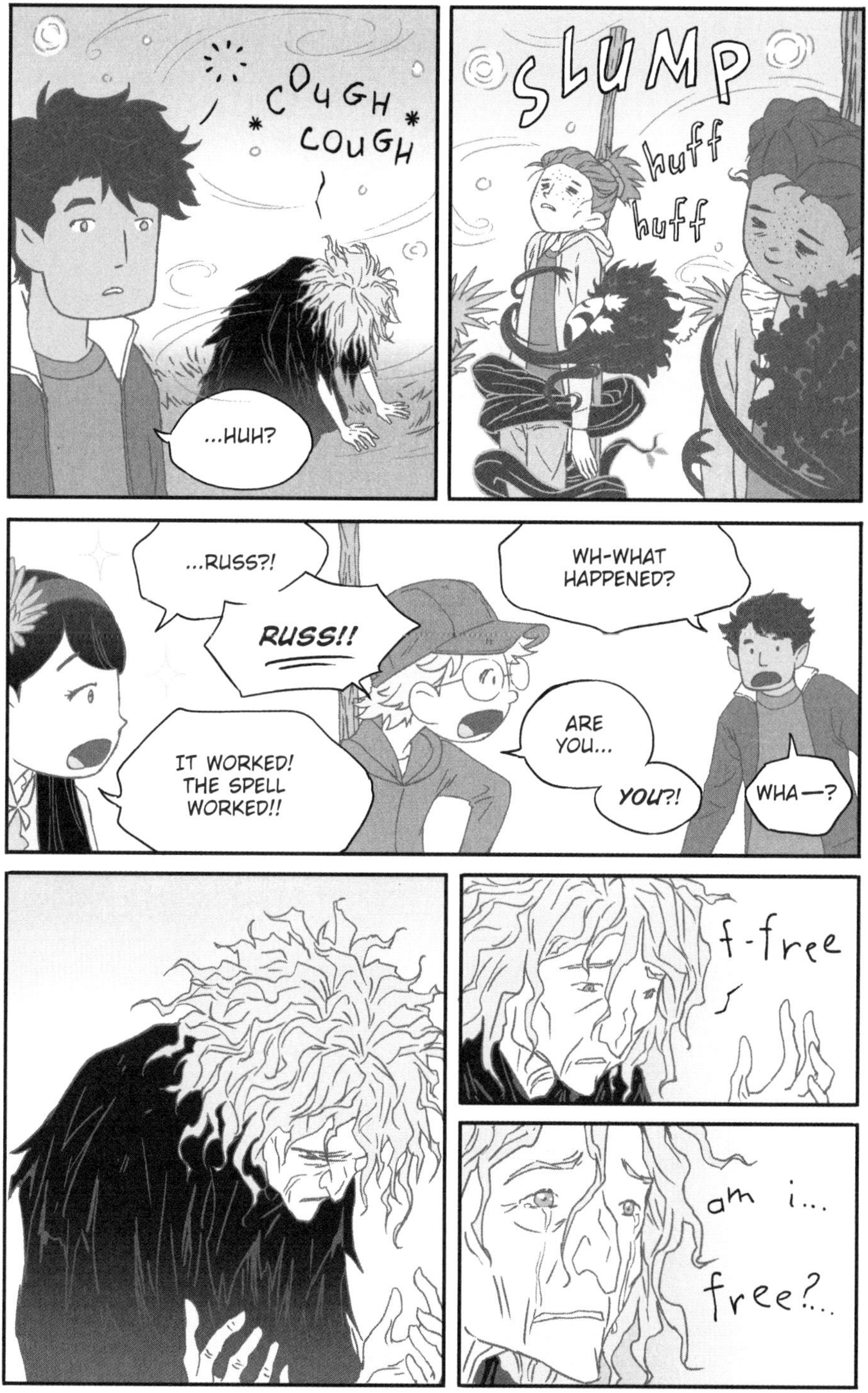
COUGH
COUGH
...HUH?
SLUMP
huff
huff
...RUSS?!
RUSS!!
WH-WHAT HAPPENED?
IT WORKED! THE SPELL WORKED!!
ARE YOU...
YOU?!
WHA—?
f-free
am i...
free?...

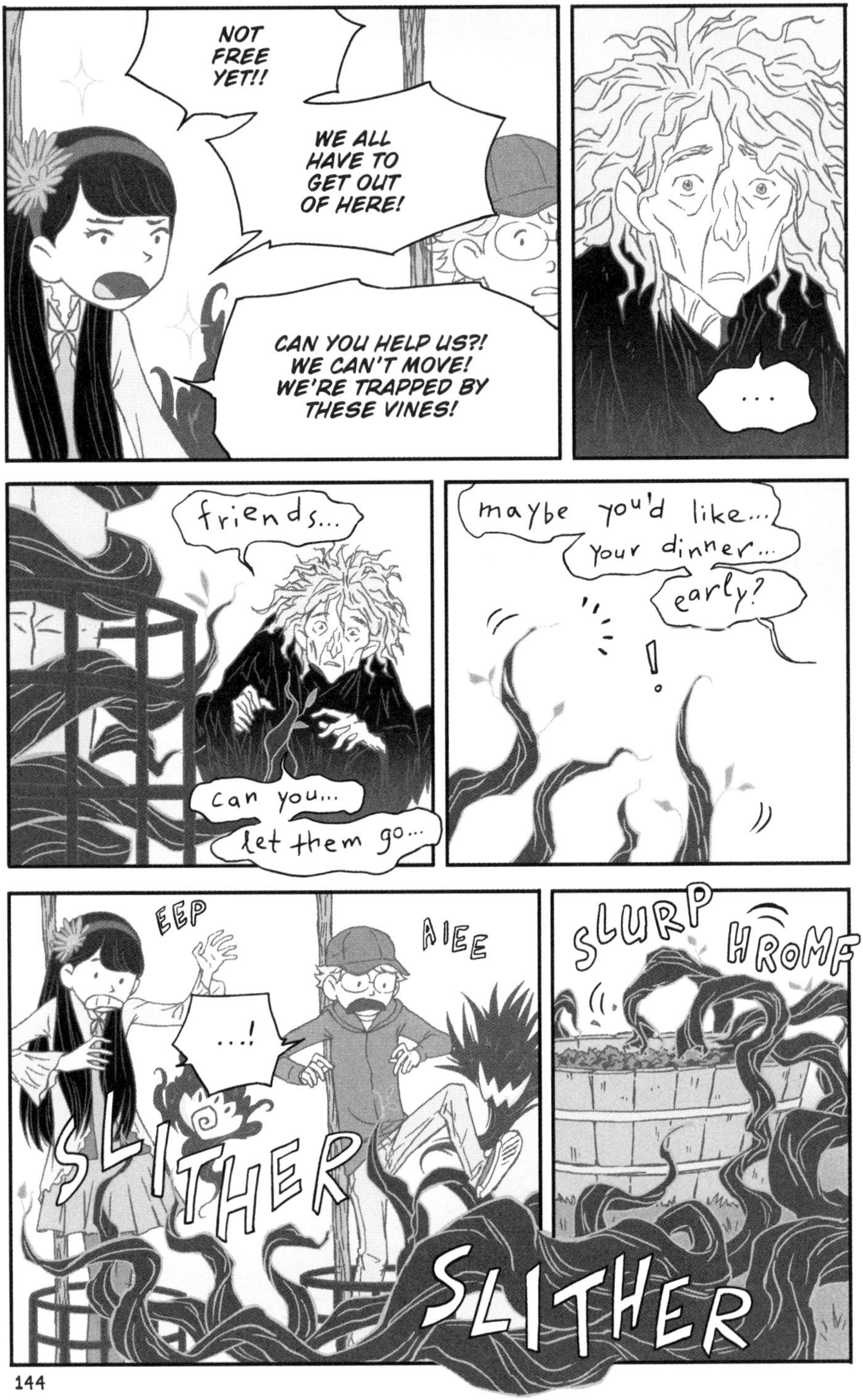
NOT FREE YET!!
WE ALL HAVE TO GET OUT OF HERE!
CAN YOU HELP US?! WE CAN'T MOVE! WE'RE TRAPPED BY THESE VINES!
...
friends...
can you... let them go...
maybe you'd like... your dinner... early?
!
EEP
AIEE
...!
SLITHER
SLURP
HROMF
SLITHER

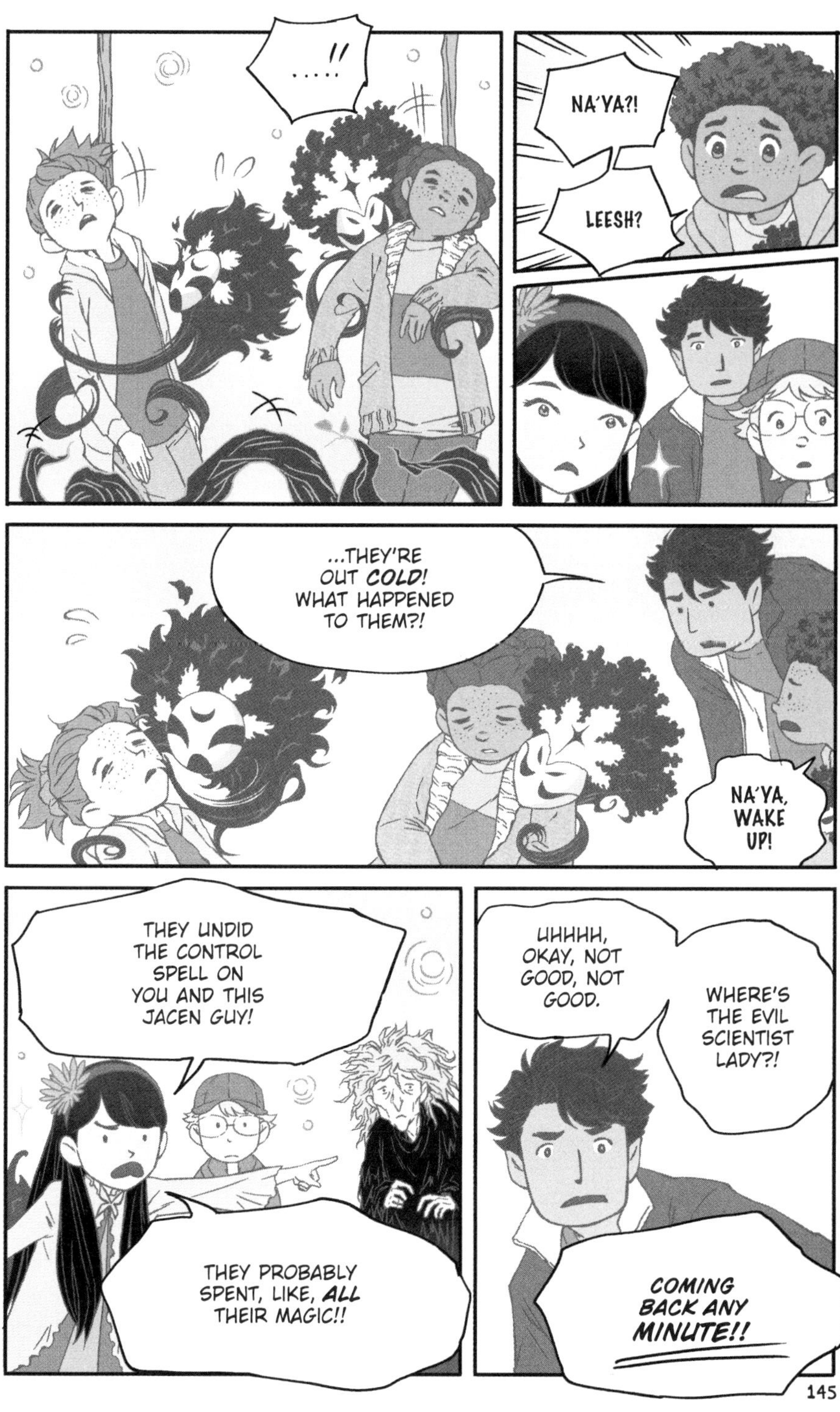
......!!
NA'YA?!
LEESH?
...THEY'RE OUT COLD! WHAT HAPPENED TO THEM?!
NA'YA, WAKE UP!
THEY UNDID THE CONTROL SPELL ON YOU AND THIS JACEN GUY!
THEY PROBABLY SPENT, LIKE, ALL THEIR MAGIC!!
UHHHH, OKAY, NOT GOOD, NOT GOOD.
WHERE'S THE EVIL SCIENTIST LADY?!
COMING BACK ANY MINUTE!!

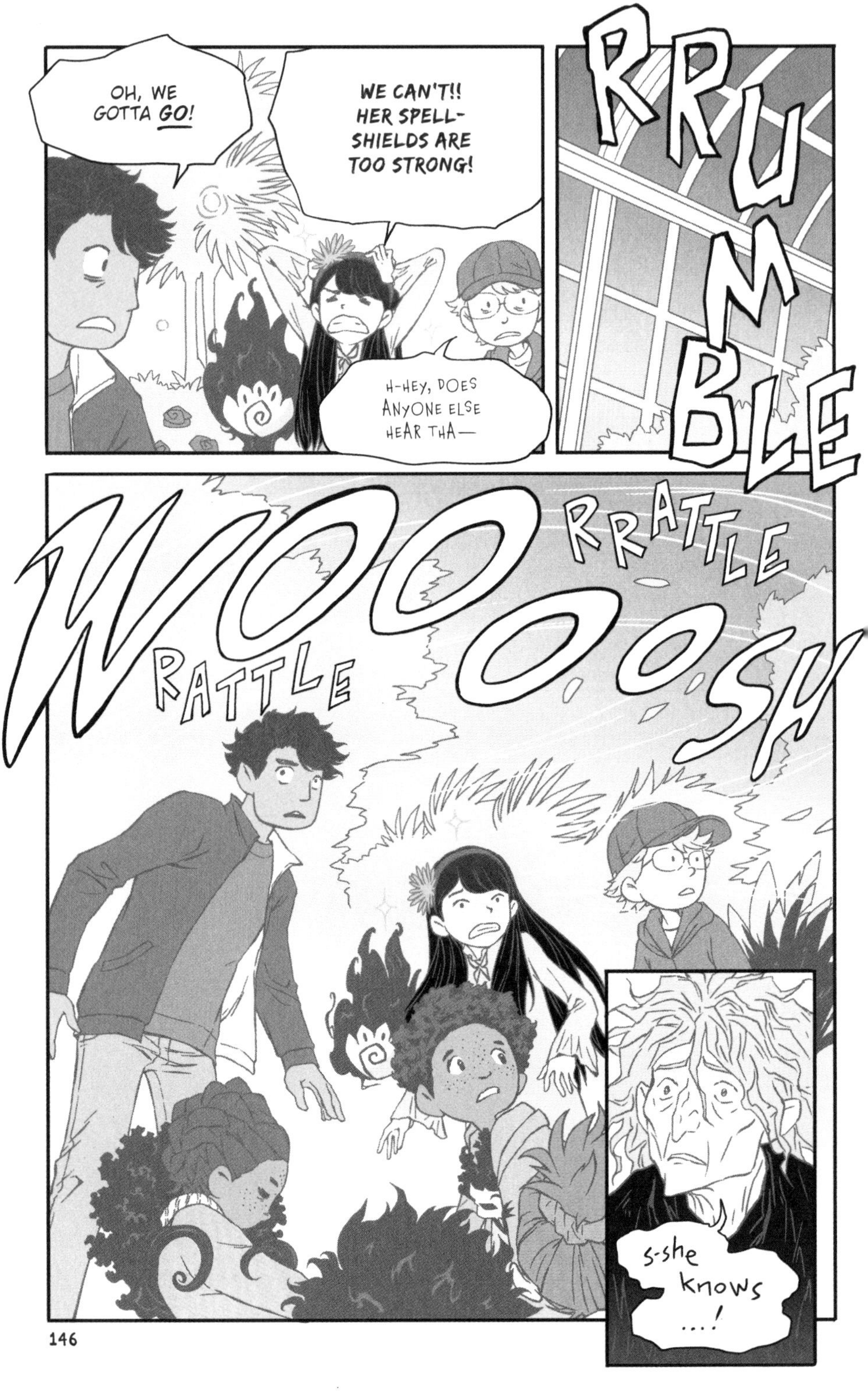
OH, WE GOTTA GO!
WE CAN'T!! HER SPELL-SHIELDS ARE TOO STRONG!
H-HEY, DOES ANYONE ELSE HEAR THA—
RRUMBLE
WOOOOOSH
RRATTLE
RATTLE
s-she knows ...!

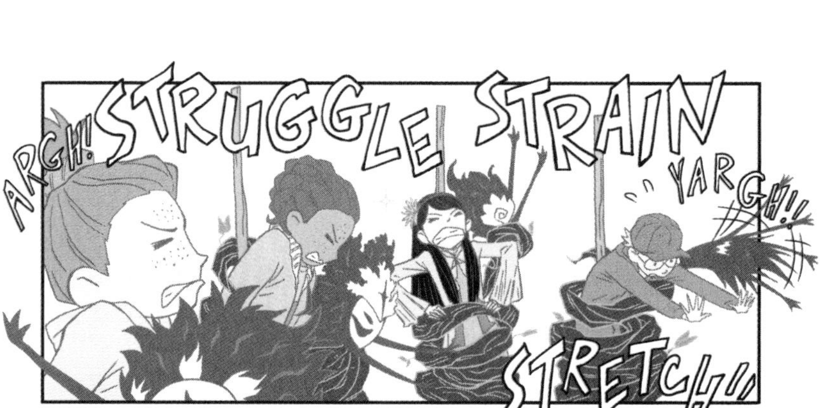
ARGH!
STRUGGLE
STRAIN
YARGH!!
STRETCH!!

Chapter 6

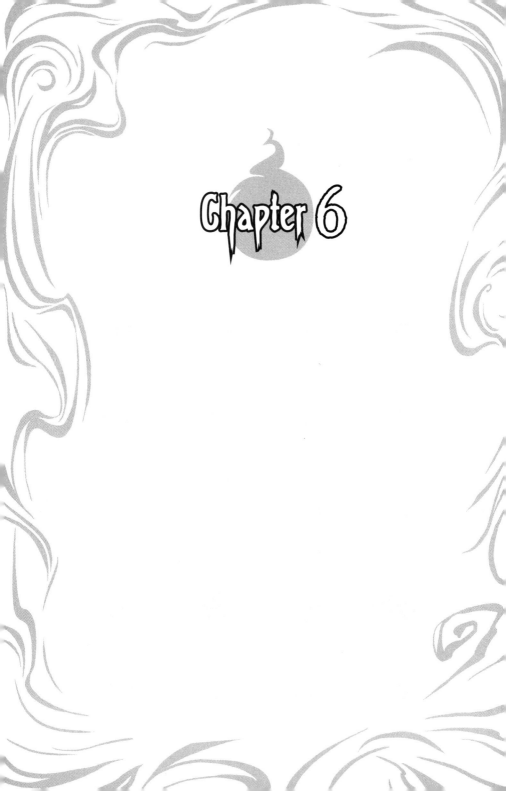

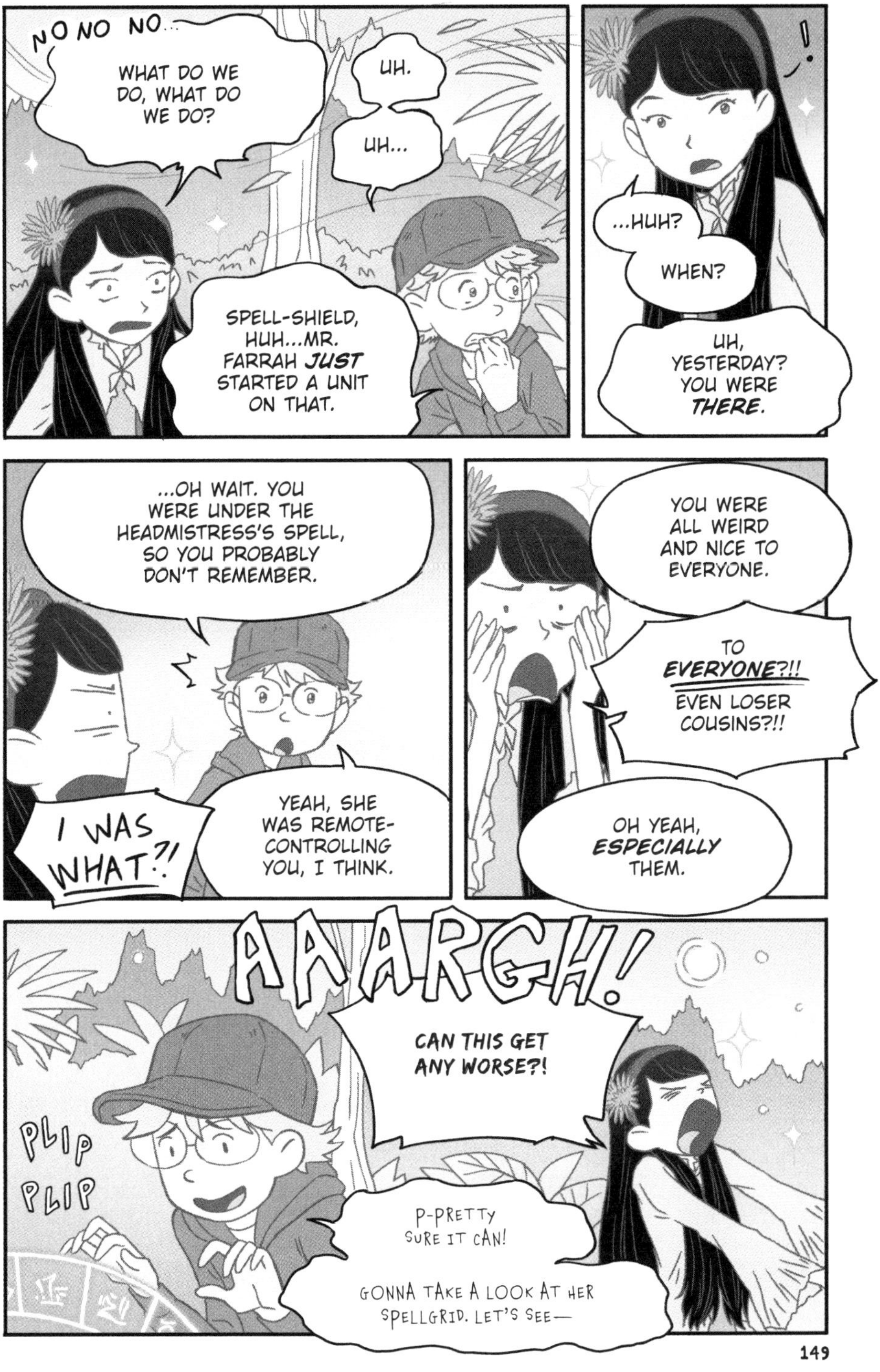
NO NO NO...
WHAT DO WE DO, WHAT DO WE DO?
UH.
UH...
SPELL-SHIELD, HUH...MR. FARRAH JUST STARTED A UNIT ON THAT.
!
...HUH?
WHEN?
UH, YESTERDAY? YOU WERE THERE.
...OH WAIT. YOU WERE UNDER THE HEADMISTRESS'S SPELL, SO YOU PROBABLY DON'T REMEMBER.
I WAS WHAT?!
YEAH, SHE WAS REMOTE-CONTROLLING YOU, I THINK.
YOU WERE ALL WEIRD AND NICE TO EVERYONE.
TO EVERYONE?!! EVEN LOSER COUSINS?!!
OH YEAH, ESPECIALLY THEM.
AAARGH!
CAN THIS GET ANY WORSE?!
PLIP PLIP
P-PRETTY SURE IT CAN!
GONNA TAKE A LOOK AT HER SPELLGRID. LET'S SEE—

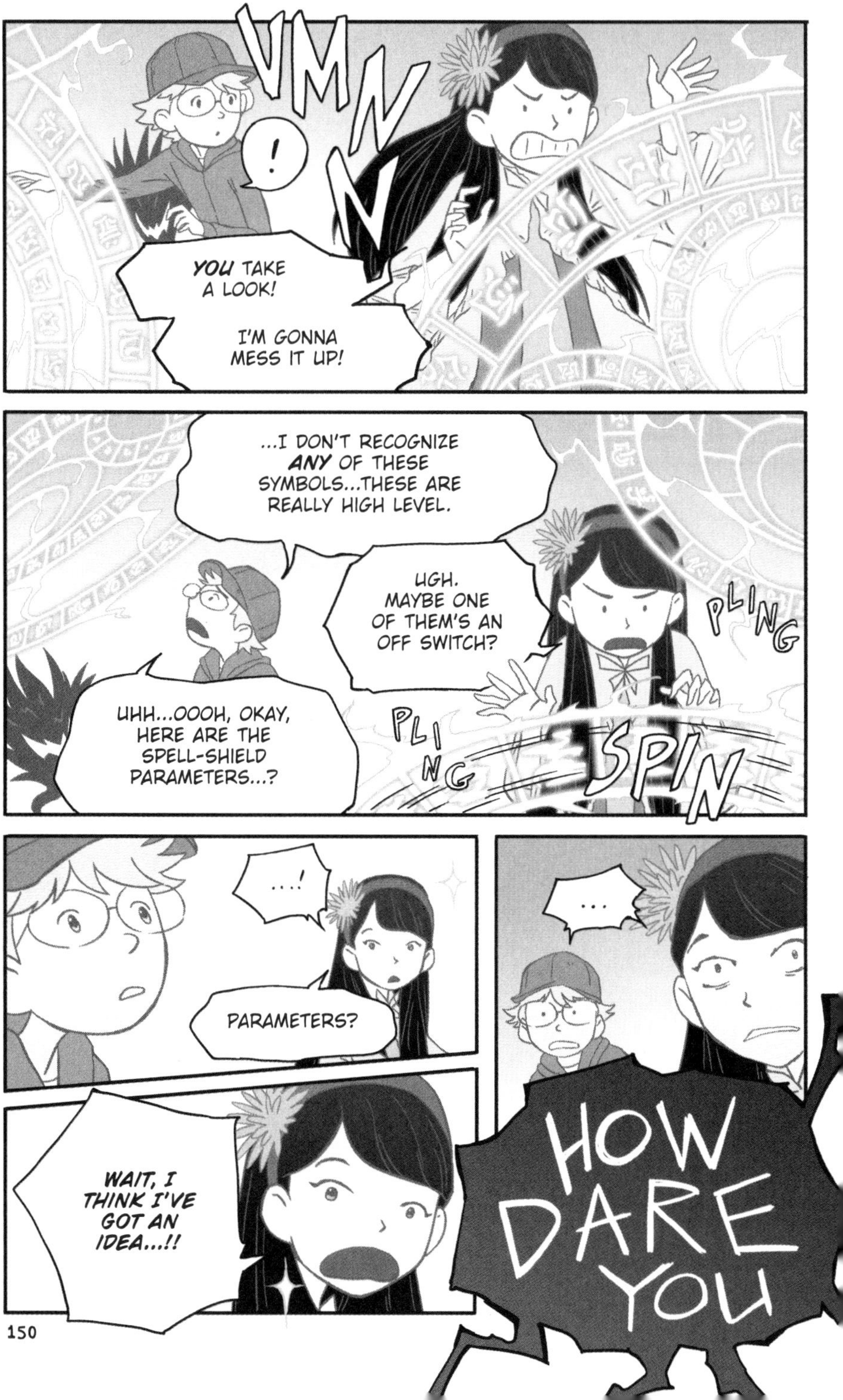
VMNN
!
YOU TAKE A LOOK!
I'M GONNA MESS IT UP!
...I DON'T RECOGNIZE ANY OF THESE SYMBOLS...THESE ARE REALLY HIGH LEVEL.
UGH. MAYBE ONE OF THEM'S AN OFF SWITCH?
PLING
UHH...OOOH, OKAY, HERE ARE THE SPELL-SHIELD PARAMETERS...?
PLING
SPIN
...!
PARAMETERS?
WAIT, I THINK I'VE GOT AN IDEA...!!
...
HOW DARE YOU

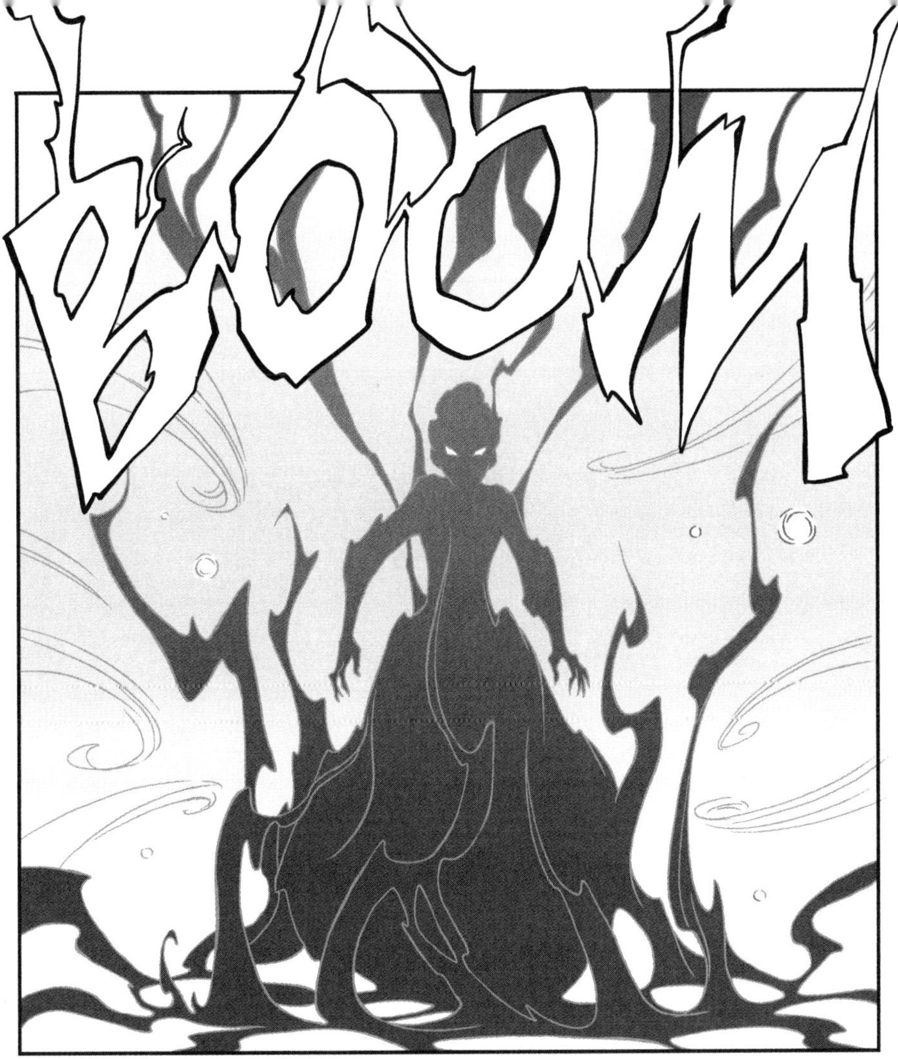
BOOM

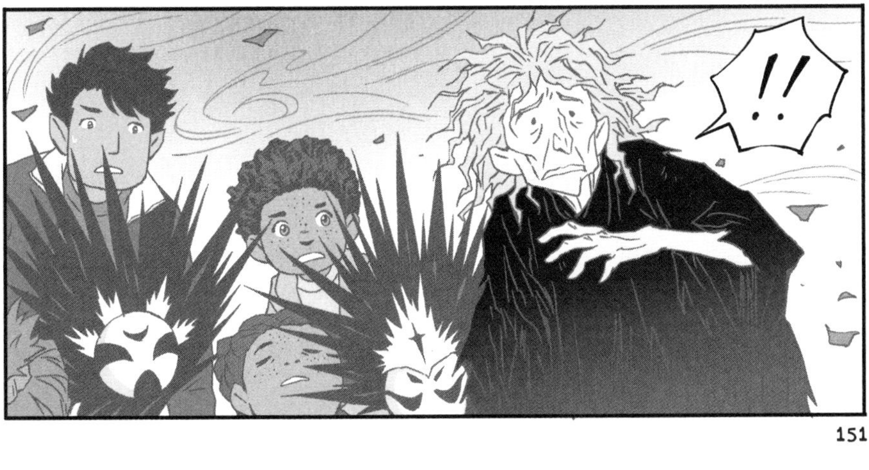
!!

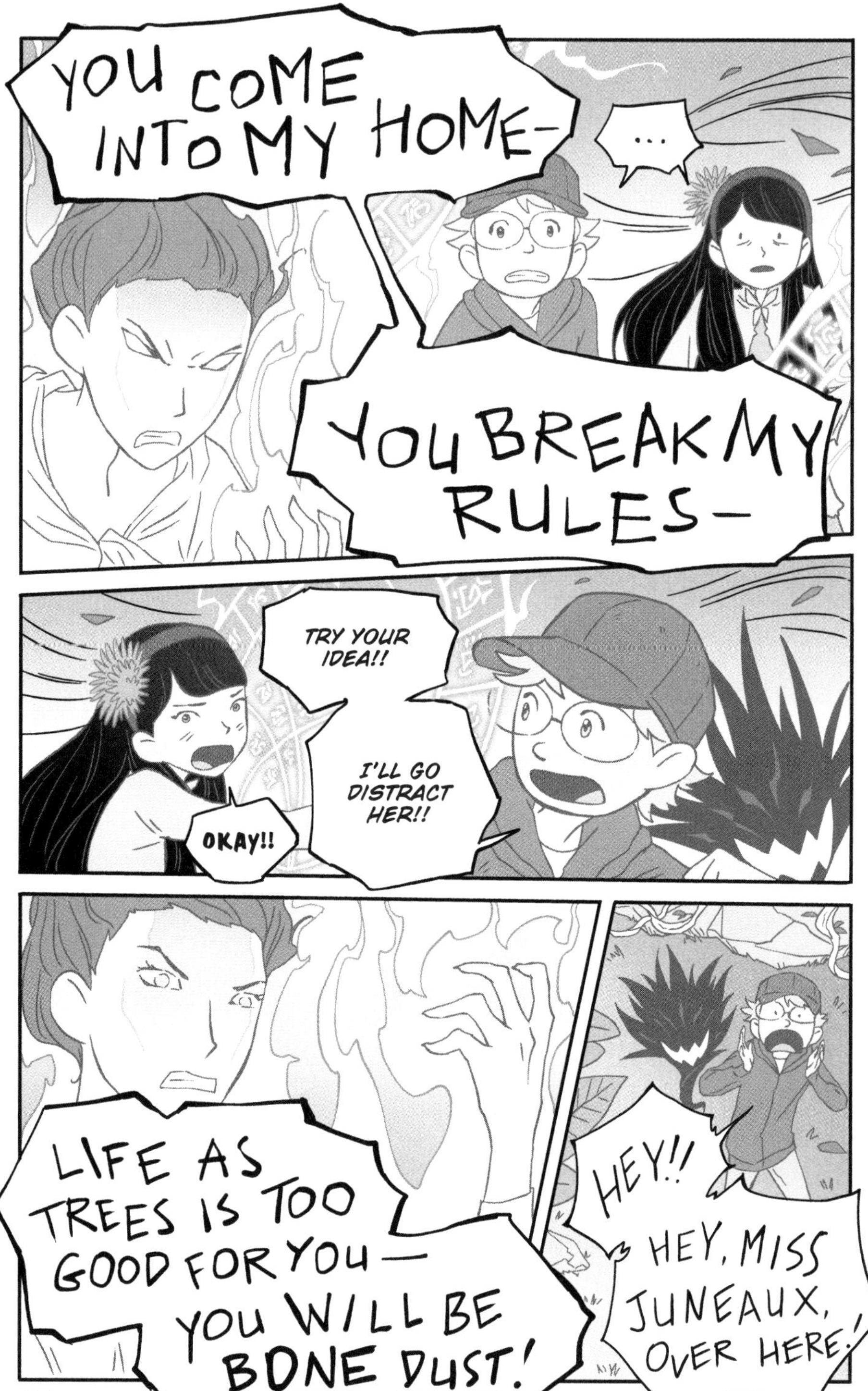
YOU COME INTO MY HOME-
...
YOU BREAK MY RULES-
TRY YOUR IDEA!!
I'LL GO DISTRACT HER!!
OKAY!!
LIFE AS TREES IS TOO GOOD FOR YOU-
YOU WILL BE BONE DUST!
HEY!!
HEY, MISS JUNEAUX, OVER HERE!

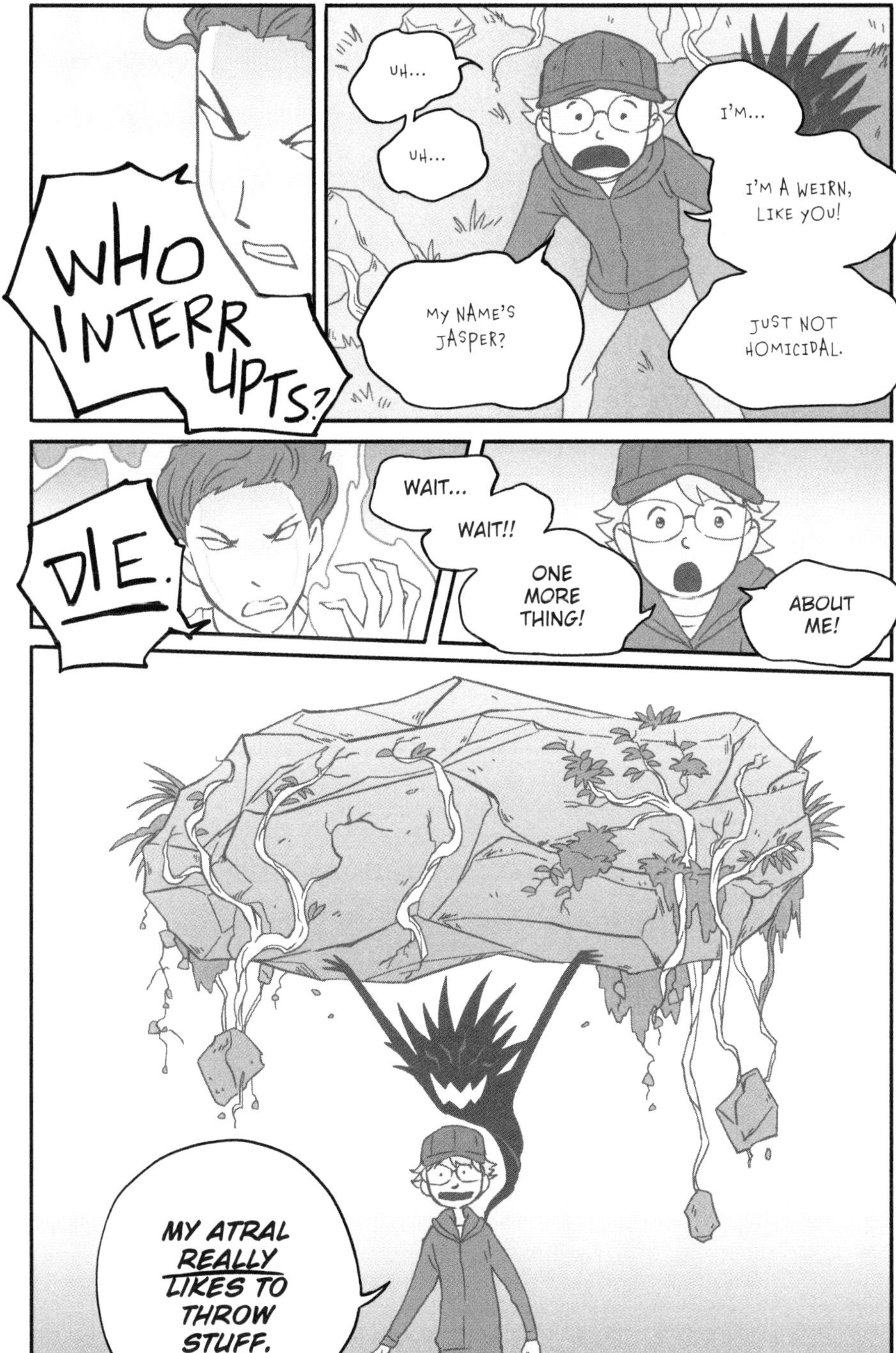
WHO INTERRUPTS?
UH...
UH...
MY NAME'S JASPER?
I'M...
I'M A WEIRN, LIKE YOU!
JUST NOT HOMICIDAL.
DIE.
WAIT...
WAIT!!
ONE MORE THING!
ABOUT ME!
MY ATRAL REALLY LIKES TO THROW STUFF.

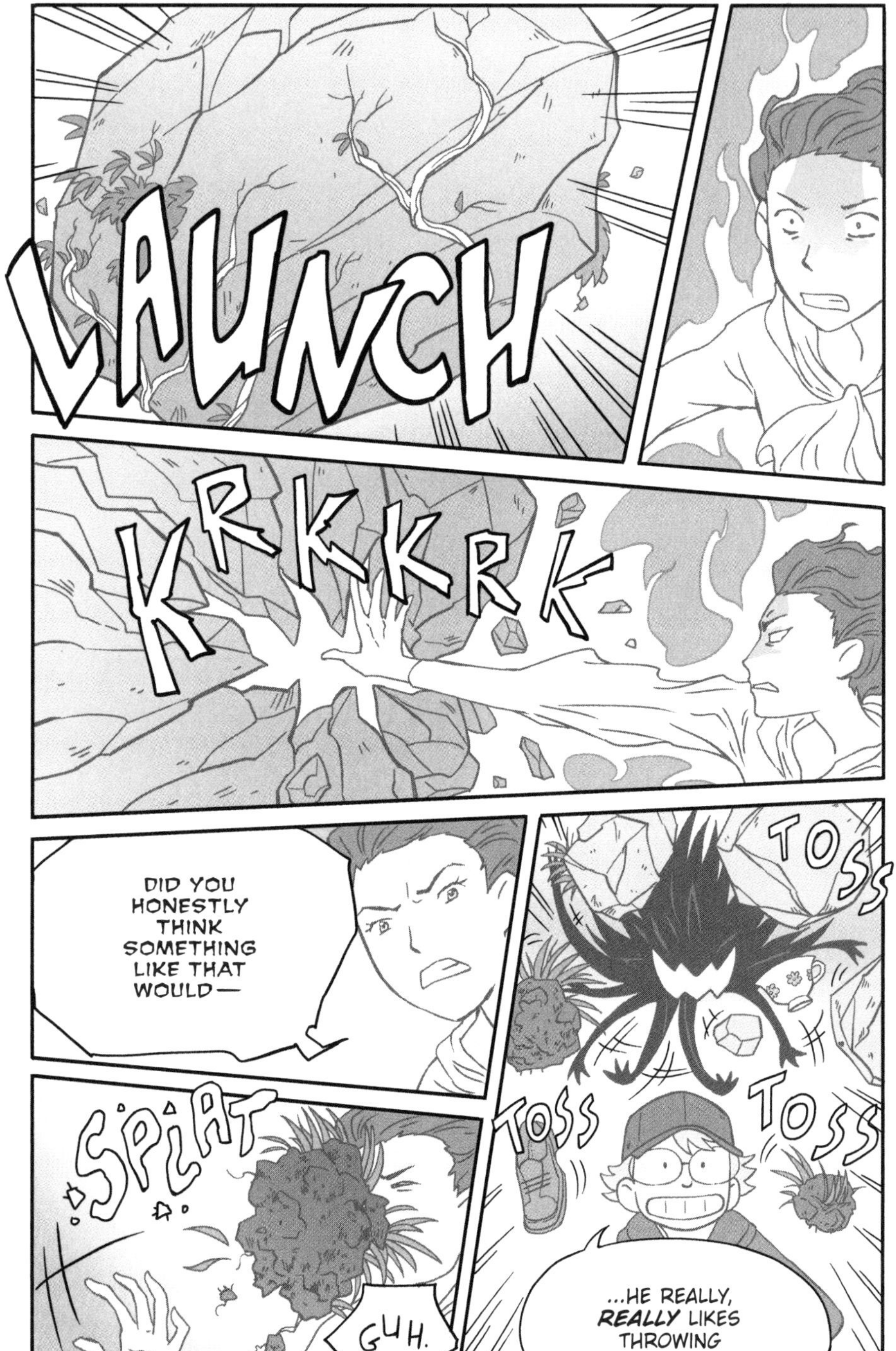
LAUNCH
KRKKRK
DID YOU HONESTLY THINK SOMETHING LIKE THAT WOULD—
TOSS
SPLAT
TOSS
TOSS
GUH.
...HE REALLY, *REALLY* LIKES THROWING STUFF.

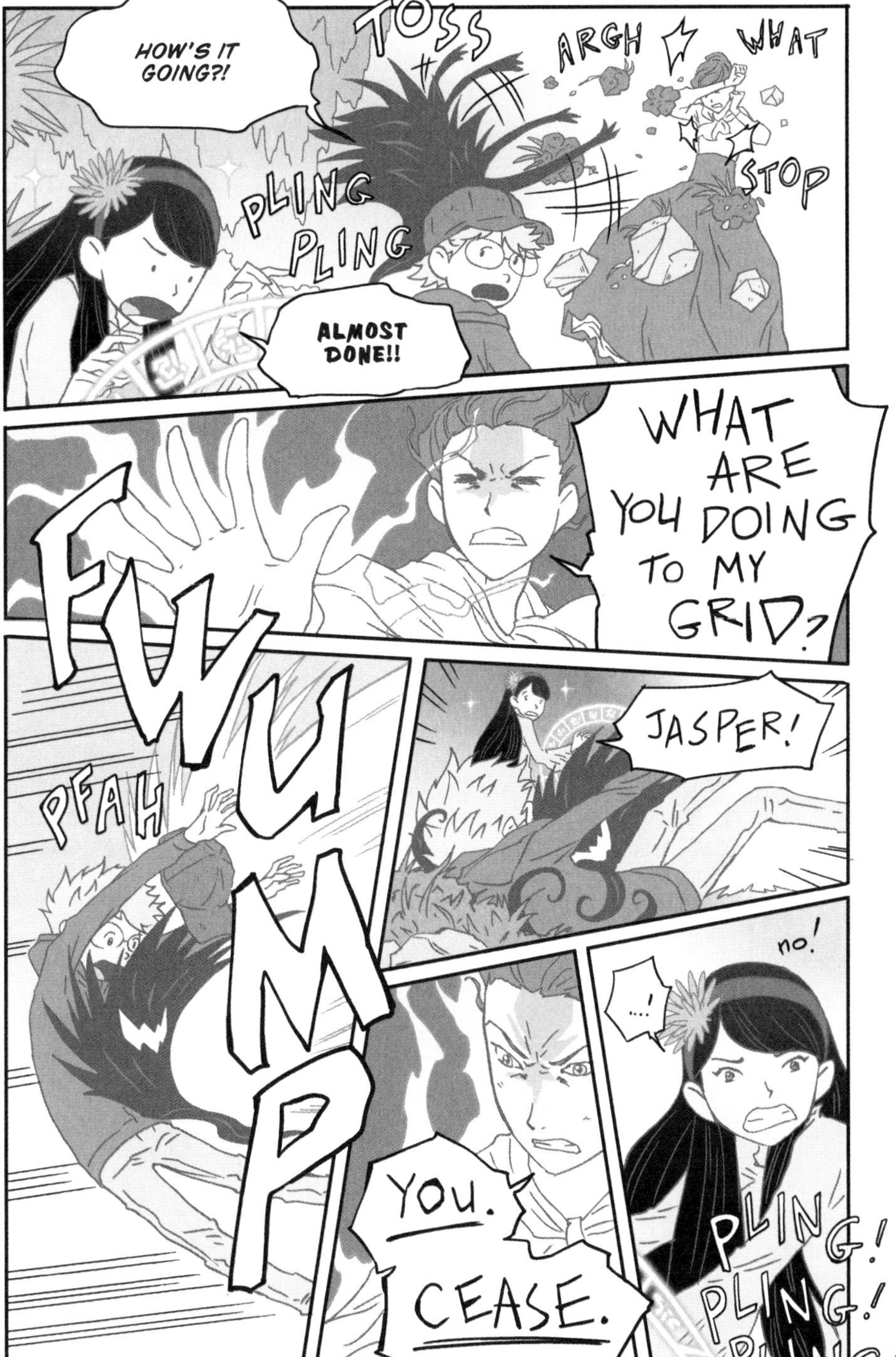
HOW'S IT GOING?!
TOSS
ARGH
WHAT
STOP
PLING
PLING
ALMOST DONE!!
WHAT ARE YOU DOING TO MY GRID?
FWUMP
PFAH
JASPER!
YOU.
CEASE.
no!
...!
PLING!
PLING!
PLING!

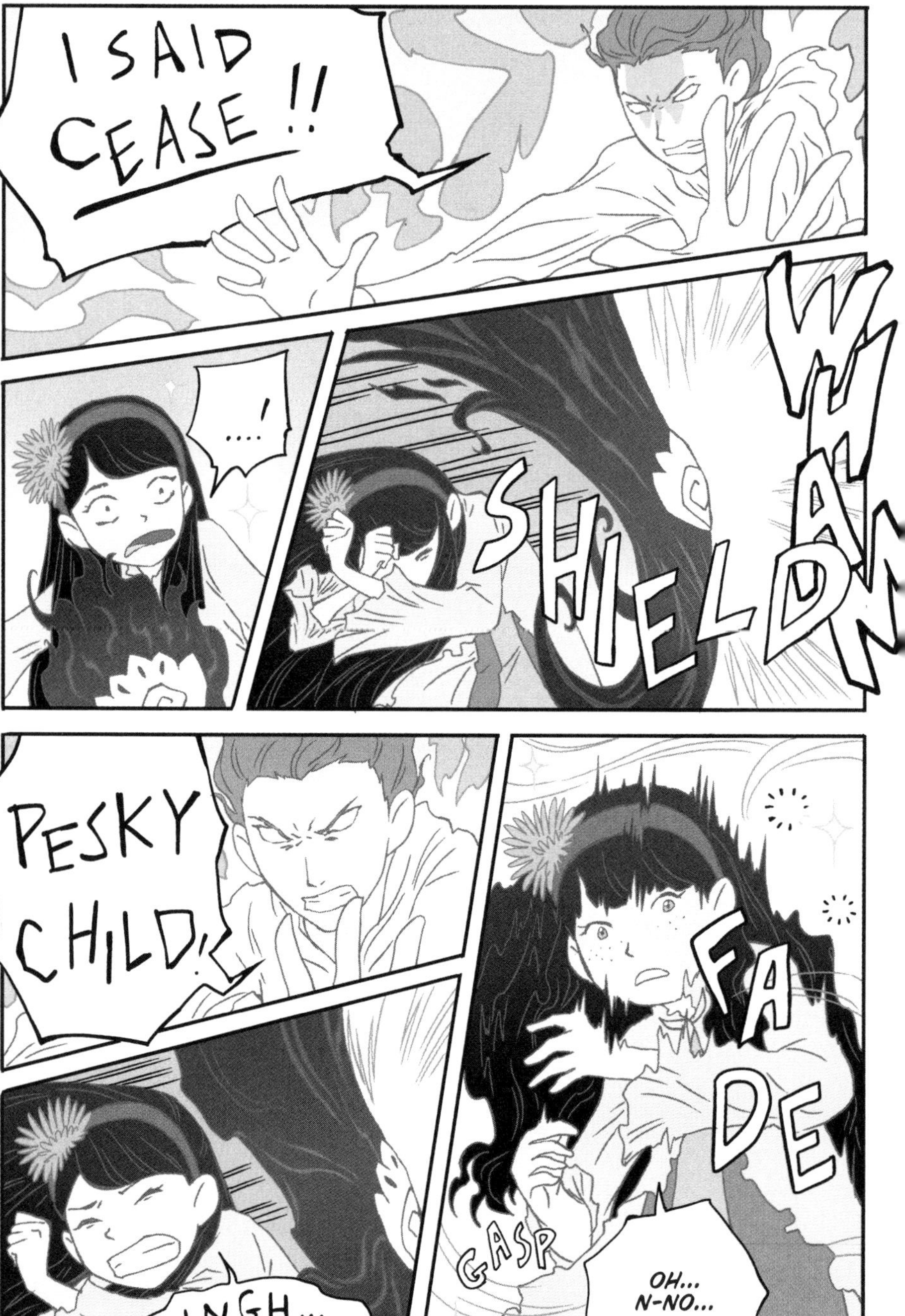
I SAID CEASE!!
....!
SHIELD
WHAM
PESKY CHILD!
NNGH... H-HOLD... ON...
FADE
GASP
OH... N-NO...

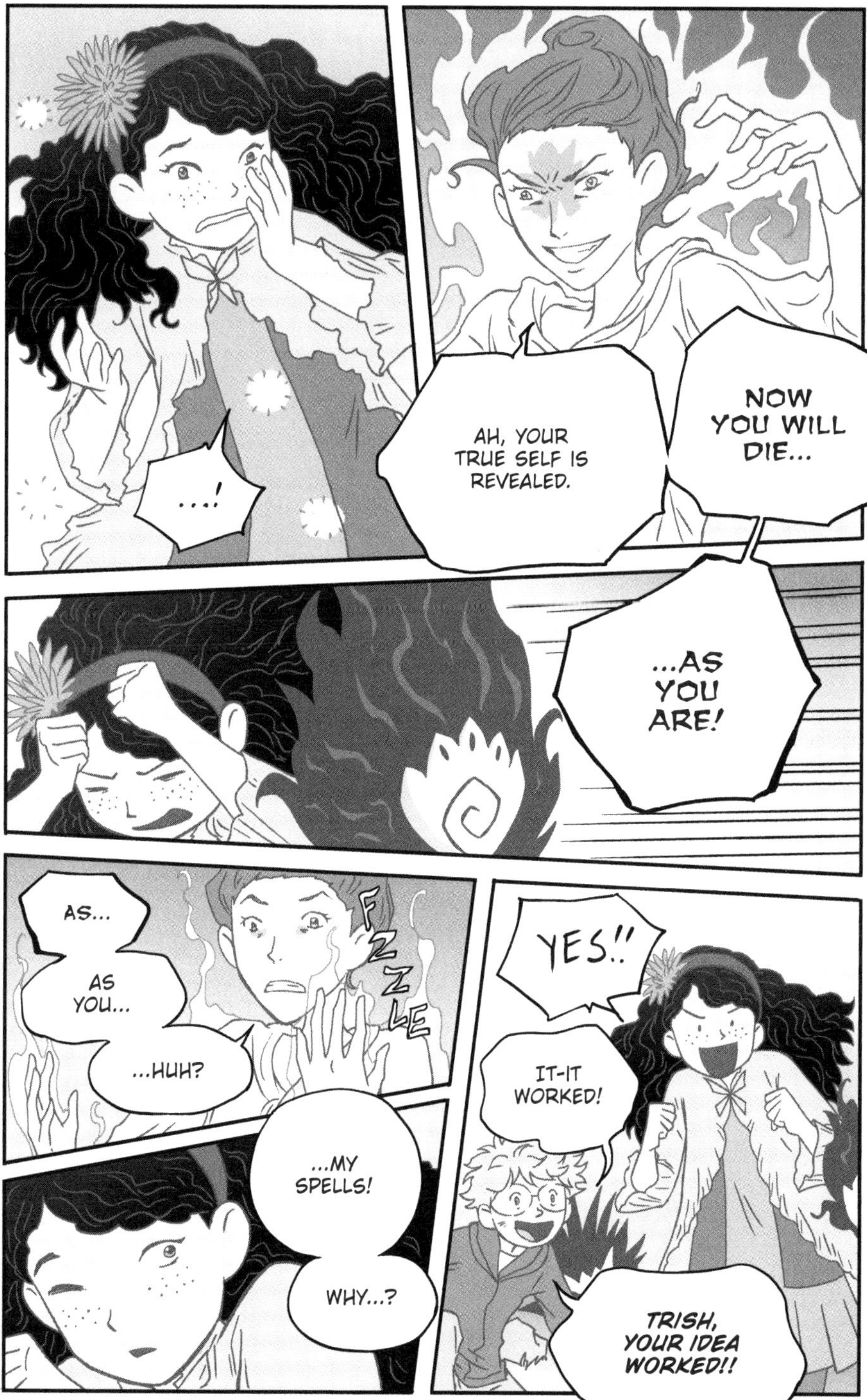
...!
AH, YOUR TRUE SELF IS REVEALED.
NOW YOU WILL DIE...
...AS YOU ARE!
AS...
AS YOU...
...HUH?
FZZZLE
...MY SPELLS!
WHY...?
YES!!
IT-IT WORKED!
TRISH, YOUR IDEA WORKED!!

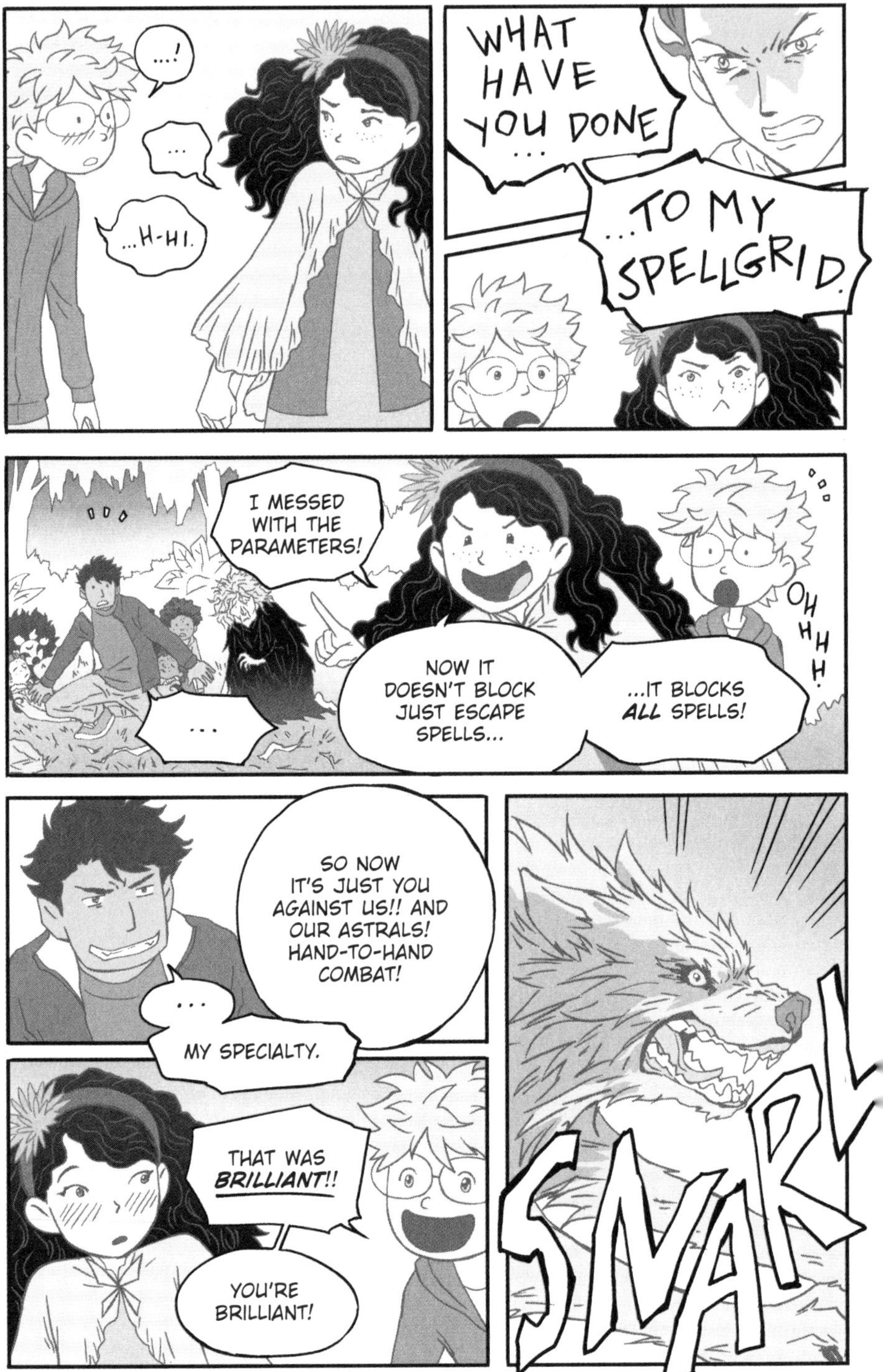

....!
...
...H-HI.
WHAT HAVE YOU DONE ...
...TO MY SPELLGRID.
I MESSED WITH THE PARAMETERS!
...
NOW IT DOESN'T BLOCK JUST ESCAPE SPELLS...
...IT BLOCKS ALL SPELLS!
OHHHH.
SO NOW IT'S JUST YOU AGAINST US!! AND OUR ASTRALS! HAND-TO-HAND COMBAT!
...
MY SPECIALTY.
THAT WAS BRILLIANT!!
YOU'RE BRILLIANT!
SNARL

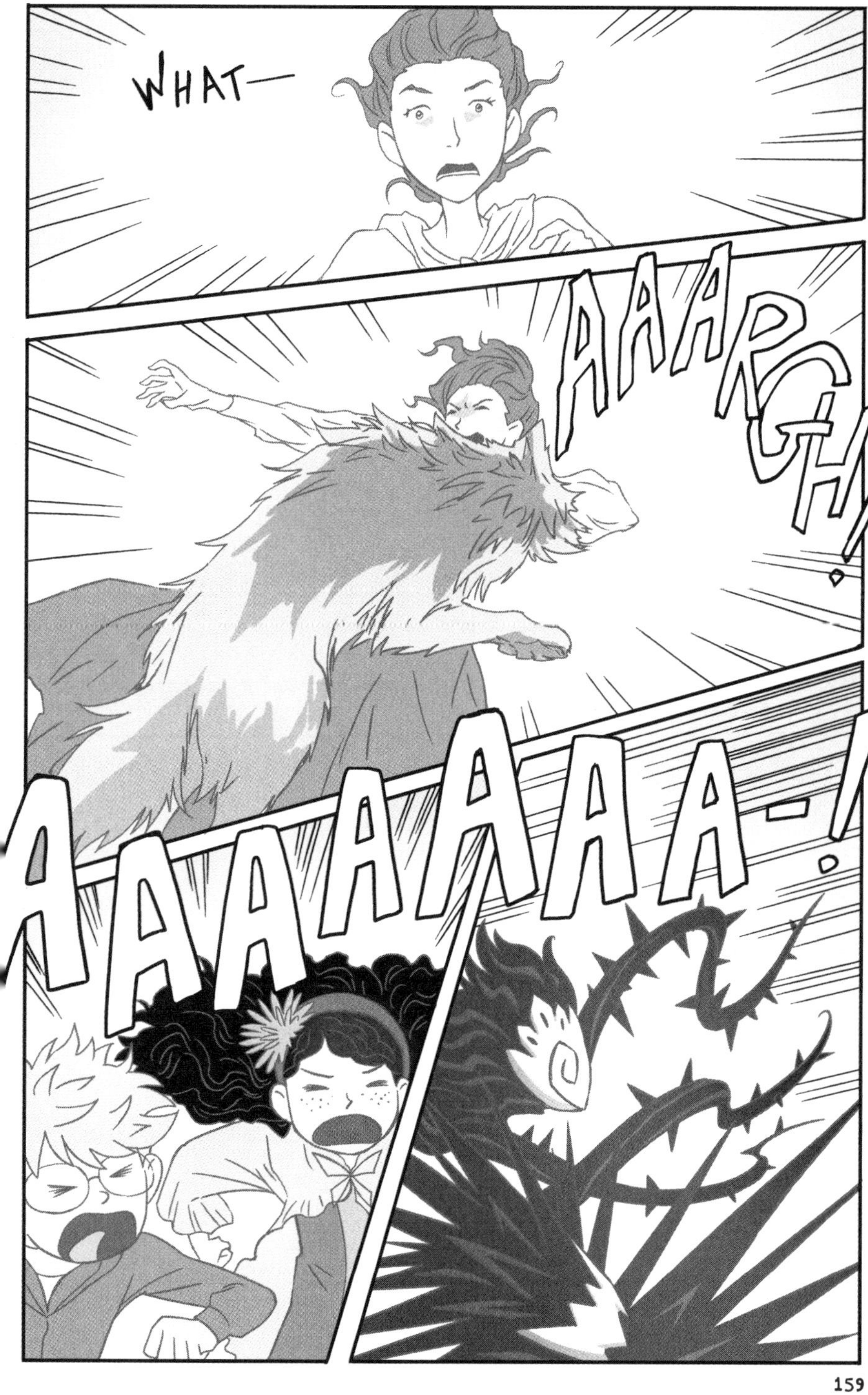
WHAT—
AAARGH!!
AAAAAAAA-!!

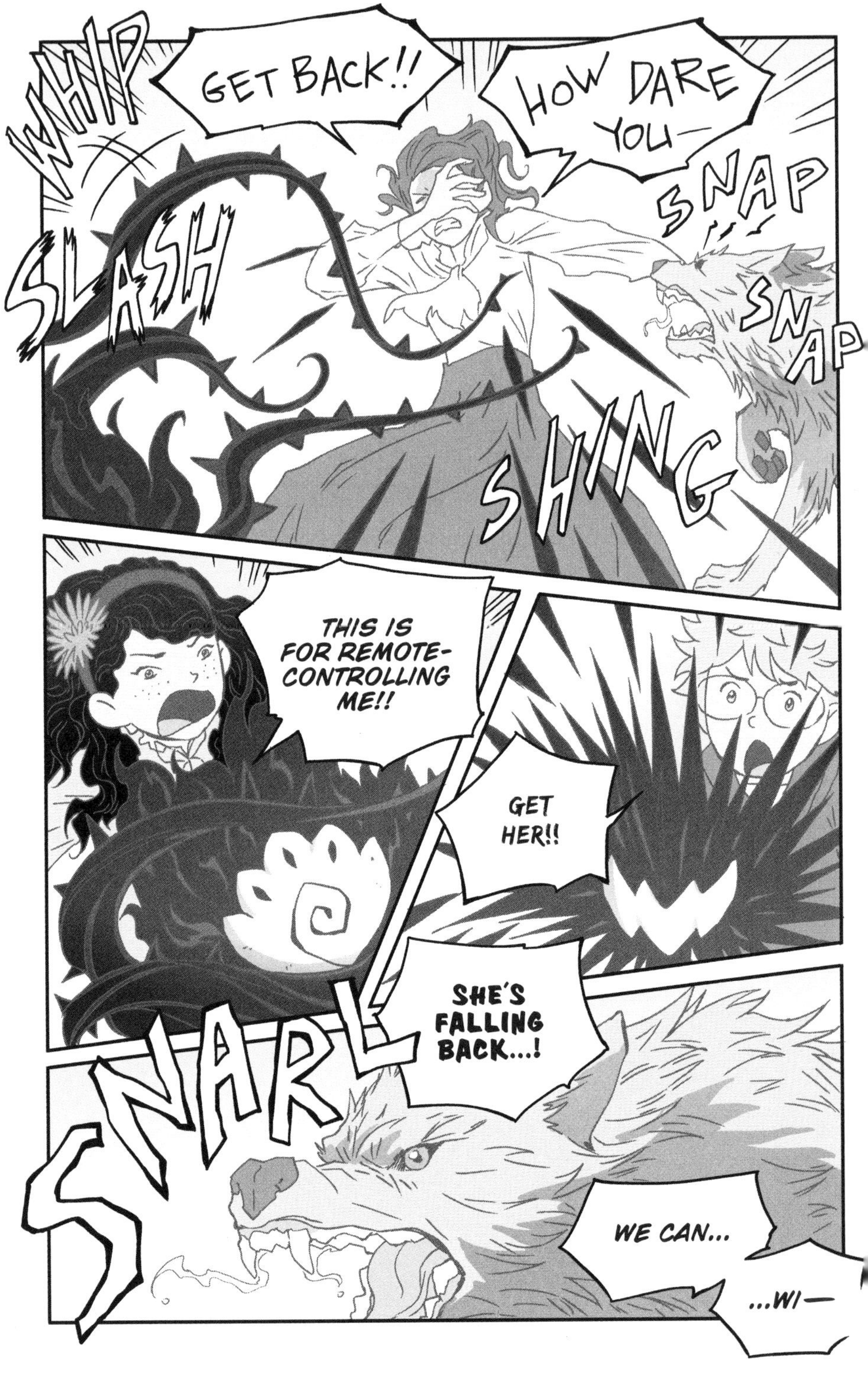
WHIP
GET BACK!!
HOW DARE YOU
SLASH
SNAP
SNAP
SHING
THIS IS FOR REMOTE-CONTROLLING ME!!
GET HER!!
SHE'S FALLING BACK...!
SNARL
WE CAN...
...WI—

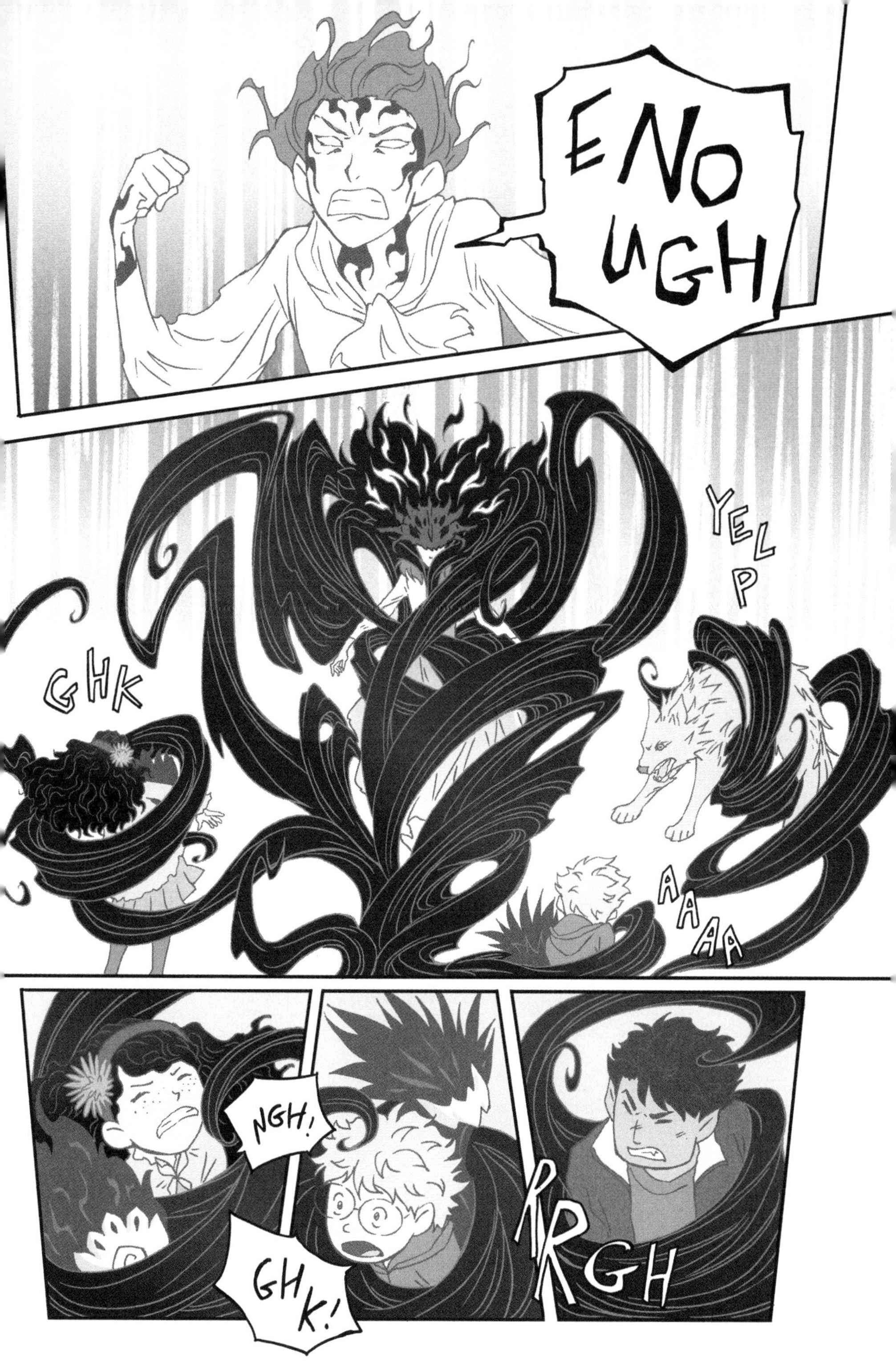
ENOUGH
YELP
GHK
AAAA
NGH!
GHK!
RRRGH

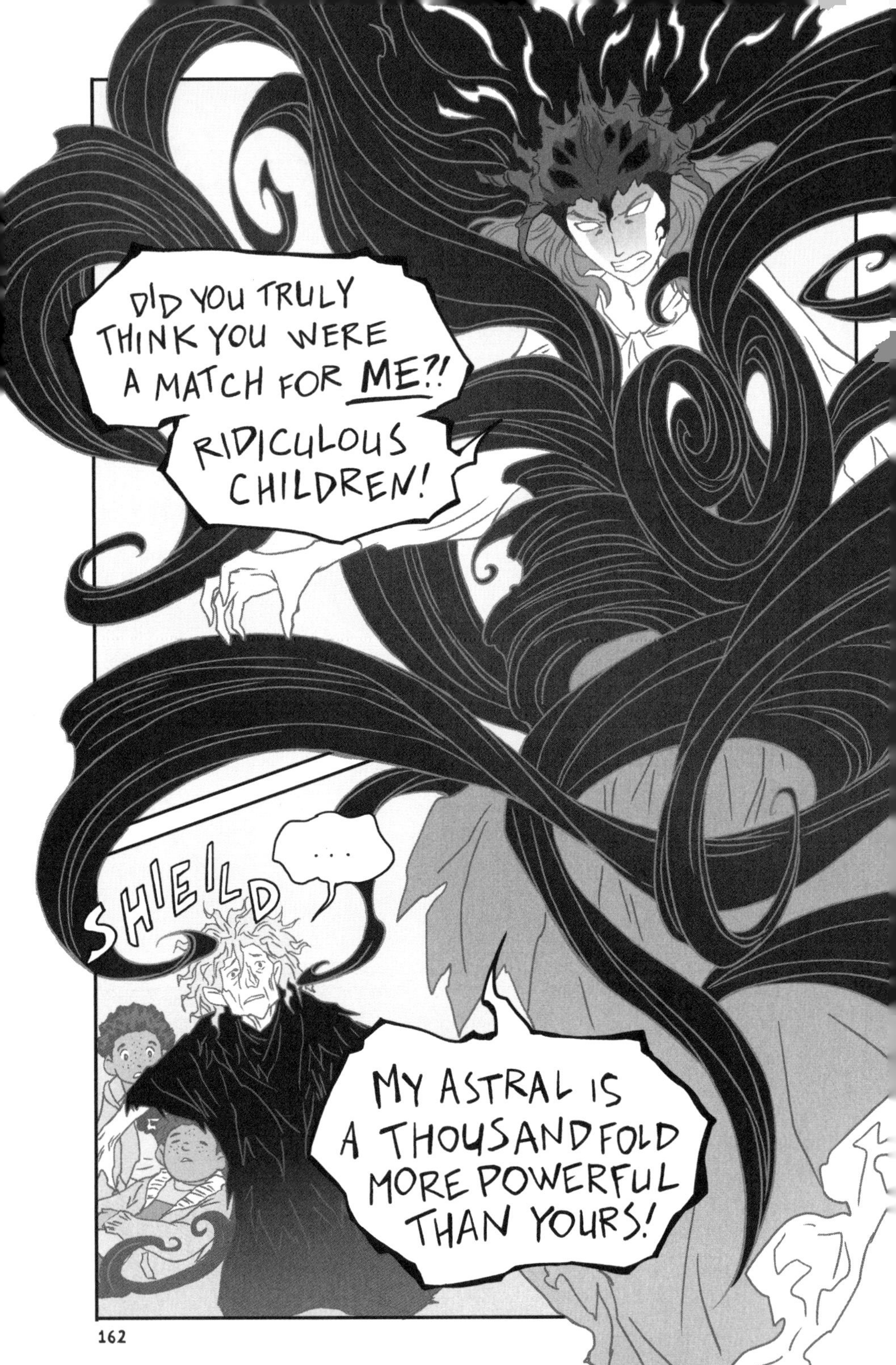
DID YOU TRULY THINK YOU WERE A MATCH FOR ME?!
RIDICULOUS CHILDREN!
SHIELD
...
MY ASTRAL IS A THOUSANDFOLD MORE POWERFUL THAN YOURS!

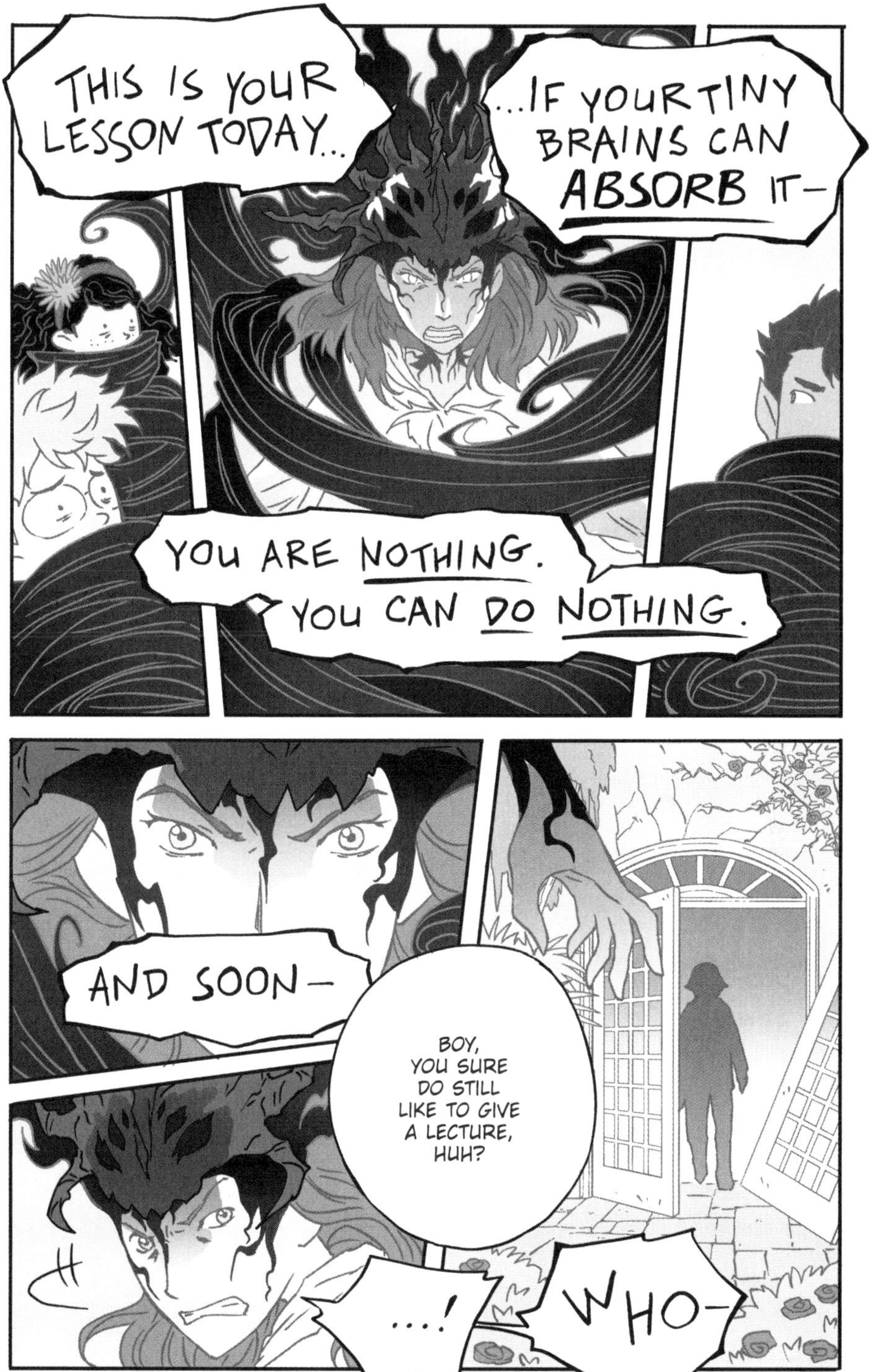
THIS IS YOUR LESSON TODAY...
...IF YOUR TINY BRAINS CAN ABSORB IT—
YOU ARE NOTHING.
YOU CAN DO NOTHING.
AND SOON—
BOY, YOU SURE DO STILL LIKE TO GIVE A LECTURE, HUH?
H
...!
WHO—

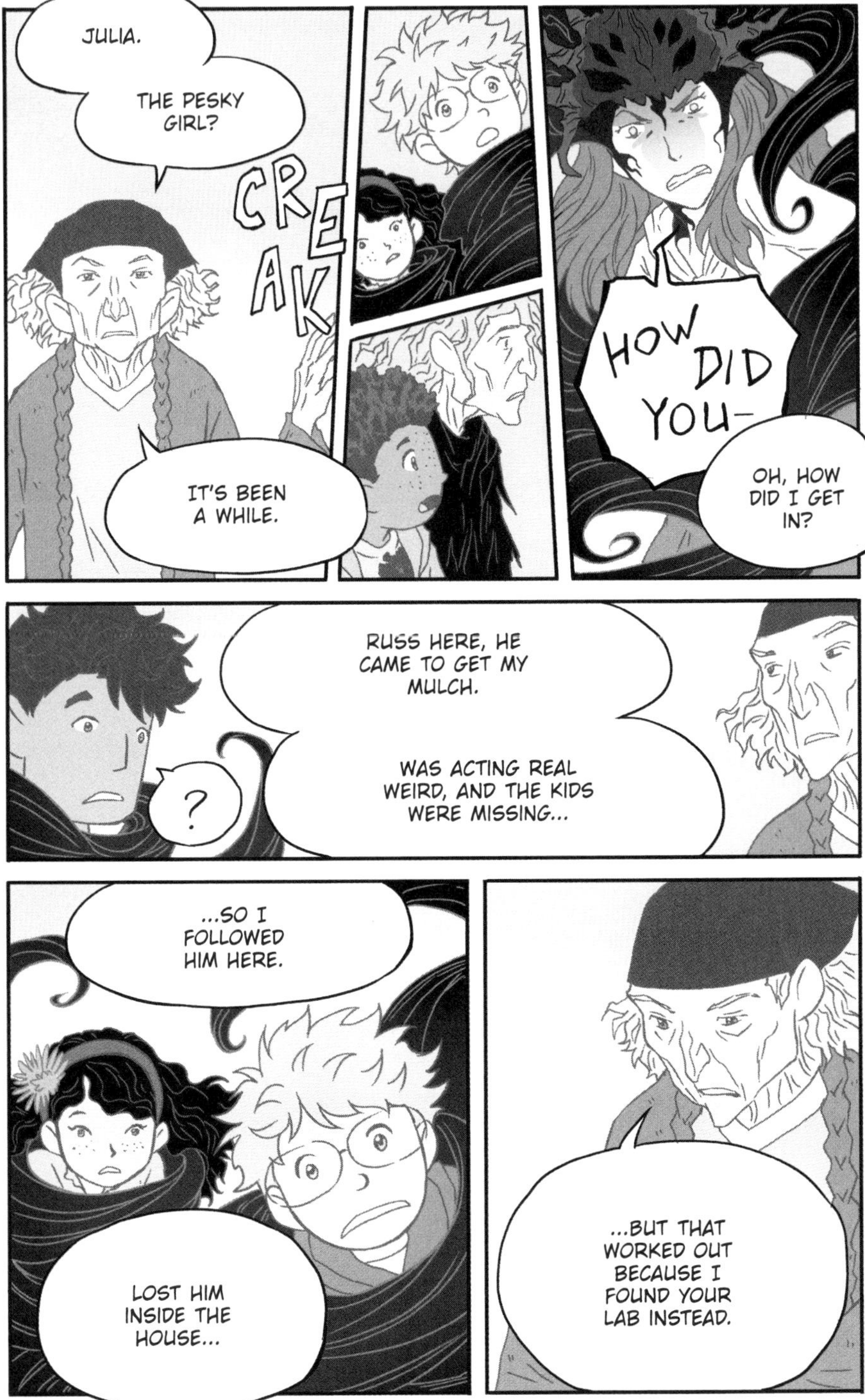
JULIA.
THE PESKY GIRL?
CREAK
IT'S BEEN A WHILE.
HOW DID YOU-
OH, HOW DID I GET IN?
RUSS HERE, HE CAME TO GET MY MULCH.
WAS ACTING REAL WEIRD, AND THE KIDS WERE MISSING...
?
...SO I FOLLOWED HIM HERE.
LOST HIM INSIDE THE HOUSE...
...BUT THAT WORKED OUT BECAUSE I FOUND YOUR LAB INSTEAD.

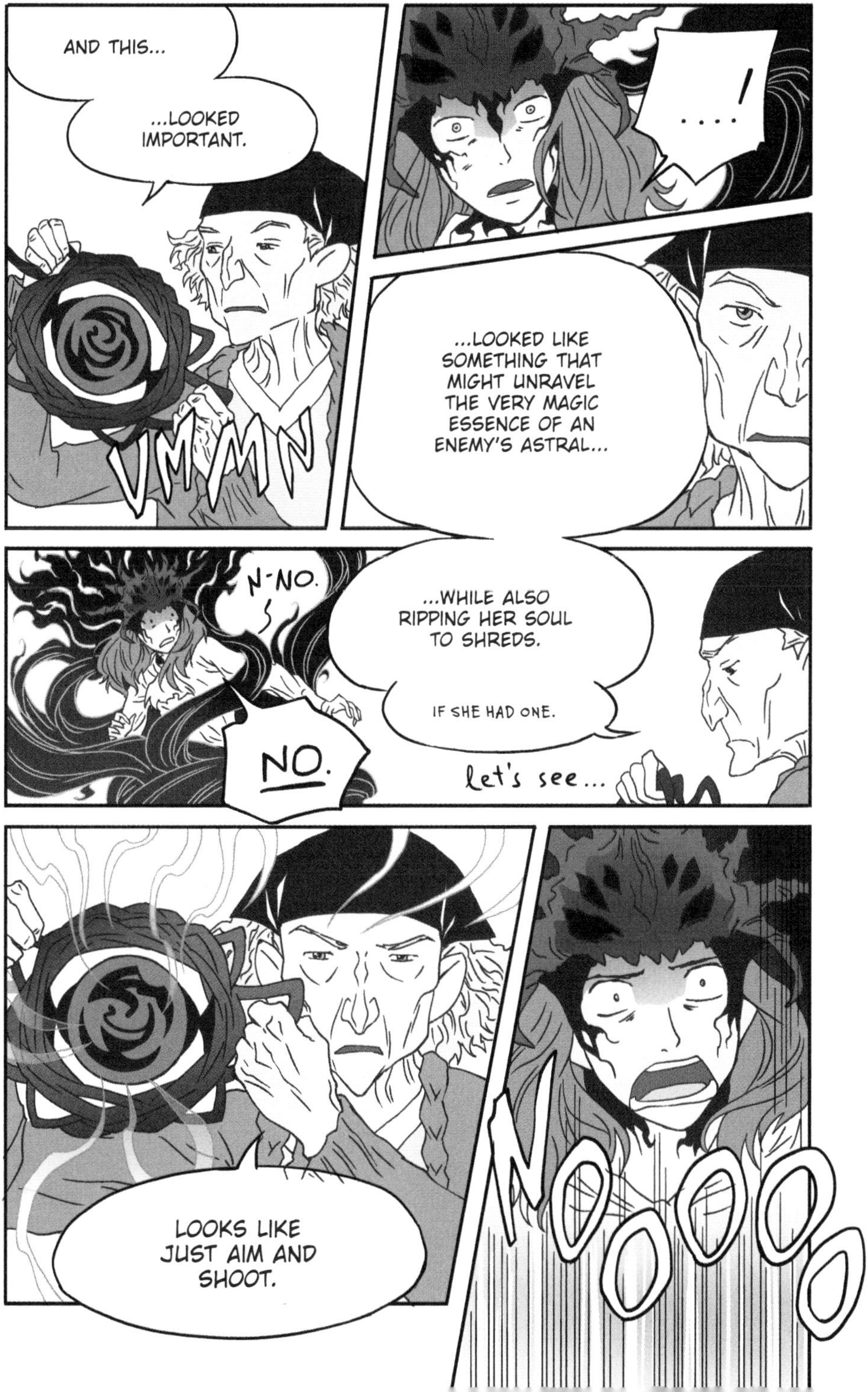
AND THIS...
...LOOKED IMPORTANT.
VMMN
....!
...LOOKED LIKE SOMETHING THAT MIGHT UNRAVEL THE VERY MAGIC ESSENCE OF AN ENEMY'S ASTRAL...
N-NO.
...WHILE ALSO RIPPING HER SOUL TO SHREDS.
IF SHE HAD ONE.
NO.
let's see...
LOOKS LIKE JUST AIM AND SHOOT.
NOOOOOO

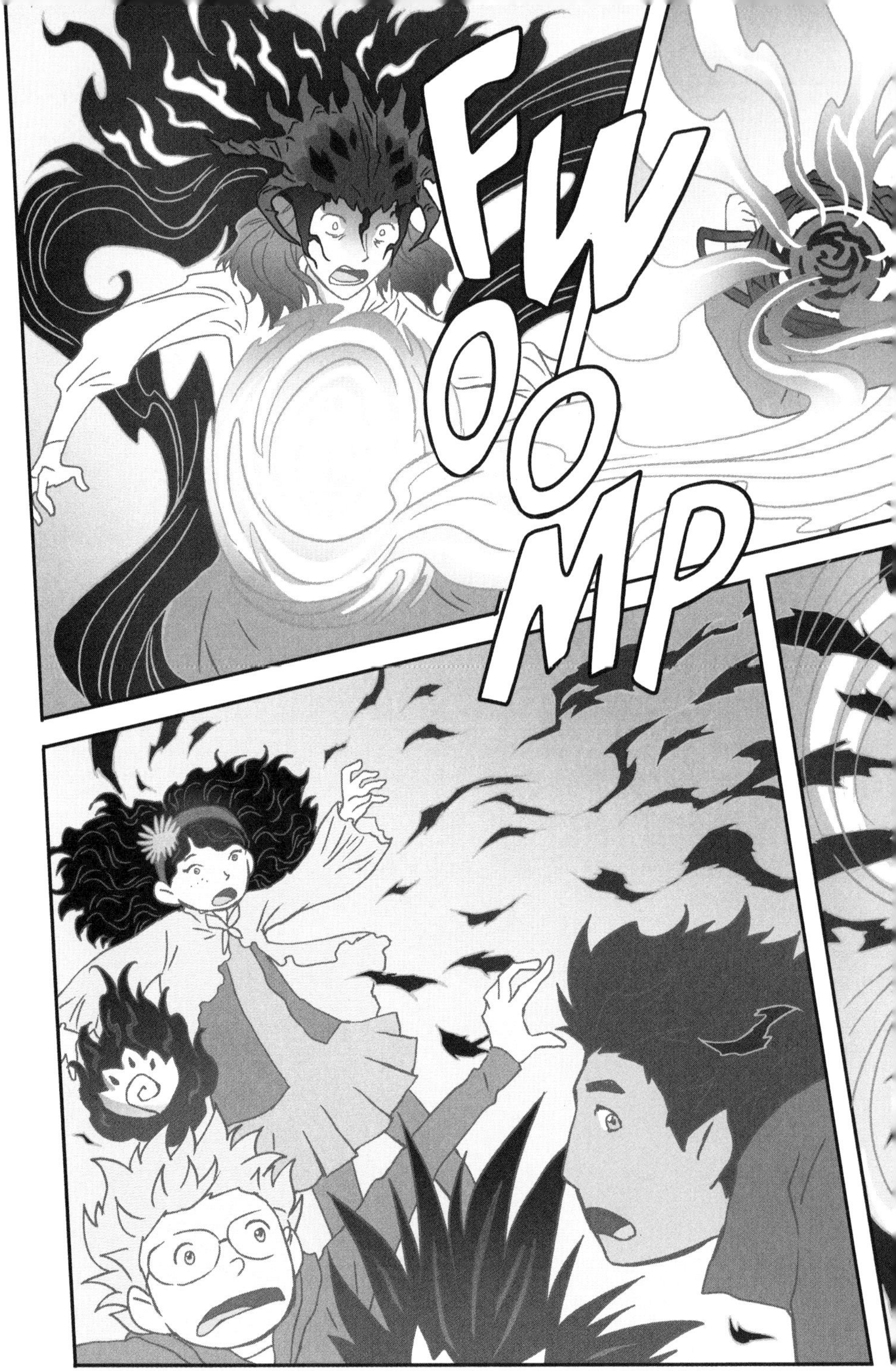
FWOOOMP

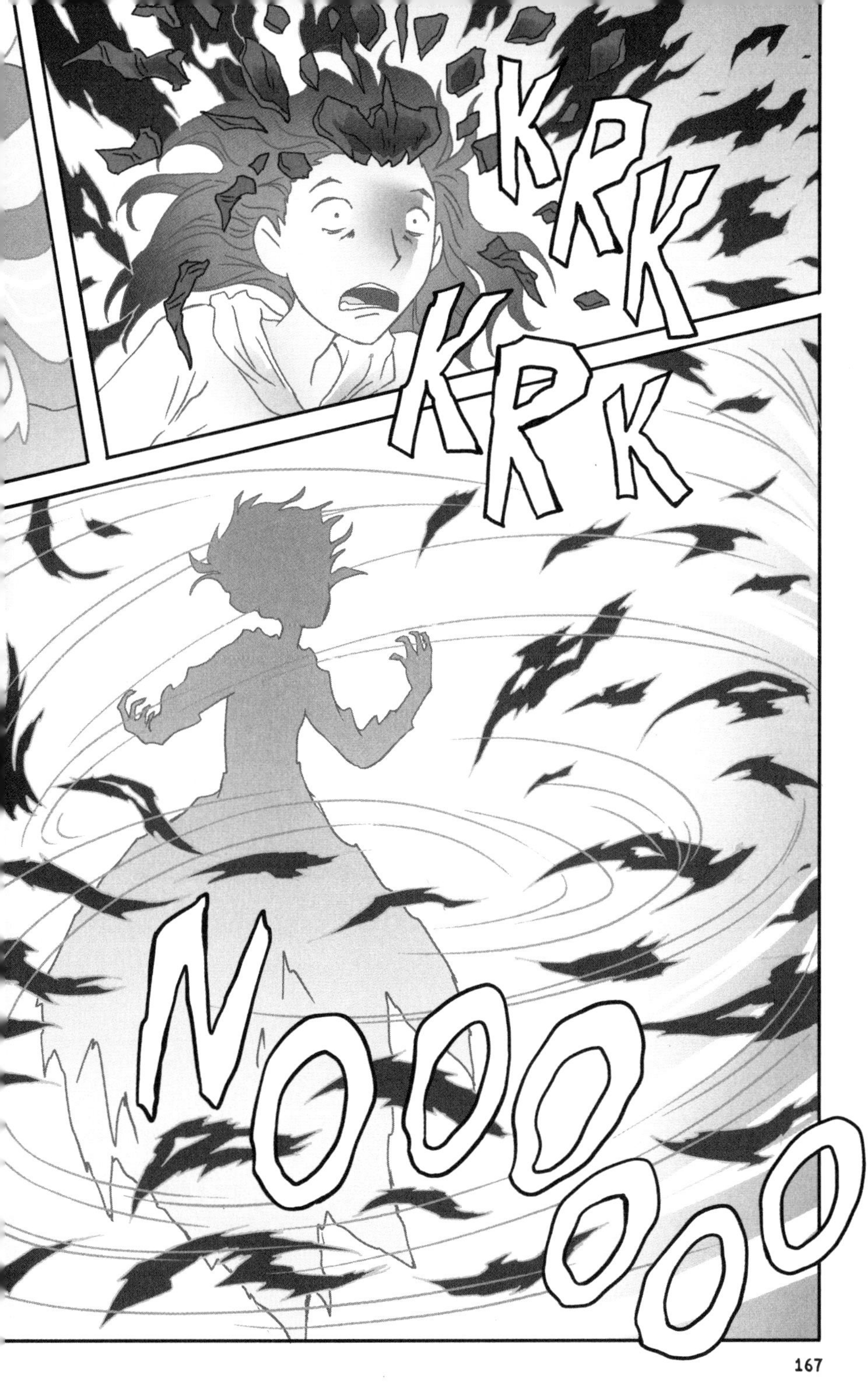
KRK
KRK
KRK
NOOOOOOOO

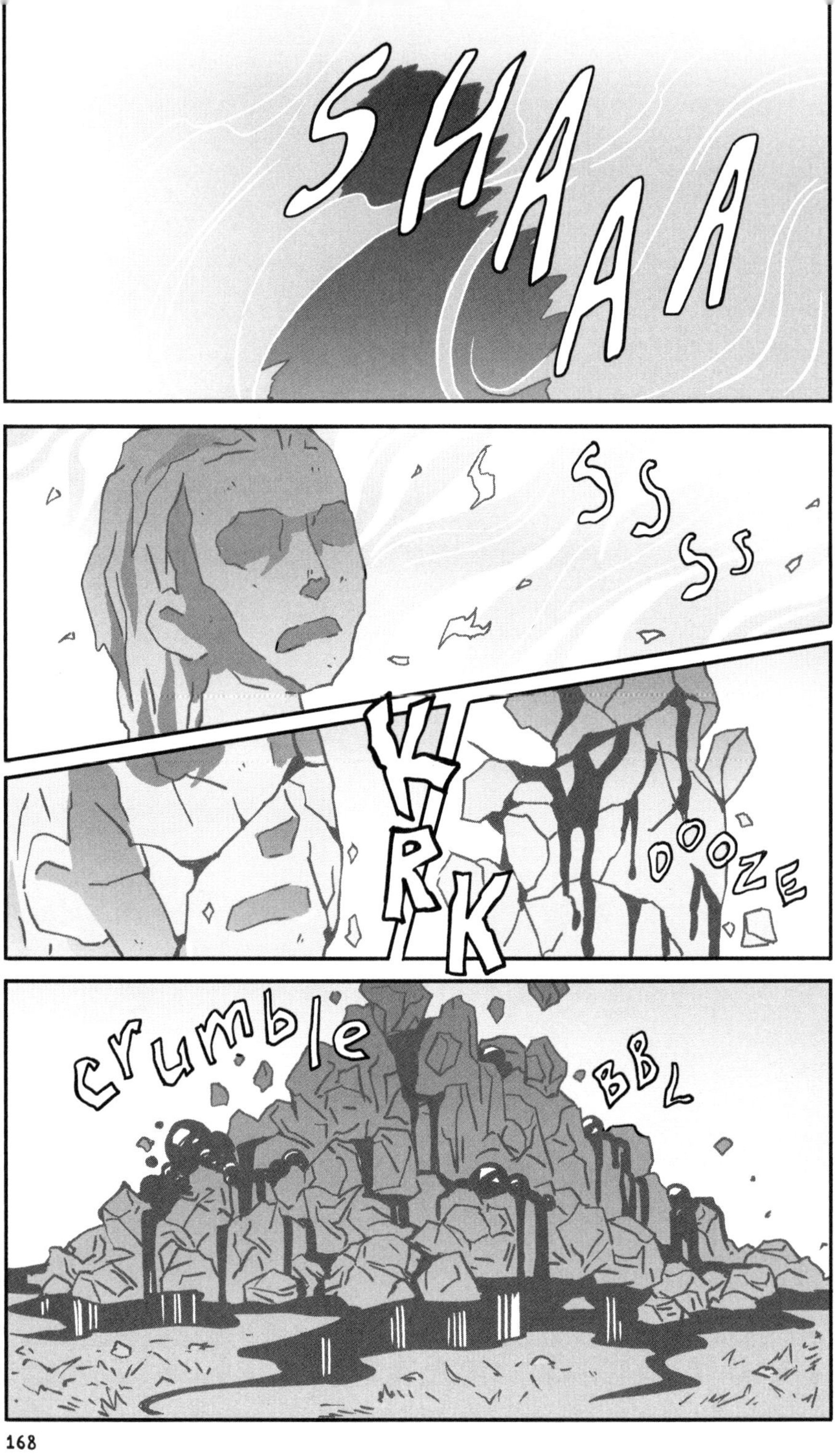
SHAAAA
SSSS
KRK
DOOZE
crumble
BBL

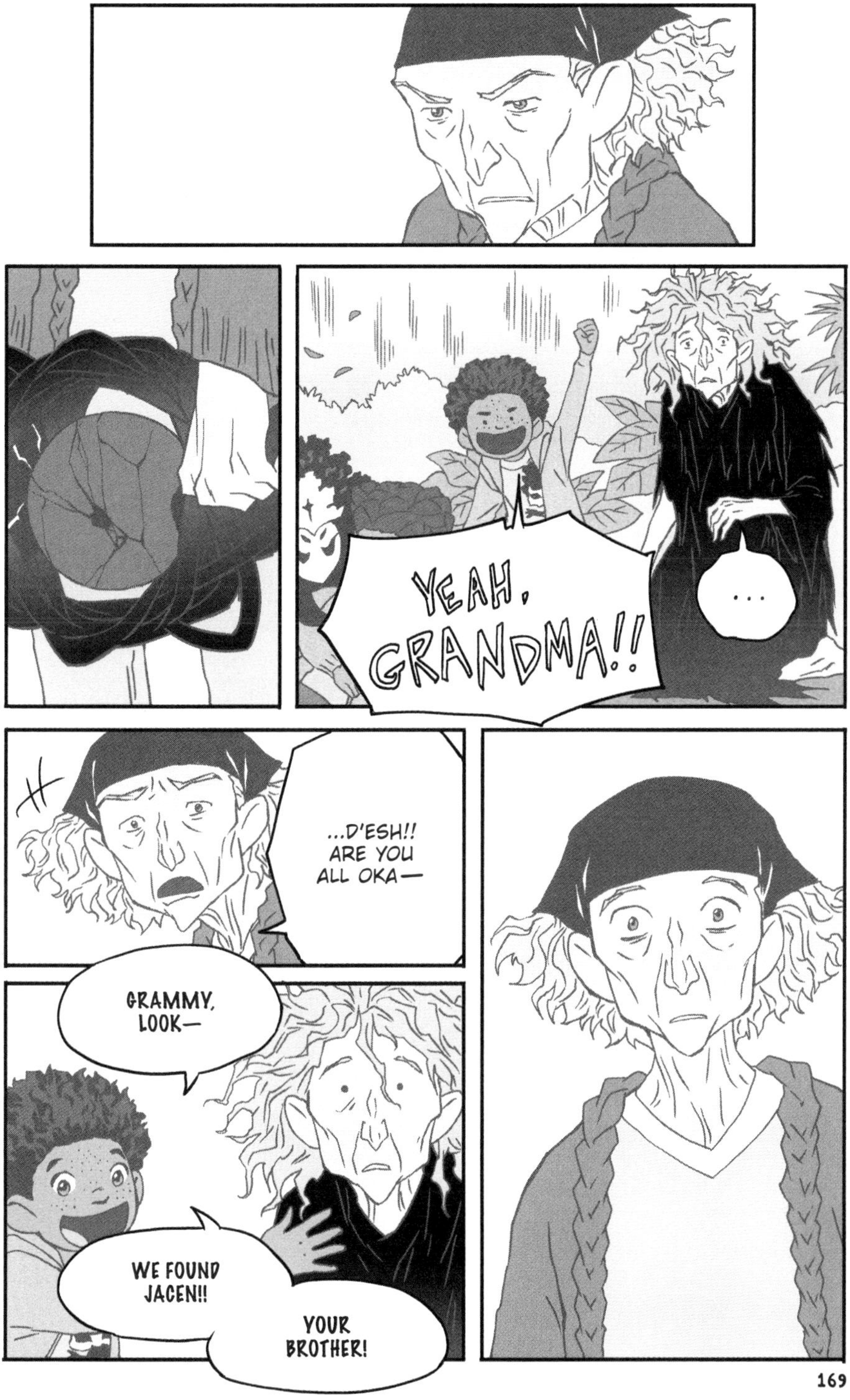
YEAH, GRANDMA!!
...
...D'ESH!! ARE YOU ALL OKA—
GRAMMY, LOOK—
WE FOUND JACEN!!
YOUR BROTHER!

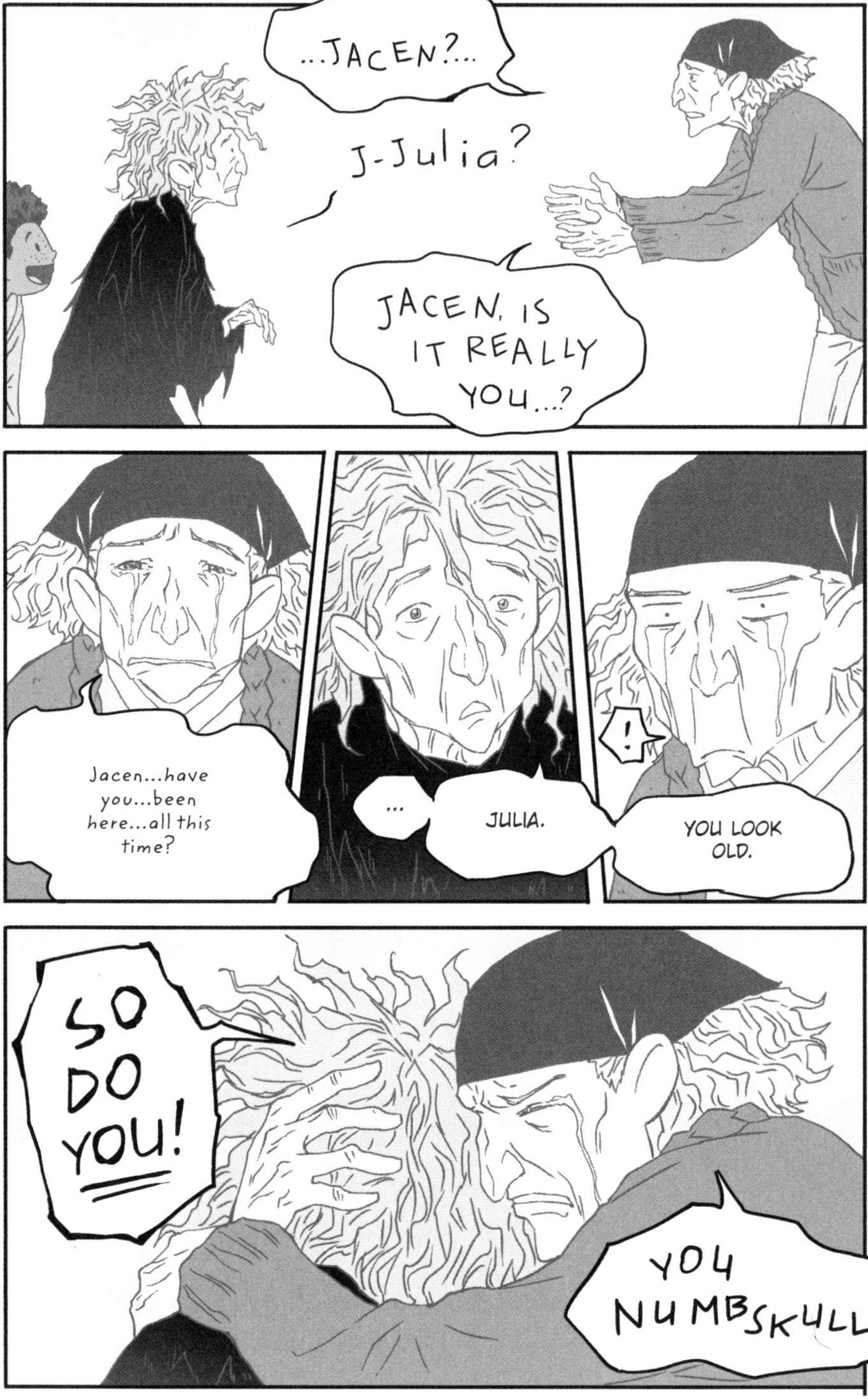
...JACEN?...
J-Julia?
JACEN, IS IT REALLY YOU...?
Jacen...have you...been here...all this time?
...
JULIA.
!
YOU LOOK OLD.
SO DO YOU!
YOU NUMBSKULL.

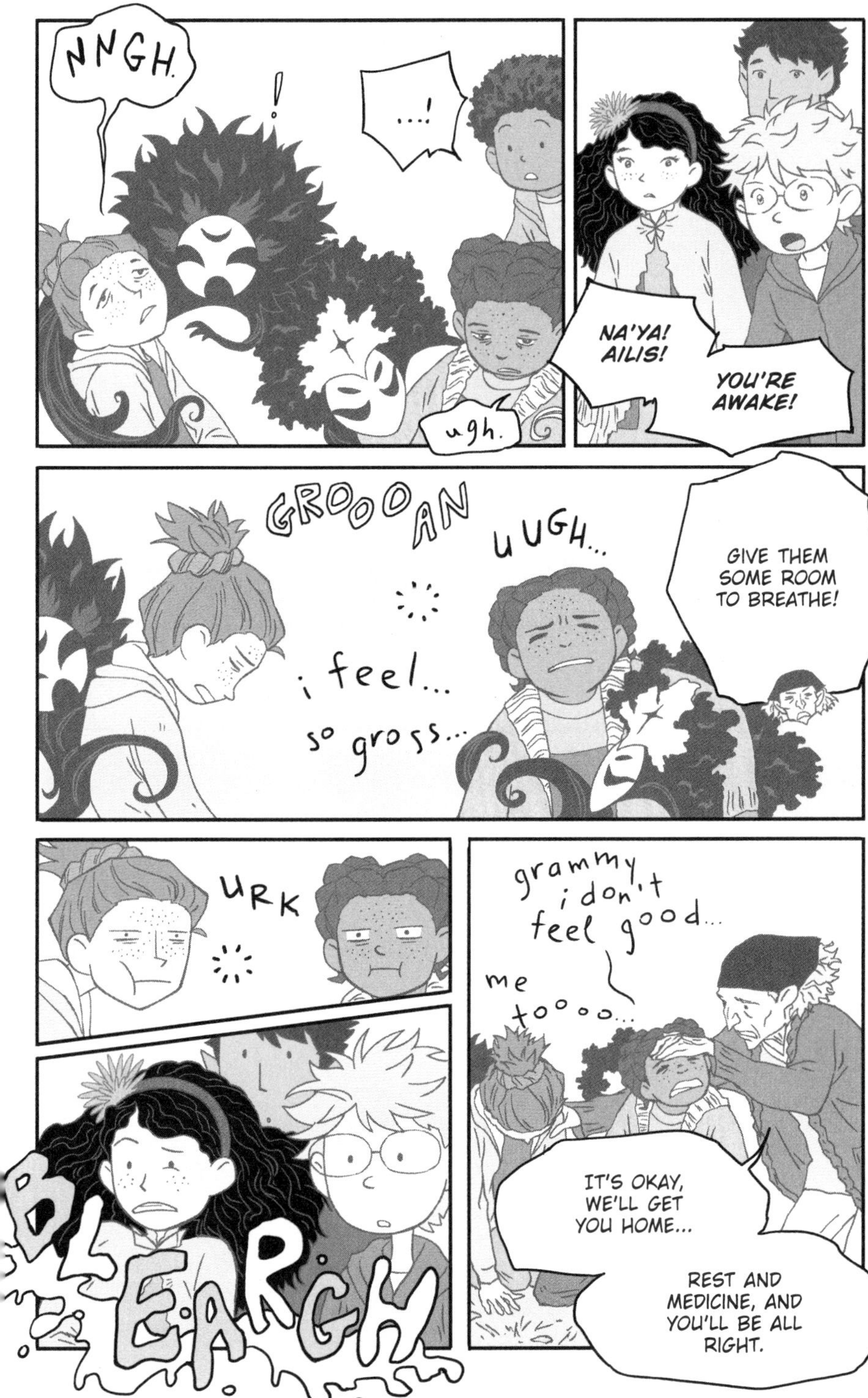
NNGH.
!
...!
ugh.
NA'YA! AILIS!
YOU'RE AWAKE!
GROOOAN
UUGH...
i feel... so gross...
GIVE THEM SOME ROOM TO BREATHE!
URK
BLEARGH
grammy, i don't feel good...
me toooo...
IT'S OKAY, WE'LL GET YOU HOME...
REST AND MEDICINE, AND YOU'LL BE ALL RIGHT.

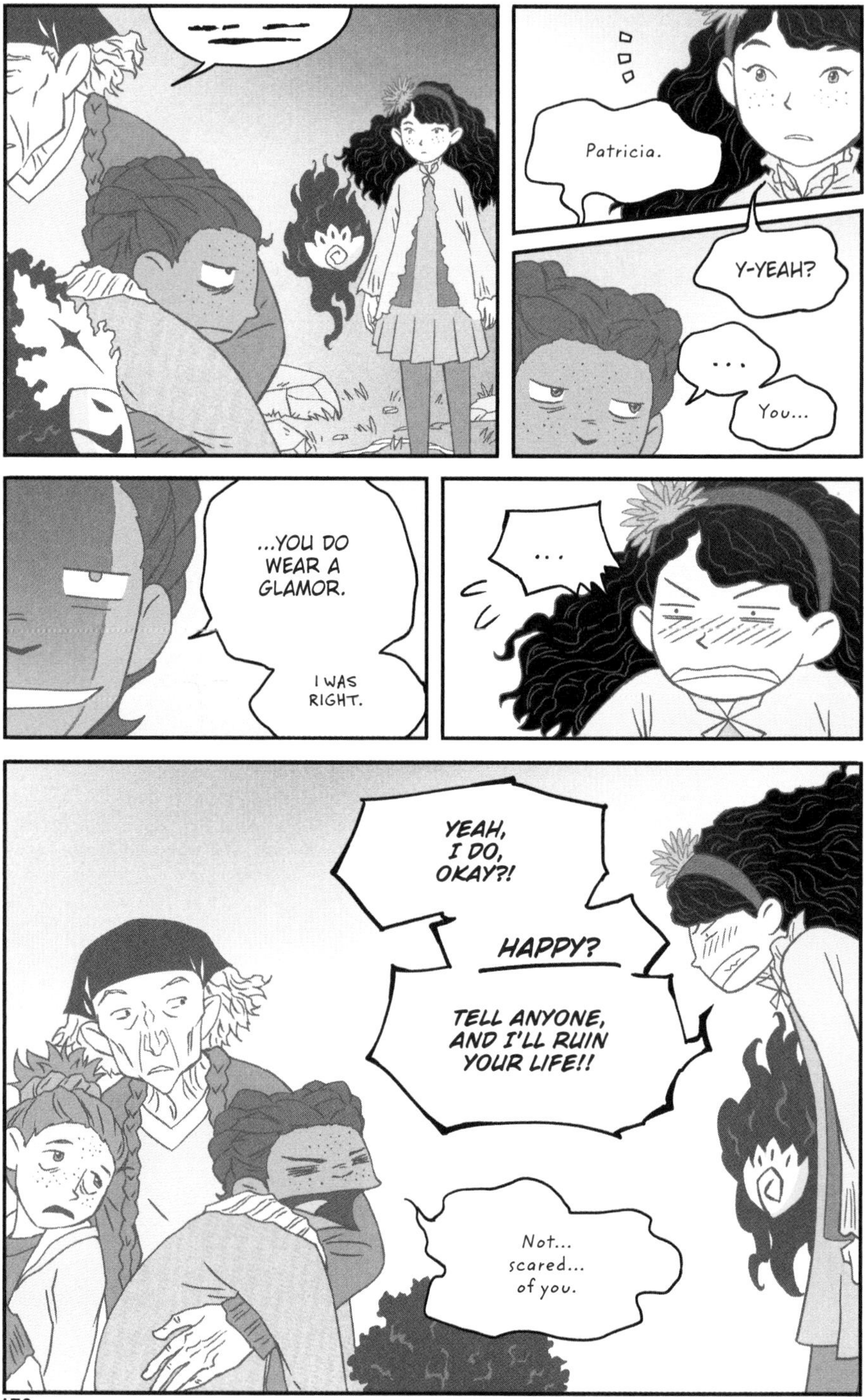
Patricia.
Y-YEAH?
...
You...
...YOU DO WEAR A GLAMOR.
I WAS RIGHT.
...
YEAH, I DO, OKAY?!
HAPPY?
TELL ANYONE, AND I'LL RUIN YOUR LIFE!!
Not... scared... of you.

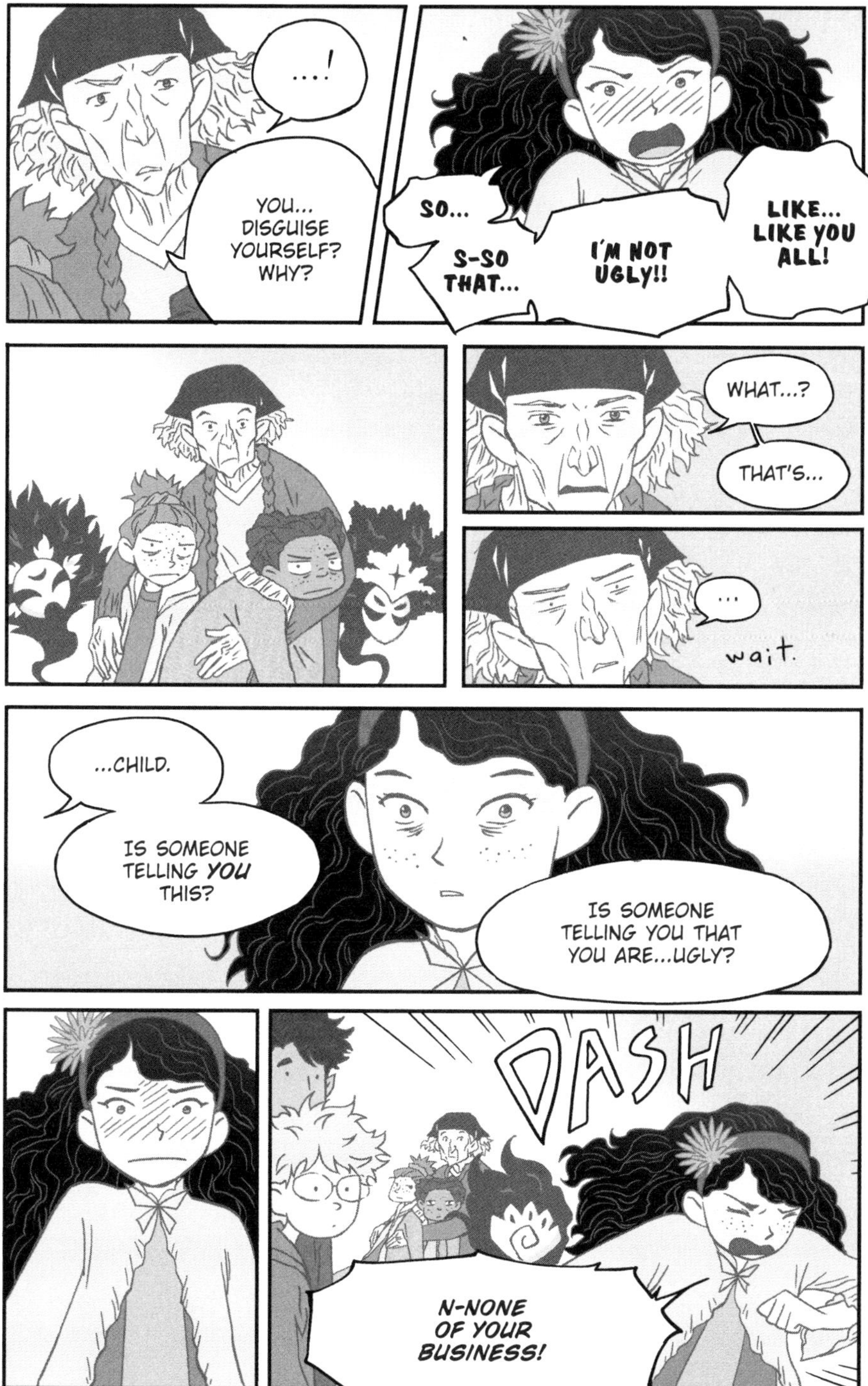
...!
YOU... DISGUISE YOURSELF? WHY?
SO...
S-SO THAT...
I'M NOT UGLY!!
LIKE... LIKE YOU ALL!
WHAT...?
THAT'S...
...
wait.
...CHILD.
IS SOMEONE TELLING *YOU* THIS?
IS SOMEONE TELLING YOU THAT YOU ARE...UGLY?
DASH
N-NONE OF YOUR BUSINESS!

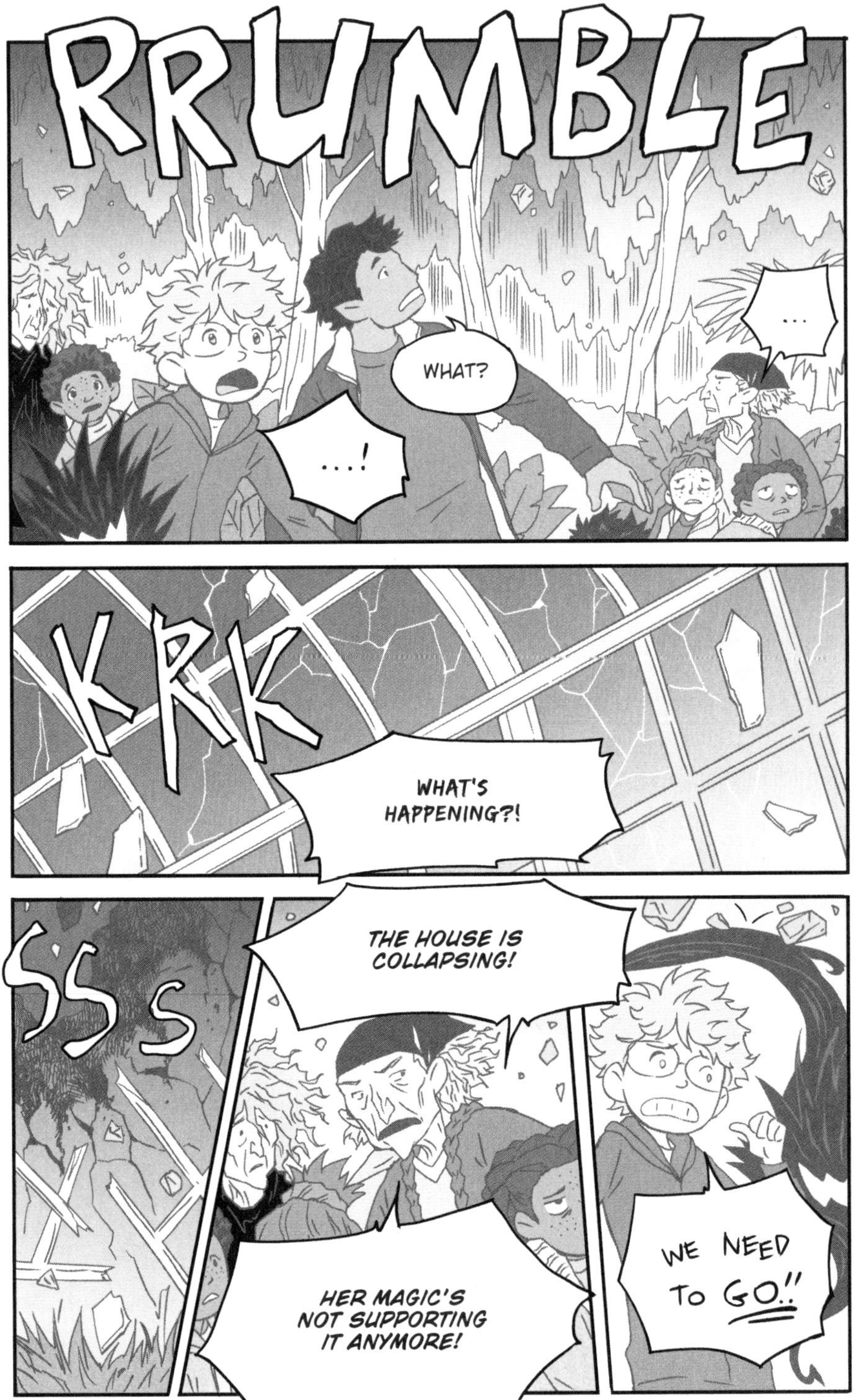
RRUMBLE
...
WHAT?
...!
KRK
WHAT'S HAPPENING?!
SSS
THE HOUSE IS COLLAPSING!
HER MAGIC'S NOT SUPPORTING IT ANYMORE!
WE NEED TO GO!!

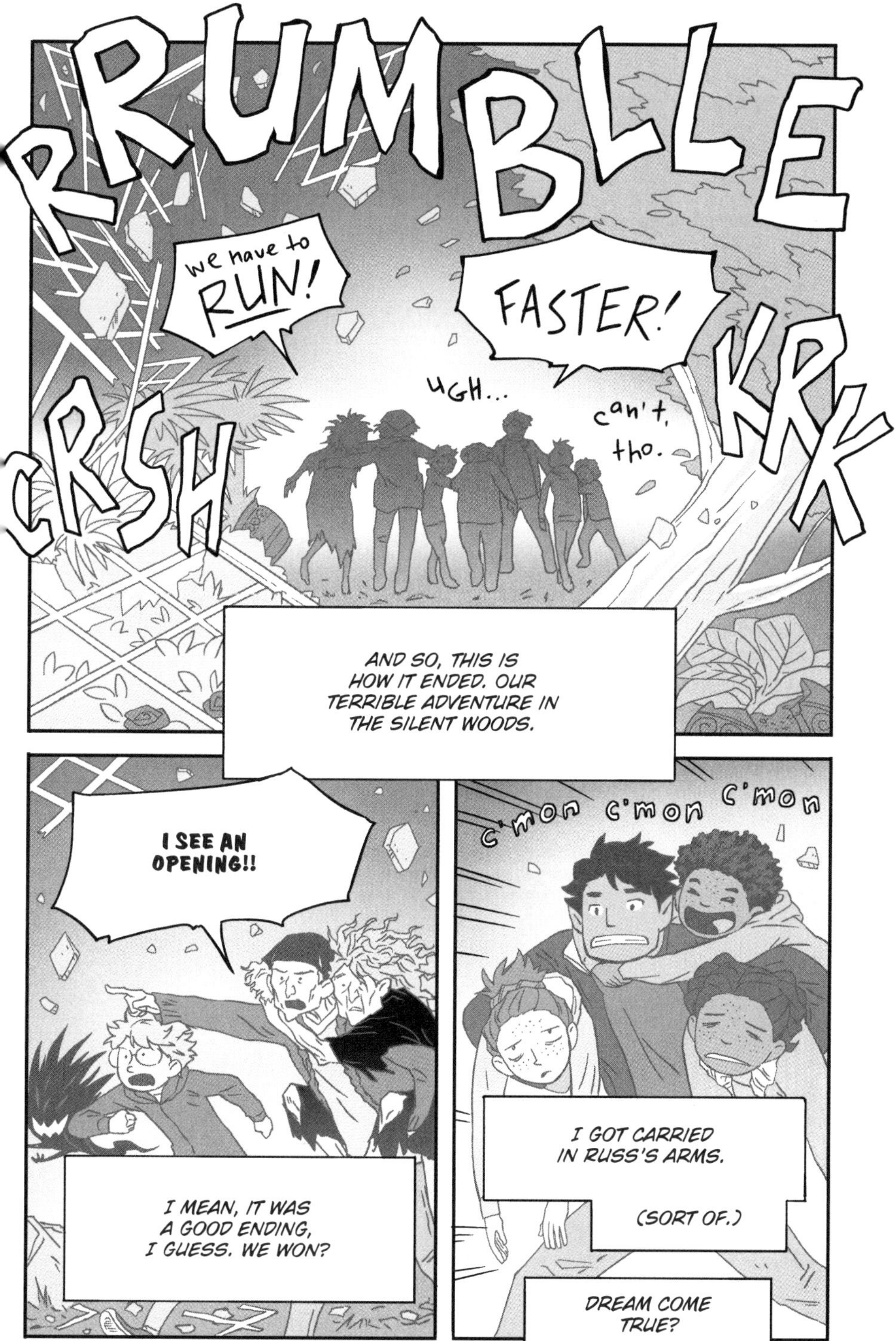

RRUMBLE
we have to RUN!
FASTER!
CRSH
UGH...
can't, tho.
KRK
AND SO, THIS IS HOW IT ENDED. OUR TERRIBLE ADVENTURE IN THE SILENT WOODS.
I SEE AN OPENING!!
I MEAN, IT WAS A GOOD ENDING, I GUESS. WE WON?
c'mon c'mon c'mon
I GOT CARRIED IN RUSS'S ARMS.
(SORT OF.)
DREAM COME TRUE?

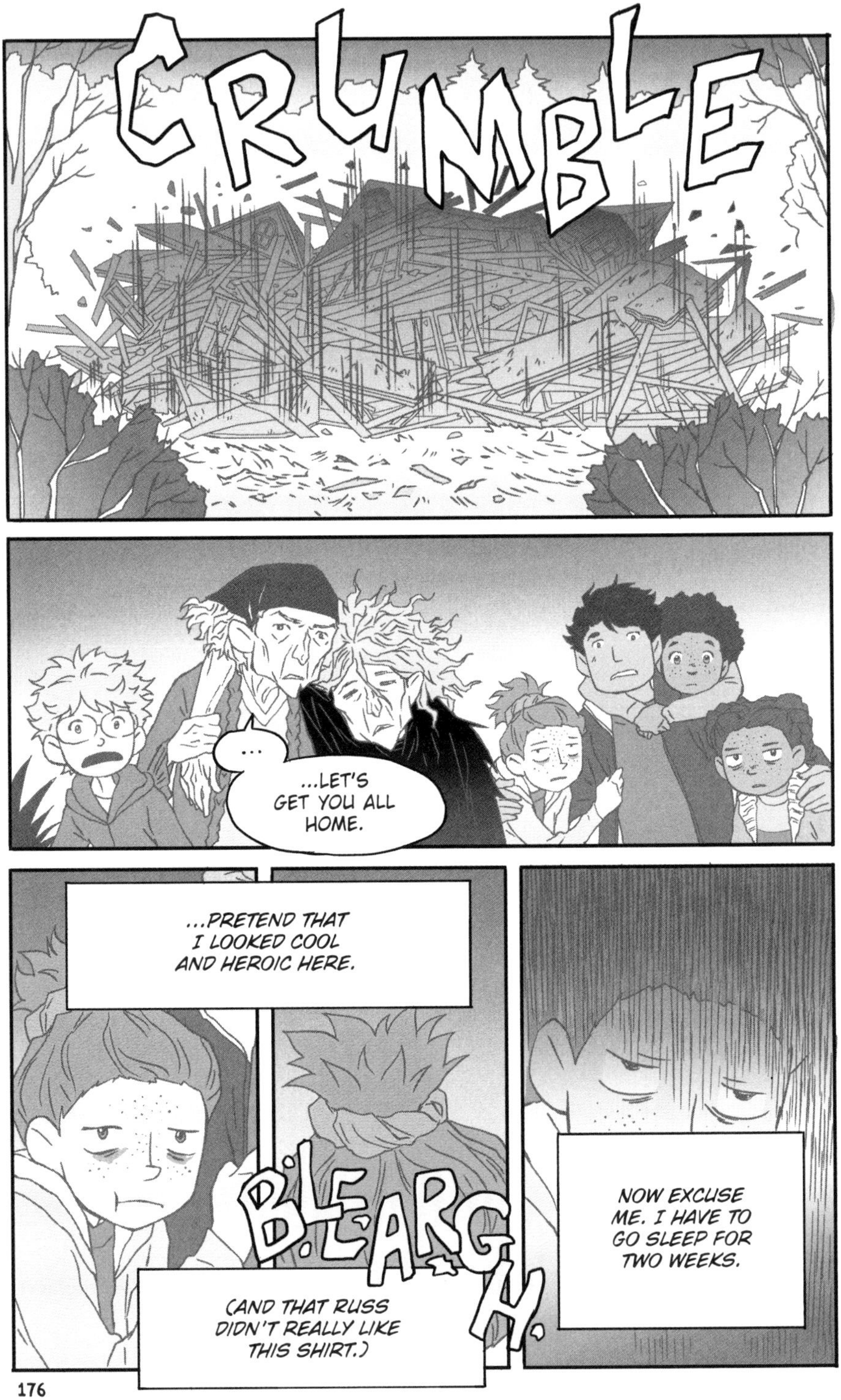
CRUMBLE
...
...LET'S GET YOU ALL HOME.
...PRETEND THAT I LOOKED COOL AND HEROIC HERE.
BLEARGH.
(AND THAT RUSS DIDN'T REALLY LIKE THIS SHIRT.)
NOW EXCUSE ME. I HAVE TO GO SLEEP FOR TWO WEEKS.

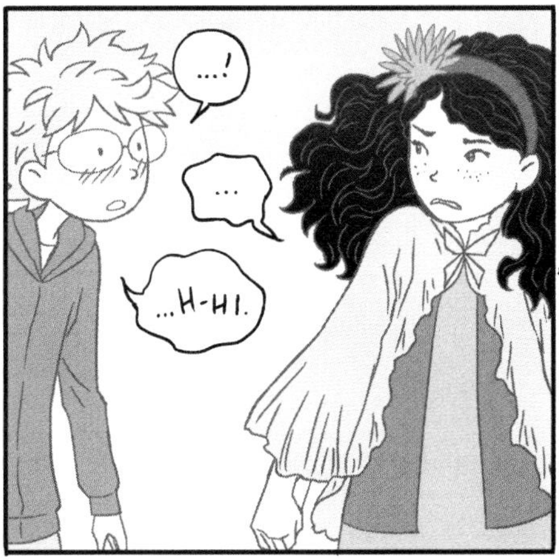
...!
...
...H-HI.

Epilogue

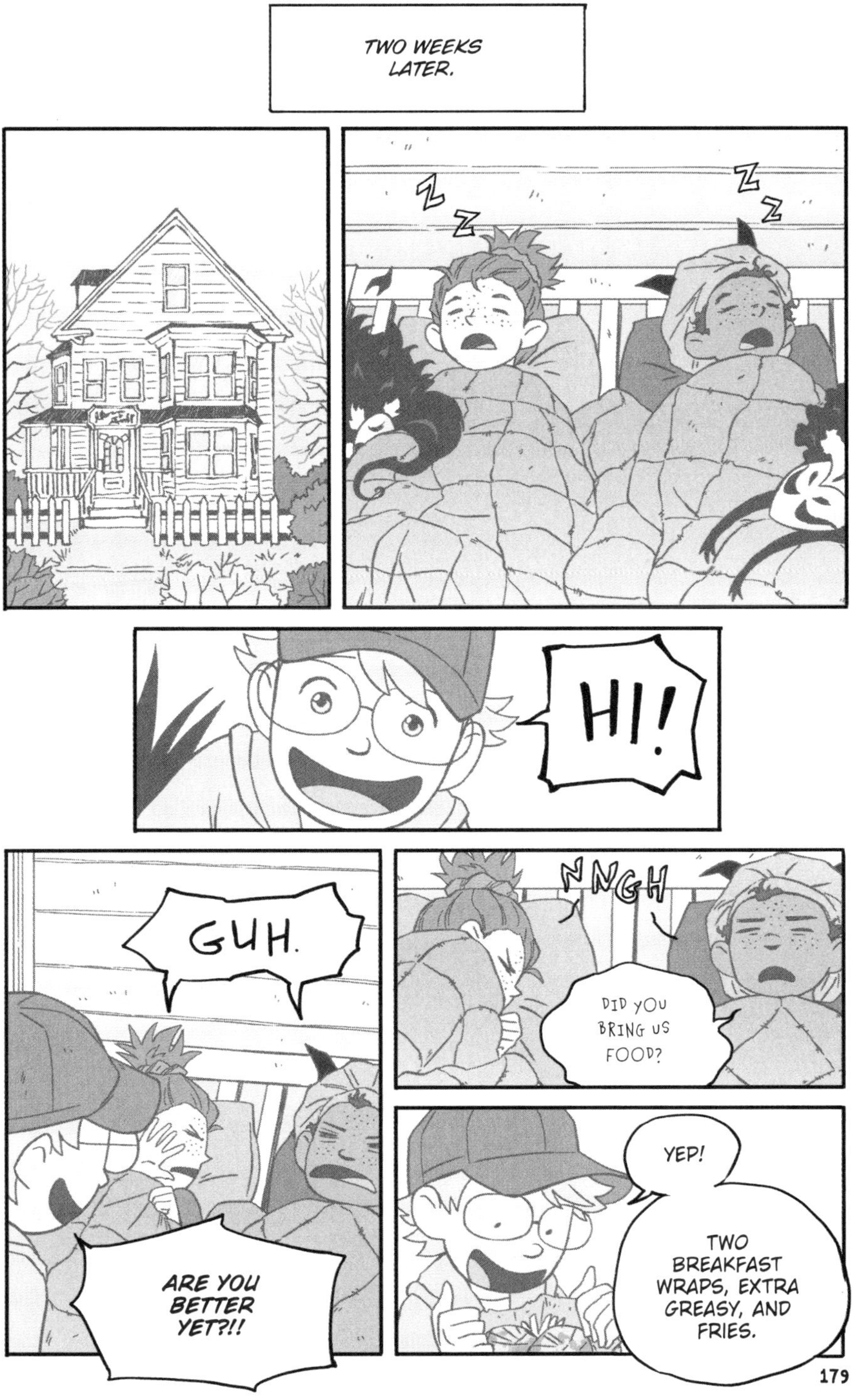
TWO WEEKS LATER.
Z Z
Z Z
HI!
GUH.
ARE YOU BETTER YET?!!
NNGH
DID YOU BRING US FOOD?
YEP!
TWO BREAKFAST WRAPS, EXTRA GREASY, AND FRIES.

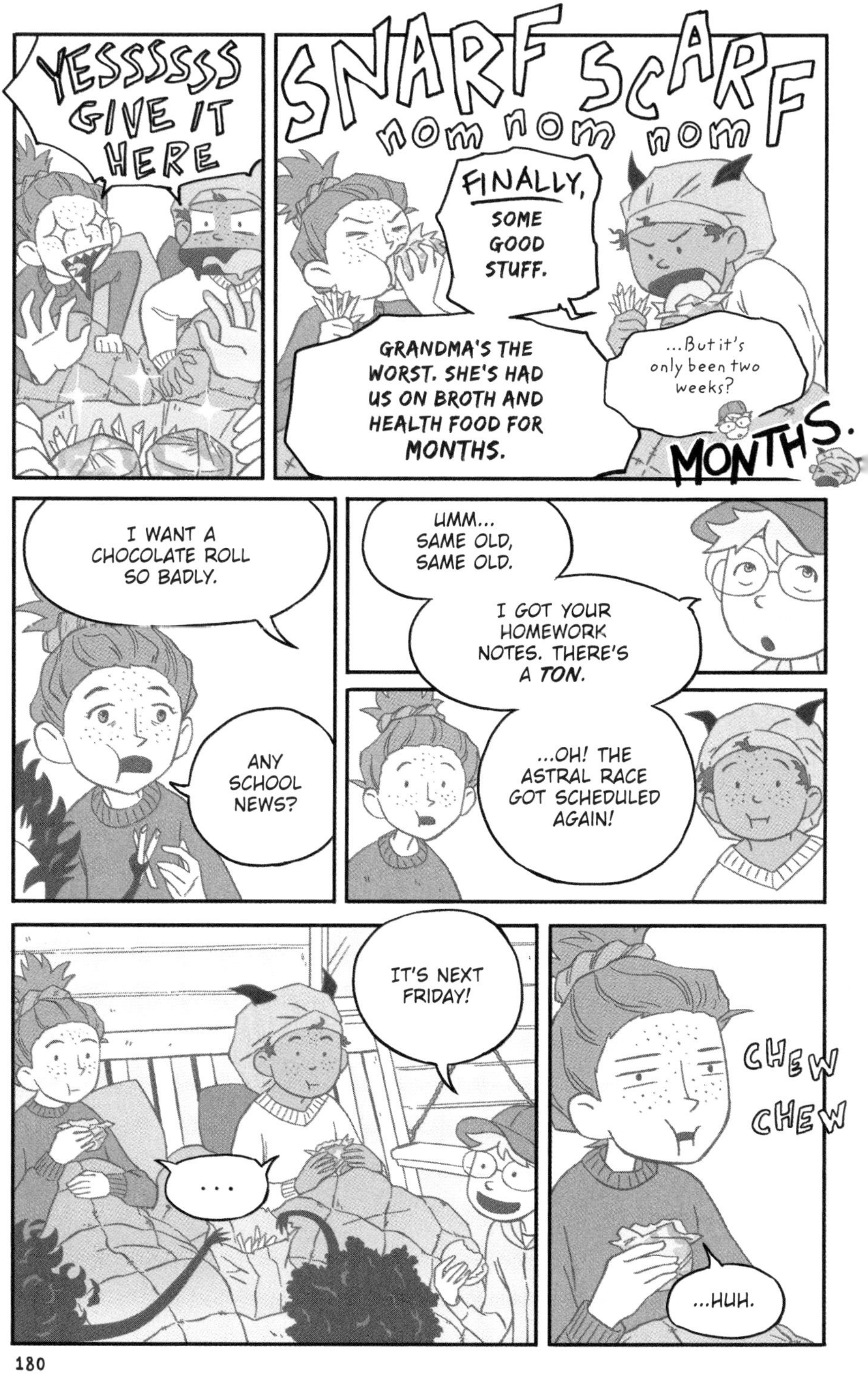
YESSSSSS GIVE IT HERE
SNARF SCARF
nom nom nom nom
FINALLY, SOME GOOD STUFF.
GRANDMA'S THE WORST. SHE'S HAD US ON BROTH AND HEALTH FOOD FOR MONTHS.
...But it's only been two weeks?
MONTHS.
I WANT A CHOCOLATE ROLL SO BADLY.
UMM... SAME OLD, SAME OLD.
I GOT YOUR HOMEWORK NOTES. THERE'S A TON.
ANY SCHOOL NEWS?
...OH! THE ASTRAL RACE GOT SCHEDULED AGAIN!
IT'S NEXT FRIDAY!
...
CHEW CHEW
...HUH.

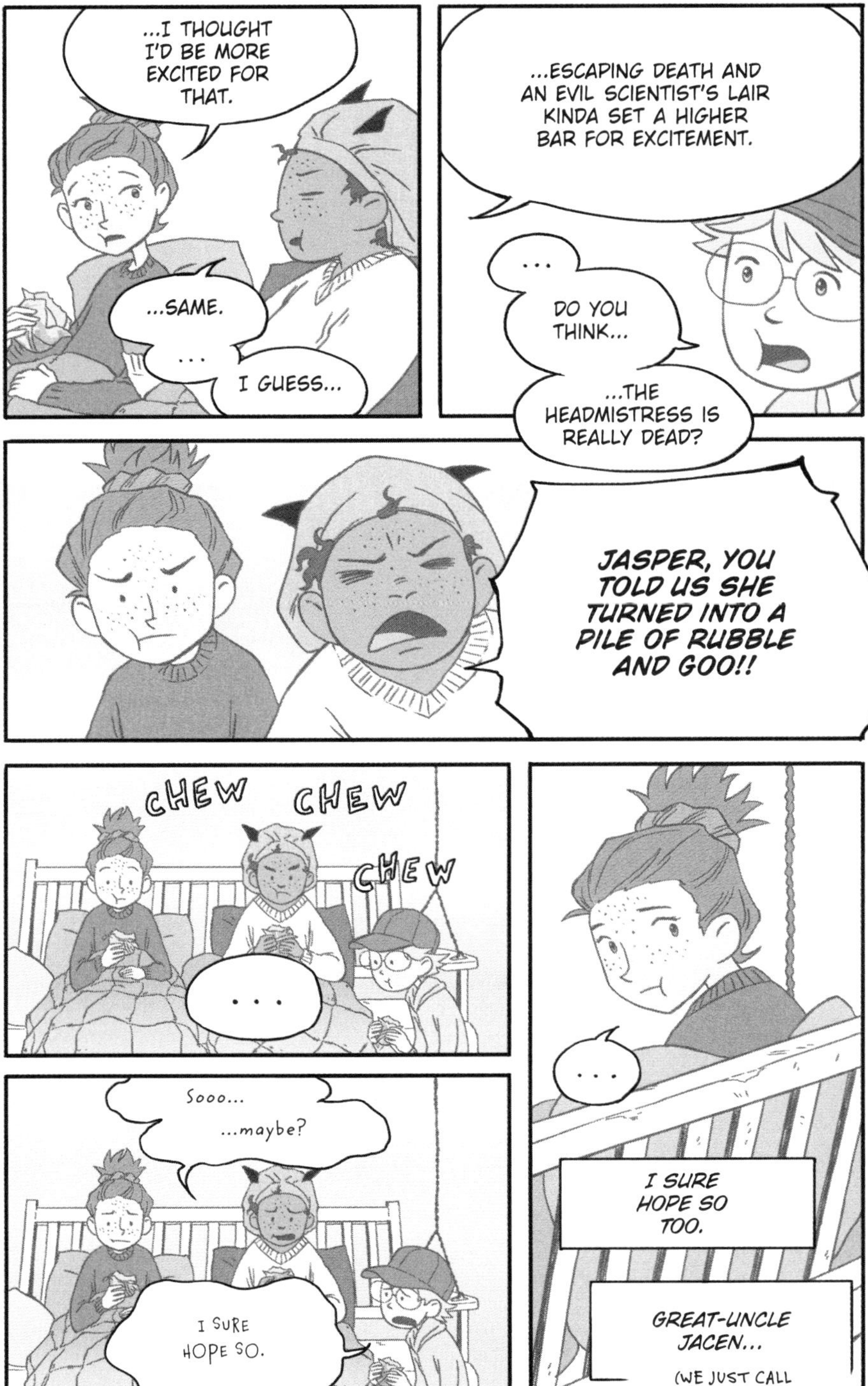
...I THOUGHT I'D BE MORE EXCITED FOR THAT.
...SAME.
...
I GUESS...
...ESCAPING DEATH AND AN EVIL SCIENTIST'S LAIR KINDA SET A HIGHER BAR FOR EXCITEMENT.
...
DO YOU THINK...
...THE HEADMISTRESS IS REALLY DEAD?
JASPER, YOU TOLD US SHE TURNED INTO A PILE OF RUBBLE AND GOO!!
CHEW
CHEW
CHEW
. . .
. . .
Sooo...
...maybe?
I SURE HOPE SO.
I SURE HOPE SO TOO.
GREAT-UNCLE JACEN...
(WE JUST CALL HIM UNCLE)

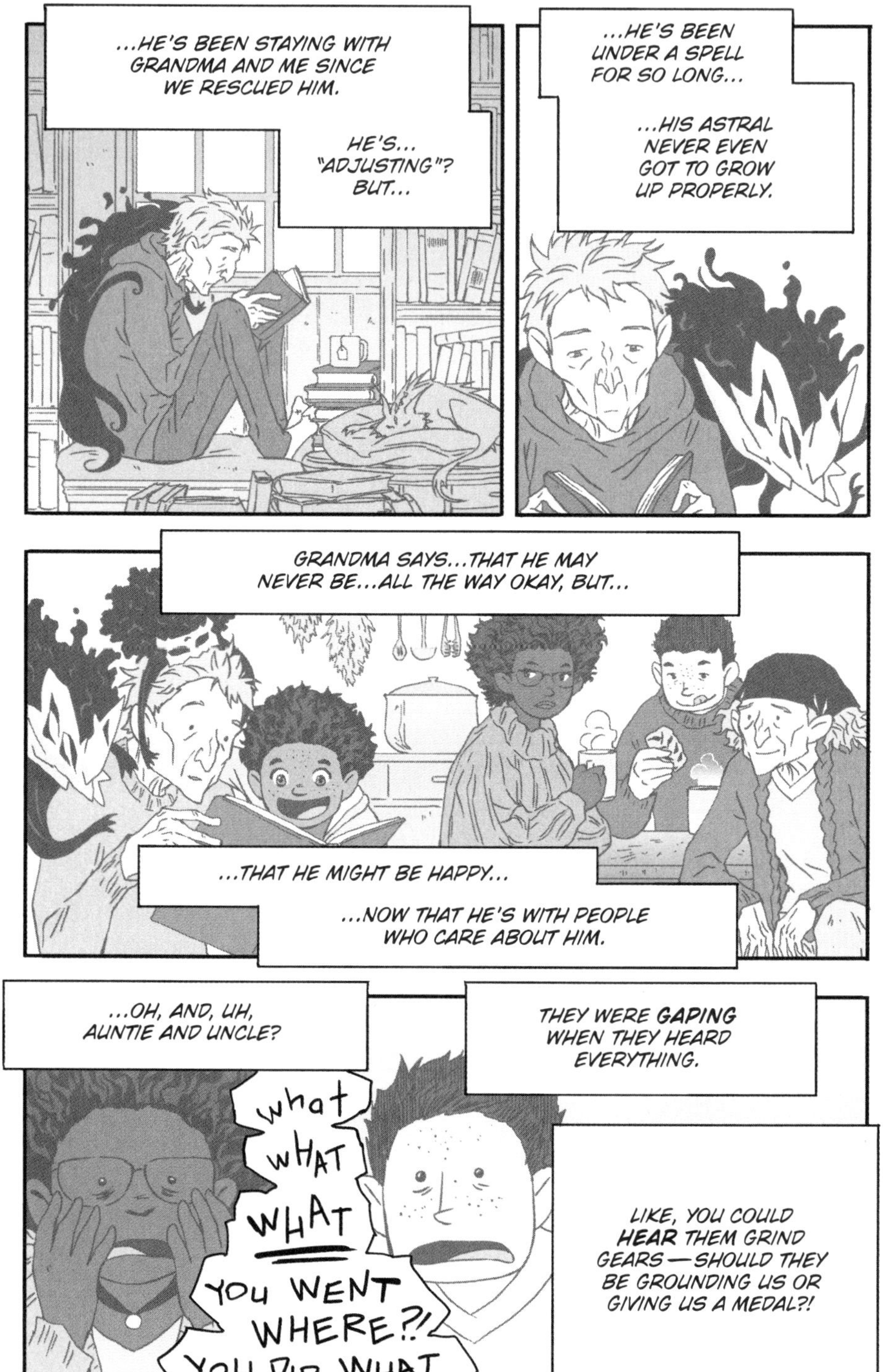
...HE'S BEEN STAYING WITH GRANDMA AND ME SINCE WE RESCUED HIM.
HE'S... "ADJUSTING"? BUT...
...HE'S BEEN UNDER A SPELL FOR SO LONG...
...HIS ASTRAL NEVER EVEN GOT TO GROW UP PROPERLY.
GRANDMA SAYS...THAT HE MAY NEVER BE...ALL THE WAY OKAY, BUT...
...THAT HE MIGHT BE HAPPY...
...NOW THAT HE'S WITH PEOPLE WHO CARE ABOUT HIM.
...OH, AND, UH, AUNTIE AND UNCLE?
THEY WERE GAPING WHEN THEY HEARD EVERYTHING.
what WHAT WHAT YOU WENT WHERE?! YOU DID WHAT
LIKE, YOU COULD HEAR THEM GRIND GEARS—SHOULD THEY BE GROUNDING US OR GIVING US A MEDAL?!

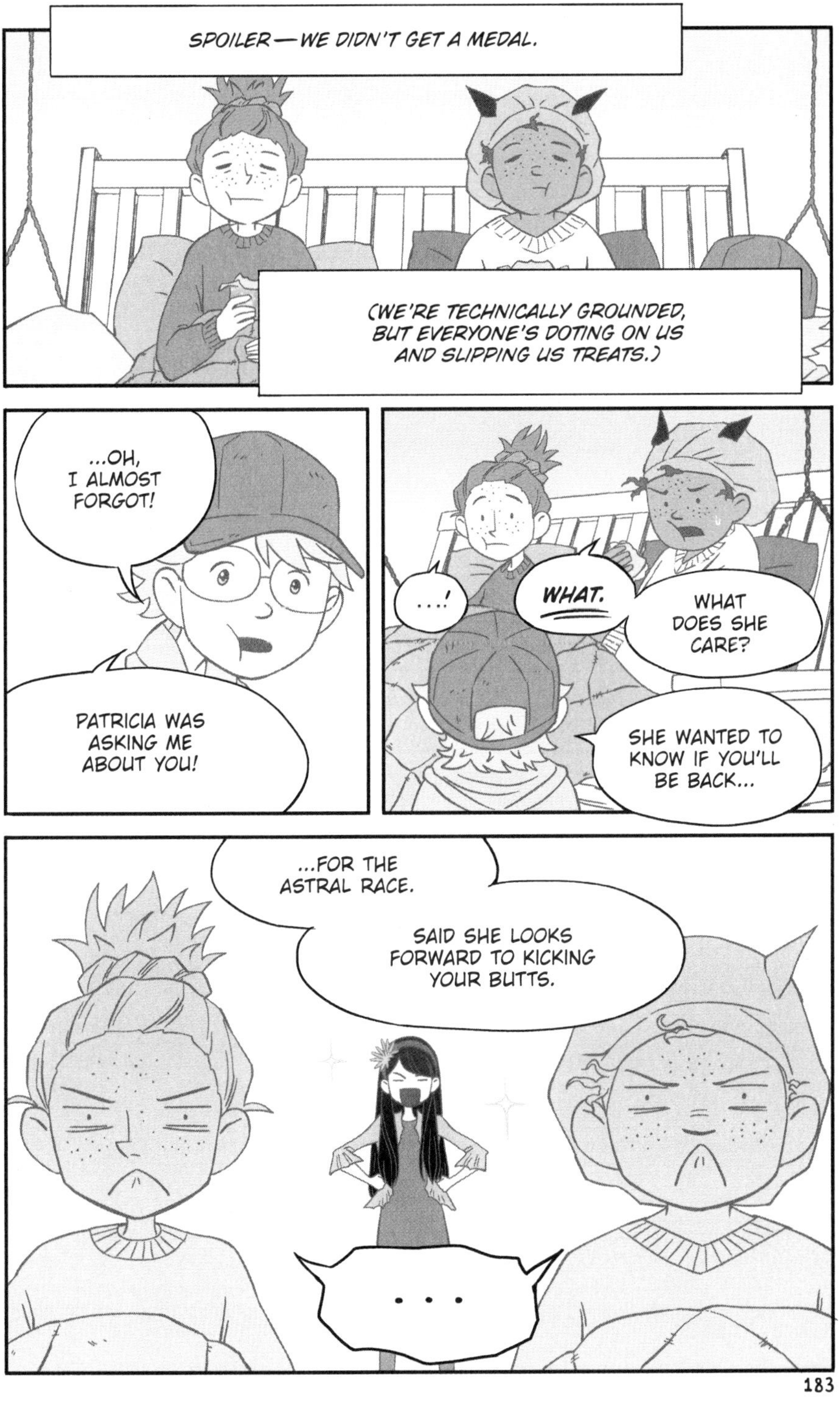
SPOILER—WE DIDN'T GET A MEDAL.
(WE'RE TECHNICALLY GROUNDED, BUT EVERYONE'S DOTING ON US AND SLIPPING US TREATS.)
...OH, I ALMOST FORGOT!
PATRICIA WAS ASKING ME ABOUT YOU!
....!
WHAT.
WHAT DOES SHE CARE?
SHE WANTED TO KNOW IF YOU'LL BE BACK...
...FOR THE ASTRAL RACE.
SAID SHE LOOKS FORWARD TO KICKING YOUR BUTTS.
. . .

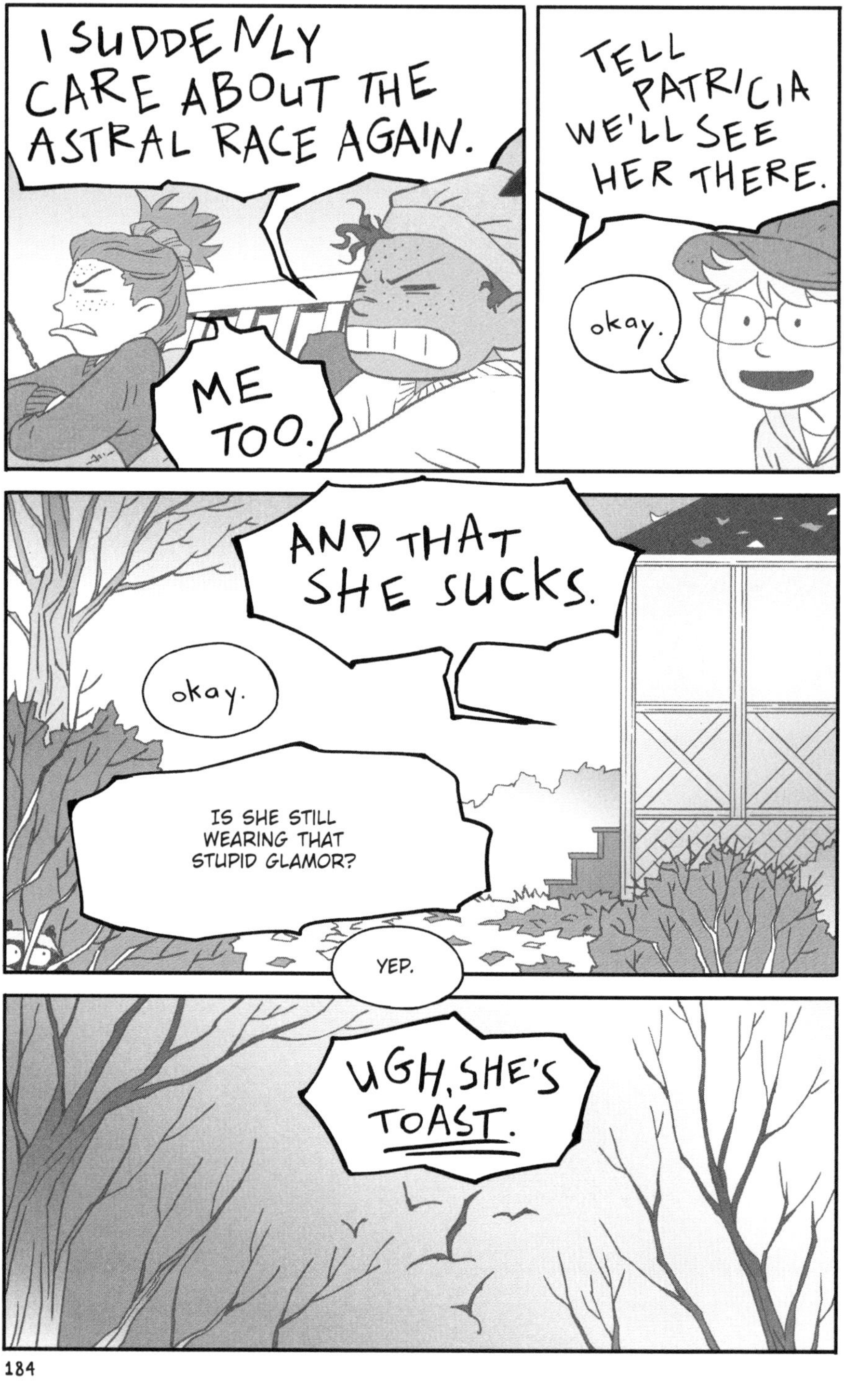
I SUDDENLY CARE ABOUT THE ASTRAL RACE AGAIN.
ME TOO.
TELL PATRICIA WE'LL SEE HER THERE.
okay.
AND THAT SHE SUCKS.
okay.
IS SHE STILL WEARING THAT STUPID GLAMOR?
YEP.
UGH, SHE'S TOAST.

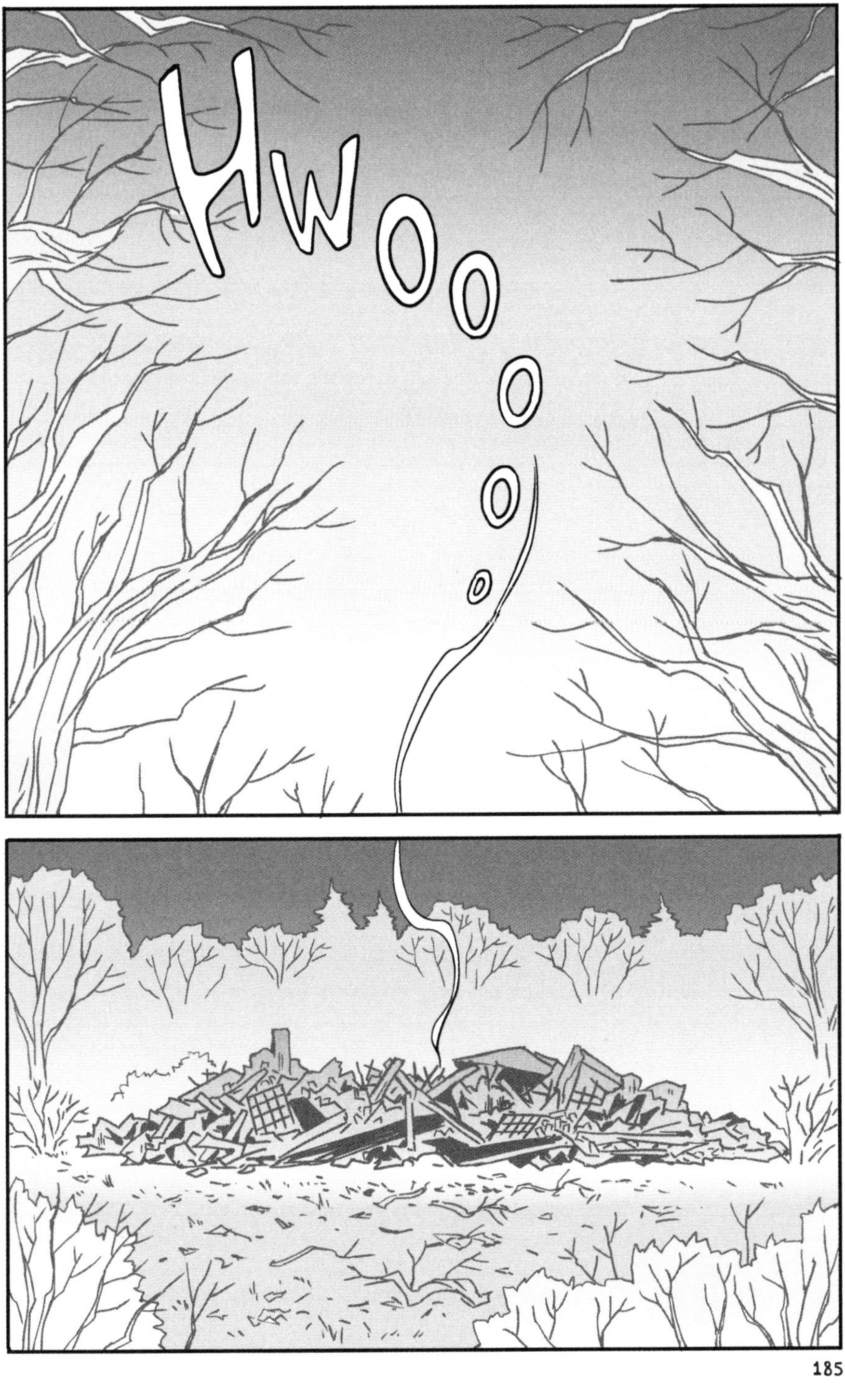
HWOOOOO

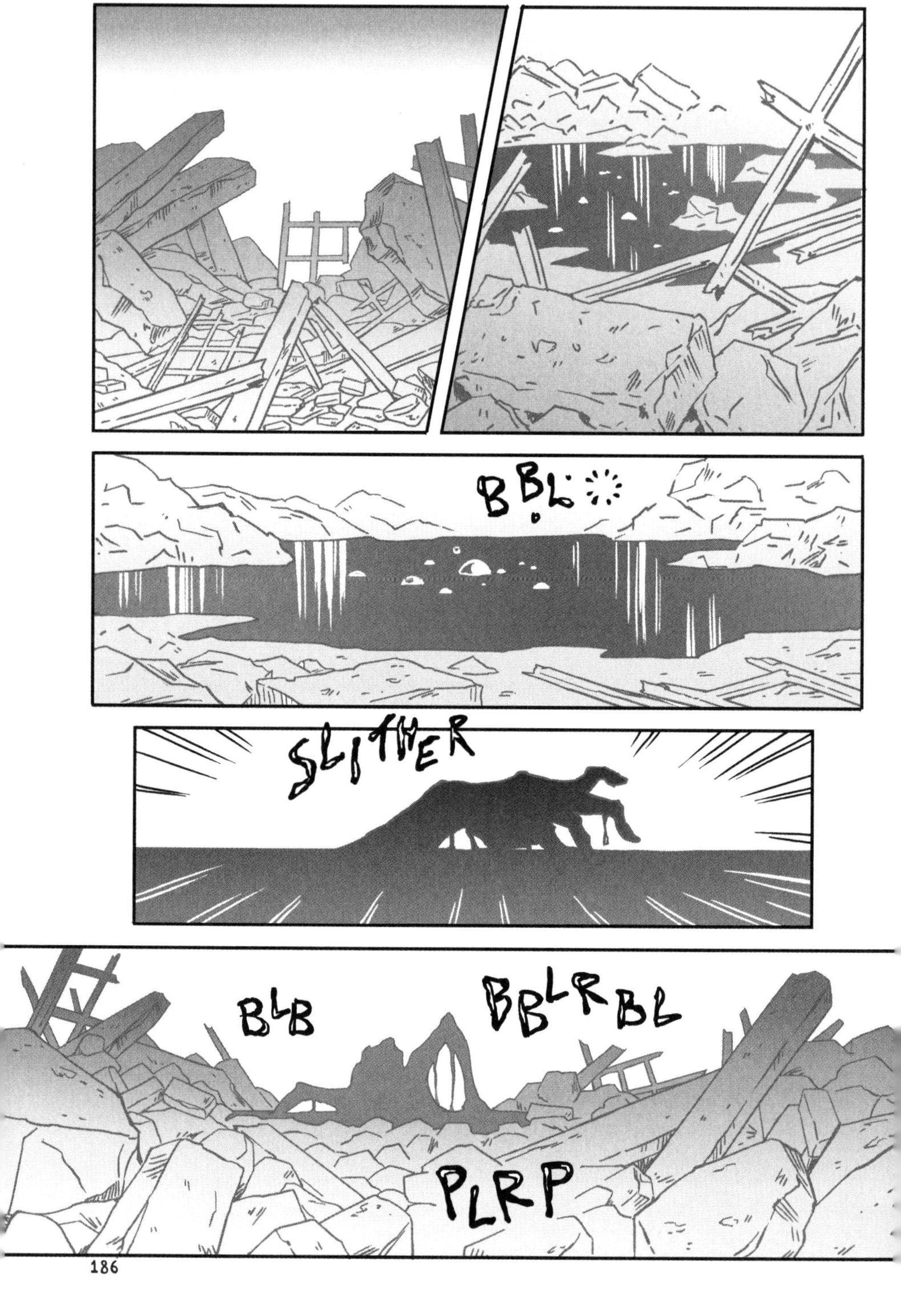
BBL
SLITHER
BLB
BBLRBL
PLRP

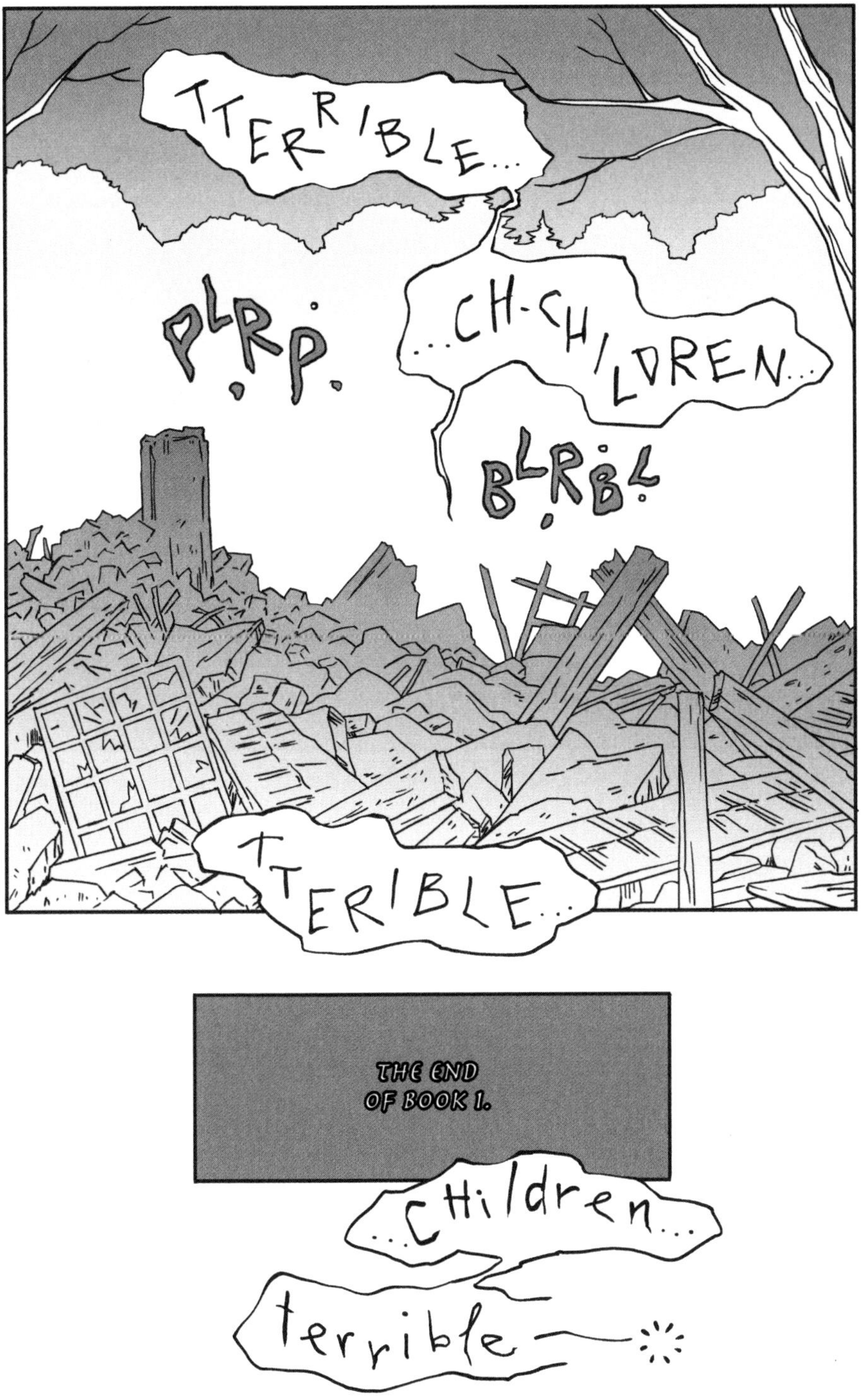
TTERRIBLE...
PLRP
...CH-CHILDREN...
BLRBL
TTERIBLE...
THE END OF BOOK 1.
...CHildren...
terrible—

FROM the AUTHOR

I MISSED DRAWING ASTRALS SO MUCH!!

I first started writing about the Weirn Books world back in 2007 (over a decade ago!! Aaaaa!!) and my favorite thing about it (besides the awesome magic, sharp-witted heroes that make bad life decisions, and a sprawling mysterious world to explore) was ⚡☆ASTRALS☆⚡!! I WANT ONE. Can't wait to get started on the next adventure for Ailis, Na'ya, and their crew. ...Right after I get, like, 10 weeks of sleep (take THAT, Ailis). Some snapshots from the book production:

We moved!

bye, house! see you on google maps

MOVING IS A SPECIAL KIND OF ENDURANCE TEST that i can't recommend

books book books books books books books books

SO MANY BOXESSSss...

huff huff

my son got sick a lot...

...and shared it with my husband and me.

nⁿhgh

The last few weeks of page production were especially rough, and while my husband was trying to hold our lives together, his beard made a triumphant comeback!

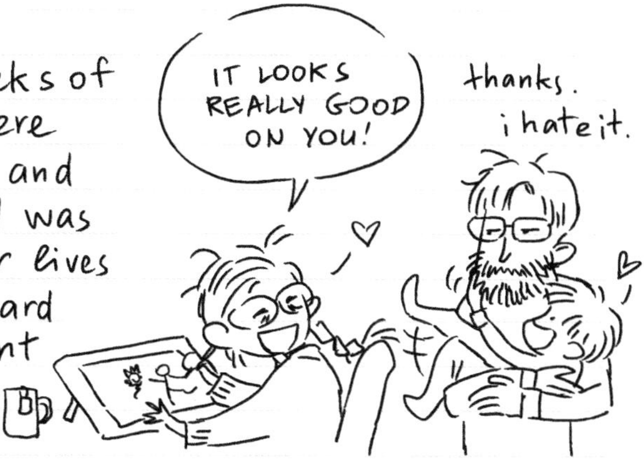
IT LOOKS REALLY GOOD ON YOU!
thanks. i hate it.

Getting this book finished up and out the door was an incredible team effort and I am so ridiculously grateful to these amazing people:

Patrick

JuYoun

Melissa

Effie

Young

JY production team!

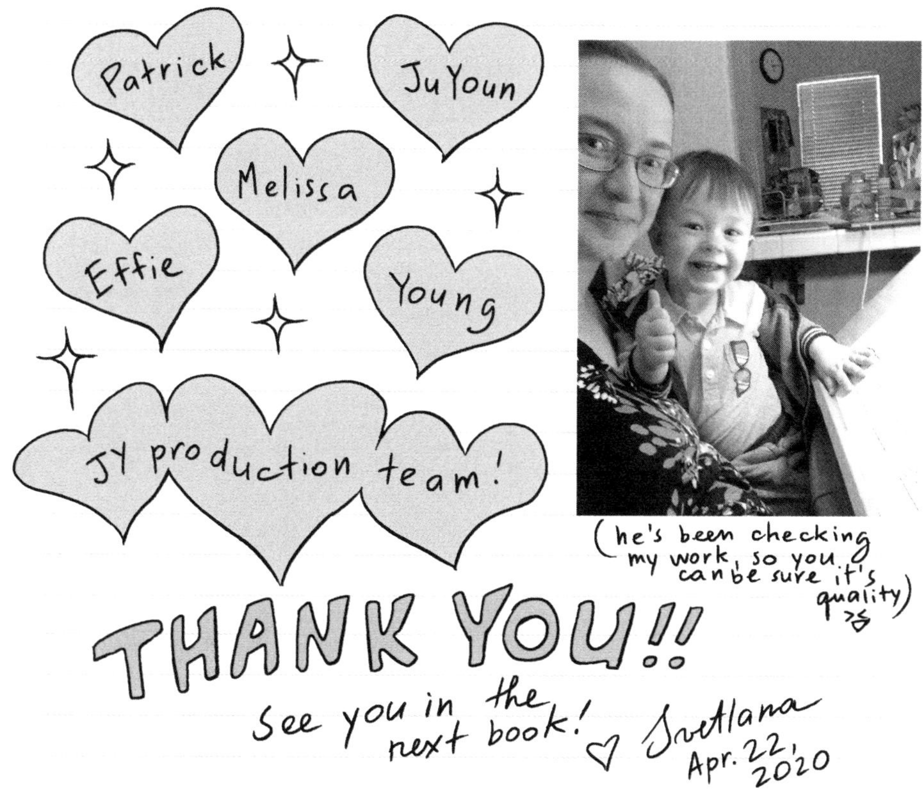

(he's been checking my work, so you can be sure it's quality) ᔕ

THANK YOU!!

See you in the next book! ♡ Svetlana
Apr. 22, 2020

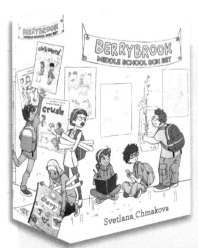

...AND FOR READERS WHO'VE GRADUATED FROM MIDDLE SCHOOL—

Nightschool
THE WEIRN BOOKS
Collector's Edition

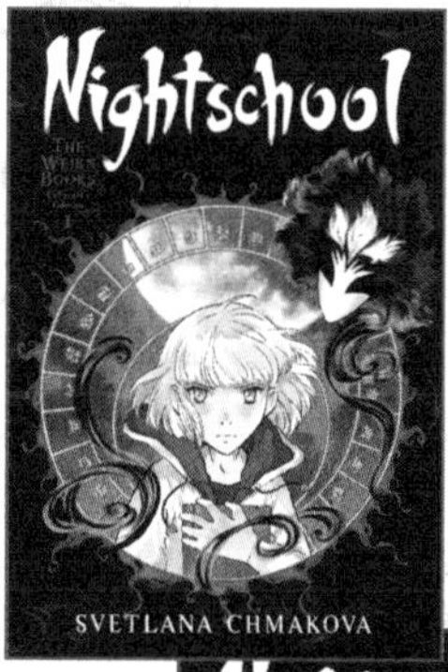
Nightschool
The Weirn Books
1
SVETLANA CHMAKOVA

Explore the Night Realm once again with NIGHTSCHOOL collector's omnibus editions!

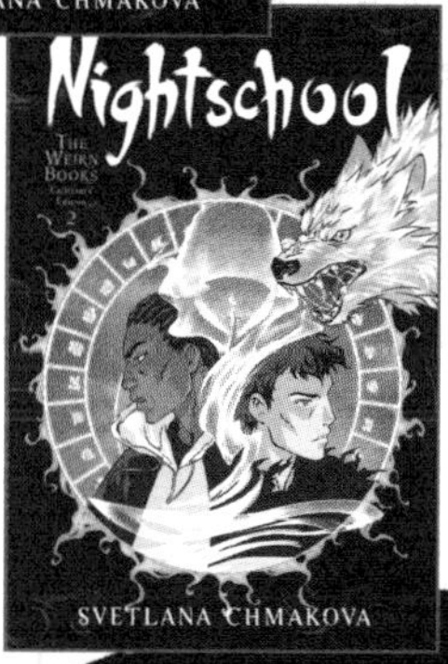
Nightschool
The Weirn Books
2
SVETLANA CHMAKOVA

Nightschool answers the age-old question—Where do demons get their diplomas? Schools may lock up for the night, but class is in session for an entirely different set of students. In the Nightschool, vampires, werewolves, vampires, and weirns (a particular breed of witch) learn everything from calculus to spell casting. Alex is a young weirn who has always been homeschooled, but dark forces seem to be drawing her closer to the Nightschool and the mysteries within.

WITCH & WIZARD

The graphic novel adaptation of JAMES PATTERSON'S *New York Times* bestselling YA series!

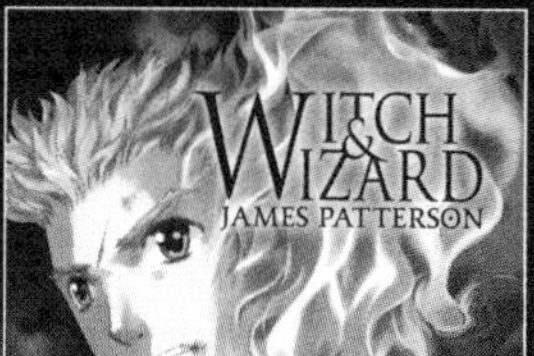
WITCH & WIZARD
JAMES PATTERSON
1

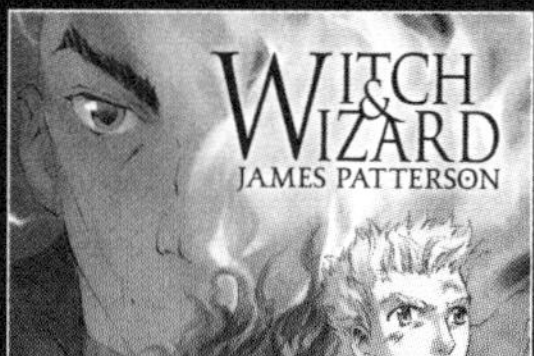
WITCH & WIZARD
JAMES PATTERSON
2

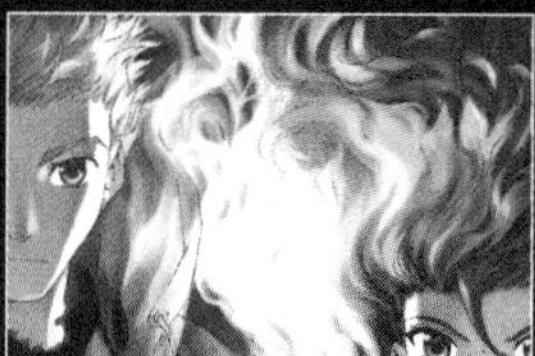
WITCH & WIZARD
JAMES PATTERSON
3

Visit yenpress.com for more information.

Yen Press

Svetlana Chmakova was born and raised in Russia until the age of sixteen, when her family immigrated to Canada. After receiving a Classical Animation diploma from Sheridan College, she quickly made a name for herself with graphic novels such as the award-winning urban fantasy *Nightschool: The Weirn Books* and the manga adaptation of *Witch & Wizard* by James Patterson. Her acclaimed Berrybrook Middle School series, which has been nominated for multiple Eisner Awards, has captivated readers of all ages since the publication of its first volume, *Awkward*, in 2015 and has made her one of the most beloved creators in the world of middle grade graphic novels.